D1446775

Suddenly Strangers

Suddenly Strangers

Surrendering Gods and Heroes

Brad L. Morin & Chris L. Morin

đ

Aventine Press LLC

Published by Aventine Press, LLC
2208 Cabo Bahia
Chula Vista, CA 91914, USA

www.aventinepress.com

Library of Congress Cataloging-in-Publication Data
2004091313

ISBN: 1-59330-111-1
Printed in the United States of America

Contents

Introduction

The news of our unthinkable fall from grace fell hard upon the ears of those who knew us best. "What has happened to Brad?" one baffled friend asked another. "You have no idea of the seriousness of this," said someone of Chris's transgression. "That is a more serious offense in the sight of God than murder or adultery—you don't understand that."

In surrendering our gods and spiritual heroes, we induced severe anguish and fear in family and friends. The reaction was anticipated but still genuinely troubling to us. Quite suddenly, many of those once close to us ceased to recognize the essence of who we were. Added to that was an inner turmoil that ruled and haunted our every thought. As we continued on our startling journey, we struggled with the loss of our exalted place in time and space, lamenting the disarray of our once well-ordered universe.

We are brothers who consider ourselves well brought up in The Church of Jesus Christ of Latter-day Saints, commonly referred to as the Mormon Church. Casting off the faith of our venerable ancestors had once seemed unfathomable. Yet, the day came when nagging inconsistencies caused us to step back and take a careful look. As Mormons, we once believed that all apostates from our faith were inspired by dark desires—to be feared, to be shunned, to be spoken of in hushed voices. Now, one forbidden look began our journey into the false and damning shadows that we had once so discreetly cast upon others.

As brothers, we share many common interests, the most obvious being our graduate degrees in mathematics and our teaching professions. Yet, our independent natures lead to vigorous debate and genuine disagreement between us. As a result, the reader may become aware of some small inconsistencies in the book. For example: one of us insists on capitalizing pronouns referring to God, while the other insists on using lower case. Still, we hope that intertwining our experiences and observations will add breadth and an understanding of the tumultuous journey that we and many others have made.

Acknowledgements

Of all the people we wish to thank, first would be our parents and siblings. The positive influence of their lives has inspired us in ways we will not try to enumerate. Today, they may regret our writing this book, which questions their cherished beliefs; still, should any good come from these pages, we give credit to their influence.

We would like to thank those outside the Church who, looking past our naive arrogance, befriended us and, in the process, gently opened our eyes to the "outside" world. After leaving the Church, we gained therapeutic insights into our past by reading stories on the Internet of many who had struggled along the same path.

There are many who have helped in the actual writing of this book. To Reb Staks, who saw our horrendous first draft and yet took the time to suggest many improvements to a story that she thought worthy of telling; to Brent W. Hughes, Robert Reiser, Dr. Jim Harris, Norma P. Ashton, Heather Ashton-Summers, Annie Sargent, and Paul Richards, who at varying stages offered significant criticism; to Ren Draya who provided much-needed editing; to Greg Meyer, Melba Buxbaum, Jeoffroy de Laforcade, Joe Clark, and many others, who read our work in progress and gave us reason to believe that others would find our story engaging; to these and many others, we are grateful.

Last of all we would like to thank our wives and children. They have endured our somewhat reclusive journey and have supported our authoring efforts, which, as far as they could tell, might have resulted only in a personal catharsis.

While we owe thanks to many, we take full responsibility for all inaccuracies in this book. We hope the reader is able to see past the unintentional errors and perhaps learn something beneficial from our story.

Chapter 1

All-American Family

Brad

There was no swimsuit competition. That may explain why the show made only one appearance on national television. In August of 1971, the nation had the opportunity to watch the All-American Family Pageant, held in Lehi Acres, Florida. They saw Anita Bryant pause and stoop to pinch the cheek of one cute little full-faced boy with a smile few could resist. That was my ten-year-old brother, Chris, one of the children in the good-looking family from Utah. I was the only missing family member, serving a mission in New Zealand for the Mormon Church.

The pageant included a family from every state in the U.S. plus one from the District of Columbia. Our family performed on the show, getting third place in the talent competition. In the overall competition for the All-American Family, we finished among the final five. However, what I liked best about my family was that out of the spotlight and in the privacy of our home, we remained an All-American family.

As Chris and I reflect upon our early years, many memories and emotions stir. Thirteen people under one roof had its

> Life does not offer anything sweeter than the love of dear ones and the sharing of time together.
> —Paul H. Dunn, *Ensign*, November 1977, p. 21

challenges, but our fond recollections overwhelm the unpleasant ones. We were the second and ninth in a family of eleven children, all born within a fifteen-year period. For us, the middle-class upbringing brought its share of excitement and anxiety, with parents and siblings tightly woven into every aspect.

Some scenes come clearly to mind as I think of our early years. I see myself with brothers and sisters working in the garden, milking cows, and playing football on the front lawn. I recall some competitive, marathon basketball games. There was golf in the cow pasture with a single club to share, a pitching wedge—watch those fresh hazards. (Some golfers think that hitting out of a moist sand trap is messy. Our purist tendencies quickly waned.) I recall a variety of rowdy games, broken bones, concussions, stitches, near drownings, my spirited horse named Rebel, a game that involved tripping fleeing siblings with a fifteen-foot bull whip, killer Frisbee, and Mom telling me one more time that I just play too rough. We occupied one long pew in church each Sunday. We gathered for morning and evening prayer. Mealtime was inevitably an event. I have fond memories of singing around the piano, and some stimulating political and gospel discussions. I still see myself as a young boy coming home from school each noon to have tuna sandwiches and home-bottled cherries or peaches with Mom. There were large family reunions with a host of uncles, aunts, and cousins whom I admired.

Not to claim myself a quick study as a lad, I did overcome some adolescent foibles at an early age, having said my last youthful swear word and smoked my last cigarette by age four. The smoking was a one-shot-deal that did not go very well. I did not know to inhale and I was annoyed that my cigarette would not maintain a visible flame. My older friend ran out of matches trying to accommodate me. Worse still, afterward, Dad noticed that my five-year-old brother and I smelled like smoke. I can still recall part of his lecture: "President McKay doesn't smoke." (Dad was referring to our beloved Mormon prophet.)

I do not remember where we learned swear words, but I believe my last swear word as a youth occurred while tromping up the road with Dad and my older brother Art, who was five, to stop the water from flowing down our ditch when it was not our turn to irrigate. (Stealing irrigation water, critical for crops and gardens, was frowned upon.) Dad wondered aloud about who had opened the head gate, allowing the water down our ditch. Art and I knew better than anyone just who had opened the head gate. Dad's displeasure appeared to be without a clear target. As we sanctimoniously trudged up the road with Dad to amend the infraction, I thought it best to reinforce our heretofore silent denial with an emphatic: "Damn those people who did it, huh, Dad!" He was quick to inform me that cursing would not be necessary, probably aware of just whom I was damning.

In 1955, I turned five. Shortly thereafter, we moved from Lindon, Utah to a neighboring town, Provo. There, across the street from Utah Valley Hospital, we lived until 1964. Mom made her almost annual trip across the street to bring home another sister or brother. The last six children joined us during those eight and a half years in Provo.

I have pleasant memories of the Church members there in Park Ward (Mormon congregations are called wards). They brought a variety of meals into our home while Mom recuperated from the delivery of each baby. It seemed we never ate so well. I marveled that so many kind people lived in our small corner of the universe. I thought Provo had to be the best place in the world to grow up.

Mom and Dad have lived their whole lives faithful and committed to the Church. They instilled their faith in their children. We thrilled to hear stories from Dad's two-year church mission, with every repeated telling. I decided early, along with most of my siblings, to go on a full-time proselytizing mission when old enough. The Church expected it of able young men at the age of nineteen and allowed interested women to go at age twenty-one. Out of the thirteen of us, including both Mom and Dad, eventually ten went on missions. I was proud of my family's faithfulness.

The nickname, Mormon Church, comes from the *Book of Mormon*. The Church claims that this book is scripture, a history of God's dealings with the early American inhabitants, translated from gold tablets through inspiration by God's prophet, Joseph Smith. Faithful church members believe Joseph Smith's endorsement found in the introduction of the 1981 copyright version. It says the book is "the most correct of any book on earth, and the keystone of our religion, and a man would get nearer to God by abiding by its precepts, than by any other book."

I have fond memories of Mom reading the *Book of Mormon* stories to us in the evenings before bedtime. At an early age, I learned to love the book and the people in it who showed such faith, courage, and commitment to the Lord. I found it comforting and stirring to see how the Lord watched over those who loved and served Him.

I remember the night that Dad explained to us in detail the plan of salvation. We learned of our pre-earth existence, in which we had existed as spirit sons and daughters of godly parents, and of the various degrees of glory that one could inherit after this earth life. I was affected by this revelation, having never before heard it presented so clearly and completely. It left me in awe, with a greater desire to be a good person. Attending second grade at the time, I wondered who of my classmates understood these sublime truths.

Church attendance came automatic for us. We did not always find services interesting, but we were well behaved, even in the long meetings on those uncomfortable pews. I knew it was the right place to be on Sunday. I do remember missing church once as a boy, without a good reason. On this occasion, some of us were playing football over at the high school, not our usual Sabbath activity. We either lost track of time or conveniently chose to ignore it. We arrived home too late for the evening Sacrament Meeting—an hour-and-a-half meeting that consisted of praying, singing, taking the sacrament, approving ward business, and listening to lay member sermons. That afternoon, Mom and Dad had no knowledge of our whereabouts and surprisingly had little to say when we returned home too late for the meeting. I do not remember that a good time ever again got in the way of church.

The lessons we learned in our home went beyond faith and church dogma. One neighborhood incident comes to mind, in-volving a ten-year-old boy, Gene, with one crippled leg. A year younger than I, he could be aggressive at times. One day, through that all-seeing kitchen window, Mom saw some of us shove Gene to the ground. She brought it up later, saying that we should have shown more kindness. We tried to explain Gene's obnoxious ways, but that did not sway her. My heart was pricked, and I made a greater effort to be kind to Gene. As a result, he no longer seemed so mean and, not surprisingly, appreciated my new attitude.

One of my favorite memories of sibling unselfishness took place during my freshman year in college, when money was tight. My younger brother Burke, about ten years old, sent a dollar to help me out. That sacrifice probably exhausted his funds, but it carried me a long way.

Family reunions were an important part of our growing-up years. More recently, the most elaborate of the yearly reunions involved our parents and their posterity. I was proud of, grateful for, and comfortable with the fact that we were all committed members of the Church. In addition, there are Lyman reunions on Mom's side and Morin reunions on Dad's. I developed immense love and respect for my extended family, almost all devoted members of the Church.

Because we often sang in the home as a family, music became an important part of my life, especially the hymns and songs tied to my faith. Some of my siblings developed remarkable singing voices. I do recall discomfort over one song we sang in the home. Dad had fallen in love with a song written especially for young girls in the Church, a specific age group known as Gaynotes. We were hip enough as young boys to recognize how foolish it was for us to be singing a girl's song that started out: "I will be a gay note." When Dad decided that our family would sing this song as a special musical number for the congregation in church, mutiny erupted. To our great relief, our protests succeeded.

We were not the Cleavers. We were not the Waltons. We were not the Bradys, Partridges, or Huxtables. We were an All-American family of our own making. It was a life rich in the common joys. In the summers, we mixed the mundane responsibility of raising a garden and a few farm animals, with the more exotic attempts to raise pollywogs, baby squirrels, and hawks. In the winters, we repaired sleighs that others had thrown away, then we found hills fast enough to lose teeth and win stitches. The occasional angry moments, accompanied with blows in rare instances, never lasted long. When Mom broke her arm picking apples—hours after Burke broke his arm while playing quarterback for the junior high school football team—we all pulled together to keep the home running smoothly. (Mom concluded that football was too rough. We concluded that picking apples was too rough.)

When Marilee won her piano competitions, we all rejoiced. When Chris won the state wrestling tournament, we were all there hollering. When Dad came down with another case of "running for political office," we eagerly joined the campaign. Chris, as a child, prayed for his pet worms, while Mom and Dad, daily, prayed for all of their children. We learned to forgive. We learned to share. We learned to sacrifice. We learned to love. For many years, it was my desire and intent to have at least ten children of my own.

Chris

So blind is life, so long at last is sleep,
And none but Love to bid us laugh or weep.
—Willa Cather, "Evening Star", *April Twilights*, 1903

In significant ways, Brad's childhood differed from mine. He was born into a small family and watched it grow as nine younger siblings were born. When he went away to college, he left a home full of brothers and sisters. I was born into a large family and watched it shrink as older siblings left the nest. I was one of the last to leave home. But from either vantage point, the scene was a pleasant one.

As one of the older children, Brad enjoyed the adoration and loyalty of his younger brothers and sisters. As one of the younger children, I relished the thoughtful attention and affection from the older siblings. They took me to movies, taught me to read, gave me my first birthday party, and let me hang around with them and their friends. Only once did I suffer an accidental hatchet blow to the head. (It earned me seven stitches, some candy, and sympathy from the whole family.)

A large picture of Jesus was prominently displayed in our home. I considered it the most important fixture in the house. His kind eyes conveyed a sense of peace and gave our home a feeling of his presence, generating a spirit of love among family members. Nothing brought me more comfort than knowing that this merciful, all-powerful being ruled the universe. The stories and songs about Jesus were my favorite.

Just as this picture was a central fixture in our home, the Church was an integral part of our family. Its teachings guided our daily family activities and our individual lives as well. Before the family prayer each morning, we usually sang a song accompanied by Mom or a sister at the piano. Then we took turns, each of us reading two verses from our individual copies of the *Book of Mormon*.

Mom and Dad instilled in their children the hopes and expectations, based on Church teachings, that if we all lived worthily and remained true to our Mormon faith, then even after this life we would continue as a family. Nurturing these "eternal families" is a fundamental theme of the Church, and *family home evening* (one night a week spent as a family) is one tool the Church uses to bring families closer together. Dad had taken to heart a prophet's promise that parents who hold family home evening would not "lose" one child in eternity, so holding family home evening was as automatic as attending Sunday meetings.

Mom wrote a song, our family song, which expressed our view that "families are forever." The song was updated as our family grew, and we sang it at family gatherings. Each child, in-law, and grandchild—eventually some seventy in all—was acknowledged by name in one of the choruses.

A mother of eleven children faces a daunting task in keeping up with the mundane daily chores. Surely Mom felt overwhelmed at times and doubtless she felt considerable stress occasionally, but I never saw any sign of it. She did more than just cope; her unselfish attitude, her firm yet consistently gentle manner, and her unconditional love for her children engendered in us a love for her that could be earned in no other way. I marvel at the sacrifices she so willingly made. Surely her faith buoyed her up. She knew that if only she could do her part, nothing could sever our family ties.

When I was five years old, we moved to Tabiona, Utah, where I had my first look at life in a small rural town and the work that can come with it. Over the next decade—first in Tabiona, and then in Richmond, Utah—Dad spent hundreds of hours with us boys on our little family farm of fruit trees, chickens, turkeys, pigs, sheep, horses, and dairy cows.

One day each spring, we made a family affair of planting a huge garden. Each of us was given a task we were capable of accomplishing, along with appropriate instructions. The furrows were not always straight, nor were the seeds always planted at the right depth with correct spacing. Nevertheless, Mom and Dad usually let our work stand. It gave us a sense of accomplishment to contribute. Although we children did not share Mom and Dad's enthusiasm about the garden, we did a surprisingly good imitation of a well-organized, industrious, and happy work crew.

At harvest time, we played different guessing games as we shelled peas or cut green beans on the back porch. We must have looked as if we were enjoying ourselves, because, on occasion, some neighborhood children would ask if they could help.

In 1970 when I was a fourth-grader in Richmond, Utah, we moved up the road to a house with a small orchard. While picking apples, our thrifty nature surfaced—we refused to waste the apples that had fallen to the ground. This otherwise useless fruit was put to use in an occasional good-natured "apple war." We were careful not to throw the good apples at each other in those wars—unless, of course, we ran short of either bad apples or good nature.

Over the years, Dad taught his own children in over twenty classes at the junior high and high school level. He was well liked by the students, and had earned a reputation at North Cache Junior High School for his jig dancing, but it was a performance seldom given. In the two years I had him as a math teacher, only once did I see him grant the students' request for an in-class performance. His was not your run-of-the-mill jig. It was a stand-on-the-desk-and-dance jig, a get-out-of-the-way-or-a-flying-book-will-knock-you-out jig. With books, paper, and other desk paraphernalia scattered over the floor, Dad finished his jig and stood there on his cleared desk—a dancer on his own little stage. And the crowd cheered.

Some of our most enjoyable times at home were spent sitting around the table, eating snacks and discussing religion, politics, or current events. (We sometimes could not limit ourselves to one topic at a time, a practice that confused some visitors until they got the hang of it.) Our discussions were thought-provoking, humorous, informative, and civil. Discussions on religious issues always promoted faith. As firm believers, nobody expressed doubt regarding Church doctrine; nobody questioned Church leaders.

Two observations of friends who participated in some of our discussions capture our typical family behavior. One friend was impressed that despite the difference in age and experience, the older children would listen to the youngest child, Carolyn, and consider her views. Another observed that if we were snacking on cookies, whoever got the last cookie invariably split it with a sibling.

This unselfish attitude did not diminish as we grew older. As a single man working in the oil fields of Texas, I stayed with a sister, Marilee, and her family for several months. Twelve years later, my family of five stayed with a sister, Lynette, and her family. During those two months, the strain from having two more adults and three more children in their small home was either well hidden or nonexistent.

Christmas with ten siblings was a treat. We did not have enough money individually to buy everybody a present, so we organized ourselves into groups and pooled our money. I remember going to a big department store with several groups of tiny shoppers. We consulted Mom for ideas, and then avoided duplicate presents by clearing with her our final selections. We looked forward to the joy our gifts would bring others.

On Christmas morning, the younger children waited upstairs with anticipation until the older boys had milked the cows. Then we all gathered downstairs, and Dad read the Christmas story from the Bible. With all those presents waiting to be opened, Dad's scripture reading was not the focus of my attention, but it helped remind me that there was more to Christmas than presents. The morning's enjoyment was prolonged as the gifts were passed out and opened one at a time. The gifts, however, were not the best part of the holiday. Burke (one year older than I) put it best one year when Mom asked what he wanted for Christmas. He said he did not need any gifts; having the entire family home for Christmas was enough for him.

Our respect for each other came as second nature. One day, when I was about five years old and before I could properly pronounce the *r* sound, we were all visiting in the front yard with a friend of some of the older children. This boy said something in response to a comment I had made. Imitating my speech, he thought to get a few laughs at my expense. Nobody rebuked him for his mockery;

nobody said anything to indicate their disapproval, but nobody laughed either. Looking around, he realized his comment had been completely ignored. It was a kind but clear message that we were more than just siblings; we were friends.

Chapter 2

Rapt in the Faith

Chris

Mormonism is a way of life in which Mormons immerse themselves. A church mission—particularly for the young men—is a rite of passage, a primer for a life of devotion to the Church.

> Let us here observe, that a religion that does not require the sacrifice of all things never has power sufficient to produce the faith necessary unto life and salvation.
>
> —Joseph Smith, Lectures on Faith 6:7

It is by design that virtually all active adult Mormons are kept busy with two or more church jobs, or *callings*. There is also a host of other demands on a Mormon's time. Among other things, they are admonished to read scriptures as a family each day, read scriptures as an individual each day, keep a personal daily journal, do genealogy work, and do temple ordinance work for the dead on a regular basis (at least monthly). The commandment to keep a one-year supply of food also takes time and effort, as does the obligation to share the gospel with others. Mormons are enveloped in these and other Church activities. This time commitment (not to mention *tithing*, the donation of ten percent of one's income to the Church) creates a culture that binds Mormons to the Church as well as to each other.

|The Mormon Church is| the only true and living church upon the face of the whole earth.
—Revelation to Joseph Smith, *Doctrine and Covenants* 1:30

The Church makes some strong claims, which Brad and I took to heart. It teaches some very appealing doctrines, in which we found comfort.

In the temple ceremony, for example, Mormons hear that exalted men and women will become "Gods and Goddesses." One of the most repeated quotations in the Church is a statement of Lorenzo Snow, the fifth president of the Church. He said, "As man is, God once was; and as God is, man may become." Mormons believe that a person must participate in certain ceremonies in order to be exalted. These ceremonies, or ordinances, must be performed by the proper priesthood authority, which Mormons believe can be found only in their Church. Mormons do genealogical research to find the names of the deceased so the necessary ordinances can be performed vicariously for them in Mormon temples.

The President of the Mormon Church is considered to be a prophet who is God's representative on earth, and his words take precedence over the words of previous prophets and the scriptures.[1] Mormons are taught that the Lord will never allow the prophet to teach us false doctrine or lead us astray.[2] Mormons believe that the first prophet in these "latter days" was Joseph Smith. Through him, God restored the fullness of the gospel that had been lost through apostasy after Christ was crucified. The beginning of the restoration was the *first vision*, in which God the Father and his son Jesus Christ appeared to the fourteen-year-old boy, Joseph Smith.

Mormons express their belief or "knowledge" of the truthfulness of the above teachings by *bearing their testimony*, in which they often say, "I know the Church is the only true and living church on the face of the earth," or simply, "I know the Church is true." This summarizes their belief that only the Mormon Church is led by a prophet who receives modern-day revelation from Jesus Christ, that only the Mormon Church teaches the fullness of the gospel, and that only through the Mormon Church can one gain exaltation.

As a boy, I thought the missionary homecomings were the only church meetings that ended too soon. In these homecomings, I loved to hear the missionaries tell stories of how the Church changed the lives of people whom they had taught, and how the Lord blessed

And if it so be that you should labor all your days in crying repentance unto this people, and bring, save it be one soul unto me, how great shall be your joy with him in the kingdom of my Father.

—Doctrine and Covenants 18:15

and protected the missionaries. I found it incomprehensible that some returned missionaries became inactive in the Church after having had such experiences.

I never doubted that I would serve a mission for the Church. Admittedly, I had some apprehensions about going on a mission and perhaps I did not look forward to it with as much anticipation as some young men did, but I understood my responsibility to share the gospel with others.

In 1979, soon after my nineteenth birthday, I received a call to serve a mission in Korea. As did other missionaries of my era, I started my mission in the Missionary Training Center in Provo, Utah. Our demanding daily schedule was set for us. Each day we had one hour of supervised physical activity and eleven hours of class, most of it studying Korean. Class ended at 10:00 p.m. and I often woke up at 5:00 a.m. to get a little extra study time.

After two months of intense study of the Korean language, six of us were sent to join the other 150 missionaries already in the Korea Pusan Mission. Most Koreans were shocked to meet Americans who could speak Korean or who even *tried* to speak Korean; they often thanked us for learning to speak their language. Church members and nonmembers alike were generous with their meager possessions, and they treated missionaries with the utmost respect.

I grew to love the culture and people of Korea. Knocking on doors, I met many wonderful people. One woman was not interested in our message, but she appreciated our hard work, and she bought a *Book of Mormon* for us to give to someone else who could not afford to buy one. On another day, a family let us in during a rainstorm. Although they were not interested in our message, they kept us, for a while, in their home and out of the rain.

My first few months in Korea seemed perfect. Each of my first three senior companions was a dedicated missionary, and we baptized ten people. I was comfortable in my role as the junior companion, working to be a senior companion for the second half of my mission.

After five months in Korea, I received the overwhelming assignment to be a senior companion. I thought I had been making sufficient progress to receive this calling after another six months. However, my previous two companions had indicated to Ho Nam Rhee, president of the Pusan Mission, that I was ready to be a senior companion. I believed they had done me an injustice, and that President Rhee was acting on faulty information. In three days, I would be transferred to an unfamiliar city of three million people. I would have a companion who knew less Korean than I did, and I would be expected—somehow—to find, teach, and baptize people with whom I could hardly communicate.

A conversation with a Korean sister missionary magnified my feelings of incompetence. Upon learning I would soon be a senior companion, she asked me a question that I did not understand. She repeated the question, and again I did not comprehend. She asked the question a third time, speaking slowly and clearly. When I still did not understand, she gave up and translated her simple question into English: "Do you hear and understand Korean well?"

Some of the other missionaries got quite a chuckle out of this "conversation," but I felt embarrassed and humiliated. I put aside the pressure I had once felt to find converts and lowered my expectations, hoping only to keep from looking like a fool.

I wanted to postpone the responsibility of senior companion for a few months. However, that sort of thing is not done, and my training was to follow those in authority. I respected President Rhee, believing he had been called of God. Before the three days had passed, I decided that success was up to me. I needed faith and the resolve to work hard; God would make up the difference as he had with so many other missionaries. Concerning faith, I felt like the man who said, "Lord, I believe; help thou mine unbelief"(St. Mark; 9:24). The hard work would come easily because this was a cause in which I believed. Praying as never before, I determined to redouble my efforts.

At first I found my solace in small successes. After one week as a senior companion, I noted in my journal how my companion and I had talked with a married couple for about an hour, and we "were able to communicate fairly well." This type of visit was commonplace for many missionaries, but to me it was a huge accomplishment.

Before long, I got out of the try-not-to-look-like-a-fool mode and went forward with some hope and confidence. Within five weeks we had one baptism, and we soon had a few more; the one that sticks out in my mind is Brother Che. A few weeks after his baptism, I saw him waiting at the bus stop, and he looked like a different man. Whereas he had once seemed unsettled and unsure of himself, he now seemed happy, confident, and at peace. I was grateful to have played a part in blessing his life with the gospel. I now had a missionary story of my own, and could add my testimony to the testimonies I had heard as a child. God is aware of our efforts, and he rewards hard work and faith.

Thereafter, each new responsibility I received required abilities that I did not have, although none was nearly as overwhelming as the "premature" call to be a senior companion. On subsequent assignments, my attitude was that God would make up for my shortcomings if I did my best.

As my mission continued, President Rhee called me to positions of greater responsibility, including the assignment to help the other missionaries better learn the Korean language. Then, when he called me to be one of his assistants, he unknowingly fulfilled a prophetic statement in a priesthood blessing I had received two years previously. This blessing—a patriarchal blessing[3]—said that I would be called to "help supervise and teach other missionaries how to do their work." The realization of this part of my patriarchal blessing was one more witness of Mormonism.

While I served in this position, an American elder admitted to a sexual indiscretion with a young woman, a violation of the Church rules of chastity. President Rhee was considering if the young man's mission should be immediately terminated. He discussed the incident with me and asked what I thought should be done. Although the missionary had done nothing against the young woman's will, I assumed Church policy would dictate that he be sent home early.

However, I was unfamiliar with Church policy on such matters, so my answer was noncommittal.

President Rhee probably had known all along what should be done. He explained that the gospel was meant to help people; he wondered what course of action would do this young man the most good. He noted that sending the missionary home would be devastating; his embarrassment for receiving a dishonorable release from his mission could keep him away from the Church for the rest of his life. President Rhee did not send the missionary home, and in the process, he taught me a powerful lesson about extending charity and withholding condemnation.

After my mission, I served as a gospel doctrine Sunday School teacher, counselor and president in the youth organization for boys, bishop's executive secretary, ward mission leader, and in several elders quorum presidencies.[4] One of my favorite Church assignments was teaching the children of the Church.

Still, of all my Church callings, none has influenced my life as much as did my mission. Those two years of teaching and testifying had a tremendous impact on my thoughts and actions. Having served in some leadership positions myself, I gained a greater desire to support those who were called to positions of responsibility for which they had not sought, and for which they often felt unqualified. When my mission ended, my resolve to stay true was uncompromising. My faith, I thought, was unshakable.

Brad

Wherefore, whoso believeth in God might with surety hope for a better world, yea, even a place at the right hand of God, which hope cometh of faith, maketh an anchor to the souls of men, which would make them sure and steadfast, always abounding in good works, being led to glorify God.
—*Book of Mormon*, Ether 12:4

I often reflected upon this verse. My hope for a better world burned brightly. The anchor to my soul felt secure. In my moments of greatest trial and in my moments of greatest peace and contentment, I felt to praise God for His goodness and blessings. Some intense spiritual experiences reinforced my commitment to God and His Church. I made a conscientious effort, with spotty success, to improve myself and to make life better for those around me.

I served as a missionary in the New Zealand South Mission from 1969 to 1971. I did not attain the leadership stature that Chris attained on his mission, nor was I particularly forceful or dynamic as a missionary. I sometimes worried about my tendency to be overly respectful of other's choices and their desires to not be proselytized. There were times, it seemed, when God inspired my mission companion and me in our efforts to spread His word. However, when our bumbling efforts were unaccompanied by His influence, I assumed He knew of my need to learn some lessons the hard way. Still, I felt special in His eyes and felt He was mindful of my desires to please Him.

As a missionary, one of my most satisfying times was with Elder Bollinger in a lovely little town called Wiaroa. The children, unusually friendly in that paradise of a town, would shout "Hi Elders" as we biked down the street in the heat and humidity, fully armored with our dark suits and ties. Maybe they were laughing at us, but at least they appeared happy and it rubbed off on us. All of the faithful members of the Church in Wiaroa were Maori, or at least Polynesian, and they adored the missionaries. We met in a beautiful little white chapel. We successfully brought new converts into the Church, and we made many friends.

I recall an interesting encounter while in Wiaroa going from door to door. The man who answered this particular door seemed pleasant enough, but, upon hearing our message, challenged us with, "You just believe it because you need the security it offers." My retort, which I considered God-inspired for the occasion, followed: "You don't believe because you don't want the responsibility of living God's commandments." That impression satisfied me as to why some people refused to believe in God's only true church. The man at the door seemed to respect my response, but not enough to invite us in. Sometimes we took pleasure in the very small victories.

I left New Zealand, content that God was satisfied with my efforts to bring souls to Him. My commitment continued. I was prepared to "waste and wear out my life" building God's Kingdom here on earth.

I returned to Brigham Young University, BYU, where I received Bachelor of Science and Master of Science degrees in mathematics. My years there were enjoyable and productive. One memorable responsibility at BYU was serving as first counselor to Bishop Bill Aaron in the BYU 69th Ward. During that time, my brothers Ben and Chris accepted calls as elders quorum president and the bishop's executive secretary respectively. I started out uneasy about the near monopoly the Morin boys had on the leadership positions in the ward, but none of us had asked for the callings and I did enjoy working with my brothers. We shared our convictions, an apartment, a reputation for pranks with water balloons, many cherished acquaintances, and much more.

My time in the 69th ward included some memorable social events and service projects that generated many friendships; however, these occasions were mixed with some sobering experiences. As a member of the bishopric, for instance, I occasionally participated in church courts for members who had committed transgressions that threatened their fellowship and/or membership in the Church. These were considered to be courts of love, used to regulate levels of participation or membership within the Church and to help the individual return to the path of righteousness. During the proceedings, I saw the acute discomfort felt by these "transgressors." Some were people I respected, whose commitment was not so different from mine. From these and other experiences, I concluded that I had exaggerated the fallen nature of those who err.

Bishop Aaron was solicitous of everyone in the ward. He expressed his confidence in me, which I appreciated and from which I benefited. When a head injury disabled Bishop Aaron for a month, I temporarily inherited his responsibility for the ward, with the help of the second counselor, Eric Hubner. It was a new experience to rub shoulders with the other bishops in the stake (an organizational unit in the Church consisting of about eight to ten wards) and with the stake president. I enjoyed it.

By late 1984, Chris and Ben had both married and were no longer in the ward. Bishop Aaron was released from his calling, and I accepted the call to be First Councilor to the new bishop in the same BYU Ward. The new bishop, whom I will call Bishop T, initially depended heavily upon my experience and familiarity with the ward. After several months I felt dissatisfaction coming from Bishop T for reasons that may have been justified but which I failed to fathom. I seriously considered asking for a release from my position, but I concluded it was God's call, not mine.

Again, I participated in some church courts held for members of the ward. It disturbed me that Bishop T never referred to the atonement of Christ and never mentioned the Savior in these courts. He seemed bothered when I emphasized Christ's atonement for our sins—a critical doctrine in the Church. We could be forgiven and our sins would be forgotten because of Christ's sacrifice. Knowing of His love, His mercy, and His willingness to remove our sins gave us hope in our endeavor to sanctify ourselves. How could Bishop T, ignoring this tenet, help these struggling souls back into God's fold?

By early 1985, the situation compounded. Bishop T expressed increasingly unorthodox views about the nature of God, that God was a male and female, literally a single being. He did not appreciate the challenge when I asked, as delicately as possible, for sources to this doctrine. As a reference, he mentioned *Ancient Texts and Mormonism*, by Eugene Seaich. I found and purchased the book in the BYU Bookstore for $6.95. The bishop's theology seemed horribly amiss, but confidence in my spiritual views had been misplaced before so some research seemed appropriate. After finding the references that justified Bishop T's beliefs, I rejected them as ideas of a scholar gone astray.

Aware of the stigma and the dangers of finding fault with one's leaders, I fretted over my next step. A week later in our bishopric meeting, a stunning attack on my morally conservative views and on my being single at age 34 left me reeling. I set up a time to meet with President B.

President B hesitated to jump on my bandwagon, maybe recognizing my concerns as overplayed and too personal. I asked for an immediate release and determined to attend a non-student ward. My concerns continued for the students in the ward; as a result, within days, I requested one more meeting with the stake president, a meeting that was to include Bishop T. It did not go well. Only the stake high councilman, Lloyd Eldridge, seemed to share significant concerns about Bishop T.

Spiritual distress rocked me for weeks as I questioned my inspiration and worthiness. Brigham Young once said: "One of the first steps to apostasy is to find fault with your Bishop; and when that is done, unless repented of a second step is soon taken, and by and by the person is cut off from the Church, and that is the end of it. Will you allow yourselves to find fault with your Bishop?"[5] Was I unknowingly on the high road to apostasy? Within a few months, I received a call to be elders quorum president in my new ward, bringing welcomed reassurance that God still trusted me.

Within a year, a new bishop had replaced Bishop T. Another year later, I got word from the stake president of Bishop T's excommunication. The ominous shadow of apostasy had overtaken Bishop T. I felt relief. I felt vindicated. Years later, I heard an account of Bishop T's disastrous effect upon the students within the ward. I wondered if the account was true; if so, I had done too little to prevent this upheaval of youthful faith. In summer of 1992, a chance meeting with Bishop T's wife (former wife at that point in time) gave me further reason, sound or not, to justify my original concerns about the bishop's spiritual stability.

During those years, I continued my commitment to the Church; however, persistent questions haunted my deepest thoughts. How often did God allow his servants to act without inspiration? How often were church leaders called without His inspiration? Were my observations of the ward members under Bishop T an anomaly, or did the pervasive assumption of inspired leadership create sheep-headed followers in the Church who were afraid to question leaders, discounting their own God-given intelligence and inspiration? Wondering about the balance between following leaders and following my own conscience, I decided to accept the consequences of my future actions based upon my own sense of right and wrong—while soliciting God's help.

Chapter 3

Fallible Minds

Brad

The aplomb with which I approached religious and po-

Ignorance more frequently begets confidence than does knowledge.
—Charles Darwin, *Descent of Man*, Introduction

litical issues did not come from a thorough understanding of the facts; it came from the conviction that God inspired my views. As a faithful Mormon, having received the gift of the Holy Ghost by authorized servants of God at the time of my baptism, I could expect God's inspiration. I put great confidence in this gift, one available to every member of the Church. Any evidence that contradicted my spiritual convictions was usually dismissed as twisted or incomplete. Six years after my fallout with Bishop T, three stunning discoveries dramatically diminished my self-assuredness.

Years earlier, in the 1960s, I wholeheartedly supported U.S. involvement in the Vietnam War, believing we were defending the world against communism. Those who protested the war were, in my mind, out of harmony with God's enlightenment and good old American patriotism. I looked with disdain upon all anti-war demonstrators.

It came as a surprise that not all *good* people shared my view, but I continued to take my cues from Mormon Apostle Ezra Taft Benson. On May 6, 1969, he gave a devotional talk at BYU entitled,

"Vietnam—Victory or Surrender," advocating that we "launch a massive military campaign" to defeat the "godless Communists." He even advocated going after Communist China. I still have the audio tape of that speech. My heart told me that anyone who bucked this sentiment had rejected the enlightenment of God's spirit.

After the war, I became aware of the increasingly popular view that the U.S. involvement in the Vietnam War was immoral. This appeared to be a misguided shift in the thinking of the masses; I considered myself above the foolishness of the oftentimes muddled popular thinking. Two decades later, the extent of my ignorance became evident. I had known virtually nothing of the history of Vietnam, part of French Indochina for a time, and their struggle for independence from France. It came as a surprise to me that initial U.S. involvement, starting shortly after World War II, was not to fight communism; rather, it was to support French rule over the Vietnamese efforts for independence.[6]

Sometime around 1991, I became deeply troubled upon seeing the documentary "Vietnam: A Television History." I witnessed history, saw interviews with those involved, and concluded that the U.S. lacked justification for its actions in Vietnam. U.S. war tactics ultimately became frantic and often horribly inhumane, with the South Vietnamese in the countryside paying the dearest price for supporting Ho Chi Minh's communist government over the French-installed regime. Identifying whether Ho Chi Minh was a liberator, unifier, despot, or some unfathomable mix became less important to me. In the end, nothing excused American equivocations, excesses, and atrocities.

I was alarmed by the discovery of my own moral arrogance, by how condescending and intolerant I had been of those who, in the end, had known the circumstances much better than I. I recoiled to think of all the people killed and maimed—on both sides of the conflict—because uninformed partisans like me had supported such a war.

Reflecting on other dearly held convictions, I asked: "What else might I be *sure of* that is not so?" What I identified as God's spiritual assurances had led me to a horribly erroneous conclusion. Thus began a faltering self-examination of my own virtue, a personal expedition that slowly gathered steam through the 1990s.

About the time I experienced this jolt over Vietnam, I made some belated discoveries about the American Civil Rights Movement. Our parents emphasized compassion for others and fostered the courage to stand up against injustice. In spite of this, and due to my ignorance of racial issues, I grew up with strong sentiments against the Civil Rights Movement. I felt certain my feelings reflected the teachings of Church leaders, though I could not recall any specific sermons to that effect. I often wondered, in later years, about my *spiritual conviction* against this movement. Only recently have I verified that at least two Mormon Apostles—Ezra Taft Benson and Mark E. Peterson, leaders whom I revered—had spoken vigorously against the Civil Rights Movement.[7]

During my college years, vocal complaints and demonstrations were directed against the Church for its views on Blacks. Brigham Young University basketball and football teams encountered serious protests. Some demonstrations were merely inconvenient. Others were ominous and threatening. In my mind, these demonstrations further justified the fears and rhetoric against Blacks and against those supporting the Civil Rights Movement.

I did not understand the plight of the American Blacks. I felt they demanded more than their reasonable rights. At the time, around 1970, my unfavorable view of the immortalized Martin Luther King Jr. seemed to be in harmony with most of my Utah peers. Over the years, as I picked up a piece of history here and there, my views softened toward the late Reverend King and Civil Rights. Then one night I saw a documentary on the Civil Rights Movement.[8] I saw old news footage that left me stunned. I learned of abuses against Blacks—atrocities which many Americans had known about for years. I watched interviews and heard the stories of Blacks and Whites who stood up for Blacks' voting rights. The stories of the Black and White Civil Rights workers who were beaten and murdered left me numb. I could not help but mentally don my armor for a battle that had long passed me by.

How could I have been so wrong on this crucial issue? For some people in the South, it was the difference between freedom and repression, justice and inequity, life and death. How could my revered leaders have been so misguided? The answers came slowly as I peered from my dark corner of ignorance. I had much to learn about myself, human nature, and the subtle mechanics of mass delusion.

My intentions had been good, but it dawned on me that in all those years, God had not been in my corner on all of life's important issues.

The gift of the Holy Spirit . . . quickens all the intellectual faculties, increases, enlarges, expands, and purifies all the natural passions and affections . . . It inspires virtue, kindness, goodness, tenderness, gentleness, and charity. —Parley P. Pratt (early Mormon apostle), quoted in James E. Talmage, *The Articles of Faith*, pp. 487–488

On March 3, 1991, three Los Angeles police officers were caught on video beating a Black man named Rodney King. He had been pulled over for speeding and reckless driving. He was drunk and had ignored the police lights and sirens. The video of the beating, shown around the world, quickly became big news, shocking many viewers. At least another twenty law enforcement officers were present and had witnessed the beating, not including the two in the helicopter supplying the lighting.

I was aghast. For me, this incident became the defining moment for the term *police brutality*. Before Rodney King, I assumed police officers were justified in their rough treatment of suspects; I gave little credence to claims and talk of police brutality. After watching the beating, I acknowledged the likelihood of past injustices and of current unacceptable attitudes. I wondered how often this kind of abuse happened with so many officers present—and no video camera around.

My dismay grew when I started hearing justifications for this kind of police conduct. On one occasion, while watching a rerun of the King beating, I heard someone justify the police action with: "But he is trying to get away! He is trying to get away!" What I saw was an already beaten and helpless man, on the ground, struggling to ward off the vicious blows, struggling to escape a terrifying situation. The difference in our interpretations left me dazed. At a loss for words, I left the home of this individual whom I considered an example of virtue and goodness.

Because I seemed out of step with so many faithful Saints (faithful Church members accepted the title of Saint), I questioned my initial conclusion, but only for a moment. I refused to accept the King beating as justified. Then, in private, my passions exploded. My reaction, silent fury, kept me from all sleep for two nights. I was on leave from teaching at the time. Alone in my home, I fumed and paced. At odds with some of God's most dedicated disciples, I told myself that living in hell would be preferable to a society that condoned this injustice. My intense desire for better relations between races fueled my anger, to the point of incongruity.

My fury was unhealthy. I finally recognized that it could take me, like a runaway team of horses, where I should not go. With an almost reluctant grasp on the rein of reason, I tempered my passions. It was easy to spot fanaticism in others but difficult to notice it in myself or my beloved causes.

Mental and spiritual agitation took its toll. An incorporeal shiver traversed the entire essence of my faith as I struggled with the fallout. As Mormons, we held that our unique endowment of the Holy Ghost would guide our thoughts and actions to a higher level of virtue, putting us more in harmony with God than was any other group on earth. I had taken this claim seriously, but now my confidence waned. In considering the justice of the King beating, my impressions from the Holy Ghost differed wildly from the impression that many faithful Saints received from *their* Holy Ghost. Maybe I lacked enough righteousness to merit the gift. Maybe it was a very part-time gift. Maybe it did not exist, except as a self-generated impression.

Before my enlightenment on Vietnam and Civil Rights, I occasionally took note of an odd group of people, those

> The solid earth! The actual world! The common sense! Contact! Contact! Who are we? Where are we?
> —Henry David Thoreau, *The Main Woods*, p. 70, Princeton University Press 1974

who seemed genuinely convinced of their own fantastic fabrications. They could, at times, successfully fool no one but themselves. It seemed they could, at will, lose touch with reality. Maybe some of them belonged in asylums, but most of them seemed to function satisfactorily amongst the rest of us.

Before long, I saw a tendency for self-deceit in varying degrees within a variety of people. Some had convenient memories; the facts supporting their cherished view came readily to mind, while the facts discrediting their outlook were easily forgotten. Some could accept a bogus argument if it supported their agenda but could readily see through the same species of false reasoning when used against their own guarded convictions. Some welcomed only the flattering stories about their favorite politicians or spiritual leaders and only the unflattering characterizations of people who preached a different gospel. Some made sweeping generalizations from a set of very incomplete facts; they then manifested total blindness to new and valuable information. Often, one's concept of reality depended upon what they wanted reality to be. In most of these cases, they considered themselves honest people, but they let their fears and fancies rule their minds.

I puzzled at length over this inclination for self-deception. It seemed to be such a curious and unproductive addiction. In 1990, I took greater notice of my own tendency for self-deception as I began to uncover serious flaws in my worldview. I realized that the lies that had long preserved my false beliefs were the lies that I told to myself. I awoke to the fact that *I am the master of my own deceit*.

The stories I believed and the observations I embraced generally harmonized with what I wanted reality to be. For example: In sporting events when passions ran high, the games my team lost due to incompetent officiating were far more numerous than the victories due to incompetent officiating. I had been too willing to believe the worst of the other team, the rival school, someone in the other political party, leaders of other nations, people of other races, and most significantly, those who conscientiously rejected the faith I revered.

My suspicions of some beliefs appeared to be well founded. I scoffed at those who deny the Holocaust, those who believe that the earth is flat, those who believe that their failures and fortunes are tied to the stars, and at the accompanying stories used for justification. I saw a host of senseless claims being whispered or shouted in the world, claims void of any compelling logic, claims that no one needed to believe; yet, they found acceptance. By the end of 1991, I became alarmed by profound flaws in my own convictions.

Still, when it came to religion, I continued to criticize the beliefs and practices of all faiths—except my own. On that front, I considered my unquestioning faithfulness to be a virtue.

On March 28, 1997, news came of a cult mass suicide in Rancho Santa Fe, California. This group, Heaven's Gate, consisting of thirty-nine people who committed suicide, apparently thought they were catching a flight on a space ship coming in the tail of the Hale-Bopp Comet. Upon seeing old videos of the two leaders Ti and Do, and some followers, I recognized troubling similarities to my approach to religion. Suddenly, I looked upon blind faith with new eyes, observing the way it shoved aside reason and natural inquiry, sometimes leading to absurd acts. Illusions are often naively foisted upon self and others; yet, even with well-intentioned innocence, unwanted results can be far-reaching and ruinous to people's lives. I saw fear and distrust coming from self-righteous delusions, greasing the gears and powering the engines of humankind's most horrific and destructive acts.

But for all my thoughtful observations, I remained guilty of inflicting a class of injury of which I was still oblivious. It was not violent. It was not loud. It would never be splashed across the headlines or the ten o'clock news. It was in the shadows. It was personal. In 1997, I still had only an inkling of the destructive role which I played in the lives of others, from the questioning youth to the sweet old non-believing lady across the back fence.

The Truman Show provides an interesting analogy. Truman (played by Jim Carrey) was unaware that he was on camera twenty-four hours a day in

> Either you think — or else others have to think for you and take power from you, pervert and discipline your natural tastes, civilize and sterilize you.
> —F. Scott Fitzgerald, *Tender Is the Night*, 1934, Book 3, Chapter 7, p. 290

a phony and manipulated environment for the live viewing pleasure of the world. When he started uncovering clues to the deception, some of his viewers thought he might unravel the secret of his existence. Truman's "creator," the individual controlling Truman's phony world, assured them that Truman would not want to leave his *perfect world*. In explaining Truman to the television viewers, the creator said: "We accept the reality of the world with which we are presented." He also said of Truman, "If his was more than just a vague ambition, if he was absolutely determined to discover the truth, there is no way we could prevent him." Then he added, "Ultimately, Truman prefers his cell."

In the end, the creator made a final effort to stop Truman's attempt to escape. He told Truman about the evils of the real world, then said: "In my world, you have nothing to fear." Truman had to choose between a familiar, safe, pretend world and a frightfully insecure reality.

Chapter 4

Living the Great Plan of Happiness

Chris

One Sunday, while living in Tabiona, Utah, our bishop wanted each person in the congregation to bear his or her testimony. Starting with those in the back of the chapel, each member of the congregation, in turn, stood up and bore testimony. As my turn drew closer, I became increasingly uneasy, afraid of speaking in front of the whole congregation and unsure of what to say. "I believe the Church is true" would have been an honest statement, but "I know the Church is true" seemed to be the only acceptable testimony. In retrospect, the pressure I felt was probably more imagined than real. However, being six or seven years old at the time, and wanting to fit in, I stood and said that I knew the Church was true.

> I have seen several entirely sincere people who *thought* they were (permanent) Seekers after Truth. They sought diligently, persistently, carefully, cautiously, profoundly, with perfect honesty and nicely adjusted judgment—until they believed that without doubt or question they had found the Truth. *That was the end of the search.* The man spent the rest of his life hunting up shingles wherewith to protect his Truth from the weather . . . from that day forth, with his soldering-iron in one hand and his bludgeon in the other he tinkered its leaks and reasoned with objectors.
>
> —Mark Twain, *What Is Man?* Section IV

As a youth, I envied fellow Mormons who could point to a certain special spiritual experience and say unequivocally: "That is when God gave me a witness of the truthfulness of the Church." Although an irrefutable witness never came at any one time, as far back as I can remember, I had believed that the Mormon Church was true. My faith increased over the years, due in part to what I considered spiritual experiences.

I had been taught, and I believed, that a person cannot be truly happy without the gospel as taught by the Mormon Church. Church teachings seemed to lead to a happy life, and I had it from very reliable sources that the Church was indeed true. By the time I left for my mission, my faith in the Church was solid. Upon returning, the combination of my observations, my study, and my spiritual experiences gave me the confidence to state with conviction that I knew the Church was true: Mormonism was the only source of lasting happiness.

After my mission, I attended BYU, living with Brad and two other brothers, Ben and Charles. There I met Connie, and in 1984 we were married in the Idaho Falls Mormon temple. I hoped to build our home on the gospel foundation, as had my parents; a prominent wall of our modest newlyweds' apartment displayed a large picture of Jesus.

While at BYU, I occasionally encountered ideas which were unnerving or inconsistent with my beliefs. For example: similarities between the Mormon temple ceremony and Masonic rituals,[9] Joseph Smith's strange account of the first vision,[10] some of Brigham Young's teachings, Joseph Smith's claim that he had translated the Kinderhook plates (which later proved to be counterfeit),[11] Church leaders buying forgeries in the 1980s from Mark Hofmann and then deceiving law enforcement officials about issues connected with these forgeries,[12] and the Church's policy to withhold embarrassing historical documents from scholars both inside and outside the Church.

I encountered a smattering of these issues in gospel discussions at church or school, or by reading newspapers or books by Church leaders. Yet, I could not investigate them further without challenging my complete trust in the Church and its teachings. It was the church to which my parents, my siblings, and all of my friends belonged. I had spent two years on a mission for the Mormon Church, and I was attending a Church university. I believed my recent temple marriage with Connie would continue through the eternities if we remained faithful to the Church. Immersed in the Church and content in my beliefs, I felt no need to dig deeper.

Upon hearing troubling issues, my first impulse was to simply ignore the problem, continuing on as if I had not read what I had just read, or heard what I had just heard. Questions that could not be ignored were handled in one of two ways. Whenever possible I would—on the spot and with little or no knowledge of the facts— state with conviction that matters were being misrepresented or taken out of context. If that approach did not work, I did as Church leaders taught and "put problem issues on the shelf." That is, I simply put such issues aside and assumed that, some day, when I was better prepared for the truth, I would understand. As it turns out, this approach was tantamount to my preferred first response of just ignoring the issue. I easily dismissed all but two matters that kept surfacing: the Church policy toward Blacks, and the question of polygamy.

In the summer of 1978, the year I graduated from high school, the Church had ended the policy of withholding the priesthood and temple blessings from Blacks. I had rejoiced for the Blacks and felt vindicated in my belief that the Church was not racist.

Only later did I give serious and semi-independent thought to the pre-1978 Church policy toward Blacks. We were told that this policy was similar to Jesus telling his apostles not to teach the Gentiles. A few members suggested that God instituted the practice because Church members (Whites) were not ready for Blacks to join the fold. Some Church leaders supported this explanation—or so I heard. I struggled to subdue my unsettled feelings as my views became more progressive.

Polygamy was the second matter I had difficulty resolving. I had always been inwardly embarrassed over Brigham Young's fifty-two wives. (By some accounts he had more, and by other accounts he had fewer. I had been taught he had fifty-two.) Fifty-two wives appeared a bit excessive, but maybe I misjudged Brigham. While some early Church leaders apparently thought there was no limit to the number of wives a man could have,[13] there is evidence that Brigham

put the limit at one thousand.[14] (Perhaps he should be commended
for his moderation.) My discomfort was mostly with the practice of
polygamy, not with the polygamists themselves; they were simply
striving for exaltation rather than damnation.[15]

One account of polygamy held particular interest for me. In
1879, Ben and Mary Perkins, with a company of Church members,
were called by Church leaders to leave their home in Cedar City,
Utah and help settle Southeastern Utah. Ben and Mary asked Mary's
nineteen-year old sister, Sarah, to help care for their four young
children on this difficult trip. Sarah consented, leaving her parents'
home to assist on this original *hole-in-the-rock* journey, which is
legendary among Southern Utah Mormons. Intended as a six-week
trip, it ended up being a six-month trek. Sarah then stayed for almost
six more months to help with Mary's newborn. Sarah grew close to
Mary and her five children.

Years earlier, Ben had received a priesthood blessing ad-
monishing him to take a second wife; now he saw in Sarah the
fulfillment of that commandment. Before Sarah returned to her
parents' home, Ben was more than a brother-in-law; he was a
suitor on a mission from God. Sarah respected Ben, sixteen years
her senior, but she felt no romantic love for him. She balked at his
proposal of marriage and returned home single.

The next year Ben and Mary visited her parents' home. Sarah had
heard Mary's heartfelt reservations about, and her parents' vigorous
objections to, Ben's proposal. She reiterated her reservations to him.
However, with a mandate from God, Ben took Sarah to talk with the
bishop and his counselors. Although she still did not love him (he
had never courted her), this group of men convinced her that it was
God's will that she marry. She acquiesced, but her obedience cost
her dearly.

Sarah's marriage to Ben in the fall of 1881 was not a festive
occasion. There was no celebration of marriage for Sarah, just a se-
cretive ceremony with no family in attendance. There was no happy
honeymoon; Ben dropped her off at his sister's house at 3:00 a.m.
then returned home to his first wife, Mary. There was no romantic
love for her new husband, just an assurance of having complied
with God's command. Her parents followed through on their threat
to shun her. Mary had consented to Ben entering polygamy, but felt

bitter toward Sarah. Sarah could not appear in public with Ben for fear of federal marshals on the prowl for polygamists. (They eventually caught him, and he served six months in prison for "marrying too much.")

For most of Sarah's married life, Ben lived in another town with Mary. He was out of town for the births of all ten of Sarah's children whom she raised virtually by herself under destitute circumstances.

Despite the hardships she suffered, Sarah defended polygamy in her journal; she taught her children and grandchildren that God had ordained polygamy. One of those granddaughters, Rene Lyman, is my mother, and she passed this conviction on to me. However, as an adult, when I read Sarah's account, I began to wonder about the anguish and misery caused by polygamy. Even so, I told myself to not question the Lord's methods.

> "Mormonism" is true in every leading doctrine, or it is false as a system altogether.
> —Brigham Young, 1865, *Millennial Star*, Volume 27, pp. 675–676

There is an analogy between my life as a mathematician and my life as a Mormon that may be useful in understanding how I could dismiss so many problems over the years.

As a Mormon, I often thought in absolute terms. For example, I "knew" the *Book of Mormon* was true; I knew that Joseph Smith was a prophet; I knew that the Mormon Church was the only true church on the face of the earth.

As a mathematician, I often think in absolute terms. I never look at a proposition as being "mostly true" or "kind of true." It is either true or false; the difficulty lies in proving it one way or the other. When a proposition has been proven, it is then called a theorem and it is considered to be (absolutely) true. With the theorem as a basis, other propositions (corollaries) can be shown to be valid. If I never question the validity of the original theorem, I am stuck with all the corollaries that follow from it, no matter how strange they may seem. On the other hand, to reject even one valid corollary requires that the theorem be discarded. This calls into question the truthfulness of all the other corollaries that followed from the theorem, no matter how interesting, useful, or beautiful they are.

Consider the parallel view expressed by Joseph Fielding Smith, who became the tenth Mormon prophet: "Mormonism must stand or fall on the story of Joseph Smith. He was either a prophet of God, divinely called, properly commissioned, or he was one of the biggest frauds this world has ever seen. There is no middle ground."[16]

Of course, the analogy breaks down. As a mathematician, I have been willing to question a corollary. I would take another critical look at the proof of the original theorem if it led to conclusions which appeared to be false. But as a Mormon, I never took a second look at anything which might cause me to reject the Church. It simply never occurred to me that my faith might be ill founded.

This unwillingness to re-evaluate my faith came with a price. The more I ignored my own thoughts in order to align my thinking to prescribed ideas, the more I lost touch with my own sense of right and wrong, and the more I lost confidence in my own judgment. I became more dependent on the source of authority as to the correct course of action. At times, I asked not: "What is right?" or "What is wrong?" but "What do the 'authorities' say on the matter?" Something precious is lost in such a process, even if one is following a prophet who will never lead us astray.

One day at BYU, I read an article about a case the American Civil Liberties Union (ACLU) had taken all the way to the Supreme Court. The suit defended the right of some Native American Indians to use a controlled substance, peyote, in their traditional religious ceremonies. Up to that time, I do not recall ever having agreed with the ACLU on any issue. In my mind, the ACLU used twisted logic and distorted the spirit of the law to justify a case. The article seemed to confirm my conservative, Republican, Mormon opinion—another case of the ACLU gone amuck.

Then the article mentioned some of the organizations in agreement with the ACLU, among them the Church of Jesus Christ of Latter-day Saints. Oops! A little chagrined, I decided that there might be something to this case after all. I quickly reread the article, and this time I acknowledged the validity of the ACLU arguments.

I gave little thought to my about-face, a turnabout based solely on the fact that the Church agreed with the ACLU. I believed in the teaching that "when the prophet speaks, the debate is over."[17] My intellectual independence would have been best described as "free thought—on a leash."

I tried to cultivate compassion for those whose lives lacked meaning for want of the fullness of the gospel. However, this compassion was sometimes over-shadowed by my view that their lack of

Believing that only your group has the complete truth does not cultivate a willingness to learn from others. Believing that God has given you a special gift of discernment does not foster respect for the judgment of those who have no such gift. Being among God's chosen people does not increase your sense of brotherhood with the rest of humanity.

—clm (Chris L. Morin)

happiness was self-imposed through their rejection of Mormonism. When comparing Mormons with non-Mormons, my views agreed with those of Church leader Joseph Fielding Smith:

> We are, notwithstanding our weaknesses, the best people in the world. I do not say that boastingly, for I believe that this truth is evident to all who are willing to observe for themselves. We are morally clean, in every way equal, and in many ways superior to any other people. The reason is that we have received the truth, the gospel of the Lord Jesus Christ.[18]

Mormons were more righteous because we had the fullness of the gospel, and we had the fullness of the gospel because we had been more noble in the pre-existence, or pre-earth life. Many times as a boy, I heard the local Church leaders teach that we—the youth of the Church—were among the most valiant spirits in the pre-existence, that we had been held back by God to be born in the latter-days, into Mormon homes, to help prepare the world for the second coming of Christ. Even as a youth, I balked at this doctrine, but I could not refute it without rejecting the teachings of the prophets and apostles in Salt Lake City. For example, Ezra Taft Benson—an apostle, and later the president of the Church—taught the following about those "born under the covenant." (A child born to parents whose marriage was sealed in a Mormon temple is said to be "born under the covenant.")

My brethren and sisters, it is my conviction that the finest group of young people that this world has ever known anything about has been "born under the covenant" into the homes of Latter-day Saint [Mormon] parents.[19]

This doctrine has been reiterated through the years.[20] The fact that it applied to me was established in my *patriarchal blessing*, a special priesthood blessing considered to be personal scripture for the recipient. My patriarchal blessing included the following statement:

> You are a choice son of our Heavenly Father, and through your faithfulness, through your study and diligence, you gained great knowledge in the pre-existent life and through your faithfulness, you earned the right to come to this earth through this choice lineage, that you might be blessed with the Gospel of Jesus Christ.

After leaving Utah, I heard less of the doctrine that faithfulness in the pre-existence earns one the right to be born into a Mormon home. However, a few years ago here in Illinois—the Land of Lincoln—those attending a Mormon youth conference were told that they had been more valiant in the pre-existence than had Abraham Lincoln. The evidence: they were Mormons; they had either been born into a Mormon home or they had been born into a time and a place where they could, and would, hear and accept the truth as taught by the Mormon Church. Abe, of course, had not been a Mormon.

For Mormons, since personal righteousness in the pre-earth life so greatly influences the family and circumstances into which you are born, your family's worthiness is an indication of your own faithfulness in the pre-existent life. This doctrine, at least on the subconscious level, stroked my ego very nicely. Other Church members were disheartened by its logical implications. For example, the beliefs and actions of an unbelieving parent imply that a believing child lacked the obedience in the pre-existence to be born through a more "choice lineage." Such judgments, although subtle and seldom acknowledged, can have a detrimental influence on relationships between non-Mormon parents and their Mormon children.

There were other yardsticks by which I could measure the worthiness of Mormons as well as non-Mormons. Compliance with the Word of Wisdom was one of the most obvious measures. (The "Word of Wisdom" is the Mormon health code. It disallows use of tobacco, alcohol, coffee and tea.) When I saw someone sipping coffee, for instance, I saw someone who was not among God's chosen people.

Similarly, clothing was a yardstick. Worthy adult Mormons are to wear the temple garment at all times; this "Mormon underwear" would be exposed if one wore a sleeveless shirt or shorts that were higher than the knees. Adults who wore such clothes were very conspicuous in Utah where I grew up surrounded by active Mormons. Even wearing long pants and a long-sleeve shirt, non-Mormons or unworthy Mormons are often easily identified by looking at their chest and observing they are not wearing temple garments under their shirt. It was common practice to identify people in this way. Although nobody formally taught me to do so, I developed a habit of identifying those who were not temple-worthy Church members and judging them as not being on the path to salvation as was I.

As for Mormons who suffered a divorce in this family-oriented church, I judged them as falling short. Although I considered my judgment to be measured and merciful, my inclination was to believe that—as my wife Connie had been taught in a religion class—"Failure in marriage is almost total failure."

I did not acknowledge the arrogance of the judgments I passed upon others; indeed, for the most part they were subconscious thoughts. Neither did I consider how the judgmental Mormon doctrine must have induced anguish in some Mormons who did not measure up.

While the effects of some Church doctrines may be elusive, there is nothing subtle about the exclusion of inactive or non-Mormon parents at the temple wedding of their Mormon child. They simply are not allowed at the ceremony. Connie's parents are not Mormons; her mother waited outside on the temple grounds, while worthy Mormons attended our wedding. Her father stayed home, having previously felt the sting of exclusion from the temple wedding of his oldest daughter.

The exclusion of Connie's parents from our wedding upset her. I tried to show sensitivity to her feelings, but I thought to myself that she overstated her parents' plight. Given that they had not accepted the gospel that could make their family an eternal family, then surely missing our wedding could not be that important to them.

The Mormon Church compares itself favorably to all other churches. In the *Book of Mormon*, an angel taught the prophet Nephi that in the latter-days there would be only two churches. One is the church of the Lamb of God, and anyone not belonging to it belongs to the "church of the devil . . . the whore of all the earth."[21] Clearly, ours was the church of the Lamb of God; all other churches together formed the church of the devil. In the book *Mormon Doctrine,* Bruce R. McConkie identified the Catholic Church as "the great and abominable church," a "satanic organization." It is the "mother of Harlots," and the Protestant churches are its "harlot daughters."[22]

McConkie later served for years as an Apostle, and during my youth, he was considered by many as *the* expert on Mormon doctrine. Although later editions of *Mormon Doctrine* took a softer stance toward other churches, I understood that the reason for the change was not because McConkie had been incorrect, but because the truth had been too offensive to people outside the Church.

According to Joseph Smith, Jesus spoke of ministers of other religions saying: "those professors were all corrupt, they draw near to me with their lips, but their hearts are far from me."[23] Similarly, in my monthly temple attendance while at BYU, the ceremony represented ministers of other religions as working under the direction of Satan. This steady diet of dogma left me with little regard for other religions, and little respect for their leaders.

Upon graduating from BYU and going on for graduate work at the University of Texas at Austin, I was comfortable in my cocoon of devotion. My faith was firm, my mind was set, and my feet were planted solidly on the gospel sod.

To preserve my belief in the fallen nature of those foreign to me, I must remain ignorant of who they really are—ignorant of their hopes and fears, ignorant of their unselfish deeds, and ignorant of their noble desires.
—clm

While surrounded by Mormons in Utah, my view of non-Mormons had been one-dimensional. I had little chance to observe the love that non-Mormon parents feel for their children; I knew only that they did not accept the church that could make their family an eternal family. I had little firsthand knowledge of their efforts to make this world a better place; I knew only that they ignored God's commandments to a wicked and unhappy world. They sought rewards of worldly riches and thought to get to heaven without the required ordinances. Because I had virtually no opportunity to associate with non-Mormons, they were defined by my perception of their non-Mormonism, little else.

One day in Austin as I was leaving the university to go home, I saw one of my professors with his wife and daughter. He introduced us and we talked for a minute. Although I admired his intellect and character, I had two thoughts that reveal the deep misconceptions I had of non-Mormons. My first thought caught me by surprise; this professor, a non-Mormon, loved his family as much as any Mormon father loved his family. Next, the thought came that his family, unlike mine, was not an eternal family. My assumptions about non-Mormons were effortless and automatic, and they continued to influence my views of non-Mormons.

Nonetheless, while living in Austin, I did take advantage of this first significant opportunity to develop close friendships with non-Mormons. One such friend was Davis, a fellow graduate student in mathematics. We spent hours talking about religion, and I gave him a copy of the *Book of Mormon*. He read it from cover to cover, then did some research on the side. He next read the *Pearl of Great Price*, another Mormon book of scripture. Interestingly, of all the people I had baptized or taught on my mission, nobody had ever put in this much effort to learn about the Church. I had been taught that sincere seekers of truth, those who were honest and pure in heart, would recognize the truthfulness of the Mormon Church. But Davis remained unconverted. I tried not to speculate as to what personal faults might be preventing him from seeing the truth of the matter.

After his research, Davis raised some questions. For example, although the *Book of Mormon* spoke of horses in America between 600 B.C. and A.D. 421, there is no evidence of the modern horse in America until the Spaniards introduced them about 1,000 years later. (A prehistoric species of horse had died out thousands of years before *Book of Mormon* times.) Davis pointed out that the *Book of Mormon* is strikingly similar to *View of the Hebrews,* a book published in a neighboring county several years before Joseph Smith published the *Book of Mormon.* Although Davis' concerns had merit, I dismissed them all without any analysis. Certain that the *Book of Mormon* was true, I could not waste my time trying to refute every accusation made against it. After all, there is no need to be objective when you know you are right.

During this time, I developed friendships with the local ward members in Austin that I will cherish for a lifetime. When Connie had severe health problems, they brought us meals, watched our children, and on one occasion washed our laundry. Their kindnesses supported my view that Mormons were unique.

However, you might say that Isaac and Marilyn—our neighbors and friends—were evidence to the contrary. They too brought us meals, watched our children, and helped in other ways when Connie was not well. I had never known kinder people, and "They weren't even Mormons!"

From a distance you look like my friend, even though we are at war. From a distance I just cannot comprehend what all this fighting is for.
—"From a Distance" as popularized by Bette Midler

Although I whole-heartedly accepted the Church teaching of respect and love for all humankind—all of us being children of God—I had through the years developed an us-against-them attitude concerning non-Mormons. Maybe this mindset was due in part to my belief that non-Mormons belonged to the church of the devil while Mormons belonged to the church of the Lamb of God. Maybe it was due in part to hearing time and again of the persecution against early Mormons and of the martyrdom of Joseph Smith. With constant reminders of the wickedness of the rest of the world, my us-against-them attitude was never seriously confronted until I moved to Texas and developed friendships with Isaac and Marilyn, Davis, and other fellow graduate students. In the following years, my new view of non-Mormons would be a constant thorn in my side, challenging my belief that Mormons were God's chosen people.

In 1993, after finishing my Ph.D. at the University of Texas, I accepted a position at Blackburn College, and we moved to Carlinville, Illinois with our three children. (Our fourth child was born eighteen months later.) In Austin we had non-Mormon friends, but with many other Mormon students nearby, we had spent more time socializing with members than non-members. On the other hand, when we moved to Carlinville, we had to drive twenty-five miles to attend church, and ours were the only Mormon children in town.

I had concerns about our children socializing almost exclusively with non-Mormons. Would these associations undermine the values we sought to instill in our children? Would there be any Mormons for them to date? Would they fall in love with, and marry, a non-Mormon—a marriage out of the covenant? Still, the better acquainted I became with our children's friends, the less these questions concerned me.

My superficial yardstick continued to measure non-Mormons as coming up short on a number of insignificant issues. Yet when I considered the important matters, such as how one treats humankind, the differences were unnoticeable. Our exclusive claim to salvation—which seemed based only on the Mormon ordinances we received—made me uncomfortable. I wondered about many of my non-Mormon friends and acquaintances. If they did not accept the saving ordinances in this life, would they accept them in the next? The answer to that question seemed completely irrelevant. Regardless of which ordinances they received in this life or the next, their actions told me that they deserved the best that God had to offer.

When we moved to Carlinville, our oldest child, Carissa, started first grade.

All animals are equal; but some animals are more equal than others.
—George Orwell, *Animal Farm*

She began to see the possibilities and opportunities of life that lay ahead. Sometimes she wanted to be a teacher. Sometimes she wanted to be a scientist who studied and helped animals. (She started an "Animal Helpers Club" with her siblings.) Sometimes she wanted to help save the rain forests. Sometimes she wondered if, somehow, she could do all of the above. As a father, I shared in Carissa's excitement about all that life had to offer, but I worried that she might be missing her true calling. The Church teaches that refusing to bear children is a serious sin,[24] and that a woman, whenever possible, should stay home with her children while her husband earns the living.[25] That option did not fit Carissa's life plans.

I was torn. How could I teach her God's plan for women without denying her dreams, crushing her enthusiasm, and forcing her to confront her fear of bearing children? I rode the fence on this issue; I told her about the joys of parenthood, and occasionally I told her that the most important thing a woman could be was a good wife and mother. Then I diluted the significance of that statement by saying that the most important thing a man could be is a good husband and father. I never did give her the straight Mormon view of the role of women. In fact, the Church's doctrine on the marriage relationship was sometimes fuzzy. For example: "In marriage neither the man nor the woman is more important than the other; they are equal partners, although the man is the head of the house."[26] Connie and I often discussed the meaning of this doctrine.

> And whoso shall ask it in my name in faith, they shall [through the power of the priesthood] cast out devils; they shall heal the sick; they shall cause the blind to receive their sight, and the deaf to hear, and the dumb to speak, and the lame to walk.
> —God (as reported by Joseph Smith). *Doctrine and Covenants* 35:10

Mormons believe that the Melchizedek priesthood is the power by which God created the heavens and earth. This is the same priesthood which is held by virtually every worthy Mormon man who has been a Church member for over a year. This power can be utilized through priesthood blessings bestowed by two or more men who lay their hands on a person's head while one of them pronounces the actual words of the blessing. The men are taught that if they are righteous, the Lord will—through the Holy Ghost—inspire them to give the appropriate blessing. The power of a priesthood blessing can heal the sick, cause the blind to receive their sight, the deaf to hear, the dumb to speak, and the lame to walk. I had even heard, and believed, stories of people who had been raised from the dead by a Mormon priesthood blessing.

Over the years, I noticed that women of the Church generally had more faith in the healing powers of the priesthood than did the men. Women were more likely than men to suggest that a sick person receive a blessing. Maybe that is because the women have never experienced the anxiety of laying their hands on the head of a sick person, waiting for inspiration from God as to how to bless the sick person—and waiting. . . .

Despite my best efforts to live righteously and prepare myself to give priesthood blessings, whenever I found myself giving one, I did not get a clear message as to the blessing God wanted me to give. Of all the thoughts running through my mind, I wondered which of them came from God, and which were of my own making. Feeling no inspiration after a brief, uncomfortable wait, I felt compelled to say something, so I would give a noncommittal blessing and state that its fulfillment depended on the Lord's will and on the faith of those involved. If the person got better right away, it could be attributed to the priesthood blessing. Otherwise, I could conclude that one or more of us involved in the blessing did not have the faith to heal or be healed. Or, perhaps it was not the Lord's will that the person be healed right away. (Actually, my record was quite impressive; nobody died, and only one came close.)

In one case, I thought my blessing had helped in the healing of a man's eye, but other than that one time, it appeared that nature merely took its course. The sick people who received a blessing from me eventually got better, as did those who had not received a priesthood blessing. Though my priesthood blessings did not result in physical healing, thcy did seem to bring emotional comfort to the people blessed. I wondered if this relief was due to the visit from concerned friends, the priesthood blessing itself, the prayers we offered, or a combination of all these. In any case, I concluded that I did not have the faith necessary to actually heal the sick, and deep inside I felt like a pretender for trying to do so.

The Colorado Indians experienced a . . . culturally induced delusion when they climbed to a mountaintop to fast until the Great Spirit came to them. Every Indian boy who had to pass through this rite of puberty wasn't allowed to eat anything until he reported that the Great Spirit spoke to him. Every young man in the tribe actually hallucinated hearing and seeing the Great Spirit. But his hallucinations were not psychotic; it was simply something that the whole culture believed in to the point of mass delusion.

—Zev Wanderer and Tracy Cabot, *Letting Go*, Chapter 3

In 1996, I chaperoned a summer youth conference. The youth played games, danced, and listened to sermons and testimonials. The conference ended with many of the youth expressing gratitude for having feasted at a spiritual banquet. I said nothing to discredit their view, yet I could not shake the feeling that the youth had simply felt some powerful emotions, which—with a little help from a few adult leaders—they had interpreted as spiritual experiences.

By this time, I had begun to recognize the faulty reasoning that I, and other Mormons, had used to support our beliefs. For example, when a missionary escaped danger, it was attributed to the Lord watching out for his servants. However, if a missionary tragically died, we did not question the lack of protection from the Lord.

We sometimes falsely labeled our thoughts and impressions as inspiration from the Holy Ghost. Once, Connie received a priesthood blessing, after which the wife of the man who gave the blessing told Connie that she and her husband had both felt inspired that I should drop out of school rather than finish my doctoral degree. I did not accept their advice as inspiration from God.

We did a poor job keeping track of supposed prophecies and inspired priesthood blessings. Some prophecies surfaced after, rather than before, their fulfillment. No matter, we still passed them around as evidence of latter-day prophets. Some prophecies and blessings did not pan out. We ignored the ones we could;[27] some, we declared, would be fulfilled in the next life.

Often, Mormons (myself included) pointed out how our version of the gospel was so logical, and easy to understand. Yet when a contradiction reared its ugly head, the mantra changed to, "the gospel is not supposed to be logical, it takes faith." If science supported some

Church teaching, we pointed to those facts as support for our views; but in cases where science disagreed with us, we noted the flaws and inadequacies of science—"the wisdom of this world is foolishness with God" (I Corinthians 3:19).

With a feeling of "by their fruits shall ye know them" we were quick to point out the humanitarian efforts of the Church as evidence of its truthfulness. However, we downplayed the good motives and humanitarian efforts of other churches. Strange as it may seem, some Mormons even said that no other Church makes claims as strong as ours, and that the strong claims themselves are evidence of the Church's truthfulness.

I had concluded that humans are, to some extent, would-be sculptors trying to mold reality to fit their perceptions. Nonetheless, I was troubled to see that we Mormons were also guilty of such behavior; with prophets to give us truths directly from God, we Mormons could, and should, support our beliefs with honest analysis and sound logic.

To what extent did my beliefs skew my judgment? Despite having no discernible doubts about the Church being true, in the early 1990s, I did begin to wonder if I held any religious misconceptions. I recalled how, in 1890, some Mormons had refused to accept the new Church policy which ended the practice of polygamy; they still held firm to the words of the late Brigham Young and others on the issue. I also remembered how, in 1978, some Mormons rejected the new revelation from God that Blacks should now be given the priesthood; again such holdouts had confused a long-time Church policy with eternal truth. Were all my beliefs based on truth? Or, was I like those people who held some beliefs based on current policy rather than unchanging truth? Surely there was no need of an overhaul of my beliefs, but perhaps a little fine-tuning was in order.

In the spring of 1996, I had been looking forward to a *60 Minutes* interview between

> **My role is to declare doctrine. My role is to stand as an example before the people. My role is to be a voice in defense of the truth.**
>
> —Gordon B. Hinckley, in *Larry King Live*, aired September 8, 1998

Mike Wallace and Gordon B. Hinckley, the president of the Church. The program aired on April 7 and included this dialogue:

Mike Wallace: Are there any conflicts between your convictions about families and women's roles with the family and the aspirations of some women to occupy leadership positions in your church?

President Hinckley: We have a few women who feel that women should hold the priesthood. We have a great women's organization. I believe it is the largest women's organization in the world—our women's Relief Society. They have their own officers who preside over their own organization. They carry forward a tremendous program of education among women. I think they are happy. They are doing a great work . . .

Mike Wallace: Why must only men run the Church?

Many of the people listening to this broadcast would object to the Mormon policy toward women. Knowing the Church policy, I expected to see a courageous prophet (Hinckley) who was unafraid to state that withholding priesthood from women is a simple matter of revealed doctrine. Hinckley did not answer as I expected.

President Hinckley: 'Only men' do not run the Church. Men have their place in the Church. Men hold priesthood offices of the Church. But women have a tremendous place in this church. They have their own organization. It was started in 1842 by the Prophet Joseph Smith, called the Relief Society, because its initial purpose was to administer help to those in need. It has grown to be, I think, the largest women's organization in the world with a membership of more than three million. They have their own offices, their own presidency, their own board. That reaches down to the smallest unit of the Church everywhere in the world.

Mike Wallace: But they don't have the power.

President Hinckley: They have office. They have responsibility. They have control of their organization.

In the Mormon Church, women do not hold the priesthood, and without the priesthood a woman can never be prophet; a woman can never be an apostle; a woman can never be a stake president or a bishop. Any time a Mormon is asked to accept a Church job, it is a man who does the asking. Every officer in the Church's "great women's organization," is given her assignment by a man. Mike Wallace saying, "only men run the Church," seemed to be a fair assessment. Hinckley's denial troubled me.

Try as I might to live the "great plan of happiness" which Church leaders talked about—and which was available only through the Mormon Church—it

> The more closely you personally adhere to [God's] plan for you on Earth, the greater will be your happiness, fulfillment and progress.
> —Mormon apostle Richard G. Scott, "The Joy of Living the Great Plan of Happiness," General Conference, October, 1996

did not seem to be working for me. What was wrong? Some of my ancestors had crossed the plains with Brigham Young, making heroic sacrifices so their descendants could enjoy the blessings of the restored Church. Why did I find such scant happiness in making the relatively small sacrifices required of me? Why couldn't I enjoy the Church for which they had so valiantly sacrificed?

True, some of my Church service was worthwhile, and I enjoyed teaching children the principles which led to happy, productive lives. However, it seemed that many of my activities were driven by policy, rather than need. There were always meetings to go to, assignments to visit people who did not really want or need to be visited, and struggles to get unwilling boys to participate in the weekly youth activities. (I certainly empathized with the boys; I remembered feeling the same way at that age.) I had serious doubts about the effectiveness of some of my Church service—which cost me dearly in time away from my family. I told myself that at least our children would learn from my good example in doing what the Church required.

Feelings of inadequacy and guilt for not doing enough were substantial byproducts of my Church membership. With the time commitments to the Church and with my mind continually focused on the afterlife, I often found it difficult to enjoy the moment and savor the good things in this life. Perhaps I had taken too much to heart the idea expressed by Spencer W. Kimball (the president of the Church who called me on a mission) when he said: "Since immortality and eternal life constitute the sole purpose of life, all other interests and activities are but incidental thereto."[28] In any case, I had trudged along, with the present held captive by my aspirations for eternity.

Yet, I had reservations about eternity. I had given my time, my money, my heart and my soul to living the gospel, yet the longer I lived this "great plan of happiness" the more miserable I felt. What were the implications of following the plan for eternity? Maybe I was not suited for godhood and the fullness of joy that God had to offer; perhaps for some people the happiness part of the plan does not kick in until the next life.

The Church's stance on missionary work is exemplified in the oft-quoted phrase "Every member a missionary." Although I felt duty-bound to find converts, I wondered: Would I be doing my non-member friends a favor by introducing them to a Church that was a source of turmoil for me? They seemed to be missing nothing for lack of the Church. Since they could accept the gospel in the next life and still achieve exaltation, my half-hearted efforts at converting them were simply attempts to do as I had been commanded. With so many advantages of Church membership apparently limited to the next life, at times I was envious of non-Mormons. Life outside of the Church looked attractive, and I wanted out. I could see three ways to leave.

I could stop going to church, refuse all church callings, and become inactive. However, I still believed the Church was true, and I did not want to influence our children to reject the very Church which could lead them to their salvation.

The second option was to commit a grievous sin for which I would be excommunicated; this option never appealed to me.

The third way out of the Church was to be falsely accused of committing a grievous sin. In my solitary pondering, I reasoned that in a few years, after my innocence became known, I would be allowed to come back into the Church. Perhaps I would feel differently about things by then. Unfortunately, this path out of the Church depended entirely on someone falsely accusing me of a sin worthy of excommunication, an unlikely event.

By 1996, I admitted to myself that I was losing my faith, a sure sign of some wickedness on my part—or so I had been taught. Unable to ascertain my wickedness, I persevered with the hope that I could recover my faith. My outward devotion to the Church hid my dilemma from others, including Connie whose faith I did not want to disturb.

I read to our children almost every night. For years, most of these readings had been from either the *Book of Mormon* or the Bible. More and more, I found myself turning to the teachings of Jesus. Among my personal favorites were parts of the Sermon on the Mount, the story of the good Samaritan, and the incident of the woman taken in adultery, about which Jesus said, "He that is without sin among you, let him first cast a stone at her" (St. John 8:7). I became aware of spending more effort instilling a sense of love, kindness, and acceptance for others; I spent less time installing dogma such as "we belong to the only true church on earth."

Although I no longer said such things as "I *know* the Church is true," I still had a functioning testimony. I tried to live by faith rather than by the sure knowledge, which others appeared to have. I told myself, "It is my actions

> One of the saddest lessons of history is this: If we've been bamboozled long enough, we tend to reject any evidence of the bamboozle. We're no longer interested in finding out the truth. The Bamboozle has captured us. It's simply too painful to acknowledge, even to ourselves, that we've been taken.
> —Carl Sagan, *The Demon-Haunted World,* p. 241

that are important, not what I know or don't know for certain." A sure knowledge could come in the next life. For now, I just needed to believe harder.

In the fall of 1997, I became the mission leader for our ward, a ward that is approximately a one-hour drive from one end to the other. I enjoyed visiting the prospective members, and I hoped the gospel would make their lives better. However, try as I might, I could not muster the appropriate enthusiasm for missionary work. In a sermon to the whole Church, President Hinckley had expressed some of my own concerns when he said that conversion to Mormonism in most cases "involves setting aside old habits, leaving old friends and associations, and stepping into a new society which is different and somewhat demanding."[29] I often saw, or played a part in, a well-intentioned effort by ward members to "love someone into the Church." But, the members simply could not sustain their efforts. After being loved into the Church, the converts often left their long-time circle of friends and family only to have the shower of special attention from the ward members soon dwindle to a trickle. In my experience, some converts made new Mormon friends, and the transition into the Church went well. Some did not, and they aborted the transition. Others seemed to be caught in a lonely state of limbo, trying to hang on and do as they were taught, but never finding a niche in the ward. I saw enough unhappy endings that my zeal for missionary work diminished significantly.

In the spring of 1998, the two full-time sister missionaries in our ward visited a man who expressed an interest in Mormonism. Their visit ended abruptly when he indecently exposed himself to one of them. Upon departing the area, the two missionaries left a note for their replacements, a warning not to visit this man lest they too be exposed to his obscenities.

A few months later, this man again contacted the Church and said he would like a visit from the missionaries. The new sister missionaries decided to ignore the warning of the previous sisters. They asked if I could go with them to visit the man, thinking that my presence would discourage a repeat performance. My job as ward mission leader was to help the missionaries, so I immediately agreed that I should go with them rather than have them visit this man by themselves. But after some thought, I told them no, I would not go with them. I would not waste three hours away from home to visit a man whose interests were so suspect. More importantly, with all the children—including four of my own—who attended our three-hour block of Sunday meetings, I did not want this man hanging around the church. I considered it my duty to tell the missionaries that I thought it a bad idea to visit this man at all.

One of the sisters got angry with me. She said that it was her job to teach the gospel and it was not her position to deny this man if he expressed a desire to learn about the Church. The sisters would find another priesthood holder to accompany them on the visit.

I understood the zeal of the sister missionaries. I recalled my desire, as a full-time missionary in Korea, to share the blessing of the gospel with others. However, I also remembered the pressure to find and baptize people. I had been taught in the Missionary Training Center that there were people out there who would accept the truth only from me. Thus, if I did not do my part to find and teach them, they may not have the chance to accept the saving ordinances until the next life. Missionaries feel additional pressure to produce: pressure from peer missionaries, the mission president, and their parents who spend thousands of dollars to support them. Weekly productivity—which is measured not only in baptisms but also in the number of hours spent actually teaching the gospel—is reported to the mission president. Yes, I well understood the sister missionaries' desire to get into this man's house to teach.

Later that summer, the Elders Quorum Presidency suggested an open house at the church, an evening when members could bring their friends to learn about Mormon beliefs. As the ward mission leader, it fell to me to organize the event. Although I gave out assignments and oversaw preparations for the evening, I had deep reservations about the prospect of an open house. I tried, but failed, to identify the reasons for my extreme discomfort. The sister missionaries may have recognized my reservations, and remembering my unwillingness to accompany them on their visit to the exhibitionist, they apparently doubted my devotion to the Church. They were scarcely civil to me. That summer of 1998 involved some of the least pleasant church work of my life.

Although the sister missionaries suspected a lack of faith on my part, I did not believe that doubts about my Church devotion were justified, and I foresaw no metamorphosis of my beliefs. True, I did acknowledge to myself that there was a serious problem, but I could not easily identify its source because my practice had always been to ignore exactly those matters that would cast doubt on the Church. Even as I recognized my waning testimony, somehow I still firmly believed the Church was true. Surely the fault was with me, not my religion.

Chapter 5
The Tip of the Iceberg

Brad

When Jesus asked the twelve disciples if they were also going to abandon him, Peter answered, "Lord, to whom shall we go? thou hast the words of eternal life."[30]

> If the people will only be full of good works, I will insure that they will have faith in time of need.
> —Brigham Young, 1855 *Journal of Discourses*, Vol. 3, p. 154

Peter's courageous devotion put a lump in my throat and sent a euphoric shiver down my spine. Yet, although I found inspiration and solace in the music, the doctrines, and in the stories of heroic faith, and although I steadfastly refused a deeper look at discomforting rumors about the Church, unwelcome inconsistencies gathered. Like the visible tip of an iceberg at sea, the discrepancies hinted at a massive, incongruent foundation.

In the summer of 1985, having recently dealt with heretic Bishop T, I made a discovery about the fallibility of the latter-day prophets that shook my spiritual foundations. During a visit with my brother Art, in Santa Barbara, he showed me some statements of Brigham Young about the "Adam-God theory." This involved the belief (currently doctrine for some fundamentalist Mormon groups) that Adam and God-the-Father were the same being.[31] This doctrine is foreign and unacceptable to virtually all mainstream Mormons today. Earlier, whenever I heard of references to Brigham Young's Adam-God theory, I assumed it was just some detractor's twist on the words of an inspired prophet of God. Even with the flexibility of modern-day revelation from God, I believed that Church doctrine persisted unchanged. In truth, I had not previously known even the simple details of this Adam-God doctrine. I believed the denials by Church leaders when they insinuated that the doctrine had not been Brigham Young's teaching.[32] The few people I had questioned on Adam-God were either ignorant of it or did not admit knowing the details. There in Santa Barbara, for the first time, I read Brigham's own words on the Adam-God doctrine. Stunned, my immediate thought was that he meant something else or that the sources were not reliable. I read each of Brigham's statements several times. They were too clear and there were too many of them to dismiss. They came from the *Journal of Discourses*, speeches given to the Church membership in the 1800s, recorded by and preserved by the early Mormon Church. At one time Church members were encouraged to read these discourses, but that encouragement has long since ceased.

In my heart, the reliability of a prophet's doctrine—a cornerstone for my beliefs—had received a considerable blow. Over the next few weeks, I convinced myself that the Adam-God doctrine must not have been important, or else the Lord would have corrected His prophet, Brigham Young. I wondered how often the Lord let errors by the prophets go unchecked. I heard rumors of other troubling issues from the *Journal of Discourses*, like *blood atonement*.[33] I had no time or desire to pursue them. I made some painful adjustments in my rationale then told myself that all was well in Zion. (Mormons claim to be descendants of Israel, intent on building a New Jerusalem, *Zion*, on the American continent.)

In 1990, the Mormon political arena presented new challenges to my faith. Although politically conservative myself, I started to lose taste for the extremism I saw amongst many Mormon conservatives. Some members of the Church quoted Prophet Ezra Taft Benson to back up their claims of a worldwide monetary conspiracy, the evils of the United Nations, the wickedness of the liberal agenda, and a variety of fanatical, right-wing political views. I still upheld Benson as the prophet, but it required continuous rationalization.

An incident in 1997 exposed the petty vindictiveness of a group of political conservatives in the Utah State Legislature against the well-known Utah resident, Robert Redford. Irritated by Redford's support for more wilderness area, some of the state legislators attempted to turn part of his land into a wilderness area. (He owns the Sundance Ski Resort and some pristine land around it.) The effort to take Redford's land failed, but the Republican support for this legislation was substantial. Redford must have been amused. Shortly afterward, he established some of his land for wilderness preservation purposes.

I once took great pride in Mormons and their goodness. I bristled whenever I heard others criticize Utah Mormons. Now I saw, repeatedly, that the political party I supported and the people I defended no longer appeared so exemplary. Either our latter-day saintliness was waning, or I was becoming more aware of my religion's weaknesses. Or, I was developing an unreasonable view of some whom I did not understand.

I grew uneasy as I considered this religious-like zeal for right-wing political issues, tied tightly to God's will by some of our best Saints. Were my religious convictions similarly motivated by a false zeal?

As Mormons, we put great emphasis on having the only true church. At times, we

Most people are willing to take the Sermon on the Mount as a flag to sail under but few will use it as a rudder by which to steer.
—Oliver Wendell Holmes (Internet)

seemed so caught up with maintaining the banners of certitude and righteousness that we neglected our steering mechanism. While greatly concerned about the infectious influence of others' lifestyles upon our children, we frequently seemed oblivious to the highly contagious nature of our own intolerance. At times, the practical side of goodness was shoved aside for the intense emotional or spiritual experience or in the interest of maintaining a *pure* society. I wondered if our prayers for the destitute were too often a substitute for service. If my sincere prayers for the poor and the needy were acted on by God, then the good I did in the world quite possibly rivaled that of Mother Theresa—without the sacrifice or the discomfort of mixing with the undesirables.

Throughout my life, there were moments when I thought I felt God's inspiration: reading scriptures, helping others, praying, seeking personal direction, and listening to and reading speeches made by leaders of the Church. This inspiration was the bedrock upon which my faith rested. Yet, this "still, small voice" of inspiration was proving to be somewhat unreliable. Was it a self-generated experience? Was I falling for a counterfeit feeling, occasionally or even all of the time? Was I not worthy? Was I out of place asking these questions?

It occurred to me that some of my spiritual feelings might be a sophisticated pretense. Pretending seemed common enough in the Church. Some Church members became caught up in their emotions, stretching stories, misrepresenting events, making bold claims based on little more than wishful thinking or unbridled devotion. In 1991, one of the most popular leaders in the Mormon Church, Paul H. Dunn, was exposed for misrepresenting several fantastic personal experiences.[34] These false stories had once generated wonderful spiritual emotions in myself and others. What other inspiring, false stories had I heard and believed?

I did not react harshly to the startling news of Paul H. Dunn's deceptions. He attempted to inspire good in others. However, news of his hyperbole bolstered my skepticism for many a miraculous claim.

The following years produced additional troubling disclosures. Some public posturing and statements by leaders of the Church fell below the standard of integrity I had expected. One example of widespread pretense dealt with the aging prophet. By the summer of 1993, the prophet and president of the Church, Ezra Taft Benson, no longer spoke publicly. He delivered his last public address during a Mormon conference session in 1989, the year he turned ninety. During that address, I became uncomfortable as he wandered with his words and thoughts at the pulpit. As he struggled, I silently prayed for him. I accepted the fact that a prophet could grow old and lose his bearings. In 1993, I winced when some members and even leaders of the Church covered up or denied Benson's failing capacity. They may have denied his susceptibility to the natural course of aging because of their desire to present him as always in contact with God.[35] Steve Benson, an editorial cartoonist for the *Arizona Republic* and 1993 Pulitzer Prize winner—and grandson of the ailing prophet—complained publicly that his incapacitated grandfather was being represented by Church leaders as still able and functioning. Steve lamented that his grandfather was publicly displayed and manipulated much like a mannequin in a store window.[36]

I had no way of knowing the complete truth on these matters, but I had seen evidence of the prophet's decline. If Steve's perceptions were in error, I could certainly allow him this mistake. If he was right, then we should accept the prophet's decline and move on. Mormon attacks on Steve seemed unreasonable. When he later left the Church, I considered his apostasy to be a big mistake, but I placed some of the blame on Church members. Shortly after Steve Benson's public complaint, the acting leader of the Church, Gordon B. Hinckley, conceded that President Benson could not participate in leadership decisions. By then it had become public that total legal control of the Church's corporation had been transferred from President Benson to counselors Gordon B. Hinckley and Thomas S. Monson four years earlier.[37]

In September of 1993, six outspoken members of the Church, branded as intellectuals, were excommunicated or disfellowshipped. That was fine with me, an orthodox Mormon. One of my favorite Church leaders, Apostle Boyd K. Packer, had played a behind-the-scenes role in two or more of these church courts. Had I known about it, I would have been supportive of Packer, but a subsequent false denial of Packer's involvement troubled me. Apostle Dallin H. Oaks, aware of Packer's actions, publicly denied any knowledge of Packer's role. Steve Benson claimed Oaks was lying. I kept track as a small public skirmish unfolded between Steve Benson and Oaks. Oaks finally publicly admitted that he had known of Packer's involvement.[38] Packer's involvement struck me as insignificant. But, lying about it seemed out of place for God's anointed. I puzzled over why Oaks initially felt a need to deny anything.

This deceitfulness caused me to reflect upon a story found in the *Pearl of Great Price*, a book that I revered as God's word re-

> 'Tis his honesty that brought upon him the character of a heretic.
> —Benjamin Franklin, speaking of Dr. Priestley in a letter to Benjamin Vaughan of England

vealed to Joseph Smith. Abraham and his beautiful wife, Sarai, were traveling to Egypt. On the way there, God advised Abraham to deceive the Egyptians by pretending Sarai was his sister. (This detail differs slightly from the Bible version.) The deception was to keep Abraham safe from a covetous Pharaoh.[39] I hesitated to be critical of anything that God chose to do, but it did not fit my picture of Deity. It seemed God had better ways of doing His work than by encouraging deception in His servants. If He was not, after all, a God of truth, then what a quandary we would be in. Rather than give up my view of God as truthful and forthright in all his dealings, I questioned the scriptural account of Abraham.

I began to wonder about some of the other stories in the scriptures. Past leaders of the Church had differed as to the extent of the symbolism in the earth's creation story. I had heard little debate on the story of an earth-encompassing flood;[40] without question, I took the story of Noah literally, as had most, if not all, of the current Church leaders. One day while conversing with a respected colleague, a biologist, my curiosity about Noah and the flood was further piqued.

The variety of animals on the earth is astounding. There are over 2,500 species of frogs and toads alone. Did some of them evolve in the 4,400 years since the flood, or did Noah really get them all on the boat? Maybe some of these 2,500 species of frogs and toads could tread water for long periods. Did God supply the transportation for the penguins and the polar bears, or did all of the animals live close by? What about all the little critters that live on the beach and rely on the tides for their existence? I wonder if Noah helped to get all the varieties of kangaroos, plus the other pouched marsupials, back to the piece of land that became Australia. What about the unique creatures isolated on the Galapagos Islands, Borneo, or a number of other exotic islands?

According to the flood account, waters covered the mountains. Where did all the water come from? Where did it all go so quickly—in just a matter of months? The atmosphere could not hold that much water without the atmospheric pressure crushing the life from many living organisms. The erosion would have been tremendous. How were the polar ice caps affected? (The polar ice caps have recorded significant aspects of the history of the earth.) How did vegetation survive the flood? What about the freshwater lakes and freshwater animals and plants? The ecological devastation would have been profound. I understood that God had miraculous powers, but he would have had to perform an ocean of miracles to make up for the flood miracle and then, for some reason, alter significant evidence. I thought about the song where the lady swallowed a fly then proceeded to swallow bigger and bigger animals to eat the previously swallowed creature.

What of the rainbow? I had been taught that rainbows did not exist until after the flood.[41] Had the laws of physics changed? Were the refraction properties of light in water not constant? I saw no end to the questions.

There appeared to be a host of easier ways to destroy the wicked. But then, maybe I mistakenly thought that God practiced economy of effort. The whole story seemed out of character for the God in whom I believed. The chances of this being an exaggeration of a much smaller local flood seemed good. I thought I ought to believe the more respectful and reasonable picture of God's nature. I revealed my concerns about the Old Testament to no one.

Looking beyond Christianity, I saw a host of unusual religions, ancient

> Error of opinion may be tolerated where reason is left free to combat it.
> —Thomas Jefferson, 1st Inaugural, 1801

and modern-day, where people clung to foolish and unproductive beliefs. Surely God would hold us accountable for the stories we believed and the creeds we chose. I recognized that any ardent follower of an unfounded belief could fall back on unexplainable faith when reason or evidence threatened, thus preserving a false persuasion. However, I considered that my situation differed in one key aspect: as a Mormon, my successful recognition of the true faith was a result of my inherent love for truth and my desire for righteousness. God's spirit spoke to my soul. My authentic religious experiences were immune to temporal verification or analysis. Or, was this just my last, sacred level of rationalization, momentarily secure behind reluctant inquiry?

Although still a keystone for my faith, the *Book of Mormon* started to pose some difficulties. Prophecies, fuzzy doctrines, and elements of some stories emerged which made me uneasy. I found the occasional doubt—I should emphasize occasional—creeping into my mind as I continued to study the *Book of Mormon*. One day, I became alarmed by a time-line issue but feared delving into it.[42] For a while, I resisted the urge to pin it down, sensing that my faith in the book was slipping, not wanting to leave the door open for the great deceiver, Satan. My effort to douse or ignore these suspicions left me feeling duplicitous. I kept my concerns to myself, thinking someday they would be answered. My public defense of the *Book of Mormon* would be vigorous, my questioning would be cautious and directed only to God.

This account provides only a smattering of my troubling observations. I neither sought nor read material critical of the Church and its claims. I looked harshly upon the Tanners, *Sunstone*, and *Dialogue*—people, groups, and publications[43] with less than flattering things to say or less than supportive views to share about the Church. Yet for me, a faithful reading from the scriptures and the words of the Church leaders had produced incongruities.

My subconscious concerns surfaced in a disturbing, recurring dream, I found myself wandering down a great dark hallway. In my attempt to return to the light, I was set upon by Satan. The struggle was frightening. I always succeeded in getting back, but Satan jeered that someday I would wander too far and he would have me. I recited the dream to Ben, a brother, concluding that I needed to be cautious or Satan would find my Achilles' heel. However, I did not mention the discrepancies in my faith.

My efforts to substantiate the Church's basic claims continued successfully. In fact, the data still appeared lopsided. I had a ready list of reasons why the Church had to be true. There was the Church's influence for good upon its members. The phenomenal, worldwide growth of the Church had been prophesied, as had been Joseph Smith's fame. Eleven witnesses testified to seeing the Golden Plates,[44] none of whom had ever denied their testimony, or so I heard. Brigham Young may have erred on the Adam-God theory, but his other teachings stood out as noble and inspiring, or so I reasoned. Conscientious men led the modern Church. They were only men, subject to faults, but as a whole they demonstrated goodness and dedication. The *Book of Mormon* might have some faults, but I recognized that my analysis was also incomplete. I continued to think of the *Book of Mormon* as God's doing. It was, overall, inspiring with its stories of courage and faith. Surely, by now the book would have been exposed as a fraud if fabricated by Joseph Smith. In fact, the evidence against Joseph Smith would have to be utterly overwhelming at this point, one hundred and seventy years later, if the remarkable claims about ancient American inhabitants were his own creations.

I wanted to believe. I had a great desire to believe. I chose to take my chances with the Mormon Church with whatever faults it had. Maybe the last days, before the Second Coming of Christ, would produce perilous times, and maybe there would be wickedness, deceptions, apostates, and wolves amongst the flock. Maybe there would be events that would shake some people's faith, but I intended to stay with the ship. How tragic it would be, I thought, to yield to deceit and fall away with the Second Coming imminent.

Chris knew nothing of my attempts to explain the inconsistencies in my faith. I knew nothing of his struggles concerning the Church and the issues that he had set aside unanswered. We each pondered in solitude when questions arose concerning our faith.

In 1996, before marrying, I expressed a few of my troubled thoughts to my fiancée, Cathy, an active, believing Mormon. I did not want to surprise her later with my questions. After we married, I continued to be aggressive in support of our religion, encouraging our joint prayers and scripture study, serving as a ward mission leader until moving from Provo to Spanish Fork, Utah in 1997.

Chapter 6

Critical Discoveries

Brad

The practice of polygamy by faithful Mormons in the 1800s was at times an embarrassment

to me but never a threat to my faith until December of 1997. It was then that the long-ignored, ugly rumors came to life. For me, the rumors had started eighteen years earlier during a memorable discussion with three associates. I considered all three—Matt, Mark, and Gordon—to be intelligent and committed to the Church. They had encountered evidence, which they considered credible, that Joseph Smith had taken other men's *current* wives and had them sealed (married) to himself for eternity.

This claim appeared as utter nonsense to me. Like every good Mormon I knew, I accepted polygamy (or rather polygyny, one man with multiple wives) but not polyandry (two or more men married to a single woman). Surely, taking another man's wife was an anathema. Though reticent to offend my associates, I gave their story no credence in 1979. When they asked why I refused to believe it, I inferred that their source was not trustworthy. Their intent was not to destroy my faith, yet I found the claims offensive; my *heart* told me such evidence could not be so. I felt no need to check their sources.

Two years later, in 1981, while on the faculty at Northern Arizona University in Flagstaff, I heard a fellow faculty member, Valeen Tippetts Avery, speak on a book she was co-authoring with Linda King Newell. The book, *Mormon Enigma: Emma Hale Smith*, was released in 1984. (Emma was Joseph Smith's first wife.) I remember closing my mind early during the one-hour presentation (I pulled out my copy of the *Book of Mormon* and read it) because of the troubling picture painted by Avery involving Joseph Smith's many polygamous relationships.

I believe it was this encounter with Avery that triggered a singular debate with myself as I walked out to the parking lot one day at the University. The question came to me: "What would I do if I found out the Church was false?" Recoiling at the thought, I concluded that it was unwise and even spiritually unhealthy to "entertain doubts." I told myself something like: "Addressing the question would be as useless as considering how a flat earth would affect my thinking." Certainly, I did not want to offend God.

My refusal to entertain the subject did not last long. The discord I felt in running from the question led me to a head-on confrontation with the unnerving query. First of all, I decided that discovering the Church to be false would unequivocally be the most devastating thing that could happen to me. After fleeting consideration of this worst scenario, I concluded that if the Church turned out to be false, I would continue to seek out God and persist in my efforts to do right, to be honest, to live a moral life, and to be kind to others. Vaguely realizing the shallowness of my considerations, I dropped the discussion with myself and effectively put the experience away for sixteen years, along with what I heard of Avery's disturbing comments.

Around 1987, I again ran into some related claims, which I refused to believe. A Sunday School teacher by the name of Todd Tippetts, while giving some lessons on early Mormon history, commented on the deception employed by the prophet and other Church leaders in their practice of polygamy. I cannot remember all that was said, but clearly Tippetts put some of the early Church leaders in a bad light. His approach was not faith promoting, and I thought he should be removed as a Sunday School teacher.

About that same time, I ran across a book review in the Provo newspaper about a title mentioned earlier, *Mormon Enigma: Emma Hale Smith,* by Newell and Avery. Reading only a paragraph or two reintroduced the polygamous claims which I found so repugnant. I did not finish reading the book review. I applied Apostle Boyd K. Packer's suggestion that:"teaching some things that are true, prematurely or at the wrong time, can invite sorrow and heartbreak."[45]

Not until December of 1997 did I seriously consider investigating the claims, which I continued to encounter. Another book review in the Provo newspaper served as catalyst. It was about the book, *In Sacred Loneliness: The Plural Wives of Joseph Smith,* written by Todd Compton. This time I finished the review. It exposed me to additional claims concerning Joseph Smith's practice of polygamy. I was deeply disturbed. The reviewer considered the book objective and well documented. Compton, a member of the Mormon Church, had access to pioneer records, diaries, and reminiscences. I wanted to read his book and debunk it or verify the claims. On several occasions I almost purchased the book, but each time the guilt welled up: Where was my faith? How could God support me if I so acted on these doubts? I renewed my efforts to build my faith with good works, study, and prayer, but my concerns did not go away.

As the months went by, I took note of the parochial intolerance for liberals, gays,[46] and Mormon apostates. It occurred amongst my peers, in the local news, and in some of our Sunday meetings. In January of 1998, I encountered a display of racial bigotry against Mexicans, Blacks, and Jews. Though it was little more than idle chat from an in-law, a devout Mormon, it was persistent and it left me furious. (My intolerance for intolerance must be my most paradoxical vice.) I did not consider racial bigotry to be a common problem within the Church, but my fury broke as I unleashed my general complaint of Mormon intolerance on the next set of listening ears I found. My parents must have wondered why I was unloading all my frustrations on them, but in fact, I had unloaded but a fraction. The most troubling issue went unmentioned. Not having checked out the new polygamy questions, I realized these concerns might be falsely based. No doubt, my parents were startled when I told them I was reevaluating my faith in the Church. That may have been an exaggeration on my part. It would have been more accurate to say my faith was troubled; a thorough analysis of my doubts did not begin for several months.

As 1998 progressed, I tried to immerse myself in the gospel. I wrote a story about the boy who supplied the loaves and fishes for the miraculous feeding of the five thousand by Jesus. The idea came one night as Cathy and I read the New Testament. I had many questions: Was the boy alone? Where was his family? Why did he have food while no one else seemed to have any? Had he come from farther away than others in the group to hear the Savior? How did this event affect his life? I undertook research to keep the story consistent with the time and place. Focusing my thoughts on this project helped me recover some spiritual confidence.

I continued with my approach to pray harder, be better, study more, and to exert more faith. Still, I failed to attain the lofty degree of spirituality that I believed necessary for a sure witness from God.

Early in February, while in this quandary, I was given the opportunity to be ordained a high priest. Having been married over a year and having reached the age of forty-seven, it seemed to be an appropriate step, but I balked. (I had previously served in two bishoprics, usually requiring the office of high priest, but college student wards were exceptions to the rule.) I informed the bishop of my troubled faith, desirous of working some things out before taking that step. He concurred, and I appreciated his confidence and patience.

Fix reason firmly in her seat, and call to her tribunal every fact, every opinion. Question with boldness even the existence of a God; because, if there be one, he must more approve of the homage of reason, than that of blindfolded fear.
—Thomas Jefferson's letter to Peter Carr, August 10, 1787, *Life and Selected Writings of Thomas Jefferson*, edited by Koch and Peden, 1993, p. 399

On May 27, 1998, I left for a three-day bike ride in Canyonlands National Park. One biker from our company, Rob, was a respected friend of thirteen years. We once served together in an elders quorum presidency. I rode with him on the three-hour drive to Canyonlands, giving me opportunity to cautiously broach some of my spiritual concerns.

Rob had recently returned, with his wife and two children, from living in Japan. I engaged him in discussion about the U.S. dropping the atom bomb on Hiroshima and Nagasaki. Afterward, I warily brought up evolution.[47] I had been a diehard critic of Darwin's theory of evolution but was starting to wonder about some of my information. I did not know Rob's views but was willing to hear anything he had to say about it. At this point, he informed me that he and his wife, Susan, had left the Church a month earlier. Without any of the warning signs I would expect from an apostate, his admission stunned me.

Rob knew of my past commitment to the Church. He did not know how I would react to this revelation. I assured him of my respect for his views, and I found him willing to answer my questions, but he volunteered little information beyond that. I kept him busy with questions whenever we were isolated from the others over the next three days.

There within the aboriginal setting of Canyonlands, full of exotic and imposing formations, reaching back in time beyond countless generations of ancestors; forbidding, unyielding, inspiring, and sobering, I honestly faced the unthinkable. I poured out my heart to God for guidance, and I milked Rob for all I could get of his thoughts. It is likely that I read the *Book of Mormon* each evening, for that was my habit. At the end of the three days, I drew two conclusions: (1) the time had come for some serious research, no matter who in the Church frowned upon it; (2) I must prepare myself in every possible way to receive all that God was willing to make known to me—if He was there and listening to my desperate appeal.

I did not believe everything Rob told me, though I respected his fair-minded and open analysis. His intelligence and integrity deserved some consideration. I had to either verify or dispel my doubts. I asked if he had read Compton's book (the book my conscience prevented me from buying). Yes, he had the book at home and was reading it. In his typically unselfish manner, he offered me his copy, willing to finish it later. At the end of the three-day ride, I obtained the book and started reading.

My deep-seated skepticism did not easily depart: Was the book reliable? Was it well documented? Was it full of shallow accusations and insinuations or did it contain cogent information? Was the author making up bogus journal entries for these women, Joseph Smith's polygamous wives? It took several weeks of checking faithful Mormon sources before I became satisfied with the answers to those questions. Though I found the devil in the countless details, four things stood out.

- Joseph Smith did indeed marry other men's wives for eternity. Did the husbands know, and were they members of the Church? Were the marriages consummated? Is there any evidence of children from Joseph in any of these relationships? The book addresses these questions, but for me their answers were less important. However, the concept of *eternal families* was a critical part of my Mormon faith, and something seemed horribly wrong about men losing their wives and children to Joseph Smith for eternity.
- Joseph Smith sometimes told the woman or girl whom he was "courting" that her marriage to him was God's will, that she had been given to him by God. Some of his wives received a promise of exaltation—for her and her family—for accepting the marriage proposal. These promises, mentioned several times in the journals left by Smith's polygamous wives, struck me as cheap exaltation for the women and girls—and their loved ones. It sounded dreadfully suspicious.
- He deceived Emma, his first wife, about his marriage relationships with other women.
- He went to great lengths to deceive the Church as a whole, as well as the public, concerning his polygamous activities—a necessary deceit, I suppose, because polygamy violated Illinois State law. Consider the following Mormon scripture:

All legal contracts of marriage made before a person is baptized into this Church should be held sacred and

fulfilled. Inasmuch as this Church of Christ has been reproached with the crime of fornication and polygamy, we declare that we believe that one man should have one wife, and one woman but one husband, except in the case of death, when either is at liberty to marry again.
—1835 publication of *Book of Commandments*, Section 101, paragraph 4.

This book of new Mormon scripture, later called the *Doctrine and Covenants*, consisted mostly of God's revelations to Joseph Smith. Though Smith did not write this section on marriage, it was sometimes referred to as one of his revelations. Quoted by Mormon leaders before Joseph's death and even ten years afterwards, it was useful for denying that Mormons believed in polygamy (see chapter 15). This section remained in Mormon scripture for forty-one years, until the dead prophet's revelation on plural marriage first appeared in the *Doctrine and Covenants*.

The day when Smith received his revelation on plural marriage is unknown, although "It is evident from the historical records that the doctrines and principles involved in this revelation had been known by the Prophet since 1831."[48] The revelation remained unrecorded until July 12, 1843 and unpublished for several more years; it was not placed in the scriptures until 1876.

An example of Joseph's deceit comes from one of my ancestors, Eliza Maria Partridge, who, at the age of twenty-two, married Joseph Smith on March 8, 1843. Her sister, Emily Dow Partridge, age nineteen, had married Joseph, age thirty-seven, just four days previously. Strict confidentiality reigned; initially, neither sister knew of the other's marriage to Joseph. Both marriages remained unknown to his first wife, Emma.

A short time later, Emma agreed to allow Joseph to take other wives, as long as she could choose them.[49] She chose the Partridge sisters. Because Emma did not know that Joseph had already married the two sisters, the marriages were performed again, secretly, but this time in Emma's presence, by Judge James Adams on May 11, 1843. But, Emma's approval soon waned. In a matter of months, Emma insisted that these marriage covenants be broken and that the Partridge sisters move out of her home and out of town. Emily wrote: "Joseph came to us and shook hands with us, and the understanding was that all was ended between us."[50]

At first, they struggled with the new divine order of marriage, but the Partridge sisters became convinced that God had given them to Joseph. Later, Emily's writings show that she felt herself being cast off too easily. Yet, she was quick to soften her heart toward the man she revered as a prophet of God.

After Joseph's martyrdom in 1844, Emily went on to become a polygamous wife of Brigham Young. Eliza married Apostle Amasa Lyman, my ancestor. Their own accounts of these polygamous relationships, living in poverty and apart from their revered husbands, dashed my belief that polygamy was instituted, in part, to take care of the women.

Possibly the youngest girl to marry Joseph Smith was Helen Mar Kimball, at the age of fourteen.[51] Helen's journal offers abundant evidence of her reluctance to marry Smith. After the initial shock of a proposal to marry Joseph Smith, delivered by her father, Joseph himself came to talk to Helen about "the principle of Celestial marrage [sic]." In her memoirs Helen wrote, "After which he said to me, 'If you will take this step, it will ensure your eternal salvation & exaltation and that of your father's household & all of your kindred.['] This promise was so great that I willingly gave myself to purchase so glorious a reward." Yet, it is clear from Helen's writings that she continued to be deeply troubled by this step and by the ways in which it affected her early years. Her fifteenth birthday was still three months away when she secretly married Joseph. She continued to live at home, but her young friends, unaware of her situation, did not understand the change in her social interactions.[52]

Another of the more memorable stories in Compton's book concerns Henry Jacobs and his wife, Zina Diantha Huntington.[53] Zina at first had rejected Joseph Smith's proposals for marriage; she was engaged, or nearly so, to Henry Jacobs. When Joseph did not show up to perform the ceremony, John C. Bennett performed the marriage between Zina and Henry Jacobs. Later, when Joseph was asked why he had not come, "He told them the Lord had made it known to him, she was to be his celestial wife." Joseph talked of an angel with a drawn sword and of losing "his position and his life" if he did not establish polygamy.[54] She finally acquiesced. On October 27, 1841, a few months after marrying Henry Jacobs, Zina was married again, to Joseph Smith.

Henry and Zina continued to live as husband and wife. Leaving out some of the twists in the story, we move on to February 2, 1846. Following the death of Joseph Smith, the temple ordinance of his celestial marriage to Zina was performed by proxy in the Nauvoo, Illinois Temple. While Zina was sealed to Joseph for eternity, she was sealed on that occasion to Brigham for time (married for this life); then she went on living with Henry Jacobs. On May 22, 1846, Henry, Zina, and their two sons were part way across Iowa in the effort to go west with the Saints. Henry was driving the wagon in this most trying of circumstances for his family; the last son had been born, en route, one month earlier. On this day, Henry was unexpectedly called on a mission, by Brigham Young, to England. After serving a faithful mission, he returned—to no one. His wife and sons were now Brigham's.

Henry never ceased to love his wife and boys. His letters over the years to his family are heartbreaking. They expressed his love, his loneliness, and his confusion over this whole affair. They made me weep. They still make me weep. How many wives did Brigham Young need? When I first read this, my wife and I had a second son on the way. My empathy for Henry was intense. Silently and passionately, I cursed both Joseph and Brigham.

My nineteen-year defense of Joseph Smith and his polygamous practices was without foundation. Greatly disturbed, I wondered: What else had I believed? What else had I defended? What else had I claimed to know based upon falsehoods which I had read, heard, or deduced? To what had I given testimony, based upon what I felt, which was simply not true? My whole world took on the aura of a bad dream.

Of course, I had to be certain. I continued my efforts to find critics of Compton's book, specifically by faithful Mormons familiar with Church history. I obtained comments from several, including an e-mail response from Danel Bachman, at the LDS Institute of Religion in Logan, Utah. I consulted with Lyman Platt, a cousin and an accomplished genealogist and historian. I also obtained a copy of a review of Compton's book, before it was published, done by Richard L. Anderson and Scott H. Faulring from FARMS (Foundation for Ancient Research and Mormon Studies), an educational foundation affiliated with Brigham Young University.

Some of the complaints expressed in their reviews sounded reasonable. Compton did make some assumptions and drew some conclusions which I thought fair to question, yet the protests against his scholarship were of minor concern. Some complaints against him were ill founded and of the name-calling variety. For example, the FARMS reviewers referred to Compton as a feminist. They did not dispute that Joseph Smith practiced polyandry (one woman with two husbands); rather, they acknowledged this practice.[55]

The major complaints I had about polygamy were verified—verified by every single qualified Mormon source I found. (This does not include the Church leaders who had neither studied nor seemed interested in pursuing the history.) Apparently, Joseph Smith was a fallen prophet. Some people may justify his actions or overlook them, but I kept thinking of Matthew 7:20: "By their fruits ye shall know them."

> Ignorance is preferable to error, and he is less remote from the truth who believes nothing than he who believes what is wrong.
> —Thomas Jefferson, *Notes On the State of Virginia*, 1782

The imposing journey had begun, a journey for which I was frightfully unprepared. This spiritual exodus was at times awful, at times amazing, and a full-time disruption to everything else in my life for months. Two years earlier, I had taken an extended leave from Utah Valley State College, eventually resigning from my tenured position. My time spent working on my software business dropped to almost nothing. Almost every waking moment was consumed with my asking and attempts to answer new questions. These were troubling questions, questions whose answers would affect my wife, my relationship with family and friends, my one-year-old son, Caleb, and—for all I knew—my eternal future.

In my mind, the *Book of Mormon* had not yet fallen with the prophet Joseph Smith. Joseph may have been inspired of God, then lost favor with Him. I had read through the *Book of Mormon* about once a year since my mission for the Church—thirty times in all. My love for the characters and principles in the book was deep set, as was my tendency to forget about the troubling questions. Suddenly, I discovered that polygamy was not the only issue which I had stubbornly defended in ignorance.

While searching for faithful Mormon commentary, I stumbled onto *Studies of the Book of Mormon* by B. H. Roberts. Roberts, a respected Mormon historian and a general authority of the Church, was asked by Church leaders in 1921 to address some questions on the *Book of Mormon*. His research produced troubling information, but he did not publish his writings; his fellow Church leaders did not like his observations. His descendants gave the manuscripts to the University of Utah library where they remained for years. Interest in the manuscripts started to build; as a result, they were published in 1985.

Some Mormon scholars claim that Roberts was playing devil's advocate. Others believe he had experienced a phase of personal doubt and thus questioned the *Book of Mormon*. That debate made little difference to me. I focused on Roberts' exposure of troubling problems with the *Book of Mormon*. Though I conceded that some of his conclusions were hasty, most of Roberts' discussion was enlightening and rational. He pointed out inconsistencies in the *Book of Mormon* which I had previously noticed in my studies, and several more with which I was unfamiliar. Here they were gathered before me, neatly compiled into a troublesome collection.

Roberts commented on the dearth of evidence supporting the *Book of Mormon*, evidence that such a prosperous civilization should have left behind.[56] I took note of some of the "historical" details from the *Book of Mormon*.

- Their domesticated animals included: horses, asses, oxen, cows, sheep, swine, goats, and elephants.
- Numerous battles were described in which they used swords, breastplates, arm-shields, and head-plates
- The metals they used included iron, copper, brass, steel, gold, and silver.

- There was mention of machinery and "tools of every kind."
- They coined money and the value system was described in detail.
- Chariots were used. "And there were many highways cast up, and many roads made, which led from city to city, and from land to land, and from place to place."
- Some cities were fortified with stone walls and with banks of earth so high that the enemy's stones and arrows were not effective.
- There were "many books and many records of every kind."
- They spoke altered Hebrew and sometimes wrote in re-formed Egyptian.

Can we find a place in the Americas that indicates the existence of this civilization? For many years, I believed that such evidence was abundant and in the hands of the Mormon scholars. The time had come for my own personal research, research which should provide significant information, unless God was changing and covering up evidence to test the faith of His Saints.

If a thousand old beliefs were ruined in our march to truth we must still march on.
—Stopford Augustus Brooke (Internet)

Apologetic Mormon scholars had answers, but none that satisfied my concerns. A few questioned the modern evidence on some issues. Others accepted the modern evidence but claimed the translation of the *Book of Mormon* to be less than perfect. Some claimed that the location of this civilization was yet to be found, for the obvious reason that no location had provided the expected evidence. Some of them ignored Joseph Smith's claims, which extend the *Book of Mormon* lands from Central America into North America.[57] It is claimed that Hill Cumorah, in Western New York, was a major battleground in the demise of two great nations (the Nephites and the Jaredites). In addition, Joseph pinpointed the location of at least one prominent *Book of Mormon* city, Manti, as being in Randolph County, Missouri.[58]

One point, which I thought significant, dealt with the wheel. The two separate groups that came over from Jerusalem would likely have brought the concept of the wheel; there was also mention in the *Book of Mormon* of horses and chariots. Yet, the Native Americans did not use the wheel for transportation. I wondered how the Indians, the purported descendants of the people of the *Book of Mormon*, had lost the use of the wheel—every tribe and nation. A few wheeled toys have been found, dating back to that period, but I found no indication of the wheel ever being used for transportation in Pre-Columbian America. It dawned on me that the *Book of Mormon* is impressively irrefutable only if one resists looking at all refuting evidence.

Archeologists have noted some relatively advanced civilizations in Central and South America. I once operated under the impression that these discoveries occurred after the writing of the *Book of Mormon*, bolstering my belief that Joseph Smith could not have written about them without divine intervention. Reading from *View of the Hebrews* put the first dent in that reasoning; I found that by 1823, much was already known and proposed about past American civilizations. Although this observation proves nothing, it effectively removed the first tangible prop I had used for the *Book of Mormon*.

View of the Hebrews was written by Ethan Smith in a county adjacent to Joseph Smith's home county. (Some Mormon apologists claim Ethan Smith was not even in the same state. They are right, but adjacent states can have adjacent counties, as in this case.) Published in 1823, with a second edition in 1825, just two years before Joseph claimed to have received the gold plates, Ethan Smith's book speculated as to the ancestors of the Native Americans. Ethan put forth claims and ideas which I had long assumed to be original to the *Book of Mormon*. Yet, problems ran much deeper. B. H. Roberts noted a host of parallels between the two books. He assembled twenty-two pages of parallels and claimed there were many more. I could not dismiss these compelling parallels as easily as had some defenders of my now fading faith. My last-gasp attempt at explaining *View of the Hebrews* was to credit Satan with inspiring the author Ethan Smith in a clever effort to thwart God's purposes for the *Book of Mormon*.

Mormon apologist responses to *View of the Hebrews* fascinated me. One scholarly defender published one hundred differences between the *Book of Mormon* and *View of the Hebrews*,[59] concluding it unlikely that Joseph had used *View of the Hebrews*. Furthermore, I wondered if other sources existed, to which Joseph Smith had access, which would have made writing the *Book of Mormon* humanly possible. The book was too great a work for one man to write, or so I had been told.

During my years as a faithful Mormon, I was convinced, and had stated it as fact to others, that the archaeological evidence in support of the *Book of Mormon* was substantial. Apparently, other Mormon faithful had fallen into the same trap; we believed whatever we heard that supported the *Book of Mormon*, bypassing scrutiny and representing it as fact. Total honesty had been shoved aside for the good of the cause which I *knew* to be true. As with most Mormons, it was not my intent to be dishonest; rather, my intellectual shortcuts were born of a passion for my beliefs—and the notion that some truths were tricky to establish, requiring a selective perspective.

It was involuntary. They sank my boat.
—John F. Kennedy's response to being called a hero. *American Quotations*, 1965, Carruth and Ehrlich, p. 111

Within a month of the epochal bike ride, I concluded that "the good ship Zion," the Church, was not taking me to the Promised Land. I prepared to abandon ship.

My business income and expenses made it difficult to compute the tithing (ten percent of one's income) which I owed the Church, but I had set aside enough to cover my obligation. I gave the bishop a check for $3,300. (I was later amused to read Prophet Joseph F. Smith's statement: "No man will ever apostatize so long as he will pay his tithing."[60]) The check would more than cover tithing and other offerings that I would have given as a faithful member of the Church. Though I considered my trust to have been violated, I wanted to depart having completed as many personal obligations as possible.

I made my last monthly home-teaching visits. I did my last church cannery assignment.[61] I went to my last priesthood meeting. I tore up my *temple recommend*.[62] I went shopping for new underwear, unknown to Cathy, who maintained her belief in the Church. The special undergarments that I had worn for twenty-nine years, considered sacred by all faithful Mormons, would no longer be appropriate for me. When I returned from shopping, I took the momentous step of changing my underwear. I wondered if Cathy was prepared for me to shed this last evidence of my sacrosanct temple covenants, though she recognized its likelihood. That night, I undressed after the lights had been turned out, then kept my distance in bed. I did not want to face her disappointment. Except for time spent with my one-year-old son, the only respite from this extended and deepening nightmare was sleep, but once again, sleep came fitfully.

Some people leave the Church out of anger. Some leave so they can pursue forbidden paths. Some join fundamentalist break-offs from the Church. Some leave because they perceive the Church as a controlling, evil organization. I parted for none of these reasons. I concluded that the Mormon faith survived because of misconceptions and subtle, well-meant deceit, driven by pride and by promises to die for. Now I understand that many people leave because they honestly feel that Church dogma is based upon illusions. Pretending to believe would not work for me. No matter how noble the Church's intentions and accomplishments, I could not remain part of an organization whose bold claims appeared so utterly inconsistent with my observations. I had taken faith in the Mormon Church as far as I could. Now that faith had vanished, leaving an all-encompassing hole as big as my universe. The time had come to move on, but how, to where, to what?

Chapter 7

The Hell of Heaven Gone Wrong

Brad

> Belief is desecrated, when given to unproved and unquestioned statements for the solace and private pleasure of the believer.
> —Clifford (As reported by William James in *God*, 1996, edited by Timothy A. Robinson)

Like Lot's wife fleeing Sodom, I could not depart without a backward glance. In fact, I asked myself repeatedly if I had made a terrible mistake in rejecting the Church. Was there some hidden motivation within me that I failed to acknowledge, something about which I was not being honest, which drove me to this conclusion? Was there something amiss in my life that allowed Satan to deceive me? Was I just being really stupid? Would my still-believing wife and our son pay a heavy price for an epic spiritual blunder on my part?

Time and again, I reviewed the pertinent information upon which I had based my decision. Joseph Smith's approach to marriage did not strike me as inspired or holy. The number of wives seemed excessive. The story of an angel with a drawn sword, threatening to slay him if he did not practice polygamy,[63] sounded inconsistent with the Mormon concept of free agency.[64] The guarantee of exaltation, promised to several women for marrying Joseph Smith, seemed like either cheap salvation or spiritual bribery. Taking a fourteen-year-old as a wife—with little regard for her hesitancy—reached the depths of abject self-interest. Taking other men's wives and children to be his own, having them sealed to himself for eternity, struck me as utterly contemptible. And significantly, Joseph Smith's deceitful nature testified of a false prophet.

The *Book of Mormon* was the other pertinent issue. I knew it well from a life-long study of its contents. The new evidence I had before me now weighed heavily against the claim of the book's divine origin. The responses from FARMS scholars and other Mormon apologists to critics of the *Book of Mormon* were effective in knocking down some baseless criticisms, but they left my carefully gathered concerns virtually untouched.

I sought divine direction with earnestness, driven by my shaken hope for an eternal plan and life after death. I found only information that furthered my doubts. I briefly considered maintaining my activity in the Church, pretending, giving priesthood blessings in which I did not believe, participating in ceremonies where I falsely pledged myself, and saying all of the acceptable things to friends and family. I also considered lingering as an active mute, participating in service projects but holding my tongue in meetings, refusing the ordinances, and refusing to exercise the "Priesthood." Another possibility was to stay in the Church and be honest in sharing my thoughts.

None of those options tempted me. I would not pretend. I would not cling to an organization while bucking its fundamental claims. As I hesitated at the crossroads, I agonized over my next move and future family relationships.

Better dead, clean, than alive, unclean.
—First Presidency Message, Conference Report, April 1942, p. 89. (Conference Report, April 1979, pp. 41, 42)

The final decision came one awful night following a conversation with Cathy. I hoped that she would understand and share my views, but she did not. On this night of my greatest despair, like so many previous nights, sleep was impossible, but the problem went far beyond sleeplessness. My thoughts were in disarray. A lifetime of faith in the latter-day prophets and doctrines, once considered my most valued possession, had vaporized. My purpose in life was shaken to the core. My cherished view of the eternal nature of the soul had apparently been based upon a fraud and his pretended revelations. It now appeared that I must discard a portion of my beliefs and seriously question the rest. In addition, I feared a partial alienation from a very beloved family. Over and over, I reconsidered staying in the Church.

In the early hours of the morning, I got in my car and drove up Spanish Fork Canyon. Parking in the dark at the lookout over Thistle Dam, under severe stress, I attempted to reason. I anticipated the turmoil soon to enter into the lives of those I loved. I struggled to see a way out of a useless life and of spreading my despair. I fully recognized that a dead brother produced less grief than an apostate brother. I realized that a dead son would not bring the embarrassment and agony brought by an apostate son. I was aware that a dead uncle would not cast the defiling shadow of an apostate uncle. If I left the Church, my family relations would change forever. My image would be irreversibly tarnished in the eyes of some wonderful cousins, uncles, and aunts. I cowered before the ghosts of the dark side of assumed virtue. The pride I had long taken in my dedication to the Church, now like a heavy iron chain, pulled upon my failing spirits.

The considerations for Cathy and Caleb were complex. I understood the humiliation I would bring upon her and the shame Caleb would experience having a faithless father. My concern was born of a worldview still tightly tied to my Mormon upbringing.

Even in my desperate state, with no good options apparent to me, I recognized some unequivocal drawbacks to driving over the edge of the canyon. My debate with self, hindered by intense emotion and unrecognized blinders from the past, was not without reason.

Another option, excommunication, would be a softer blow to others than would my apostasy, if I could just find an excommunicable sin with which I felt comfortable. It would take more than just getting drunk, and I did not even want to do that. Another possibility was to fake an excommunicable sin. Or, maybe I could write an intellectual book critical of the Church. (No—too much work, and friends and family would still hate me.)

In my distress, I considered the option of simply leaving Cathy, Caleb, and the expected second son, starting a new life in some distant spot away from everyone I knew. I could not have handed Cathy a more devastating blow than my apostasy. If I left her, she would be free to find another believer for a husband and plan on having him for eternity, as is the Mormon belief, and my children could be raised in the faith which I thought had served me well.

My relationship with Caleb, who had just celebrated his first birthday, was my biggest concern. I was deeply devoted to this wonderful boy with his indomitable will, his unusual intelligence and curiosity, his ready, delightful little sense of humor, and his love for his dad. Yet, I had seen father-son relationships warped and mangled when non-believing fathers were reduced to second-class citizens by sons and daughters devoted to Mormonism. Because of Cathy's desire to raise her children as Mormons, my future role in the family weighed heavily upon my mind. I did not relish spending the rest of my life as "the damned one" or as the "conversion project" amongst those I most loved.

Though I was convinced on that dark night that Cathy could find a husband who would be better for her, I believed that Caleb could not possibly have a stepfather that would love him as I love him. None would spend as much time and energy trying to make him laugh, trying to spark his curiosity, trying to develop his mind, trying to teach him discipline. No stepfather could equal my patience for Caleb's difficult moments or my efforts to teach him to be fair, kind, and considerate of others. No stepfather would be as devoted to his growth and happiness. I had seen Caleb's unusual will. He would be a challenge to raise. I knew he would miss me if I left. He needed me, his dad. This conviction, right or wrong, dwarfed all other considerations.

I would pretend to nothing. I would seek God in every way possible. I would try with renewed effort to be a better person. I would love Cathy, Caleb, and the child soon to come, remaining with them as long as Cathy was willing. I would tolerate whatever others thought of me. Having once cast the subtle shadow of prejudice, though never maliciously, upon others for their non-belief, I must now be willing to dwell in that shadow. I expected that the explanations I gave to friends and family—virtually all faithful Mormons—would fall on unsympathetic ears.

Some may think me affectedly righteous or pious, or just playing the martyr. Maybe so; I will not claim immunity to such tendencies. Still, in the face of considerable turmoil, these were my thoughts; justified or ridiculous, these were my resolutions.

Some people are hesitant to share such personal views and experiences with others. For that reason I will say but little, here and afterward, of my wife's thoughts and reactions. Cathy had been thrown into an alarming situation. She thought, as a happy newlywed, that she had married someone for eternity who shared her beliefs. Now I was turning into a faithless stranger whose influence on our children would be perceived as tragic. Briefly, she knew the security of a husband who held the Priesthood of God, who could call down the blessings of heaven when faced with illness or the powers of evil. Suddenly, with one small child and another on the way, she felt alone in the battle against a wicked world.

Cathy married late, having finally found someone she was proud to call her husband. Now, virtually all of her acquaintances would feel sorry for her, praying for her eternal welfare. They would wonder just how she was going to deal with this spiritually dead-weight husband.

On occasion, while contemplating marriage during bachelorhood, I had asked myself what I would do if my spouse ceased to believe in the Church. As a bachelor of many years in a Mormon community, my circle of friends included some divorced women whose husbands had become estranged from the Church. I held a low opinion of all such men. I saw no solution to the problem of a faithless wife with children involved. Marrying well seemed like the best way to avoid the problem. My record shows many years of cautious courting; I had determined to find someone who showed unquestioning devotion to the God I worshiped. Ironically, my wife was now thrown into the very situation I had once so faithfully sought to avoid.

In spite of all her fears and turmoil, Cathy committed herself to our relationship. She continued to attend the Mormon Church but respected my thoughts and feelings. She continued to laugh at my attempts at humor. She believed we could work together to raise our children with the values we still shared. Typically, I wanted it all, to have her think as I thought, but in my rational moments, I appreciated Cathy for her tolerance and efforts to make the best of the situation.

Cathy later reminded me that it was on Father's Day of 1998 that I showed her the first draft of my official request to leave the Church. But then, bad timing seems inevitable for such an announcement.

My parents and siblings would be notified next, then the bishop. Immediate action was the only course; I could no longer comfortably serve in my church responsibilities. I knew a letter to each family member would be the best way to express myself and avoid saying more than I should. A letter would save me from the well-meant, rhetorical questions: "Have you prayed about it?" or "Have you considered how this would affect your wife and son?" My answers would mean nothing to them.

I wanted nothing of debate. I dreaded all eleven confrontations. I hoped that a personal visit or phone call, perhaps more difficult for us all, would do more to preserve our mutual love, respect, and understanding.

My feelings and thoughts were a jumble. I did not want to bring pain and turmoil into anyone's life; yet at times, I wished that everyone would stop and listen to the evidence. It seemed that no matter how bleak the truth, it was best to base one's beliefs on the available facts. I suspected that few family members, if any, would wish to check my sources or hear the whole story. Finally, I decided that when I called them I would give no reasons for leaving. That did not work. I ended up trying to answer every expressed question and even the questions I thought they were afraid to ask. Family members were stunned. My explanations were confusing, defensive, and certainly not acceptable or complete. Maybe that was best.

Chris is the brother with whom I have the most contact. I told him Sunday evening, June 28, 1998. For some reason I remember little of the visit; maybe because he had so little to say or because of the feeling of acceptance he yet expressed toward me. Maybe the trauma of the following visits to family members drove the memory of this visit from my mind.

Monday morning, June 29, I told another brother, Ben. I planned to tell him when we finished some work on the computer at my home, but I could hardly think. Finally, I stopped work and told him I was leaving the Church. Ben has always been one to allow others leeway for their beliefs and actions; he is even tolerant of a fair bit of stupidity, though mine has exceeded his limits on occasion. I appreciated his measured response, though I suppose that for him, a blow to the face would have been more welcome. We discussed a variety of Church issues. Afterward, I knew that little of what I said was complete and virtually none of it believable. It concerned me that his wife would soon know and not appreciate my desire to be first to break the news to other family members.

I will long remember the sickening drive over to another brother's place that evening and asking him to step outside for a visit. Again, there was shock upon hearing my announcement. We talked at length. He seemed convinced that most apostates attempt a return to the Church and told me of a recent example.

I do not recall whom I told next. I feared that some family members would want to spread the word before I had personally spoken to everyone. I told my parents the next morning. Mother wept and it tore me up inside. I could do nothing to console her, short of lying about my beliefs. I did promise myself that in spite of my altered beliefs, I would make every effort to be a devoted son.

I called family members all day Tuesday and finally finished with the last sibling. Although I wanted everyone to hear the news first from me, that proved impossible. Later, two in-laws who did not get my announcement firsthand accused me of being on an ego trip.

A long visit with a brother sharpened my perspective on my new situation. In explaining that I sought strictly Mormon sources for my research, I acknowledged my limited encounter with some apostate claims. I attempted to give a simple example. (Jane Law claimed that Joseph Smith had proposed to her.) He stopped me, not wanting to hear what an apostate had said. Thinking he had falsely anticipated the intent of my comment, I tried to explain, even insisting that I was going to tell him anyway—that was a big mistake. I realized that as an apostate, my opinions might be as unwelcome in the future.

After the last painful phone call, I felt a huge weight off my shoulders. I appreciated my family's lack of animosity, although the loss of their esteemed favor and confidence was keenly felt. I lamented the wasted effort they would inevitably make to reclaim my lost soul. I grieved—especially for my parents—over the discomfort, the sorrow, and the heartache resulting from my announcement. It induced in me a searing burst of disdain for the impostors responsible for creating and sustaining this collection of illusions upon which millions of believers had hung their life's faith, hopes, and family ties.

My visit with the bishop lasted more than an hour. He found my announcement troubling. After sharing some of his personal experiences with me, he asked me to reconsider and to begin a twenty-four-hour fast with him, which I agreed to do. Even after the fast, I continued to petition God for guidance, hopeful that He was there and listening. Nevertheless, my prayers were fundamentally altered. I no longer asked for assurance that the Church was true; rather, I asked for guidance to the truth, whatever it was. To eliminate biased criticism, I sought additional information about Mormonism from sanctioned Mormon history and pro-Mormon sources. But the more I learned, the worse became the picture of the Church. A few weeks later, I informed Bishop Tanner in a letter that my decision was final; my name needed to be taken off the membership records of the Church.

Chapter 8

Backing Away

Brad

My wife, parents, and siblings found themselves in a horrible situation. They feared nothing more than the intangible

We as we read must become Greeks, Romans, Turks, priest and king, martyr and executioner, must fasten these images to some reality in our secret experience, or we shall see nothing, learn nothing, keep nothing.

—Ralph Waldo Emerson, Essay I, "History"

powers of darkness and the influence that could lead them to reject this "one and only true path to God." That which could destroy the body would produce only a temporal setback. That which could destroy the soul would produce eternal damnation. That which could rob them of their children in the eternities was to be kept at bay at any cost.

Although the initial reactions were kind, I assumed the family all struggled with the implications of my decision. In a few days, I encountered significant negative effects from my announcement. My ability to anticipate family reactions was poor. Some of the surprises brought relief. Some did not.

Some of my brothers made a request that I could appreciate. They asked that I not speak to their children about my beliefs.

The request was not necessary, but they could take no chances. I had gotten along well with my nieces and nephews and knew that reports of my decision would affect these relationships.

A week or two later, Cathy, Caleb, and I attended the baptism of a niece. Although I saw reasons for not attending, I also saw reasons to support and maintain family relationships, and Cathy wanted to go. As we approached the Mormon chapel, three questions moved to the forefront of my turbulent thoughts. Who of the nephews, nieces, and extended family knew of my announcement? How would others react? Moreover, would I detract from the event by showing up? When I walked in from the back of the room and saw a row of teenage nephews looking at me, the first question was partially answered. Their frozen faces could not hide their awareness of Uncle Brad's recent and frightful fall from grace. Nonetheless, I felt accepted, except for one possible jab during the opening prayer, something to the effect, "We are grateful for the gospel in our lives, a blessing which not everyone we know is appreciative of." The prayer was given by an acquaintance, not a member of my family.

I remained in the background. I had not come to make a statement. I questioned myself on every move, uncomfortable with every option.

A phone conversation with a family member confirmed one of my fears: Some of the family looked suspiciously on my efforts to be cordial as an attempt to convert others to my heretic ways. I decided to back off in my association with specific family members until I could ascertain where my presence was welcome and where it was dreaded. I made an effort to respond to any correspondence or invitation of acceptance. While hoping that time would work her miracles, an immediate solution escaped me.

Was I interested in having others look at my viewpoint? Of course; however, I still questioned the benefits of destroying cherished illusions, and my relationship with family was more important than sharing my new, ill-formed notions. I longed to talk with others about God, life's purpose, and related topics, but needed more than the standard Mormon viewpoint.

Cathy and I were responsible for organizing the Morin family reunion for the last weekend in July of 1998. My apostasy announcement came at the end of June, a month before the reunion. Two family members asked me if we should consider canceling the upcoming reunion. Someone else said his family would not be coming for fear of how he might react to me. I could only guess what other family members felt and said amongst themselves. I expected that in time, they would regroup and try to love me back into the fold, but some were not yet ready to associate with me. I wondered how relationships would change if they ever realized the depth of my new convictions.

Cathy and I relinquished our responsibility for organizing the reunion. Family feelings seemed to mellow as the reunion time approached. With encouragement from Cathy and from others, I decided to attend the reunion. To my relief, the event went well. It appeared I could be included in the family circle without obvious discomfort to others. In the end, only one family had canceled plans to come—because they were closing on a house. The brother-in-law later made a comment in an e-mail about apostates making for "really crappy family reunions."

In years previous, I had observed how wonderful it was that all of my siblings and their spouses were believing, active members of the Church. We could talk openly and comfortably about that which gave meaning to our lives. I had enjoyed those gospel discussions and offered more than my share of input. Now, a growth more dreaded than cancer had arisen in the clan. Only time could reveal if this rather guarded kinship was worth fostering.

Before the reunion, Chris and his wife, Connie, invited Cathy, Caleb, and me to Illinois for a visit. They could not attend the reunion in Utah so a chance to spend time with them in Illinois and maintain our relationship was tempting. Furthermore, feeling like an alien in the family, I greatly appreciated the friendly gesture. Nevertheless, I declined. My business was suffering. Our finances were shaky. In addition, I was concerned about possible family suspicions over such a visit. But, Chris persisted and Cathy was willing, so we decided to go. I reasoned that the trip would

> Here lies the power. . . in helping ourselves and others to see some of the possibilities inherent in viewpoints other than one's own; in encouraging the free interchange of ideas; in welcoming fresh approaches to the problems of life; in urging the fullest, most vigorous use of critical self-examination.
> —Adlai Stevenson, as quoted in *A Chosen Faith*, by John A. Buehrens and Forrest Church, p. 81

be a good distraction for my troubled mind. Chris was the family member with whom I felt most at ease, and I hoped to maintain that relationship. I also wondered if Chris wanted to discuss my decision to leave the Church. At that point, I willingly listened to anyone's response to my concerns, and Chris's viewpoint could be valuable. I also appreciated anyone's willingness to hear my full story. We left for Illinois the day after the family reunion.

We could not have felt more welcome. We enjoyed the camping, the river running, and the company. Caleb, just over a year old, made a big splash with his cousins. Cathy had an opportunity to become better acquainted with her in-laws. In addition, for the first time in weeks, I felt the unguarded respect and acceptance I had always known from family.

On the second day of the visit, Chris raised the subject of my apostasy. Not in the least preachy, he asked a few questions and then pretty much let me unload. He made a few observations, but overall he offered little response. I desperately wanted to talk to someone who could reason with me and help me find some answers to the new questions that had erupted in my life. If he listened, maybe he would check out my story. His reaction, in effect, was silence. I could not tell if he listened just to be kind or if he actually had some respect for the issues that so troubled me. My research had been ongoing since my announcement to the family, and I had found additional verification for my concerns. My explanations to Chris were more coherent and complete than had been any of my prior communications with family members.

For the next month, Chris gave me no inkling of his thoughts. Though we kept close contact with each other, we never discussed religion during that period, with one exception; he did phone me the day after we returned home and asked me for a reference to a quotation by President Gordon B. Hinckley, the prophet of the Mormon Church.

Those who too narrowly define the experience and intelligence of others hinder the broadening of their own.
—blm

Soon after our trip to Illinois, I received a letter from a nineteen-year-old niece, showing concern over my decision to leave the Church. The following are excerpts from her letter.[65]

It is unclear to me why exactly you left the LDS church. I have heard it was influenced by mainly three things: mistakes in church history, thoughts found in "anti-Mormon" literature, and pressures or messages you received from members of the church. Whatever the reason, all three are based solely on the actions or thoughts of other people. As common as it is, I find it strange that you Brad, would base people and not God as your reason for abandoning a personal belief.

Perhaps I am wrong though. Upon choosing to leave the church did you pray to God? And if so, was the answer a feeling of peace and joy and confirmation, stronger than any you have ever felt? Did it outweigh all those feelings you received during a testimony meeting, your mission, a new convert's baptism, the temple, every priesthood blessing you have ever received or given, and the reality that God was listening as you prayed at night and your repentance on various occasions had been accepted? Did you pray with an earnest heart to know if you should leave a church you once swore to strangers was the only true gospel— And did that answer knock you to [the] floor with such an incredible force of assurance that it erased all doubts or sick feelings you had over such a choice? . . .

What glory is promised to you in leaving the church? Does any of the reading and study you have done mention amazing benefits you will receive from the world and other religions? How do these compare with those of your patriarchal blessing and covenants in the temple? As Moses said, you are a child of God and where is the glory in leaving the church? How does giving up the goal to become a perfect being, who lives eternally in a state of joy with those you love, seem glorified in any way? . . .

When I look at your life, I see a man who has been given every blessing he could want from his Heavenly Father. You have found a loving wife (once your eternal companion), received a beautiful son, and business is going well. These seem to be a testament of how your prayers were heard. And yet, have you so easily forgotten? . . .

I could go on for pages about various scenarios you will soon face, or outlets of life and personal identity you have now lost.

I admired her courage, addressing Uncle Brad with her convictions and questions. Her statements reflect my former predisposition and the predisposition of many within the Church. Within the confines of the Mormon perspective, my answers or my attempts to correct her shallow assumptions and conclusions would win little respect. There was good reason to shun my views. "Wherefore, a man being evil cannot do that which is good . . . For behold, a bitter fountain cannot bring forth good water;"[66] Siblings could ill afford to tell their children the real reasons Uncle Brad had left the Church.

The letter also exposes the errant, almost subconscious logic which I once used. It is to the effect: "The Church promises wonderful things if we remain faithful; therefore, you would be foolish to leave the Church."

I considered how my niece's parents would feel about a reply to her letter. I took a chance and answered the letter without giving any reasons for my disbelief. I thought it fair to present myself as someone still capable of reason and desirous of living a good, moral life.

Before releasing me from my church calling, a stake high councilman interviewed me. Although he may have thought me misinformed about Joseph Smith's polygamous anomalies, he was kind. One of his statements struck me. He said: "The gospel is not supposed to be logical."

Eventually, because the process of removing my name from Church records seemed to have bogged down, I made an appointment with the stake president, President Coray. In our hour-long visit, I outlined some concerns and asked to be removed from the records of the Church. He acknowledged the existence of unanswered gospel questions then submitted a number of reasons for believing and remaining in the Church. I appreciated his approach. To this day, I continue to admire many Church members who are committed to following their heartfelt convictions.

When I ceased to pay tithing on my income, after notifying the bishop in July of 1998, I suggested to Cathy that she pay tithing on her share of what I earned. When I heard that Bishop Tanner had reported me as a *full-tithe payer* at the end of 1998, I appreciated his respect for my contribution. My request to be taken off the membership rolls was granted in January of 1999.

Chapter 9

A Paradigm in Peril

Chris

The phone call came Sunday evening of June 28, 1998, while I was home with Connie and our children. Brad and I talked for a minute or two before he ambushed me with the news that he was leaving the Church. Could this really be happening? Something had gone terribly wrong. This was not a case of someone losing his testimony through neglect over a period of years; Brad had been an active and dedicated member of the Church. What had caused this seemingly sudden mutation?

> It is most astonishing to every principle of intelligence that any man or woman will close their eyes upon eternal things after they have been made acquainted with them, and let the . . . things of this world, the lusts of the eye, and the lusts of the flesh, entangle their minds and draw them one hair's breadth from the principles of life.
> —Brigham Young, November 2, 1856, *Journal of Discourses*, Vol. 3, p. 59

I had no reason to doubt Joseph Fielding Smith's teaching, "Almost without exception when a person leaves the Church, it is due to transgression."[67] Rather than confessing a serious sin and suffering the embarrassment of a Church court, some people find it easier to simply leave the Church. But as the list of possible transgressions flashed through my mind, none of them stuck to Brad. Even if he had committed the unthinkable, he would have confessed, confronting his sin head-on rather than taking the easy way out. Perhaps outright wickedness was not the reason for his leaving.

Some people leave because a fellow member or a Church leader offends them. I knew Brad had no misconceptions about the leaders being perfect, but neither is he one to react so rashly at another's misdeed. There must be something else afoot.

My racing thoughts fell deeper into disarray when Brad explained his decision. He presented evidence that Joseph Smith had married other men's wives. It was a tale I had never been told. I listened but said very little. I suppressed the urge to acknowledge that I found the evidence compelling, that perhaps he had some legitimate concerns. As he talked, I had a thought that, to me, was original. Some people leave the Church not as a result of wickedness, nor because they want to join some fundamentalist Mormon sect that practices polygamy: They leave because they believe the Church is not true and never has been true.

Although Brad's comments had been few, they had rocked the beliefs around which my life revolved. Knowing Brad as I did, I found it difficult to dismiss what he had to say.

After we hung up, I told Connie that Brad was leaving the Church. Stunned at the announcement, she asked why. I hesitated to tell her, fearing that exposure to these claims about Joseph Smith would add to the doubts she already had. Needing some time to prepare my answers to questions that would strain her faith, I asked if we could discuss it in a couple of days. She agreed to my patronizing request.

Two days later I went to Carthage, Illinois, where Joseph Smith and his brother Hyrum had been killed by a mob. The Church was making a movie, which required shooting some scenes at Carthage Jail. Several weeks earlier, the Church had asked for local members to participate as extras for the movie, and I had volunteered. I left at 5 A.M. with a young couple in the ward, and we returned home about midnight. Some of the day we spent rehearsing and shooting, but mostly I waited and thought, and talked with other extras. Most conversations revolved around Joseph Smith and early Church history.

Listening to these conversations reminded me of an experience several years earlier in Independence, Missouri. While at the visitors center of a church that had broken off from the Mormons, I had observed and listened to a group as they gathered for a church activity. I talked with one of the men who explained their beliefs. His explanations seemed too superficial to justify some of their claims, yet the gathering group exuded certitude and enthusiasm for their religion. They appeared to be in their own make-believe world, unaware of important information which surely was readily available to them. Now I saw a peculiar shadow of similarity between that scene in Independence, Missouri, and the day in Carthage.

I wondered if the other extras had heard the stories of Joseph Smith's polyandry. I wondered if there was any truth to these stories. I wondered about the story that we were filming. Had I been living in a make-believe world my whole life?

At one time in my life, I would have considered it a privilege to be an extra, even an insignificant extra, in making a movie about Joseph Smith. Surely, this re-creation of the prophet's last days would be a spiritual experience. However, considering recent events, I only hoped that the day in Carthage would ease my troubled mind. I had hoped it would strengthen my belief that Joseph was a prophet. It did not.

The next day, however, I made a conscious decision to believe as I had always believed. My decision was not based on any new facts or fresh insight; I simply decided to keep my beliefs in this particular church, much as some basketball fans keep their loyalty fixed on some particular NBA team. I made the decision while talking with Mom on the phone. Knowing that she was distraught over Brad's apostasy, and not wanting to add to her burden by admitting my own uncertainties, I reverted to my lifelong practice of repressing any bothersome questions concerning the Church. I immediately shelved these most recent disturbing questions and convinced myself, on the spot, that my lifelong beliefs were correct. I hope never again to be so deliberate in smothering doubts in order to hang on to a belief.

Over the previous few years, I had at times admitted to myself a desire to get out of the Church. Since the phone conversation with Brad a few days earlier, the thought kept crossing my mind that leaving the Church might be easier than I could possibly have imagined. Now I buried those thoughts, having decided to believe. After quelling my own doubts, I tried to quell Connie's. People often turn a tiny truth into a truckload of trash; no doubt, this was the case with the reports of Joseph Smith marrying other men's wives. From the thousands of people who knew him, surely there had been people who disliked him, people who would twist the truth and outright lie about him, enough people and lies to fill a book. Furthermore, how good could the evidence be of things that had supposedly happened over 150 years ago?

Two weeks after Brad's phone call, I helped put on a program for the youth of our ward. We played the parts of people who had died and were stuck in the spirit world, waiting for someone here on earth to do their temple work so they could be forever united with their families. Everyone, adults and youth, seemed to consider it a spiritual experience—everyone but me. Despite the best intentions of all involved, I saw it as a program that evoked powerful emotions, which were then misconstrued as a spiritual confirmation. My part in the unintentional manipulation left me feeling deceptive, so when some visitors asked us to present the program to the youth of their wards, I declined without offering an explanation.

A few days later, I drove fifty miles north to Springfield, Illinois to help in a neighborhood beautification project. Participating in the project were volunteers from a number of local congregations, including a few Mormon wards. Since most of the volunteers—both Mormon and non-Mormon—were strangers to me, here was the perfect opportunity to test the claim that Mormons have a radiance by which they can be identified in a crowd. (This radiance, the reasoning goes, is due to the gift of the Holy Ghost that is unique to Mormons, and to our wholesome living.)

The test results did not surprise me. I simply could not identify the Mormon volunteers by their radiance. Perhaps I was lacking something. The episode was not significant to me, just one more thing to think about, one more belief I had grown up with that should probably be labeled as folklore. (Any religion, even a true religion, is bound to have some folklore.)

I continued—as I had for years on other issues—trying to reconcile two conflicting views: Certainly, Brad was wrong, yet I knew that eventually an in-depth look was called for, just in case he was right. However, now was not the time.

I think a full, free talk is frequently of great use; we want nothing secret nor underhanded, and I for one want no association with things that cannot be talked about and will not bear investigation.
—John Taylor (third Mormon prophet), March 2, 1879, *Journal of Discourses*, Vol. 20, p. 264

Knowing that my testimony needed to be strengthened, I decided to give myself a year to shore up my beliefs and then take a look.

Since 1993, I had spent a lot of time with Brad. He owned a computer software company, and I had worked with him throughout the summer of 1993. Each summer from 1994 to 1997, I had gone back to Utah from Illinois and spent a week or two with him. After a day's work, we often spent the evening discussing various topics. We held thought-provoking discussions on science, math, social issues, politics, religion, and interpersonal relations. On each of these visits, I returned home with new insights and with a greater desire to be a better father and husband. It was curious, I thought, to learn this from Brad, because he was not then a father and not until my last visit was he a husband. He had weaknesses, as we all do, but I knew of no man who tried harder to do what he felt was right.

Oh, how the mighty have fallen, I now thought of Brad. This was a fulfillment of the prophecy that the very elect of God would be deceived.

I was concerned for Cathy and Caleb. Only two short years ago, Cathy had married a man who was as dedicated to the Church as one can be. Her husband was now an apostate. Caleb had, in the premortal existence, earned the right to be born of wonderful parents who could raise him in the only true church on the face of the earth. I had thought that no prophet had been born of better parents than had Caleb. Yet, by leaving the Church, Brad had betrayed his own son. Caleb's strong Mormon family had lasted only a year.

Although I had convinced myself that Brad had made a terrible mistake, I still believed he was trying to do the right thing. I prayed often throughout the following weeks that he would come back to

the Church. If angels could appear to Saul (of the Bible) and Alma
the Younger (of the *Book of Mormon*) and tell them they were
wrong, surely the Lord could do some small thing to help Brad see
the light.

I never doubted that Brad would be treated kindly by family
members, but I wondered if he was being overwhelmed by loving
and well-meaning family and friends who were trying to point out
the error of his ways. Thinking that he might want to get away for a
while, we invited him and his family back to Illinois for a visit and
a camping trip. I also planned to talk to him about his decision. I
was aware of our tendency as Mormons to be dogmatic. However,
I intended to listen to what Brad had to say. In return, surely he
would listen to my small, but potent, arsenal of logical arguments in
support of the Church.

Brad, Cathy, and Caleb came to visit on August 4. We drove to
our campsite the next day. Brad and I conversed during the three-
hour drive, while Connie and Cathy visited in the other car. We
talked about some issues that had led to his decision. Several times
he asked if I was comfortable holding this discussion with two of
my children in the back seat. Although he was careful to speak
softly, they could hear some of his talk about Joseph Smith—not
a faith-promoting topic. Despite feeling a little chagrined that an
apostate would show more apparent concern than I did over my own
children's spiritual welfare, I saw no reason to keep this conversation a secret, and I had no interest in ending the discussion. My
prepared arguments did not seem relevant, so I mostly listened and
asked a few questions.

We camped for two days. We took a float trip with one raft and
one canoe, and we enjoyed playing with our children in the river
next to our campsite. I saw a dimension to my brother which I had
never before seen, Brad as a father. He had always been a beloved
uncle and had enjoyed spending time with our nephews and nieces,
so it was no surprise to see that he was also a loving father. This
was the same Brad I had always known. He was not under the influence of Satan. He did not conform to the prophets' descriptions
of apostates, nor was he a candidate for "Son of Perdition," a phrase
Mormons apply to the irredeemably evil. Brad was the first of many

apostates with whom I became familiar over the next few years. Not one of them fit my preconceived notions of apostates.

On the drive home we continued our discussion. Brad had not made his decision based on a few isolated stories told by anti-Mormons. A number of issues had troubled him, and he had restricted his studies to sources written by active Mormons. Although he had been careful with his sources, I wanted to see with my own eyes Church records of Joseph Smith's marriage to women who were already married. However, I knew the Church would not allow an average member like me to do this; after all, the Church routinely withholds some documents from even its own scholars. Nevertheless, of the several issues that Brad discussed, there was one disturbing report that I could check out. In an interview with the press, President Gordon B. Hinckley had reportedly backpedaled on the basic Church doctrine that God was once a mortal man.

I gave Brad no indication of how deeply our conversation disturbed me. Having considerable respect for his thought processes and for the time he had spent looking into these matters, I had finally run into some controversial Church issues that could not be ignored, scoffed at, or superficially explained away. Is truth so fragile that it remains standing only if left unchallenged? I did not think so. Refusing to withdraw into my shell of faith, I again decided to look into this whole affair, perhaps in a year.

Chapter 10

Looking Behind the Curtain

Chris

A Riddle:

A man who took daily walks on the beach occasionally saw some writing in the sand. This was most peculiar, because he was on an island inhabited only by himself and some monkeys. Furthermore, he knew for a fact that no other person had been on or near the island when the writing had been done. The writing in the sand included some of Shakespeare's sonnets and the development and proof of the Fundamental Theorem of Calculus. He never had understood the proof of the Fundamental Theorem of Calculus, but this proof had been so well written, with such clear commentary, that he finally had a firm grasp of its difficulties.

Knowing that no other person had been within hundreds of miles of the island, the writing in the sand had utterly befuddled him. Every now and then, he had seen a monkey carrying a stick. But could that be the answer? How could a monkey know Shakespeare? How could a monkey give a well-written proof of the Fundamental Theorem of Calculus? It stretched his credulity to the limit, but what else could he conclude?

This is a variation of a riddle Brad once told me to support our belief in the Church. What this man on the island needs to do is examine his original conviction. Why does he believe that no other person was on or near the island? Which is more reasonable: to question his "knowledge" that no human could have written it, or to believe that a presumptuous primate did it?

The riddle is misleading, for the existence of other people nearby did not appear to be a possible explanation. However, the riddle parallels my dilemma prior to August of 1998. Figuratively speaking, I had been the man on the island, "knowing" that the Church was true. When this "knowledge" conflicted with the evidence, I failed to question the truthfulness of the Church, just as the man on the island failed to consider the possibility of humans nearby.

On several occasions I had feigned a critical look into whether or not the Church was true. But such occasions were nothing more than a few minutes of one-sided arguments supporting my beliefs. My convictions had been so strong that if I had seen a man on that figurative beach, I might have called it a monkey in a man suit. But my assumptions changed after Brad's visit. I would seek for the truth. I was now willing to question the unquestionable, to ponder the impossible. This would be more than a pretended pursuit of truth. This time I was ready for the truth of the matter; or, was I simply on the verge of a fall from grace?

Broad-mindedness leads to apostasy.
—Joseph Fielding Smith, *Doctrines of Salvation*, Vol. 3, 1956, p. 298

The day after our camping trip, Brad, Cathy, and Caleb returned to Utah. The next day, a Sunday, Connie and I spent most of the morning talking over the troubling issues that Brad had mentioned. I could not bear to follow my original plans to wait for a year before researching the disturbing reports. I would at least look into the report that President Hinckley, in talking with the press, had denied the Church teaching that God was once a man.

Briefly, the Mormon view is this: Since we are children of God, we have the potential to become, like him, a god. Since he is our father, he was once like us. He had once been a mortal man worshiping his god, and, through righteousness, he had attained godhood. Had Hinckley really denied this fundamental doctrine? I found it inconceivable that he would do so; yet if he had, it should be easy to verify.

I went to see if our church library had any recorded interviews of President Hinckley talking with the press. I felt awkward showing up at church at that time. The three-hour block of regular meetings was almost over, and I had also missed an early morning meeting with the bishop and other ward leaders. Furthermore, I was not prepared for, nor did I want to hold, my weekly planning meeting with the full-time missionaries. I checked the library and found that it did not have what I wanted. I told the missionaries that our weekly planning meeting was cancelled, and I left quickly to avoid having to explain my absence at the day's meetings. It was the first time in years that I had missed the regular Sunday meetings for anything other than sickness. It was the last time I would set foot inside the church building as a believer.

I had not yet paid tithing on my last paycheck. (This donation is required to remain a member in good standing. The money is used to build meetinghouses, temples, Church schools, and seminaries, with plenty left over for the Church to amass significant holdings.) On any previous Sunday morning at church, I would have filled out a tithing slip, written a check, and given it to the bishop. But on that Sunday morning, I determined not to give the Church another dime until I had settled the question of whether or not I was being duped by Church leaders in Utah.

By searching the Internet that afternoon, I learned that President Hinckley had reportedly made his comments in 1997 during an interview with Richard N. Ostling of *Time* magazine.[68] I went to the public library and found the issue. The cover story was an article favorable toward the Mormon Church and its members. Then I reached the part where President Hinckley refused to admit that God was once a man. What was going on here?

I looked on the Internet for more information about the interview. The Institute for Religious Research had sent a letter to the First Presidency asking about President Hinckley's comment on this doctrine. The response included the following paragraph:

The quotation you reference was taken out of context. The statement was made in response to a question about the actual circumstances and background surrounding remarks given during the funeral services of a man named King Follet, not the doctrine of exaltation and the blessings that await those who will inherit the celestial kingdom.[69]

Following is the relevant part of the interview between Ostling and Hinckley, coming after a long discussion of the Mormon doctrine of men becoming gods.

Q: Just another related question that comes up is the statements in the King Follet discourse by the Prophet.
A: Yeah
Q: . . . about that, God the Father was once a man as we were. This is something that Christian writers are always addressing. Is this the teaching of the Church today, that God the Father was once a man like we are?
A: I don't know that we teach it. I don't know that we emphasize it. I haven't heard it discussed for a long time in public discourse. I don't know. I don't know all the circumstances under which that statement was made. I understand the philosophical background behind it. But I don't know a lot about it and I don't know that others know a lot about it.[70]

I was flabbergasted at his comments. God as a man is a well-established Church doctrine. It is taught from the pulpit. It is taught in Sunday School. It has been plainly taught in a number of publications such as the Church magazine *Ensign* and Church manual *Gospel Principles,* which can also be found online at the official Church website.[71] Apostles and prophets have taught the doctrine since the 1840s. In the general conference of April 1977, the prophet and twelfth Church president, Spencer W. Kimball, quoted Lorenzo Snow who had been the fifth president:

We remember the numerous scriptures which, concentrated in a single line, were stated by a former prophet, Lorenzo Snow: "As man is, God once was; and as God is, man may become."

It is impossible that President Hinckley could honestly deny a doctrine which has permeated the Church since Joseph Smith taught it.

I felt a range of emotions. I was shocked. I felt incredulous. I was angry with myself and Hinckley. Most of all, I felt betrayed and lied to. In my various Church jobs, I had taught many times that God was once a man. I had taught that the Church was led by a prophet: a prophet who knew God as Moses knew God; a prophet like Abinadi of the *Book of Mormon* who plainly and fearlessly spoke what he knew to be true, even at the expense of his own life. I knew that the world considered this claim about Mormon prophets to be inconceivable, but I had believed it.

I recalled another of Hinckley's statements—two months after the *Time* magazine article—in the October 1997 General Conference when he said:

> I personally have been much quoted, and in a few instances misquoted and misunderstood. I think that's to be expected. None of you need worry because you read something that was incompletely reported. You need not worry that I do not understand some matters of doctrine. I think I understand them thoroughly, and it is unfortunate that the reporting may not make this clear. I hope you will never look to the public press as the authority on the doctrines of the Church.

Because I had not read the *Time* article when it first came out, this statement by Hinckley had struck me as odd when I first heard it. I had wondered what prompted the comment, but he was silent about the circumstances of his being misquoted. After reading the *Time* article, I understood what might have prompted his remark.

There was a time in my life when I might have said—without looking into it any deeper—that the statements as reported in *Time* were taken out of context, that Hinckley was misquoted. Or, I might have tried to defend what he said. However, this time I would not let a little superficial thought appease my concerns. I recalled my uneasy feeling in 1996 upon hearing Hinckley dodge some questions in his interview with Mike Wallace on *60 Minutes*. What other issues has the Church dodged? Were they hiding something?

Had I been fooled? Hinckley's Orwellian newspeak convinced me that my research into the Church had to go full speed ahead.

If a faith will not bear to be investigated; if its preachers and professors are afraid to have it examined, their foundation must be very weak.
—George A. Smith, 1871, *Journal of Discourses*, Vol. 14, p 216

That afternoon, I spent several hours on the Internet reading material I had shunned my whole life. Although the Internet contains a jumble of truths and untruths, I decided it was better to sift through them than to rely exclusively on the Church, a self-proclaimed supreme source of truth. Internet sources presented new problematic issues as well as issues I had dismissed years earlier.

Being unsure of the reliability of Internet sources, I would not discard my beliefs based on one afternoon spent on the Internet. However, two thoughts forcefully struck me. First of all, my complete, unquestioning trust in the prophet and apostles of the Church seemed more like blind faith than well-founded faith. Secondly, I noticed how well the puzzle pieces fit if one dared to consider that the Church was not true.

Concerning this first point, virtually everything I had ever read about the Church had either been published by the Church or written by some Church leader. I had not questioned such sources. A quick check of the Brigham Young manual—used throughout the Church in 1998 and 1999—revealed some subtle points that I had previously missed.

Brigham Young had dozens of wives, and he taught that the practice of polygamy was essential for one's salvation.[72] Yet in the Brigham Young manual, each occurrence of the word "wives" had been replaced with "[wife]," and there was no indication in the manual of Brigham's emphasis on the practice of polygamy, or that he and most of the early Church leaders practiced it. This lesson manual, in many languages, is being used in countries all over the world. New members will never know that Brigham or the Church ever practiced polygamy if they get their information from this lesson manual or from other recently published Church manuals. There was no doubt that the Church, embarrassed by Brigham's teachings and lifestyle, was trying to skirt the issue of polygamy.

What bothered me most about the thorough efforts to remove any hint of polygamy was the omission of Brigham's wives in the chronology of his life. The chronology mentions only his first wife and then his second wife, whom he married after his first wife had died. What about the women who had obeyed the "eternal principle" of polygamy in becoming one of his many wives? They never knew what it was like to have a husband who would devote his time and means to his one wife and their children. Following Brigham into polygamy had required a tremendous sacrifice which was now completely ignored—or hidden—so that the Church could paint a portrait of Brigham that was acceptable in today's world.

This fact about the Brigham Young manual may seem minor, but it revealed a bothersome "fudge factor" in Church publications. How could I have allowed myself to be fooled into reading only sanctioned Mormon literature?

I made a vow that I would never again so completely suspend my critical thought as I had done on issues related to the Mormon Church. Regardless of the outcome of this investigation, regardless of whether or not my faith remained intact, I resolved never again to conform blindly to the views of *any* organization. I would never again automatically accept the ideas of any group of people. I would never again walk lockstep behind any man or woman, in any aspect of my life. My attempts to keep this vow have had profound consequences that go well beyond my religious life.

The second thought that struck me that day was truly an epiphany. If the Church were not true, all the problems on the shelf would have such simple solutions, and my bewildering set of answers to a multitude of other problems could be discarded. Could it be that the *Book of Mormon* was a plagiarized creation of Joseph Smith rather than an inspired translation of an ancient record? Could it be that the *Book of Mormon* gave a Protestant—rather than the current Mormon—description of God and Jesus because that was Joseph's view when he wrote it? Could it be that some parts of it seemed like nonsense because it really was nonsense? Was it possible that the rampant apostasy in the early Church was not a result of Satan's efforts to thwart the establishment of God's church, but rather the result of Joseph's unscrupulous behavior? Was it possible that current Church leaders, at times, did not act like "prophets, seers, and revelators" because, in fact, they were not? Could it really be that simple? Maybe the proverbial monkey had not written in the sand.

From my childhood, the question had never been, "Is the Church true?" Rather, it had been: "Have you made the necessary effort to gain a testimony? If not, you need more diligence in your scripture study; you need to ponder and pray more sincerely." I was the one, never the Church, on trial. By the time I was mature enough to recognize troubling inconsistencies, my view was hopelessly jaded. Certain that the Church was true, I had been striving for spiritual enlightenment, not intellectual verification. I was thirty-eight years old, about twenty years late in taking the first hard look at my faith.

Reality, as I understood it, was on the verge of collapse.

Thus I have given a brief history of the manner in which the writings of the fathers, Abraham and Joseph, have been preserved, and how I came in possession of the same—a correct translation of which I shall give in its proper place.
—Joseph Smith, 1835, *History of the Church* Vol. 2, pp 350–351

I could not sleep well that night, so I got back on the Internet. I did more research and ordered some books, including one on the Book of Abraham. While President Hinckley's denials had knocked the breath out of me, information about the Book of Abraham—supposedly written in the ancient Egyptian language—would knock me to the canvas.

In 1799, a French soldier in Egypt discovered a black stone—named the Rosetta Stone because it was found in the Rosetta branch of the Nile River. Inscribed on this large stone was a royal decree, recorded in three different languages: Egyptian hieroglyphs, demotic script, and Greek. The ability to read Egyptian hieroglyphs had been lost in about the fourth century. In 1808, a Frenchman by the name of Champollion began working to decipher the Egyptian hieroglyphs by comparing them with the Greek version of the decree. It took fourteen years to complete the project, and the results were published in 1822. Champollion's accomplishment proved just a beginning, but it was the breakthrough needed for learning how to read hieroglyphs.

Joseph Smith, while perhaps not on the very cutting edge of translating ancient Egyptian, was apparently ahead of the curve. In 1835, some Church members purchased four Egyptian mummies and some papyri which had been buried with them. Two scrolls and several pieces of papyrus were then given to Joseph Smith, the prophet, seer, and revelator. Joseph wrote, "I commenced the translation of some of the characters of hieroglyphics, and much to our joy found that one of the rolls contained the writings of Abraham, another the writings of Joseph of Egypt."[73] Joseph Smith never gave a translation of the writings of Joseph of Egypt, but he did present a translation of some of the writings of Abraham. Joseph had very little formal education and no training in ancient Egyptian. His ability to translate came from his calling as "prophet, seer, and revelator." Joseph also explained three pictures contained in the papyri.

Evidently, Joseph became somewhat of a scholar of ancient languages. The Church history book used by several of my older siblings in their high school seminary classes said the following.

He [Joseph] began a study of Egyptian, Hebrew and Greek to enable him to better understand the Bible and ancient documents concerning God's people. This study continued at intervals until his death. His most notable achievement was the development at Kirtland of a grammar for the Egyptian hieroglyphic form of writing. It was . . . the first Egyptian grammar in America.[74]

After Joseph Smith was killed, the papyri were sold to a St. Louis museum, but they eventually went to the Museum of Chicago. For years, the papyri were thought to have been destroyed in the great Chicago fire of 1871.

Meanwhile, after years of studying the Rosetta Stone and other documents, scholars could translate ancient Egyptian with considerable accuracy. In 1856, the Egyptology expert M. Theodule Deveria, upon seeing facsimiles of the figures from the Book of Abraham papyrus, did not agree with Joseph's interpretation. (We will use the singular term "Abraham papyrus" rather than "Abraham papyri" although the original scroll has been divided into pieces.) He said the facsimiles looked as if they came from Egyptian funeral documents. Furthermore, some parts of the facsimiles appeared to have been incorrectly filled in; he conjectured that part of the original papyrus had been missing.

The Mormons were undaunted by the expert's opinion; in 1880, Joseph's translation of the papyrus, along with the facsimiles and Joseph's explanation of them, was officially recognized as scripture. Called the Book of Abraham, it is currently part of the *Pearl of Great Price,* one of the four books recognized as scripture by Mormons.

Several experts gave scathing assessments of Joseph's interpretation of the facsimiles. However, Church authorities adamantly supported Joseph. Some argued that without the papyrus it would be difficult to give a fair intellectual assessment of Joseph's ability to translate ancient Egyptian. The Church has never wavered in its claims of the origin of the Book of Abraham, which begins as follows:

THE BOOK OF ABRAHAM
TRANSLATED FROM THE PAPYRUS, BY JOSEPH SMITH
A translation of some ancient Records, that have fallen into our hands from the catacombs of Egypt.—The writings of Abraham while he was in Egypt, called the Book of Abraham, written by his own hand, upon papyrus.

I was six years old in 1966 when eleven fragments of the papyri were rediscovered in New York at the Metropolitan Museum of Art. Not all of the papyri had been rediscovered, but we now had facsimile 1. In addition, manuscripts long held by the Church, with the original English translation, give further evidence that these papyri included the papyrus Joseph translated; the margins contained a sequence of hieroglyphic characters which matched those from one of the fragments. Would the current Church leaders—following Joseph Smith's example—fulfill their roles as prophets, seers, and revelators by expounding on this ancient source of scripture? Or, would they turn the papyri over to experts to confirm Joseph's translation? This was indeed an exciting and historic time for Mormons.

I was only seven when the fragments were presented to the Mormon Church, and I was not aware of these events or their significance. I recall nothing of the anticipation Mormons felt at the opportunity to verify Joseph's claims; finally, the Church had conclusive proof that he did have the ability to translate ancient records. To Brad, who would soon be going on his mission, it was an exciting discovery which could be used in his missionary work (see Chapter 15).

The excitement, inexplicably, did not last. Evidently, the true-believing Mormons had no need of more evidence that Joseph was a prophet, and non-Mormons did not find it convincing. Consequently, when I was older, I knew almost nothing of this background to the Book of Abraham, despite having read articles from the Church magazine *Ensign* that discussed the ancient Egyptian language; they pointed to similarities between the facsimiles in the Book of Abraham and figures from other ancient documents, and they mentioned Abraham. Illustrations of papyri added to the appearance of scholarship in these articles. However, the writers did not say that these very papyri were once used by Joseph Smith to translate part of the Book of Abraham and that they were now in our possession. They did not draw the one connection which would have made the Book of Abraham an interesting topic, so I failed to see any real significance to the articles.

In short, I had seen pictures of papyri, and in the back of my mind was the lost memory that Joseph Smith had translated the Book of Abraham from papyrus, but I remembered no claims that the Church owned the very papyri that proved Joseph could translate ancient records.

I knew nothing of doubts concerning the Book of Abraham. However, while on the Internet in the wee hours of the Monday morning after Brad left, I was shocked to read accusations directed at the Book of Abraham. Some information cast doubt on the validity of the Book of Abraham; in some circles, its authenticity had been debated for years. How could I have remained ignorant of this ongoing debate? I decided to look into it.

It would take a book to cover all the issues concerning the Book of Abraham. In fact, there is such a book. *By His Own Hand Upon*

Papyrus, by Charles M. Larson, is an excellent source of information on the Book of Abraham. The preceding discussion on the Book of Abraham and the following summary touch only a fraction of what I found in his book.

Joseph's "Egyptian Alphabet and Grammar" had been forgotten for years. Its 1935 "rediscovery" in a Church vault was kept under wraps. In 1965, a microfilm copy was leaked and, the next year, published. Because the Church had not published it, this whole affair went largely unnoticed by Mormons, but the professional Egyptologists who examined the manuscript concluded that the "first Egyptian grammar in America" was gibberish.

The next year, 1966, the papyri were rediscovered in the Metropolitan Museum in New York. With it came a flood of evidence against the Book of Abraham. Facsimile 1 on the papyrus had been damaged. In fact, it was missing portions exactly where experts had claimed, since 1856, that it had been falsely reconstructed. The papyrus had been glued to backing paper; the reconstructed figure as found in the Church's publication of the Book of Abraham was sketched on the backing. A similar problem existed for facsimile 2.[75]

As for the text of the papyri, the Church was hesitant to turn them over to just any expert; they wanted one friendly to the Church. They found their man in Dee Jay Nelson, a Mormon who had studied Egyptology for twenty years. He translated the Abraham papyrus and was disturbed to find no mention of Abraham; it was indeed a common Egyptian funeral document. Other experts later identified the document as a version of the Egyptian *Book of the Dead*. It discussed Egyptian gods, spells, and pagan rituals. (It had, after all, been buried with mummies.)

What were the Church leaders to do? They did not like Nelson's interpretation, and he was unaccommodating about trying to put a favorable spin on the facts. Because Church leaders had promised members an interpretation, they turned to Dr. Hugh Nibley, a highly respected scholar in the eyes of Mormons. Nibley did not have the background in Egyptology that Nelson did, but over a two-year period, he proceeded to write a sequence of articles for the Church magazine *Improvement Era*. He did not deliver the promised translation, but he succeeded in throwing up some scholarly smoke and mirrors that intimidated the average Mormon. The Book of Abraham faded into a non-issue.

How did Mormon scholars react? Some, such as Dee Jay Nelson, simply lost their faith and left the Church. Others, in defense of the Book of Abraham, gave a sequence of ever-evolving explanations which (people on both sides of the argument will probably agree) approach the level of scholarship exhibited by Joseph's translation of ancient Egyptian.

For me, the Book of Abraham problems were just the beginning. I read from several well-documented books not sanctioned by the Church. Of all my reading, the most damning evidence was presented in the book, *Where Does It Say That?*[76] Ironically, it is merely a book containing quotations of Church leaders, most of them from the early history of the Church. However, rather than simply quoting the Church leaders, this book, compiled by Bob Witte, contains photocopies of over one hundred pages out of books published by the early Church. These photocopies prevented me and other faithful Mormon readers from concluding that these controversial teachings were either misquotes or were taken out of context.

Although I had once argued that Brigham Young had not taught the Adam-God doctrine, I had been wrong. Furthermore, Brigham's false prophecies, strange teachings, and derogatory comments about Blacks, Jews, and women could not be ignored (see Chapter 14). I found other doctrines, taught by early Church presidents, which Mormons no longer accept as true.

Joseph Smith reported a personal visitation by God the Father and Jesus Christ. This "first vision" is the very

Mormonism, as it is called, must stand or fall on the story of Joseph Smith.
—Joseph Fielding Smith, *Doctrines of Salvation,* Vol. 1, p. 188

foundation of the Mormon Church. In monthly testimony meetings, Mormons will often stand before the congregation, testify of the first vision, and say that they know Joseph Smith saw God the Father and Jesus Christ. There is no confusion in modern Mormonism about the first vision. From Bob Witte's book, I learned that this had not always been the case.

Early Church leaders, including Brigham Young, John Taylor, and Wilford Woodruff—the second, third, and fourth presidents of the Church respectively—clearly taught that the first vision was a visit from an angel.[77] Within the *Journal of Discourses,* the first reference to the Father and the Son being in the first vision came from Orson Pratt in 1859. The next mention came in 1864, but starting in 1869 the Father and Son version became more popular. After 1879, mention of the angel account ceased.

I also found confusion as to the date of the first vision. Wilford Woodruff taught that the first vision occurred in 1827.[78] While Joseph was still alive in 1840, Oliver Cowdery (who was reportedly with Joseph during several angelic visitations) corrected a previous printing error in the *Times And Seasons.* He emphasized that 1823 was the correct year of the first vision.[79] The Church now teaches that the first vision took place in 1820. The 1823 and 1827 dates are irreconcilable contradictions to the currently accepted timeline for the other visions and revelations that Joseph received.

How could there be such confusion about an issue so central to the Church? How could Joseph's close associates be so confused about such an important matter as a visit from God the Father and Jesus Christ? Perhaps it is because Joseph's explanation of the event changed through the years. Of the several contradictory accounts of the first vision which are attributed to Joseph Smith, only one is in Joseph's handwriting. It mentions Jesus Christ but not God the Father.

While considering the evidence which I had finally confronted after all these years, I asked myself what I would conclude if I were a non-Mormon looking at Mormonism for the first time. With all the information the Church provides and all the additional information that I had recently acquired, what would I do? The answer was simple. On one side, I saw the boldness of the Church's claims, supported by the sincere and forceful testimonials of its many good members. On the other side, I saw verifiable facts. My years of faith and testimony had been based on emotion and well-told—but uncorroborated—stories. Now, with the evidence at hand, it was impossible for me to believe in Mormonism.

Some would later accuse me of being too intellectual in my approach. They overestimate the intellectual effort required to make this decision. I am reminded of Dorothy being told to pay no attention to the man behind the curtain. She unveiled the Wizard of Oz, not through great mental exertion, but merely by looking. I too had been told not to "look behind the curtain," and for years—being more obedient than Dorothy—I had taken only an occasional unintentional glance. However, now having looked, the evidence was clear and compelling. I understood, as never before, the dangers of reading unsanctioned literature; I understood why the Church discourages its members from looking behind the curtain.

Chapter 11

Free at Last

Chris

"Put on the brakes," I told myself in the days after Brad's visit. For years, I had desperately wanted to leave the Church, and now the

> It is necessary to the happiness of man that he be mentally faithful to himself. Infidelity does not consist in believing, or in disbelieving; it consists in professing to believe what he does not believe.
>
> —Thomas Paine, *The Age of Reason*, Chapter 1, p. 2

path leading out was more than just a possibility; it appeared to be the only honest choice available. I wondered, "Am I just groping for an excuse to leave?" Had I done the mathematical equivalent of dividing by zero in my analysis of the evidence? No, the facts were there, and the evidence—much of it from the Church's own records—was compelling. For several years I had envisioned scenarios for leaving the Church, but this particular one had never crossed my mind. Guilt and turmoil receded; relief overwhelmed me. I was "free at last, free at last—thank God Almighty, free at last."

The Church in Salt Lake City keeps a record of every Mormon in the world. Some Mormons who lose their faith do not remove their name from Church records. However, I wanted to make a clean break from the Church, an organization that takes seriously its charge to watch over its flock. I remembered a woman who had, for years, been an inactive Church member in Idaho. She had not told the Church of her move to Austin, Texas, and thought she had left Mormonism far behind. She was shocked when I showed up at her door and announced that I had been assigned as her new home teacher. Only then did she understand the Church devotion in keeping track of, and visiting, its members. Years ago, I knew some local Church leaders who visited the post office to get the forwarding address of a member who moved without leaving a new address. It was an effective, although illegal, method of keeping track of Church members.

There is something to be said for an organization so dedicated to its members, but I wanted nothing to do with it. Our local ward included many people I considered friends. Aware of the sacrifices they made for their faith, I did not want to burden them further with the responsibility of looking after my spiritual welfare if I became an inactive member of record. Connie remained a member, so removing my name from Church records was the most I could do to distance myself from the Church.

Additionally, feelings toward Church leaders in Salt Lake City motivated me to remove my name from Church records. I had obediently submitted to their summons for thousands of dollars in tithing and years of service. They had asked for and received my sustaining vote for them as prophets, seers, and revelators. Yet they had played a major role in withholding any information which could shake the faith of their followers. Removing my name from the Church records would be my last act of Church membership, one last vote cast in silent protest for a betrayal of trust.

Four days after the visit from Brad and Cathy, I informed Bishop Gietler of my lost faith in the Mormon Church. Upon hearing some reasons for my conclusion, he expressed his view that I was still a good man. It was a response that I didn't fully appreciate at the time.

Some obligations were yet undone: as ward mission leader, I was in charge of the upcoming church open house; I had not paid tithing on my July paycheck; I had not yet done any of my monthly home-teaching assignments. These duties were all left undone. The last guilt I would feel in connection with the Church was for deserting my fellow ward missionaries, leaving them to do the last few preparations for the open house that was eleven days away. My last tithing donation to the multi-billion-dollar Corporation of the President of the Church of Jesus Christ of Latter-day Saints had been a check for tithing on my June income; unfortunately, that check had cleared the bank weeks previously. As a home-teacher, my duty was to serve my assigned families with monthly visits. As my last act of service, I left them alone for the month.

I agonized over how to inform my parents and siblings of my decision; I knew that our relationship would be forever altered. Surely my mother's heart would break. Mom and Dad considered the gospel to be the bedrock of their lives and the foundation of all the good things they had taught their children. Would they understand that I could reject the Mormon Church without rejecting their lives as examples of goodness?

Despite my anxiety over how things would work out with family, the decision to leave the Church gave me a tremendous sense of peace and relief, the likes of which I had seldom felt

Just the facts, Ma'am.
—Sergeant Friday, *Dragnet*

In the four days between Brad's visit and my talk with the bishop, I had kept Connie updated about my rapidly crumbling faith in the Church. She was shocked at what appeared to be a 180-degree turn in my views over this four-day period. It was a serious case of religious whiplash; but my turnaround was not as drastic as Connie thought. She had never been as certain in her Mormon beliefs as I had been in mine. Yet paradoxically, for years my distress had probably run deeper than had hers. Not wanting to weaken her faith, I had hidden my inner turmoil and sustained my faith with activity in the Church. Hiding my concerns from Connie had not been difficult, having never really faced them myself.

She felt my retreat was too hasty, believing that leaving one's faith was a decision that should take some time—time measured in months, not hours. She asked me to reconsider my decision before announcing it to the family. I agreed to postpone sending them the letter I had already written. As for thinking about my decision, that would dominate my thoughts for months.

Connie and I had many talks over the next few weeks. Maybe I was wrong, she suggested. Maybe I should spend more time pondering and praying. I admitted that I might be wrong, and I had not completely given up on prayer, but without more reason to believe, I could no longer honestly pray to know if the Church was true.

Connie suggested that I talk with someone, a Church leader perhaps, about my decision. But, such a discussion would likely result in my hearing another testimonial of the truthfulness of the Church. I had heard thousands of testimonies throughout my life; I had given hundreds myself. To hear one more would give me no new information. I did not want to hear another forceful statement, and I needed no help interpreting what was clearly written in the Church's own publications. I wanted only valid arguments and verifiable facts. The time for feel-good testimonies was over.

Connie asked about those occasions when the Spirit had testified to me of the truthfulness of the Mormon Church. She had a point, I admitted, but what of non-Mormons who have such feelings about *their* churches? Perhaps these feelings were nothing more than strong emotions. Furthermore, my recent feelings of peace after deciding to leave the Church felt like spiritual confirmation that my decision had been correct. Spirit or no spirit, I was not willing to ignore all the recently encountered evidence against the Church.

Connie wondered: What if Mormonism was the only way to exaltation? Was I throwing away my chance to be exalted? I replied that regardless of my actions from this point on, my faith in Mormonism had evaporated. Could I be exalted by pretending to believe? Would I be rewarded for teaching my children and others to believe that which I do not believe myself? Must I live a lie to get to heaven?

Belief was no longer an option. I was like a man living hundreds of years ago who was told by some people that the sun orbits the earth each day, while others told him that the earth turns on its axis each day. This man could honestly and reasonably believe that the sun orbits the earth. His beliefs were justified each day as he watched the sun come up each morning and go down each night. The only way he could ever come to the truth would be to learn the physics involved and then take an objective look at the evidence. After doing so, he no longer had the honest option of holding on to his beliefs.

With conflicting beliefs, what would Connie and I teach the children? I volunteered to drive them to their Sunday meetings, if they chose to go. However, our bedtime activities did change. I read the children something other than Mormon scriptures; I sang them no more songs of *Book of Mormon* heroes, Joseph Smith, or modern-day prophets.

One Sunday afternoon, three weeks after Brad's visit, some missionaries dropped by our house for a visit. They were dumbfounded when I informed them of my lost faith. As they had been taught, they did not debate the issue; rather, one responded by bearing his testimony: he knew the *Book of Mormon* was the word of God; he knew that Joseph Smith was a prophet; he knew that the Church was true. Now I understood why such a testimony so effectively ends a discussion. With no possibility for open communication and no desire to argue, I said nothing in response. We exchanged awkward pleasantries and the missionaries left.

This was my first experience of sitting on the other side of the fence as someone bore his or her testimony. It struck me how unaffected I was. How many times had I, as a missionary, left a home thinking my testimony had inspired them, when in fact they had been utterly unimpressed? How many times had I misinterpreted polite silence as awe for the message?

On the other hand, I thought of occasions when a non-Mormon had complimented the Mormon Church. How many times had the compliment been given in an attempt to find some common ground, an attempt to make a peace offering in the midst of conflicting claims to truth? How many times had I interpreted these compliments as evidence that even the non-Mormons recognize us as a cut above the rest?

As a Mormon, I held many beliefs about the central role of Mormonism in today's world:

- Technological advances in transportation, communications, and computers had been inspired by God to meet the needs of his Church.
- The United States Constitution had been inspired by God as a necessary step leading to the establishment of Mormonism.[80]

- Not only were Mormons God's chosen people, we were also the focus of Satan himself. Satan and his angels worked harder at getting us Mormons than at getting the non-Mormons.[81] Monday Night Football was Satan's response to the Mormon Church designating Monday night as *family home evening*.[82] (Satan was tempting the fathers into watching Monday Night Football rather than holding family home evening as directed by the Church.)

In short, Mormons were at the center of the universe, the focus of both good and evil forces.

The most important thing I teach my college students is to think critically; I was now embarrassed at how readily I had accepted my status as one of God's chosen people. On the spiritual side of my life, I had been a classic example of a non-critical thinker, looking only for evidence that would confirm my faith, ignoring any contradictory evidence that might drift my way. With an approach like that, how could I possibly have believed in anything else? If I had been born a Protestant and maintained this level of critical thinking, right or wrong, I would be Protestant still. If I had been born Muslim, I would be Muslim still. If I had been born an atheist, I would be atheist still. If I had been born believing in dragons, I would believe in dragons still.

No longer believing that I had the special gift of the Holy Ghost, I recognized my thoughts as just that: *my* thoughts; there was no need to speculate on which ideas originated with me and which were promptings from the Holy Ghost. There were no more futile attempts to squeeze a spiritual message out of bone-dry readings. (Over the years, my innermost thoughts had approached those of Mark Twain who said that the *Book of Mormon* "is chloroform in print."[83]) My former mistrust in scientific theories which conflict with Mormon doctrine has disappeared. I no longer spend exorbitant amounts of time attending administrative meetings and making assigned visits to people who have no need or desire to be visited. There is more time to spend in the little personal causes in which my efforts are better utilized.

Life in the Church had been a virtual reality—in many ways, a comfortable virtual reality. The proprietor had drawn unambiguous lines between good and evil, allowing me to live my life in a simple black-and-white world. In stepping out of this virtual reality, my eyes were open to a world full of colors, shades, ambiguities, and unanswerable questions. My previous comfortable answers to some important questions now seemed invalid. But, with my sudden, overwhelming ignorance came an exhilarating freedom to confront all of my beliefs, the challenge to see the world for what it really was. I was agog at the expansive world that I had always tried to fit into a neat little box.

In the next few weeks—before telling parents and siblings of my decision—I marveled at this new world and its unburdened joys. Sundays in particular were a delight. Although we had enjoyed associating with Church members in weekly meetings, any inspiration from these four- or five-hour family crusades had been effectively neutralized by sheer exhaustion; we spent the rest of the day in recovery. Now with Sunday free, we enjoyed more time as a family. We also had more free time during the week. Life was less stressful.

Although Connie sees more of a difference in me than do I, we agree that the change is for the better and that our relationship has improved since I left the Church. My oldest daughter Carissa appreciates my less rigid attitude.

Another bright spot is my son's soccer. Casey loved to play soccer, but I had been firm in not letting him play in the city league, because games were played on Sundays. Playing soccer would have required us to miss some church meetings and went against the Church teaching that we should not "shop, hunt, fish, attend sports events, or participate in any similar activities on that day."[84] With Connie's consent, one of the first things I did after making my decision to leave the Church was to sign Casey up for soccer. He enjoys playing, and I enjoy watching him play.

As the days passed, I felt a greater desire to make a clean break from the Church and to get on with the rest of my life. I had briefly considered waiting for a year before making my announcement; leaving the Church so soon after Brad's visit would surely cause family members to blame him for having drawn me over to the dark side. However, if I declined to perform Casey's baptism in a few months, then my siblings and parents would know something was wrong. Having complied with Connie's request to wait before telling my family (even Brad was unaware of my new views of the Church), after one month my announcement could not wait.

Rather than informing them by phone, I decided to send a carefully written letter. This could be read and reread, then passed on to others who could read the same message, decreasing the likelihood of misrepresentation. I sent the letter to Mom and Dad and two sisters through the U.S. mail on Thursday, September 3. I would e-mail the message to others after Mom and Dad had received theirs. Over the weekend, I waited apprehensively for the phone calls that were sure to come once the letters were received. No call came. Monday was a holiday, so I decided to e-mail the letter to the remaining family members on Tuesday, certain that the other letters had arrived.

On Tuesday morning, an e-mail came from a brother, Ben. He was unaware of my decision to leave the Church. I wrote a quick light-hearted reply to one of his comments, but hesitated in sending it. Would this note, followed in a few hours by my letter—a virtual son of perdition coming-out announcement—give Ben the impression that I had been too light-minded in my decision to leave the Church? I considered being solemn in all my communications so family members would know I understood the seriousness of my decision. However, mind-games did not appeal to me, so I sent the note to Ben, and a few hours later I sent the letter via e-mail explaining that I was leaving the Church.

The letter was addressed to my parents, siblings and in-laws. I would let each set of parents decide how, and if, they would explain the matter to their children. Following is my letter.

Dear Mom, Dad, Brothers, Sisters, and In-laws,   August 31, 1998
   I have recently felt a need to take a step back and look at the beliefs I have held from my childhood. After some very careful research and consideration I have asked that my name be removed from the records of the church.

   I remember as a boy being told many times that we need to pray to get our own testimony. I did pray many times to know if the church was true and I never felt that I got any kind of an answer. One day I realized that I already believed in the church, and that as far back as I could remember I had always believed in the church. Why then should I pray about it if I already firmly believed in it? Furthermore, why should the Lord answer my prayer for a testimony if He had already given me one? I was very satisfied with this conclusion, so I no longer prayed for a testimony but occasionally prayed that my testimony might be strengthened.

A few days ago, after coming to the conclusion that the church is not true, I wondered why I originally believed in the church. I soon realized however that believing was a very natural and reasonable thing to do. As a boy, I felt that the principles of love, kindness, integrity, morality, and other virtues taught by the church would lead to a happy life (and I still feel that way as an adult). This, weighed against any unanswered questions I may have had, firmly tipped the scales in favor of the church being true. Furthermore, when I considered my parents who were, and still are, such wonderful examples of love and integrity, and whose lives had very much been influenced by the church, the evidence was overwhelming in favor of the church. So as I said, it was a very natural thing for me to believe in the church.

From that point on, anytime something came along that I did not feel comfortable with, I dismissed it (put it on a shelf as they say), having already made up my mind that the church was true. As time went by, the issues on the shelf were piled higher and higher. By the time I took a step back and took an honest look at things, I realized that the scales had tipped, leaving me with some very serious doubts concerning the church. A vast majority of these doubts were based on things I read in the usual books a Mormon reads through the years, scriptures, teachings of Church leaders, etc., as well as some observations I have made through the years.

I thought that if my faith was based on truth, then truth would not destroy my faith. So I did more investigating, and the scales were tipped, quite convincingly I feel, against the church.

So that is where I now stand. I have tried not to make this investigation a purely intellectual exercise and this is not a decision I make lightly. I don't make it without regard to others;

knowing how it will hurt some of you makes it a terribly difficult thing to do. On the other hand, I am surprised at how comfortable I am with the conclusion that I have come to. In any case, I feel this is the only thing I can do.

I would like to say that I believe there is much good in the church, and I hope you will find much happiness in your own church membership.

Love, Chris

There was something about writing and sending this letter to my family that simplified life. It was an announcement, perhaps more to myself than to them, that I would cease to hide my doubts; the charade was over.

Although sending this letter brought relief, it also brought a fear of what my siblings would think of me. Months earlier, Mormons world-wide had read a lesson from the Brigham Young manual reminding them of the fallen nature of apostates: Apostates leave the Church because "their senses are taken from them"; apostates who were once "active, quick, and full of intelligence" become darkened, they are not able to comprehend things as they are; and the "Devil has power over them." The rewards of apostasy are "death, hell, and the grave."[85]

I compared myself to a homosexual coming out of the closet. How would my family react? In light of all that the prophets have said, Mormonism does not offer much room for a noncritical judgment of those who leave the Church—unless one employs some doublethink. No doubt, my family would think I was under the influence of Satan, but I hoped for the best. I knew they would at least be civil.

Within a few hours of sending out the e-mail announcement, I received an e-mail reply from a brother. So far, so good. He wanted to talk with me, and there was no hint of antagonism. I replied to his e-mail and we set up a time that we could talk later that night. It was the best response I could have hoped for.

A few weeks earlier, I had told my friend Davis about my decision to leave the Church. He had warned me of possible harsh reactions. I replied that my family would disagree with my decision, and it would drastically change our relationship, but they would certainly respond with kindness, as would the local ward members.

The few ward members I told had indeed reacted with kindness; preliminary indications were that family members would react in the same way. Davis's warning was proving to be a clear miscalculation, the type of misjudgment one expects to hear from those who think of Mormonism as a reactionary fundamentalist religion.

Chapter 12

Suddenly Strangers

Chris

The evening of September 8, 1998 (the day I e-mailed my announcement to the family), Connie and the children were gone for a few hours. We wanted the children to

> In the Church we are not neutral. We are one-sided. There is a war going on, and we are engaged in it. It is a war between good and evil, and we are belligerents defending the good.
>
> —Boyd K. Packer (Mormon Apostle), 1981, "The Mantle Is Far Far Greater than the Intellect," *BYU Studies*, Summer 1981, p. 267

be elsewhere when I answered the phone calls that were sure to come from family members. The television set was tuned to a St. Louis Cardinals–Chicago Cubs game. In progress was the home-run race of the ages between Sosa and McGwire. However, I could not focus on baseball, and I would not see McGwire break the home run record held by Roger Maris.

My stomach was knotted. For most of my life I had looked upon apostates as depraved degenerates. (To this day, Connie cringes when I refer to myself using that "nasty word, *apostate*.") My announcement to the family would place me squarely in the apostate world. What would they say? What would they think?

When the phone rang, I answered it with trepidation. It was a sister. After the initial greetings, our one-way conversation lasted about a minute, or maybe two. It went something like this: "When I read your letter I was disgusted. . . . We have been taught our whole lives not to read anti-Mormon literature. . . . You are a very wicked, wicked person. I don't want to talk to you anymore, good-bye." She may or may not have heard my "good-bye" before she hung up.

Although I had not expected understanding from family members, I had not expected this dire reaction. This abrupt introduction into Brad's world of the previous two months left me wondering how he had been treated. I regretted offering him little support.

A few minutes passed and I answered the phone again. It was a brother. My defenses were up, but the feared onslaught never came. He listened as I expressed concerns about a few Church issues. He acknowledged that there were questions with no easy answers. He asked if we could study some of the issues together to see if there were better answers than those I had found. I consented to his suggestion. He let me know that I was welcome in his home. He may never understand how much his kindness meant to me.

Brad

Fear is the main source of superstition, and one of the main sources of cruelty. To conquer fear is the beginning of wisdom.
—Bertrand Russell, *Unpopular Essays*, 1950, Chap. 7, "An Outline of Intellectual Rubbish," p. 106

In the afternoon of September 8, 1998, I still had no inkling of Chris's religious reversal. During the previous month, my telephone visits with him included no mention of religion. I deduced that neither Chris nor anyone else in the family had further interest in my reasons for leaving the Church. That afternoon I received an alarming phone call from a sister. It lasted only seconds and went as follows: "I am angry at you! You are a wicked, wicked, person!" I had no opportunity to respond.

A call from a brother followed within three or four minutes. It lasted a little longer and was just as troubling. It went essentially as follows: "I am going to be honest with you. I don't want to ever talk to you again. I don't want to see you again. I don't want any letters or e-mail from you. If you write a letter for the family newsletter, I will not send it out. I don't want you coming to visit on the nineteenth. I still love you, but I don't ever want to see you again."

My part of the conversation, squeezed in between his sentences, consisted of the phrases: "OK," "I understand," and "I don't blame you." The "I don't blame you" may seem a bit overdone, but I could see this brother's viewpoint if he considered me a candidate for perdition and a threat to his own family's salvation.

I failed to thank him for his forthrightness, then braced myself for more calls. I concluded that my response to my niece's letter had been found inappropriate, had been shared with others, and that the flames of fear and anger had been fanned to an inferno. Was this new sentiment universal within the family? I was badly shaken.

Early evening came as I waited for more phone calls, not thinking to check my e-mail. I felt awful for having answered my niece's letter. I continued to wonder if my reply had been misunderstood and misrepresented to others or if it had indeed been inappropriate. I pulled up my response on the computer and read it again and again.

Upon hearing a knock on the door, I felt a foreboding chill, wishing for no more confrontations with family members. I considered not answering the door but did so, apprehensively. To the brother standing there, my first words were, "Do you hate me too?" He said he did not. It seemed like an honest answer. Relieved, I knew that if there was going to be a family lynching, it would not be by unanimous consent.

I invited him down to my office. I mentioned the letter from our niece and found he had already seen it. (Apparently Mom and Dad had a copy.) I tried to apologize for my response to her, but found he knew nothing of my return letter. Initially confused by my line of discussion, he soon realized that I had not heard the latest news. Did I know of Chris's announcement? I did not. He informed me that Chris was leaving the Church.

I checked to make sure I had heard correctly. I was stunned. I felt awful for Chris, knowing full well the horror in making such an announcement and knowing the inevitable turmoil from such a change in one's life. At the same time, I felt intense relief to gain an esteemed family member with whom I could discuss the troublesome questions from which my thoughts found no escape. Chris's reflections on God and life would be most welcome. Wondering what had caused his turnabout, I impatiently waited for a chance to call him.

Another brother stopped by that evening. He expressed his acceptance and love. I recall no qualifications to his acceptance. Both brothers encountered my defensiveness that evening, but each endured it without complaint.

One family member described Chris and me as proud and arrogant over our "great" discovery about the Church. Pride and arrogance come easily enough for me, but at that time, they had no place in my disheveled world. Aware of Mom and Dad's heartbreak and suspecting a host of unsettled feelings in siblings and in-laws, I feared for family relationships. In addition, I struggled for months with the extensive fallout that comes from the total meltdown of a lifelong faith, a faith once full of hope and promise for this life and the eternities. I made no claims of a better way of life, but I knew there was much in the world to which I had previously closed my mind. Would Chris be as eager as I in the search for answers, ready to explore long-shunned avenues of knowledge?

I knew Chris would not be going to bed early that night. It was late before I had an opportunity to call and later still before I could get through. From our long conversation, I came to understand for the first time some of his inner thoughts during our discussion a month earlier and his silence on the matter in the month that followed. I was fascinated by his recent research of issues unfamiliar to me.

Within the next few days, I wrote a long letter to the family. In their eyes, I was heading for a place of torment, the exact depths still unresolved within their debates. Yet, my mind harbored a thousand shades of hope—hope ranging from family acknowledgment of Chris's and my unchanged basic natures, to their full-blown investigation of our concerns. While I wanted the depth of my conviction to be known, my eagerness to maintain long-cherished ties remained a priority.

In the letter, I tried to incorporate my sometimes-appreciated sense of humor. The same day that Cathy made ten copies of this long letter, I received the first of several troubling letters from family. After hesitating for a few more days and a few more letters from family members, I lost hope that my words would make any difference. My letter to the family was never sent.

The letters and e-mails from family members expressed varying degrees of respect and love, exhortation and reprimands, fear and ultimatums. They exposed some hasty reactions, but they also revealed deep-seated misunderstanding and distrust for the brothers who could no longer believe in their god.

Here is part of a proclamation sent by a sister to the entire family.

> I hold my testimony and membership in the Church of Jesus Christ of Latter-day Saints as my most precious possession bar none . . . more important to me than any relationship with any person or group of people. I intend to honor the promises I made in the temple.

The following advice, sent via e-mail, came from a brother-in-law. He expressed his admiration, kept his sense of humor, and spoke freely with the following thoughts:

> Just heard from Chris, and respectfully speaking, of course, I'm not so sure you didn't exert some influence there. . . . I think you need to allow people to make their own decisions without your influence. . . . Choices about religion lead to divorce, bad family feelings, and really crappy family reunions, otherwise known as dysfunctional families. People who leave the church end up with huge chips and a need to convert others to their new found philosophy.

His family had not come to the family reunion that year. Without a second thought, I considered his comment about "really crappy family reunions" to be his own rash assumption. Much later, I realized he may have heard family members express discomfort over the recent reunion.

Here is a portion from another letter sent to the entire family from a sister-in-law who knew little beyond the fact that we had left the Church.

It seems that in today's world he [Satan] gets men to think that they are the highest intelligence in the universe and as such know it all. . . . In the egotistical tunnel vision of these men who sought to dethrone god, there flamed the phantom hope that somehow they may have made the discovery of the ages. Brad, Chris, that is the feeling I get from you—that through your studies you think you figured out truths that have eluded the rest of us. . . . The reason I fear intelligence is because of the blazing self-confidence it can engender, choking out humility and the ability to rely upon God. Too many times I see people who have a small piece of the puzzle and have created an incredible picture which they believe to be right because it makes so much sense, but the real picture is so much different. . . . Brad, Chris, have your decisions brought you joy, peace and tranquility? They have not brought us these. . . . We are not angry. Only confused and sad.

In an e-mail to Chris and me, a brother expressed the following fears and demands; I suspected his sentiments were widespread with family members.

The thing that scares me most is your current beliefs. Those beliefs have the capability to destroy me and my family, and anyone who subscribes to those beliefs. . . . Nor will I risk the safety or welfare of my family. . . . Those beliefs you currently have have destroyed families. And if you have the same desire to share your current beliefs with others including me and my family, then you are a danger to me and my family. . . . You must not say anything to my wife or children about Joseph Smith or any prophet of the church, or any church leader or any church writings, or any church history. Any, and I mean any effort on your part to persuade my family to subscribe to your current beliefs will not be tolerated. I do not want any literature in my house which is contrary to what you know I believe. We read scriptures in our house. We say prayers in our house. If you visit us you will observe at least one of those maybe both. If we visit your houses we expect to be able to give thanks for the food and to read our scriptures even if in our bedroom. . . . If you look forward to enjoying my company as much as I do yours, and you make this promise, we can and will enjoy each other and each others families. If you cannot make this promise to me or if you make this promise to me and break it, my family will not associate (Face to face) with yours. . . . Is this drastic? You bet it is. I have everything I have ever wanted, to loose[lose], if I am deceived.

I expected the knee-jerk reactions to mellow. However, the family's deep-seated fears and distrust would not so easily be changed. I responded with some sharpness to the first letter from the brother-in-law but soon felt overwhelmed by the flood of communications. If my sharpness was unproductive, so was every other response I could think of. Even silence produced undesirable results.

As I read the e-mails and letters, I peered into a mirror from the past, where my prior beliefs and attitudes were clearly reflected. I had not so soon forgotten my former view on Mormon apostates. I shall not soon forget what I devoutly believed for so many years. Nevertheless, understanding family reactions did little to ease the blow of losing the confidence and trust of so many so quickly. Chris and I were described as having abandoned all the loving teachings we had received. We found no useful weapons with which to battle this formidable, phantom image.

Having become a "really crappy" family influence, an openly acknowledged threat, and an embarrassment to the clan, I committed to stay away from family gatherings. Maybe time would soften some feelings. Maybe Chris' and my efforts to tell our story and share our thoughts would provide greater understanding; however, we viewed the prospects skeptically.

In October of 1998, Mom and Dad were to celebrate their fiftieth wedding anniversary. In August, before Chris's announcement, the family had planned an October reception. It was an opportunity for eleven children, with their spouses and children, to express their love and appreciation for two wonderful parents. Mom and Dad had sacrificed most of their lives for their children. Unfortunately, their golden anniversary fell on the most tumultuous period, by far, of the family's fifty-year history.

Of Mom and Dad's eleven children, five showed up for the event. I was not one of them. I supposed myself to be the only missing child who had not offered a good excuse. It seemed that the chances for a good family attendance should have improved with my notice that I would be avoiding family activities. The celebration took place five miles from our home. Friends and relatives surely noticed how few of my parents' children were there. I grew sick as I imagined my parents—once proud of each child in their All-American family—having to justify the poor showing to their circle of friends and extended family.

I spent the day away from my home looking for an activity to distract my harrowed thoughts from Mom and Dad's hollow "celebration." When I finally came back home that night, there were cars parked in front of the house, so I drove on by and waited elsewhere for two more hours. When I came back, the cars were gone. It was late. I did not want to explain anything. I did not know how to apologize to Mom and Dad. I wanted no one telling me they missed me. I wanted no expressions of love—weary of the strange expressions of love I had been hearing. I needed to be left alone. Cathy and Caleb were the only ones I wished to see. I felt like the pain would linger forever. I presumed that other family members felt the same.

Mom and Dad did not complain. They expressed only gratitude for the part each family member played in celebrating their fifty years together.

Chris

It is unrealistic to expect people to remain ignorant indefinitely. When an individual fails to respond openly and honestly to . . . a problem it only passes the problem—and the pain of dealing with it—to someone else, multiplying ignorance and hurt in the process.
— Charles M. Larson, *By His Own Hand Upon Papyrus*, p. 181, 1992

Perhaps I was insulated, by distance, from some of the strain that Brad felt living in Utah and surrounded by family members. However, I did receive unpleasant phone calls and e-mails, enough that each ring of the phone rang like an alarm, alerting us to put on our "riot gear" and brace ourselves. I say "us" because Connie suffered through every austere attack or mild rebuke directed at me. She was only half joking when she said that she wanted to join the Witness Protection Program to get away from it all.

I did not tell Connie's family about my decision until November, which meant that reactions from the two families were spread out over a period of about four months. As the responses came in, we could not help but keep score. If we made the three-day drive back West the following summer, who would want to see us? In whose company would we feel comfortable?

Mom had dedicated her life to helping her children attain salvation so we could be together as a family in

> No other success can compensate for failure in the home.
> —David O. McKay (Mormon Prophet), *Improvement Era*, June 1964, p. 445

the after-life. I believe that nothing brings her more joy than to see her children living to attain that goal. Thus, she believed she had failed with two of her sons; she had lost them for eternity. The blow was almost more than she could bear, and she needed to wait a couple of days before she could talk to me. But, Mom would always love her children. She would never cause one of her children to question that love, and she has never been one to use guilt to coerce her children.

Mom was aware of how some of the siblings had reacted. She felt bad and maintained that it was an unthinking response rather than a true indication of their feelings. We talked of how my decision would affect Connie and our children. She expressed concern that without the Church, I would have "nothing to hang on to" in this wicked, tumultuous world. Our conversation was bittersweet; I found comfort in her reaffirmation of love, yet, I could think of little to say that would bring comfort to a mother I love dearly.

A few weeks after my announcement, my younger brother Chuck came for a short visit. He volunteered his opinion that I appeared to be happier and more at peace, now that I had left the Church. He also pointed out that, from a certain point of view, our siblings' fear of Brad and me was not unreasonable. Having rejected the church to which we had looked for moral guidance our whole lives, we had clearly undergone *some* kind of metamorphosis. How were siblings to know the extent of the change?

From the beginning, Chuck has welcomed discussions about my new views. The openness allows for honest, unguarded, and engaging conversations that help us find common ground and maintain a close relationship. Brad and I regret that such relationships have not been common since our decision to leave the Church.

If my blood kin would not believe the Gospel, I should be as much alienated from them in my feelings as I am from the people of the Chinese nation.
—Brigham Young, 1859, *Journal of Discourses,* Vol. 7, p. 175

Although all family communications soon became civil, alienation was evident. Even many of the civil communications had implications that soon began to wear me down. For example, one family member sent the following.

> Please be careful how you treat this decision around family. Be careful not to become as many people who leave the Church . . . obsessive and distant. This must be like a dagger into Mom and Dad's heart. Can I implore you to communicate with them and other family members? This can turn into a large rift and chasm if you don't tread lightly.

Another family member phoned to say he had received some very powerful spiritual witnesses of the truthfulness of the Church. When he asked what I thought of his beliefs, I responded that our conflicting views could not both be right and that his spiritual witness did not convince me. "How dare you discount my testimony?" he replied, expressing concern that I might discount his testimony to his children. I assured him I had no intention of doing so.

A sister's letter said:

> Dearest Chris,
> I got your letter. It made a hole in my heart.
> I weep for your wife and children.
> I weep for Mom & Dad.

I weep for myself.
I weep for you.
I love the gospel.
I stand committed to Joseph Smith & every prophet since that time. I stand committed to my temple covenants.
I love you.

One year later, a niece reminded me that "all is not lost," and that I still had the chance to "gain peace, joy, and hope" through the gospel that I had rejected. She questioned if I could honestly say that my life was better, that I had inner peace, and that I had greater strength to face trials. She reminded me that with the Church's help, I could still have an "impact of good . . . on the world," and she encouraged me to take another look at what I had rejected. This letter contained no hint of hard feelings, yet it was full of insinuations that reflected the teaching that "devastation . . . visits the personal lives of those who succumb to apostasy."[86]

For how many years would I need to "tread lightly" while others made blind assumptions about my life? How long would their save-our-children-from-the-apostates anxiety last? I would always be suspect because the temple ceremony unequivocally states that someone in my position would be under Satan's power. (The temple ceremony was not to be trifled with. When I first attended, commitments were made with blood oaths.) Those looking to condemn me will find sins enough—both real and imagined—to support their belief that I am a fallen man.

However, maybe I have not fallen so far after all. From the time we left the Church, people have insinuated that Brad and I have somehow always been different, that our character was flawed, that we were somehow frauds as Mormons. This rewriting of history stings. It is true that our faith had been troubled for some time, yet our sacrifices had been real; our decades of service, significant; our motives, genuine. But, when wickedness is the only explanation for apostasy, revising the past to make us marginal Mormons is a convenient way to make sense of our actions.

Each year my siblings and their spouses must pass two worthiness interviews if they wish to attend the temple. Church leaders who conduct the interviews are told they "must take exceptional care when [interviewing] members whose parents or other close relatives belong to or sympathize with apostate groups."[87] The interview consists of a series of questions, including the following.

> Do you affiliate with any group or individual whose teachings or practices are contrary to or oppose those accepted by the Church of Jesus Christ of Latter-day Saints, or do you sympathize with the precepts of any such group or individual?

I was an outsider.

In an effort to reach out, one brother told me that I need not worry about his wife having hard feelings toward me because she "is not one to hold a grudge." I wondered why she might hold a grudge against me in the first place. Then I realized that although I had carefully avoided criticizing their beliefs, my simple confession—that I do not believe the Church is true—had far-reaching implications. It said that Joseph Smith was not a prophet, and worse, that he was a fraud. And if Joseph was a fraud, the Mormon priesthood blessings have no value except as placebos; their sacred temple ceremonies are the creations of a charlatan; and the *Book of Mormon*, *Pearl of Great Price*, and *Doctrine and Covenants* are only hoaxes. If the Church is not what it claims to be, then Mormon views of eternity are nothing more than wishes resting on a foundation of mass deceit.

Coming from a traitor to the cause, these unspoken, unintended, but unavoidable insinuations must be especially hard to take. It is no wonder that when talking of how we now view each other, another brother said to me, "What we [family members] think of you is probably comparable to what you think of us."

So what do Brad and I think of our family? They are, of course, a group of individuals; but although we see some of their beliefs as misdirected, we do not consider any of them evil. The above account is a snapshot of their reaction in a disturbing situation they had never before faced. This narrow focus on their response ignores their kind hearts and commitment to principle that has otherwise defined their lives. No doubt, they pray for us and would like to rebuild our relationships.

Due to Dad's hearing difficulty over the phone, I had not talked to him since before my announcement. On several occasions over the

Recently I heard of a good man who, after being married in the temple and having four children, fell away from the Church. His physical appearance became shabby and his demeanor sad as he became a drug addict, an alcoholic, and then a chain-smoker.

—James E. Faust (Counselor to President Hinckley), 1997, *Ensign*, November 1997, p. 43

years, Dad claimed that he would love his children no matter what they did. He was true to his word; we had a pleasant visit when he and Mom came for a few days in October.

During their stay, Mom and Dad wanted to go to Church; so Connie, the children, and I went with them. I was glad to see some of the Church members that I had not seen for two months. While visiting with one acquaintance, I noticed that he kept looking down at my chest. By looking at my chest, he could see that I was not wearing my temple garments (Mormon underwear) under my shirt. (Two months earlier, I had found myself looking at Brad's chest, even though I knew he was not wearing his garments.) These downward glances reminded me that several years earlier a grave sin would have been my only explanation for an active member and firm believer who suddenly stops attending church and forsakes his/ her sacred temple garments.

My decision to leave the Church was considered a confidential matter, so most of the ward members knew nothing about it. They knew only that I had suddenly stopped attending meetings. Their thoughtfulness in trying to keep a confidence was admirable, but I had no desire to keep my decision confidential. Without the facts, people would certainly make unflattering assumptions based on Mormon doctrine.

Eight months later, in June of 1999, my concerns were confirmed when I received a letter from a woman in the ward whom I highly regard and whose company I had always enjoyed. Although one of her sons, also a member of the ward, had known for months that I had officially left the Church, she had apparently just learned of it from another woman in the ward. Her letter included these comments.

Don't give up the one thing that has been your strength. No
other activity or relationship can fill that hole inside you. Take
the Church back and give up something else. . . . I just know
that you were faithful in the pre-existence. Whatever is happening is probably just not how you envisioned things would
go. This is probably your one big test. It may be embarrassing
or just seem like too much work. . . . It's going to be hard to
get back on the path and stay there. Much harder than if you
hadn't gotten off. . . . I am sad when people leave the Church.
For some reason I am particularly sad about you.

Clearly, she believed I had done more than just conclude the
Church was not true. Yet she gave no hint of condemnation, and I
appreciated her concern. Her misreading of the situation is typical
of a Mormon who has assimilated Church doctrine.

Some friendships in the ward continued. For a time, we still
enjoyed the company of the current bishop and his wife. A former
bishop had, for years, offered us a standing invitation to spend
Thanksgiving, Christmas, and other holidays with him and his
family. They still invited us into their home. I still enjoyed their
company and valued their friendship. I still view them as models for
humanity.

Other friendships have suffered from neglect. One acquaintance,
whom I will call Mr. H, lives forty miles from me. We are in different stages of our individual lives, and we had little in common
except our faith, time spent working together in the ward missionary organization, and a mutual respect. Still, I considered Mr. H
a friend, and when I left the Church he expressed confidence in my
character. For a few months, he continued to phone me to see how
I was doing. Perhaps I did not reciprocate as often as I should have;
but in any case, without the opportunity to visit with each other
at Church, our friendship has waned—a drawback of leaving the
Church.

I complied with my wife's request to delay telling her family of
my decision to leave the Church. It was November of 1998 before I
felt the need to get this all behind me and move on with my life.

Connie's parents are not Church members, but four of her five siblings are. The father-in-law of one is a longtime Church member. He told a sister of Connie that I must have committed adultery, stating adultery as the reason people leave the Church. It was an interesting judgment to pass upon me; he lives in Idaho, I live in Illinois, and we had met only once about eight years previously. Once that misconception was cleared up, most in-laws accepted the fact that I just didn't believe.

One of Connie's sisters reacted differently. She warned Connie about leaving the Church with the second coming of Christ so near—probably within the "next six years." She compared my decision to "a matter of life and death" and suggested that Connie ask the bishop to excommunicate me rather than just remove my name from the Church records. She also wrote:

> Well first of all Chris is denying the spirit of the gift of the Holy Ghost given to him by the only true Priesthood of God. That is a more serious offense in the sight of God than murder or adultery—you don't understand that.

Connie was not receptive to her ideas.

Between family, ward members, and other Mormon friends, various explanations were given for my apostasy. Some people laid part of the blame at Brad's feet for having led me astray. Some out-of-state friends thought our current ward could have done something to prevent it. Some thought that Connie had been the root of the problem, and of course, some assumed I had committed a serious sin. Wickedness was the thread common to all theories. At times, I marvel at the refusal even to consider what seems to be a very reasonable explanation. However, I am familiar with Mormon thought processes, and quickly remember that I reasoned similarly for years.

From the time our children were born, a major focus of my life had been to teach them to love the gospel. Although in recent years I had been less dogmatic, I had done nothing to shake their budding testimonies of the Church. After leaving the Church, I did not want to yank the rug out from under them by revealing my new views, so I gave them little explanation for my lost faith. My oldest child, Carissa, knew a little more than the rest.

The previous May, when Cami turned ten, we had given her a nice set of Mormon scriptures and encouraged her to read and take care of them. She was careful to keep them in good condition, and in the evenings she eagerly read them to me. After I left the Church, I chose something other than Mormon scriptures to read the children at bedtime, but I continued to listen nightly as Cami read from her new scriptures.

One day, several weeks after she learned that I no longer believed Joseph Smith was a prophet, Cami told me, "Joseph Smith is still my favorite prophet." I had other precepts to teach my children that were more important than that the Mormon Church was not what it claimed to be, nor did I want to attack a child's treasured belief. There would come a time when she would understand the depth of my concerns about Joseph Smith; perhaps then she would choose to look into it. I told her that it was fine with me that she believed Joseph Smith was a prophet.

The fall of 1998 was a blur. On one hand, I enjoyed a tremendous sense of relief from ridding myself of an inner stress that had plagued me for some time. I had a refreshing new outlook of this world and its inhabitants. Yet at the same time, family reactions to my announcement had staggered me, and my well-defined universe had been blasted. I continued to read about issues related to the Church, and I was altogether amazed at the wealth of evidence I had so religiously ignored my whole life. Grievous losses, shocking revelations, and shattered hopes utterly dominated my thoughts, receding only slightly when I stood at the front of the classroom, trying to focus on mathematics.

At least now my struggles were out in the open. They were no longer denied, ignored, or hidden in my subconsciousness. Surely the hardest part of this journey was behind me.

Chapter 13

I Don't Want to Know

Brad

As word of our apostasy spread, Chris and I encountered the "Why?" question. I tried various responses. My incomplete explanation to one intelligent and fair-minded friend produced several of his own reasons for remaining faithful to the Church. He then closed with this pronouncement: "And if it isn't true, I don't want to know it." We left it at that.

> Man, once surrendering his reason, has no remaining guard against absurdities the most monstrous, and like a ship without a rudder, is the sport of every wind. With such persons, gullibility, which they call faith, takes the helm of reason, and the mind becomes a wreck.
> —Thomas Jefferson, Letter to Rev. James Smith, December 8, 1822. *The Life and Selected Writings of Thomas Jefferson*, edited by Koch and Peden, 1993, p. 642

It was not the first time I encountered this attitude from a faithful Mormon. I had never used those words, although my past actions may have said as much. There is some justification for such a posture. The Church provides an attractive concept of God, the soul, the eternities, and the universe. The Church provides a moral code and fellowship with others who wish to live by that code. The Church makes wonderful promises, for anyone willing to believe. But, the "I don't want to know" attitude had not prevented the surprises from springing so rudely upon me. Learning to look for and live with truth seemed better than closing my eyes and praying that the moving walkway we trod upon would deliver us to our chosen heaven's doors.

This "I don't want to know" attitude is rarely expressed so explicitly within the Mormon Church. Truth is put upon a pedestal; it is revered; it is talked about as the only way; it is said to be that which makes us free. For most of my life this reverence for truth was sincerely felt. Yet, complete and open honesty had been defined strictly within the context of loyalty to my faith. I wanted the truth but neither provided nor allowed an avenue for discovering the fallacy in my faith's foundation.

Many people—including myself—tend to avoid reality when it is distasteful. Some do not want to know if they have cancer. Some do not want to know if what they consume is bad for them. We often effectively close our eyes to future consequences in the interest of immediate gratification. We sometimes ignore the facts as if only an acknowledgment will allow the evil spell of reality to take effect.

Happiness does not require the shield of ignorance; rather, happiness is enhanced and perfected in the discovery of reality. Cowering in the shadows of circumscribed belief fills us with uneasy anticipation. Shedding our restrictive cocoon of fear and gathering the facts as we would so many delicious fruits, adds an exquisite dimension to the banquet of life.

In the end, it is not ignorance which damns us; rather, it is the love of ignorance, the devotion to ignorance, the passionate embrace of ignorance by labeling other views as evil, then relentlessly insisting: "See no evil. Hear no evil."

Fear illusion's gifts; their haunting beauty often hides treachery.
—blm

I have been asked: "Even if the Mormon Church is not true, why not remain a member for all the good it can do? What harm can there be in it?" The short answer is: commitment to an illusion requires the fettering of truth. One sacred illusion leads to another until the road back to reality is shrouded with misconceptions. Guarded ignorance becomes the norm, and truth becomes a casualty of sincerity and faith.

The following personal examples will prove nothing; they are too few and they are too difficult, if not impossible, for others to verify. Nevertheless, for me, these personal experiences help answer the question: "What harm can there be in a well-intended illusion?"

The first concern I have with the Church, despite its wonderful television and radio spots advocating family values, is that the side effects of its teachings tend to destroy some families. Chris' and my experience, as given in the previous chapters, testifies to that. In hearing and reading the stories of others who left the Church,[88] it appears that our experience with family members was not uncommon, and in fact, on the mild side. Parents are devastated. Sibling trust is lost. Divorce is contemplated and often occurs. A gulf often develops between believing children and the unbelieving parent, or the other way around. These might be excusable reactions if one assumes the validity of the teachings of the Church. However, if the Church is not what it claims then tearing families asunder is a horrible mistake with long-term and far-reaching consequences.

My patriarchal blessing, which I received as a thirteen-year-old, was similar to Chris'. Mine said:

> He [God] made you a member of his chosen people, the House of Israel. [Typically, Mormons were declared to be descendants of Joseph who was sold into Egypt.] He did this because you were obedient in the spirit world, and he caused that you should come here and live a mortal life and be a member of the wonderful family that you belong to, because of your obedience before you came.

We Mormons were the only ones with God's true authority. We were the only ones who understood or had the fullness of the gospel. We had access to special inspiration, special spiritual gifts, special prophetic leaders, and special ordinances. God expected more of us because he had given us more. With all of this came the weight of excessive pride and feelings of self-righteousness; I once bristled when accusations of self-righteousness were leveled at Church members. Now I realize that when a group claims to be "God's Chosen," an unhealthy polarization of society is inevitable—in communities, nations, and around the world.

In the Church, I often heard peer pressure talked about in negative terms, though I noticed that "good" peer pressure was employed to keep the youth faithful. At the time, the ill effects of the "good" peer pressure escaped my notice. Young men face tremendous pressure to go on missions, and young women are taught they should marry a returned missionary. As a result, those young men who do not serve successful missions often feel inferior and have little chance to win the heart of a nice Mormon girl. Some missionaries serve only because of the expectations of others, not because they want to be there or because they are genuinely convinced of or committed to the gospel. Some of them struggle with the lie they are living, uncomfortable with both their belief and unbelief. Some return home early in disgrace.

While preparing to leave on my mission, I knew a very likable young man by the name of Gordon who came home early from his mission for health reasons. We went deer hunting together one afternoon. He was clearly troubled and apologetic for his shortened mission. I offered nothing in response, thinking of the scripture: "And any man that shall go and preach this gospel of the kingdom, and fail not to continue faithful in all things, shall not be weary in mind, neither darkened, neither in body, limb nor joint."[89] Soon afterward, Gordon committed suicide. Though I can only guess why he did this, thirty years later I better understand the pressures he may have felt in disappointing those around him. Perhaps I could have made a difference.

Some young people are thrust hopelessly in the wrong direction because of peer and family pressures to follow an incongruent belief system. The suicide rate for teenage boys in Utah has been reported to be more than three times the national average.[90] For many years, I justified Utah's high suicide rate with the explanation that Satan makes his greatest effort where God's Kingdom is strongest. Now I lament the likelihood that my attitude added to the discomfort, pain, and despair of others who could not feel the spirit or could not believe. My zeal and focus may have produced some wonderful results, but at a cost that I neither acknowledged nor understood—a lopsided cost to be borne by those who did not qualify as being committed to God.

In 1969, I took a missionary preparation class at Brigham Young University. Partway through the semester, one of the young women in the class was reported as missing. One day later she was found in the mountains east of campus, very disoriented. She apparently had made an all-out effort to obtain a special witness from God. We were told by Church leaders that we could see visions if we asked in faith. Fasting can be an important step in that process. Within the Church, many scriptures and stories tell of people who experienced special manifestations because of extended fasting and prayer, often in the wilderness. I had made a number of such attempts myself with limited success, having obtained some impressions and some inner peace, but never any visitations or voices. The young woman never returned to the missionary preparation class. We were reminded by our religion professor that we should use good judgment in such efforts. Hers was one of several such efforts which I have seen gone awry. When faith is false, an all-out effort for spiritual manifestations and assurances can be detrimental to one's mental health.

Sometime around 1986, I had a mathematics student at Utah Valley Community College (now called Utah Valley State College) by the name of Jim. He was bright and hardworking, excelling in two terms of calculus. I saw him on the golf course one day and had a chance to get better acquainted while we played nine holes. He had a wife and a little girl.

Two or three years later, bombs were set off at some local Mormon churches. Another went off in the BYU library. The culprit was Jim. As I later understood the story, his little girl had died of a terminal disease. Evidently, she had been given a Mormon Priesthood blessing, and Jim felt she would recover. When she died, he vented his grief and anger on the Church.

His retribution cannot be justified, but neither is the promotion of false powers of healing.

In the New Testament, Jesus on occasion cast out evil spirits. It was no metaphorical exorcism; in one incident, the spirits were cast into a herd of swine. In the Church, we were taught that because we had this same priesthood power and authority, we could also expel evil spirits. I found myself facing such an opportunity while on my mission. One evening, we received an urgent call from a church member who said his wife was possessed. My missionary companion and I rushed to the home and found her wild-eyed, combative, and incoherent. Her husband held her while we laid our hands on her head and in the name of Jesus Christ commanded the evil spirit to leave. She calmed down. We were greatly relieved. We did not leave immediately and within minutes, her frenzied demeanor returned. We left, at a loss as to what to do.

I used to feel guilty that we had not made another effort to get the spirit/spirits to leave and stay out. It was not a missionary story I wanted to recite to others. The woman ended up in a mental institution. Now, I wonder if her disorientation was compounded by her fear of being possessed. I wonder if her husband's anxieties were compounded by the same fears. I believe that my own fear of evil spirits turned some events, not readily explainable, into unnecessarily frightening experiences. It is interesting that with the advance of medicine, we hear less of possessed people and we see more of epilepsy, Alzheimer's disease, chemical imbalances, and other medically diagnosed conditions. There is no end to the mischief of a mind fed on false, supernatural fears.

These accounts are not intended to show the Church is false; rather, if the Church is false, they suggest drawbacks to embracing the illusion.

Passing the problems of a false faith on to the next generation magnifies the potential for misery. If the Church is recognized as false, that is reason enough to act. "Truth has no special time of its own. Its hour is now — always."[91] Any success we have in out-maneuvering truth and reality will at best be temporary. Even if a false belief survives for a thousand years or longer before it dies, it will leave its wake of destruction.

My belief in the imminent second coming of Christ had an enlivening effect upon my life, but it also inspired shortsighted thinking. It smothered my concerns for many potential long-term problems: planet pollution, species extinction, the looming energy crisis, global warming, ozone depletion, dwindling resources for an expanding population, relationships between hostile nations, and nuclear or biological war. I relied on everything being put right by the Almighty; trusting in His supposed statement "there is enough and to spare;"[92] trusting in the peace Christ would bring once He returned; believing that the prophecies of forthcoming misery, war, destruction, and bloodshed were immutable, that such horrors somehow had a divine purpose.

> How many false starts and dead ends have plagued human thinking, how our biases can color our interpretation of the evidence, and how often belief systems widely held and supported by the political, religious, and academic hierarchies turn out to be not just slightly in error, but grotesquely wrong.
> —Carl Sagan, *The Demon-Haunted World*, p. 67

It is possible that some of the popular concerns for our planet are exaggerated, but with insufficient consideration I dismissed them all. The time and energy I spent seeking salvation, for myself and others, drew me away from reality. My pretend world insulated me from the natural world. I effectively became autistic: hearing without listening; seeing without comprehending; feeling, but dismissing the touch of anything that contradicted my pretend world. Without realizing it, I left it for future generations to struggle with an abused earth and with the unresolved distrust and tension between nations, ethnic groups, and heirs of incompatible religious illusions.

Chapter 14

Still Entangled, Still Engaged

Chris

Shortly after leaving the Church, I saw a website entitled "Recovery from Mormonism." Feeling no need for "recovery" and

At times, our minds exhibit all the agility of an eggplant. As the plant continues to lean in the direction of an extinct light source, so do our thoughts remain bent toward rejected misconceptions as we strain to take in new truths. Change comes slowly, and it may be the seedlings that first enjoy the fullness the new light source has to offer.
—clm

sensing that someone was being overdramatic, I didn't bother reading any of it. Leaving was simply a process of discovering the facts and moving on.

Several days later when I saw a colleague walking across the Blackburn campus, a previous bias resurfaced and I impulsively judged him as somehow lacking in virtue. This was a holdover from my long-time habit of identifying—by the clothes they wear —those who were not temple-worthy Mormons; such people were not on the path to salvation. My judgment was especially paradoxical not only because I had rejected Mormonism, but also because I was, at that instant, wearing such clothes myself. I recognized my conclusion as absurd, but could not immediately dredge these views from my mind.

On one level I had rejected Mormonism, but a lifetime of absorbing Church doctrine had instilled in me many deep-seated beliefs and sentiments. It was no easy task to identify and disentangle the views that had become incompatible with my new direction. I spent every spare moment studying Church matters. This investigation exposed subconscious biases and validated doubts that had plagued me for years. Some issues were as old as the Church itself; some were current events that had unfolded within the previous few years or even months. Not all of the following issues are directly related to lingering misconceptions; nevertheless, studying them helped me break away from a lifelong mindset.

Lying is intentionally deceiving others. . . . When we speak untruths, we are guilty of lying. We can also intentionally deceive others by . . . telling only part of the truth. Whenever we lead people in any way to believe something that is not true, we are not being honest.
—*Gospel Principles*, 1985, p.193

President Hinckley appeared on *Larry King Live*, which aired September 8, 1998. (Coincidentally, that was the day I informed my family of my decision to leave the Church. I read transcripts of the interview weeks later.) The discussion included the following dialogue.

King: . . . First tell me about the Church and polygamy. When it started, it allowed it?

Hinckley: When our people came west, they permitted it on a restricted scale.

King: You could have a certain amount of . . .

Hinckley: The figures I have are from between two percent and five percent of our people were involved in it. It was a very limited practice; carefully safeguarded. In 1890, that practice was discontinued. The president of the church, the man who occupied the position which I occupy today, went before the people, said he had, oh, prayed about it, worked on it, and had received from the Lord a revelation that it was time to stop, to discontinue it then.

While looking at the Church website, I read the following about polygamy in the early Church:

> Some early leaders and members of the Church entered into plural marriages (polygyny) during the latter half of the nineteenth century. After receiving a revelation, Church President Wilford Woodruff declared that the practice should be discontinued. That position has been reaffirmed by every President of the Church since. Members of the Church who enter into plural marriage today face Church disciplinary action, including excommunication.[93]

Polygamy was permitted when Mormons came out west, and some leaders did enter plural marriage in the latter half of the nineteenth century as stated above. However, polygamy was also permitted in the first half of the century before Mormons moved out west. In fact, before Joseph Smith was killed in 1844, he had married somewhere from twenty-nine to forty-six women.[94] When the Mormons began the trip out west, Brigham Young had married twenty-five women,[95] and every single one of the twelve Mormon apostles was a practicing polygamist.[96]

It is true that most Mormon men did not participate in polygamy. (Perhaps, as the joke goes, women of marriageable age were scarce because they were all marrying Young.) However, to say polygamy was "permitted on a restricted scale" simply does not convey the truth of the matter: *All* righteous men were admonished to take more than one wife, and according to Brigham Young and others, those who rejected polygamy would be damned.[97] President Wilford Woodruff—the president who "declared that the practice should be discontinued"—continued as a practicing polygamist. Jesus was said to have been a polygamist.[98] Simply put, polygamy was one of the defining doctrines of the early Mormon Church.

Earlier in my life, I would have said that Hinckley and the website had been honest; and strictly speaking, the statements were not false. However, now I see in Hinckley my own previous tendency: Before I could, in good conscience, convert others to my faith, I first had to subconsciously camouflage troubling facts with technical truth. Polygamy is not the only case of Hinckley's faith-inspired fudging.[99]

Incidentally, while Mormons no longer practice polygamy, there is more to the issue. When a man and woman have their marriage *sealed* in the temple, Mormons believe the couple will continue to be husband and wife in the next life if they live worthily in this life. If the man dies prematurely, the woman may marry again, but will not have both husbands in the afterlife. However, if the woman dies first, the man is free to have another woman sealed to him,[100] giving him two wives in eternity. If the second wife dies, the man may marry again, giving him three wives in the afterlife. In short, a man may have many wives in the next life, but a woman can have only one husband. Polygamy has been temporarily discontinued, but it will resume in the next world. According to *current* Mormon scripture, those who reject polygamy will be damned.[101]

I have never yet preached a sermon and sent it out to the children of men, that they may not call Scripture.
—Brigham Young, 1870, *Journal of Discourses*, Vol. 13, p. 95

Gordon B. Hinckley and Brigham Young appear to be on different ends of the prophet spectrum. President Hinckley is a former employee of the Church public relations department, and he is very conscious of how non-Mormons perceive Mormonism. On the other hand, Brigham Young made the statement, "I am satisfied that it will not do for the Lord to make this people popular. Why? Because all hell would want to be in the church."[102]

In my mind, Brigham fit the prophet mold very well with his bold and straightforward sermons. However, over the years I had encountered a few of his teachings that seemed odd.

For instance, as a missionary, I read Brigham's following instructions to women.

Do not put your loaf into the oven with a fire hot enough to burn it before it is baked through, but with a slow heat, and let it remain until it is perfectly baked; and I would prefer, for my own eating, each and every loaf to be not thicker than my two hands—you tell how thick they are—and I would want the crust as thick as my hand.[103]

Perhaps some women constantly burned their bread before it was baked through. Perhaps some women needed to hear from a prophet how to bake bread. Perhaps many of his own wives burned their bread, and they did not know that he liked his crust as thick as his hand. Was it easier to tell all of his dozens of wives with one comment from the pulpit, rather than tell each of them on an individual basis? I was not one to question a prophet of God. His advice seemed good, and I had no objection as to how he liked his bread; but his cooking instructions seemed out of place, and the focus on his personal taste conveyed a sense of self-importance. (I wonder: Does the Pope ever pontificate about his culinary preferences?)

After leaving the Church, I saw a few more teachings at which I could only chuckle. For example, Brigham Young, as the "prophet of God," taught that the sun and moon are inhabited[104] and that gold grows as did the hair on his head.[105]

Not all of his false statements were so harmless. I had previously heard, and then dismissed, claims from faithful Mormons that Brigham Young had made derogatory comments about Blacks. (Mormons believe that Blacks are descendants of Cain, the son of Adam and Eve, who killed his brother Abel.) Brigham taught:

Shall I tell you the law of God in regard to the African Race? If the White man who belongs to the chosen seed mixes his blood with the seed of Cain, the penalty, under the law of God, is death on the spot. This will always be so.[106]

He also said:

You see some classes of the human family that are black, uncouth, uncomely, disagreeable and low in their habits, wild, and seemingly deprived of nearly all the blessings of the intelligence that is generally bestowed upon mankind. The first man that committed the odious crime of killing one of his brethren will be cursed the longest of any one of the children of Adam. Cain slew his brother. Cain might have been killed, and that would have put a termination to that line of human beings. This was not to be, and the Lord put a mark upon him, which is the flat nose and black skin. Trace mankind down to after the flood, and then another curse is pronounced upon the same race—that they should be the "servant of servants;" and they will be, until that curse is removed.[107]

These teachings did not end with Brigham. After John Taylor became the third president of the Church, he taught that Blacks are the devil's representatives here on earth.[108]

Brigham also spoke ill of other groups of people. He said,

Can you make a Christian of a Jew? I tell you, nay. If a Jew comes into this Church, and honestly professes to be a Saint, a follower of Christ, and if the blood of Judah is in his veins, he will apostatize. . . . I would rather undertake to convert five thousand Lamanites [American Indians], than to convert one of those poor miserable creatures whose father killed the Savior. . . . Yea, I would rather undertake to convert the devil himself, if it were possible.[109]

I am embarrassed to have once proclaimed Brigham Young a prophet, a champion of Jesus and his teachings.

True there is a curse upon the woman that is not upon the man, namely, that "her whole affections shall be towards her husband," and what is the next? "He shall rule over you."
—Brigham Young, 1856, *Journal of Discourses*, Vol. 4, p. 57

Some of Brigham's teachings reveal a disturbing mindset toward women. Although this next statement was about the doctrine of individual blood atonement, it reveals a callous attitude toward his wives.

Let me suppose a case. Suppose you found your brother in bed with your wife, and put a javelin through both of them, you would be justified, and they would atone for their sins, and be received into the kingdom of God. I would at once do so in such a case; and under such circumstances, I have no wife whom I love so well that I would not put a javelin through her heart, and I would do it with clean hands.[110]

How did the women feel when they heard the prophet of God tell the men that they could—under certain circumstances, and with clean hands—kill one of their wives?
This next lengthy quotation illustrates that Mormon women were not as supportive of polygamy as I had once supposed. It also illustrates the profound control Brigham assumed.

Now for my proposition; it is more particularly for my sisters, as it is frequently happening that women say they are unhappy. Men will say, "My wife, though a most excellent woman, has not seen a happy day since I took my second wife;" "No, not a happy day for a year," says one; and another has not seen a happy day for five years. It is said that women are tied down and abused: that they are misused and have not the liberty they ought to have; that many of them are wading through a perfect flood of tears, because of the conduct of some men, together with their own folly.
I wish my own women to understand that what I am going to say is for them as well as others, and I want those who are here to tell their sisters, yes, all the women of this community, and then write it back to the States, and do as you please with it. I am going to give you from this time to the 6th day of October next, for reflection, that you may determine whether you wish to stay with your husbands or not, and then I am going to set every woman at liberty and say to them, Now go your way, my women with the rest, go your way. And my wives have got to do one of two things; either round up their shoulders to endure the afflictions of this world, and live their religion, or they may leave, for I will not have them about me. I will go into heaven alone, rather than have scratching and fighting around me. I will set all at liberty. "What, first wife too?" Yes, I will liberate you all.
I know what my women will say; they will say, "You can have as many women as you please, Brigham." But I want to go

somewhere and do something to get rid of the whiners; I do not want them to receive a part of the truth and spurn the rest out of doors. . . .

Now recollect that two weeks from tomorrow I am going to set you at liberty. But the first wife will say, "It is hard, for I have lived with my husband twenty years, or thirty, and have raised a family of children for him, and it is a great trial to me for him to have more women;" then I say it is time that you gave him up to other women who will bear children. If my wife had borne me all the children that she ever would bare, the celestial law would teach me to take young women that would have children. . . .

Sisters, I am not joking, I do not throw out my proposition to banter your feelings, to see whether you will leave your husbands, all or any of you. But I do know that there is no cessation to the everlasting whining of many of the women in this Territory; I am satisfied that this is the case. And if the women will turn from the commandments of God and continue to despise the order of heaven, I will pray that the curse of the Almighty may be close to their heels, and that it may be following them all the day long. . . .

But the women come and say, "Really brother John, and brother William, I thought you were going to make a heaven for me," and they get into trouble because a heaven is not made for them by the men, even though agency is upon women as well as upon men. True there is a curse upon the woman that is not upon the man, namely, that "her whole affections shall be towards her husband," and what is the next? "He shall rule over you."[111]

In my mind I picture my oldest daughter, Carissa, as a fifteen-year-old in a pretty dress as she sits in Church listening to Brigham talk of women. Being of marriageable age in the early Church, is Carissa encouraged by Brigham's sermon? Is she looking past the boys her age and hoping that Brigham will propose to her as the prophet Joseph Smith proposed to, and married, fourteen-year-old Helen Mar Kimball? Or, is she romanticizing about some other middle-aged man, hoping to become his newest, youngest, and prettiest wife?

Perhaps not.

Rather, she may be aware of the pressure exerted on some young women to accept proposals of marriage from Church leaders, so she is hoping to go unnoticed by the elders of the Church. She may be scared to death of what could happen in the next few years before she can marry some handsome young man closer to her age.

In today's Church (not to be confused with Mormon fundamentalist factions), Carissa would have no such worries. Still, fundamentalists aside, there are holdovers of the doctrine that a husband rules over his wife. For example, Church leaders would consult with me before they offered Connie a Church job. However, they would not consult with Connie before offering me a position. This is consistent with the Church handbook.[112] The temple ceremony that I attended for years was less subtle about the subservience of women. The women were told to make a covenant of obedience to the law of their husbands. The ceremony has since been modified. Women no longer promise to obey their husbands; instead, they promise to hearken to the counsel of their husbands in righteousness. Husbands make no such promise to their wives.

Some important doctrines from early Mormonism—such as Brigham's teachings on women, polygamy, and Blacks—put today's image-conscious Church in a quandary with three different groups.

- Critics who would like a renunciation of these doctrines.
- Many long-time Mormons who have been weaned on the doctrine and would be troubled by such a renunciation, which would be a concession of Brigham's fallibility as a prophet.
- Many others who have never been exposed to such doctrine. A renunciation would not keep them ignorant of these embarrassing doctrines.

Of the possible ways to deal with this dilemma, perhaps the Introduction to the 1998 Brigham Young manual is indicative of the course the Church has chosen. The introduction states, "[Brigham Young's] words are still fresh and appropriate for us today as we continue the work of building the kingdom of God." But this confident statement of the timelessness of Brigham's teachings is followed by an exhortation:

> Each statement has been referenced, and the original spelling and punctuation have been preserved; however, the sources cited will not be readily available to most members. These original sources are not necessary to have in order to effectively study or teach from this book. Members need not purchase additional references and commentaries to study or teach these chapters. The text provided in this book, accompanied by the scriptures, is sufficient for instruction.

With trust in Church leaders, most Mormons will follow this exhortation, which fairly screams, "Please do not look any deeper than this manual." Replacing original sources is one solution to the problem of how to discard antiquated doctrines.

Missionaries are told to avoid mentioning controversial issues to potential converts and new members. Missionaries are given specific lessons to teach, and they are expressly told, "Do not digress into less basic doctrine"[113] when teaching investigators and new members. This practice of giving "milk before meat" hides some doctrines from people until after they are baptized, involved in, and committed to the Church. Had I seen another organization withhold controversial teachings from new members until they were "hooked," I would have been suspicious—but, as a Mormon, I had not applied that reasoning to my own church.

Within a few months, the dismantling of my faith in the integrity of the prophets, apostles, and the Church itself, was complete. However, I still felt a strong connection with Mormons. For years, I continued referring to Mormons as "we" rather than "they". Long after I left the Church, a good friend concluded that I would always be a Mormon; in some ways, he is right. I still try to live by many of the ideals taught to me as a Mormon. It is true that these ideals can be learned elsewhere, but for me it happened in a Mormon family and with Mormon friends. My exodus from the Mormon Church is not yet complete, and probably never will be.

Chapter 15

Lies to Die For

Brad

In 1981, Apostle Boyd K. Packer delivered an address titled: "The Mantle Is Far, Far Greater Than the Intellect."[114] The expressions "the mantle of the prophet" and "the bishop's mantle" refer to the alleged aura of inspiration which settles upon the leaders called of God. Packer advocated that this mantle of inspiration was far more reliable than any scientific, scholarly, or rational conclusion. He criticized those who put the Church in a bad light with their intellectual observations, even if those observations were true. Packer's masterful way of presenting ideas is evident in the following quotation from his "Mantle" talk:

Faith, as well intentioned as it may be, must be built on facts, not fiction—faith in fiction is a damnable false hope.
—Alleged to have been said by Thomas Edison, (Internet)

> The writer or the teacher who has an exaggerated loyalty to the theory that everything must be told is laying a foundation for his own judgment. . . . In an effort to be objective, impartial, and scholarly a writer or a teacher may unwittingly be giving equal time to the adversary. . . . We should not be ashamed to be committed, to be converted, to be biased in favor of the Lord.

Chris and I were both admirers of Packer. He displayed great wisdom and effectively illustrated his teachings with stories and examples. He had a calm, forceful way of bringing home his point. Upon hearing a blunt attack on Packer's "Mantle" speech, one Sunday in 1984, I ardently defended both Packer and his ideas. At the time, no combination of words could have turned my convictions. My uncompromising zeal closed all avenues for discovering the error in my beliefs. I refused to question God's ways, not acknowledging the difference between questioning God and questioning the man I considered to be God's spokesman.

Mormons believe that all people once lived as spirit children with God. There, in a council held in heaven, Satan proposed a plan that would force everyone to be good when they came to earth to be tested and to receive a body. His plan was rejected; the plan chosen allowed for free agency. I no longer accept the "council in heaven" story, but I still believe people should be given a choice.

When a man or quorum of men assume their word is God's word and then isolate their followers from sources that suggest alternate views, it is akin to removing free agency. They, in essence, presume that only they are wise enough, worthy enough, or inspired enough to control information. If they err in their logic or inspiration, their faithful followers are doomed to the cell of ignorance. If the followers accept that the mantle is greater than the intellect, then they yield their judgment up to another; the door is opened for Waco, Heaven's Gate, Jonestown, Mountain Meadows Massacre,[115] the Third Reich, September 11, and an unending parade of horrors.

The problems do not start and end with the deaths of the innocent. The unchallenged bending of minds and wills can affect the quality of life in many ways, for people in and out of the circle of blind allegiance, for people in the present and people yet to be born.

Skepticism is the chastity of the intellect, and it is shameful to surrender it too soon.
—George Santayana, *American Quotations*, p. 99, #15

I shudder at the list of apparent falsehoods for which I would have given my life.

My intent was not to deceive so much as to enlighten others and to maintain my faith in the face of well-orchestrated deceitfulness. I wonder why I once felt it necessary to equivocate in order to uphold the truth and how I could have been so critical of others' closed minds while feigning objectivity in my own.

Packer quoted the Mormon prophet Joseph F. Smith as saying:

> There may be many who can not discern the workings of God's will in the progress and development of this great latter-day work. But there are those who see in every hour and in every moment of the existence of the Church, from its beginning until now, the overruling, almighty hand of Him who sent His Only Begotten Son.[116]

I once thought I saw "in every hour and in every moment" the hand of God in the Church's existence. I feared only the lies, not *true* history. Thus, I had followed Packer's formula and restricted my studies to sanctioned and faith-promoting writings. But even original Mormon scripture and the writings of past Mormon prophets hold stunning contradictions.

For instance, from faithful Mormon records, I discovered Joseph Smith's history of unreliable prophecies.[117] His deceitful nature first became obvious to me as I learned of his bold denials of polygamy.[118] Then I learned of the Kinderhook plates,[119] Joseph's use of a seer stone for treasure seeking activities,[120] his talk of using a divining rod for revelation from God,[121] and something of the bold eloquence of his lies about the goodness or wickedness in others.[122] Joseph's claims concerning the Book of Abraham are profoundly absurd.[123] The *Book of Mormon* generates a list of untenable assertions. Though information repudiating its validity is abundant, the book is revered by millions who refuse to hear another side to the story while at the same time claiming the evidence only verifies the book's historicity.

Likewise, I saw a side to Brigham Young which did not fit my former spiritual convictions. At times, his talk was intolerant and vicious,[124] his doctrines bizarre,[125] his pride excessive,[126] his expressions of family love a sham,[127] his touted integrity riddled with duplicity,[128] and his respect for human life counterfeit.[129]

I learned that as much as Mormons complain of being persecuted and killed,[130] they too have been guilty of killing a great number of innocent people. In addition to the Mountain Meadows Massacre there were the Morrisites, the Aiken party, the Circleville Massacre, and a host of others.[131] These killings do not fit comfortably into the Church history I once championed. They were acts by *God's chosen people*—a band of people I once revered.

I was familiar with stories of the Mormons being threatened, plundered, and driven from their homes. I had not realized that Mormons, too, had threatened, plundered, and driven others from their homes.[132]

I spent months researching Church history, impelled to obtain an accurate account and to make sense of it all. Even after leaving the Church, I was hesitant to believe the apparent depths of deception perpetuated by past Mormon leaders.[133] The extensive denials of polygamy astonished me. Though the practice of polygamy was not hidden from the Saints in Utah, it was publicly denied in Europe until 1852, deceiving newly converted Saints and Gentiles alike. The following is a portion of Apostle Orson Pratt's response to Anti-Mormons in Europe on January 15, 1850, as found in the *LDS Millennial Star 12*, pp. 29–30. At the time, Pratt had at least four wives.

12th Lie—Joseph Smith taught a system of polygamy.
12th Refutation—The Revelations given through Joseph Smith, state the following . . . "We believe that one man should have one wife." *Doctrine and Covenants*, page 331.

Another denial came from Apostle John Taylor. He published a pamphlet in Liverpool in 1850[134] wherein he said the following:

We are accused here of polygamy, and actions the most in-delicate, obscene, and disgusting, such that none but a corrupt and depraved heart could have contrived. These things are too outrageous to admit of belief; . . . I shall content myself by reading our views of chastity and marriage, from a work published by us, containing some of the articles of our Faith. "Doctrine and Covenants," page 330 . . . "Inasmuch as this Church of Jesus Christ has been reproached with the crime of fornication and polygamy, we declare that we believe that one man should have one wife, and one woman but one husband, except in case of death, when either is at liberty to marry again."

John Taylor, who later became prophet and president of the Church, was fully aware of polygamy amongst the Mormons. He had twelve wives at that time.[135]

I will describe only a few of the most obvious lies that I had told to myself

It is impossible to calculate the moral mischief, if I may so express it, that mental lying has produced in society.
—Thomas Paine, *The Age of Reason*, Chapter 1

and others in the process of defending my faith. For the most part, they followed a pattern: If the Church was true, then I knew certain claims would follow; I took the liberty of assuming those claims and then used them to prove to others the validity of the Church. Several good (or shall I say unscrupulous) examples come to mind.

While teaching at Northern Arizona University in 1982, I occasionally found opportunity to share my faith with some of my more intelligent and open-minded students. One such student, Jeff, asked for a Mormon prophecy that had been fulfilled. I showed him Joseph Smith's prophecy on the Civil War. He asked if the prophecy was put into our scripture after the Civil War or if it was there before the war. I had never asked myself that question, assuming that it had been in there all along, supposedly given on Christmas Day of 1832. I assured him it had been in our scriptures long before the Civil War. After leaving the Church, I remembered the discussion with Jeff and guessed that the Civil War prophecy, although made and recorded earlier, would not be found in the *Doctrine and Covenants* before the Civil War had occurred. I tracked it down and found that, indeed, the prophecy was not included in the *Doctrine and Covenants* until the 1876 version, after the Civil War. Closer examination revealed significant problems with Joseph Smith's *prophecy*.[136]

In 1967, I became excited about the rediscovery of the long-lost collection of Joseph Smith papyri, including the papyrus from which the Book of Abraham had been translated by Smith—at least, that was the story being told by the Church. With great anticipation, I waited for a long-overdue series of articles in the official Church magazine, *The Improvement Era*. I understood that Hugh Nibley, a celebrated Mormon scholar, was translating the hieroglyphics from the ancient documents, and I *knew* it would provide an unimpeachable testament—for those willing to listen—of the Prophet Joseph Smith's divine calling.

The series of articles found in *The Improvement Era* from 1968 to 1970 were titled, "A New Look at the Pearl of Great Price." After stalling for months (Nibley later admitted), he finally addressed the newly rediscovered Book of Abraham papyrus. My excitement immediately faded. His article made no sense. I did not know if Nibley lacked the ability to bring it down to my level of understanding, or if he was going through some heavy preliminaries before revealing some marvelous evidence. The next article produced similar disappointments. I recall being bothered by Nibley's inability to write anything useful or relevant to this historical find. Still, an alternate explanation did not occur to me.

I did not let my disappointment in Nibley keep me from repeating one of my most absurd lies. While on my mission, people occasionally challenged me with the fact that Mormons did not have the gold plates—the plates from which the *Book of Mormon* had been translated. I was quick to agree then add that we did have the papyrus from which Joseph Smith translated the Book of Abraham. I stated with conviction that this papyrus proved Joseph Smith to be a prophet. (I was not aware of anyone having been convinced by the papyral evidence, but I felt certain that if examined, the papyrus would provide the evidence.) Today, there is no parading of the rediscovered papyrus as proof of Joseph Smith being a prophet.

As the years passed, I occasionally wondered what had become of the Abraham papyrus and the opportunity to bolster the work of the Lord. Then one day I heard disturbing news of a scholar who had worked on the papyrus. He had left the Church.[137] That seemed impossible. A fleeting shadow of doubt entered my mind, but it quickly disappeared when I considered the follies of man and the ability of Satan to lead the *proud intellectual* astray. I also wondered if God tests our faith by creating contradictory evidence.

Again, I shoved these details and doubts to the back of my mind. Several months after leaving the Church, I took out all the pieces to which I had been exposed, attempting then to construct a complete picture of the Book of Abraham papyrus. I thought it would be a good issue on which to verify or invalidate my new conclusions about the Church. I told Chris as much in our visit in August of 1998. Eventually, Chris and I tracked down volumes of information from a variety of sources. Such information is not hard to find, once one gets away from the myopic approach recommended by Apostle Boyd K. Packer. While not surprised by the conclusion, I marveled at the quality and quantity of evidence available.[138]

In 1982, a non-Mormon acquaintance tried to explain that over the years, significant changes had been made in the *Book of Mormon.* Specifically, she stated that references

> It is not for knowledge to bow to faith. Rather, faith should be subservient to knowledge. Faith is no virtue. It is a necessary evil, a last resort, a substitute for knowledge when the facts are scarce. And closing our eyes and ears to new information because it contradicts our beloved faith, is akin to scorning true friends while clinging to the promises of an exotic false lover.
> —blm

to Christ had been recently added. While carefully understating my confidence in the matter, I explained the unlikeliness of her claim, telling her that my well-read, well-marked, 1920 copy of the *Book of Mormon* would not show any such changes. I further asserted that the only alterations made to the original translation of the *Book of Mormon* concerned grammar, punctuation, and the addition of chapter and verse designations. I did allow for one exception, a recently announced change referring to Native American skin color.[139]

Humored by her attempt to enlighten me, I recounted to others her absurd claims. I thought her presumptuous, telling me about a book she had never read—one I had studied devotedly for years. Sixteen years later, I discovered justification for her charge.

In at least four places, the *Book of Mormon* had been modified by placing the words "the Son of" immediately before *God,* or *the*

Eternal Father.[140] Upon discovering this, along with other significant modifications to Mormon scripture, I realized that many of
my former claims were born of a defensive, fervent faith, combined
with my naivete of original Mormon scriptures.[141]

At one time, for me, an astounding piece of archaeological
evidence for the *Book of Mormon* was the Tree of Life Stone (Izapa
Stela 5) found in Mexico. The Smithsonian Institution's Bureau
of American Ethnology published a photograph of a cast of this
sculptured, eight-foot-by-six-foot stone in 1943. I accepted and
repeated the claim that the stone matched a dream given to the
prophets Lehi and Nephi of the *Book of Mormon*. However, I was
skeptical of BYU Professor M. Wells Jakeman's claim that the
names of the two prophets, Lehi and Nephi, had been identified on
the stone. Today, many Mormon scholars dismiss Tree of Life Stone
claims.[142] As a typical Mormon, I had spent little time studying what
the scholars said—taking only their faith-promoting tidbits repeated
amongst the devoted believers.

Another of my lies, one not so easily excused or blamed
upon others, happened during my mission in New Zealand. While
teaching some teenagers about the *Book of Mormon*, I used a little
deceptive logic, reasoning calculated to bolster their faith in the
book. The ruse appeared to work, but afterwards it bothered me. I
did not forget this incident and did not repeat it. Yet, in the passion
of faith, I continued with subtle, biased deceptions relating to
spiritual things. Most of my lies remained well concealed, even
from myself. In my rational moments, I believed that unadulterated
truth was sufficient for the cause I loved.

As the years passed, I found inspiring literature from non-
Mormon authors. Around 1994, in concluding a second reading
of *The Keys of the Kingdom* (a novel by A. J. Cronin), the thought
struck me that this story inspired pure, natural goodness—more so
than did the *Book of Mormon*. I admitted such thoughts to no one at

the time. Now I see the *Book of Mormon* as a black-and-white book, unrealistic in relationship to the everyday challenges of life; full of extremes, heroes and villains; depicting a picture of a society wildly swinging back and forth between righteousness and wickedness. Virtually every conflict provides only one clear, courageous choice. Miracles are abundant and fantastic, accompanied by promises to die for. The *Book of Mormon* makes little mention of simple kindness and consideration for others; rather, it is a book for zealots and I had adored it.

Upon leaving the Church, I often wondered about the leaders whom I had so long revered. They

> **But Faith, fanatic Faith, once wedded fast**
> **To some dear falsehood, hugs it to the last.**
> —Thomas Moore, *The Veiled Prophet of Khorassan*, John Bartlett's *Familiar Quotations*, 10th ed. 1919, p. 525.

were in a position to know much of what I had found so disturbing. I wondered if they were duped or intentionally covering up. Ultimately, I concluded that they were fooling themselves by their own embellishments and distortions of Mormon history and doctrine.

In President Gordon B. Hinckley's *Compass* interview[143] for the Australian Broadcasting Corporation, he said: "We don't speak disparagingly of any Church. We simply say to people of other Churches, bring all the good that you have and come and let us see if they if we can add to it. Now that's all there is to it." The truth is that Mormon scripture, speaking of other churches, says: "all their creeds were an abomination in his [God's] sight."[144] Mormons believe that all who conscientiously reject their claims will pay a heavy price eternally.[145]

In the same interview, when asked if God had a wife—a concept unquestioned in the Church—Hinckley waffled with: "I don't know, but I suppose so. As we have a Father I assume we have a mother."

We have earlier mentioned Hinckley's lack of candor about the Mormon concept of God, the leadership role of women in the Church, and the place of polygamy in the early Church. We have noted his misrepresentation of little things like President Benson's capabilities as prophet while in his declining years. Hinckley paints a picture of Mormons innocently suffering great persecution for their religious beliefs.[146] He also played a duplicitous part in one of the most bizarre chapters in modern Church history, the Hofmann story.[147]

In his dedication of the Mountain Meadow Monument on September 11, 1999, Hinckley passed up the chance to acknowledge, and apologize for, the Mormon community's responsibility for the massacre of 120 men, women, and children in 1857.[148] The Church has effectively insulated many of its members from the details and ramifications of this ugly piece of history. Hinckley did nothing to spoil that shroud of ignorance; rather, he suggests that we forget the past—while he publicly details the injustices which Mormons have suffered at the hands of others.

The single most common and blatant error in the search for truth is to decide first what it is you want to believe.
—blm

As with past and present Church leaders, my biases were well intentioned; my concern for the Church's image was premier. Ignoring evidence, shading the facts, and perpetuating untenable but well-intentioned falsehoods were done in defense of the faith that brought salvation. Maybe this false approach resulted from the *Book of Mormon*, which teaches that knowledge of spiritual things is preceded by a desire to believe.[149]

Chapter 16

Hidden Legacy

Brad

On July 24, 1984, Ron and Dan Lafferty went to the home of their brother Alan in American Fork, Utah. The only ones home were Alan's wife, Brenda, and their daughter. With a ten-inch hunting knife, Ron and Dan slit the throats of Brenda and her fifteen-month-old daughter. Brenda, their sister-in-law, had not been willing to support polygamy, still practiced by fundamentalist groups who have broken away from the Church of Jesus Christ of Latter-day Saints.[150] Along with the rest of the Mormon community, I was horrified by the event. Few of us had any idea of the historical significance of this act.

> When fanaticism is bubbling up around us—then, habits of thought familiar from ages past reach for the controls. The candle flame gutters. Its little pool of light trembles. Darkness gathers. The demons begin to stir.
> —Carl Sagan, *The Demon-Haunted World*, p. 27

A year later, while I was still single, I became acquainted with Dan Lafferty's estranged first wife. Dan was in prison and she soon divorced him. In the time I spent with her, little was said of Dan, but she did mention the blood atonement doctrine once taught by Brigham Young. Although she expressed a loathing for the doctrine, I did not take the opportunity to learn what she was talking about. For another thirteen years, I knew next to nothing of this doctrine.

In spite of the occasional, dark insinuations, I remained certain that Brigham Young was not responsible for leading anyone into sin. His word carried the weight of scripture.[151] I continued to believe that on the important issues, "The prophet will never lead the Church astray."[152] By the end of 1998, my examination of the early Church publication, *Journal of Discourses*,[153] had shattered my naivety. Further research of Utah history in the 1800s exposed Mormon atrocities that left me reeling.

In Brigham Young's day, it was openly taught that some sins were not atoned for by the blood of Christ; some sinners had to die, shedding their blood in the process, or else forfeit exaltation. However, if they allowed their blood to be shed, they could be exalted—living as a god or goddess in the society of the gods.

> There are sins that men commit for which they cannot receive forgiveness in this world, or in that which is to come, and if they had their eyes open to see their true condition, they would be perfectly willing to have their blood spilt upon the ground, that the smoke thereof might ascend to heaven as an offering for their sins; and the smoking incense would atone for their sins, whereas, if such is not the case, they will stick to them and remain upon them in the spirit world.
> —Brigham Young, September 21, 1856, *Journal of Discourses*, Vol. 4, p. 53.

> And suppose that he is overtaken in a gross fault, that he has committed a sin that he knows will deprive him of that exaltation which he desires, and that he cannot attain to it without the shedding of his blood, and also knows that by having his blood shed he will atone for that sin, and be saved and exalted with the Gods, is there a man or woman in this house but what would say, "shed my blood that I may be saved and exalted with the Gods?"
> —Brigham Young, February 8, 1857, Ibid., Vol. 4, p. 219.

These teachings, found throughout the *Journal of Discourses*,[154] were acknowledged and defended by Church leaders in my lifetime, including Joseph Fielding Smith, who became the tenth president of the Church in 1970, and the more recent apostle Bruce R. McConkie. Both gave founder Joseph Smith credit for this doctrine.[155] Yet strangely enough, while defending the doctrine, they both vehemently denied that it was ever practiced by the Mormon Church.[156] McConkie said: "This principle can only operate in a day, as that of Moses, when there is no separation of Church and state and when the Church has power to take life."[157]

Sins that called for personal blood atonement include adultery, apostasy, stealing, a White marrying a Black, and breaking temple covenants.

> Suppose you found your brother in bed with your wife, and put a javelin through both of them, you would be justified, and they would atone for their sins, and be received into the kingdom of God. I would at once do so in such a case; and under such circumstances, I have no wife whom I love so well that I would not put a javelin through her heart, and I would do it with clean hands.
> —Brigham Young, March 15, 1856, *Journal of Discourses*, Vol. 3, p. 247.

> I say, rather than that apostates should flourish here, I will unsheath my bowie knife, and conquer or die. [Great commotion in the congregation, and a simultaneous burst of feeling, assenting to the declaration.] Now, you nasty apostates, clear out, or judgment will be put to the line, and righteousness to the plummet. [Voices, generally, "go it, go it."] If you say it is right, raise your hands. [All hands up.] Let us call upon the Lord to assist us in this, and every good work.
> —Brigham Young, March 27, 1853, Ibid., Vol. 1, p. 83. (The brackets in the text are original.)

> If you want to know what to do with a thief that you may find stealing, I say kill him on the spot, and never suffer him to commit another iniquity.
> —Brigham Young, May 8, 1853, Ibid., Vol. 1, p. 108.

Shall I tell you the law of God in regard to the African race?
If the white man who belongs to the chosen seed mixes his
blood with the seed of Cain, the penalty, under the law of
God, is death on the spot. This will always be so.
—Brigham Young, March 8, 1863, Ibid., Vol. 10, p. 110.

You may think that I am not teaching you Bible doctrine, but
what says the apostle Paul? I would ask how many covenant
breakers there are in this city and in this kingdom. I believe
that there are a great many; and if they are covenant breakers
we need a place designated, where we can shed their blood.
—J. M. Grant, September 21, 1856, Ibid., Vol. 4, pp. 49–50.

Few of today's Mormons are inclined to admit to or even believe
such doctrine, and few are aware of the influence of this doctrine
on early Utah history. The following account about the Mountain
Meadows Massacre is but one example of the fruits of Brigham's
preaching. The whole story is long and horrific, with many people
making conflicting claims, but the uncontested facts and the ad-
missions by those faithful to the Mormon Church are more than
sufficient to make the point.

If there isn't a Hell, there ought to be.
—Senator Berry of Arkansas, quoted in R.N.
Baskin, *Reminiscences of Early Utah*, p. 149

In the summer of
1857, the Fancher
wagon train attempted
to pass through Utah on their way to California. This party from
Arkansas, which consisted of approximately 140 people, made it
only as far as Southern Utah, to a place called Mountain Meadows.
Many of the families in the Fancher wagon train were related to
each other, and their wealth was substantial and obvious. The names
and origins of some members of the party are still unknown, but of
the eighty-seven whose names and ages have been identified, over
half were children sixteen years or under.[158]

As the emigrant train traveled through Southern Utah, friction
with the local Mormons intensified. Some residents in the towns
along the way later testified that Church leaders banned them from
selling supplies to the emigrants.[159] The emigrants were charged
with a variety of offenses committed against the Mormons and

Indians.[160] Adding to the tension, the U.S. army (referred to as Johnston's army) was on its way to put the Mormons in their place. President Buchanan had expressed his intent to restore respect for civil authority in the Utah territory; however, the Mormons considered themselves to be the abused party and were soon whipped into a mutinous frenzy.[161]

In addition to news of Johnston's army, word reached Utah of the murder of the beloved Apostle Parley P. Pratt at the hands of Hector McLean in Arkansas.[162] The Mormon vow to avenge the blood of the prophets[163] now included new responsibilities. Recently emphasized teachings of blood atonement likely influenced the thinking of some Saints.[164] Talk of killing the emigrants surfaced amongst the Saints in their meetings in Southern Utah.[165] Although a few men voiced disapproval, they were outnumbered and felt threatened by their fellow Saints for their dissenting views.[166]

The Arkansas emigrants finally reached Mountain Meadows where they intended to rest and prepare for the difficult trip across the desert that lay ahead. There, on or about September 7, they were attacked; they had reason to assume the assailants were Indians. Several emigrants were killed in the initial assault. They dug in and repulsed all further attempts. As the siege lengthened into days, with little water and so many young children, the party became desperate. A group of three attempted to get to Cedar City for help. In the venture, one of the three, a young man by the name of William Aiden who had joined the party in Provo, Utah, was shot by a White man. The other two escaped, temporarily. There is confusion as to what happened at this point. Either the two fled toward California or they first made it back to the emigrant camp and another attempt was made later to bring help from California.[167] The Mormons made the decision to kill all of the emigrants because the emigrants now knew of the Mormon involvement in the siege.[168]

On September 11, two Mormons with a white flag approached the beleaguered group. Surely, this desperate company of men, women, and children felt relief and hope at this opportunity for reconciliation. With no other options, they finally accepted the conditions of surrender and the Mormon promise of protection from the Indians. Still, they must have been suspicious or at least nervous, giving up their arms and relying upon their attackers to escort them safely back to Cedar City. The besieged party left their fortified camp in two groups: the women, children, and wounded went first in a group; the disarmed men followed, strung out in single file, each escorted by an armed Mormon militiaman. When the party reached the appointed spot, the signal was given. Shots rang out as the massacre began. Concealed Indians assisted in the ambush. The slaughter was quickly over and completely effective; every man, woman, and child lay dead—except eighteen children too young to testify.[169]

Anyone who has the power to make you believe absurdities has the power to make you commit injustices.
—Voltaire, 1767, alleged to be in the *Collection of Letters on the Miracles*. The quotation is found on numerous Internet sites.

Even if I were to believe every last charge against the emigrants; even if some of them were responsible for the blood of the Mormon prophets; even if I were to consider all mitigating circumstances—such as the war hysteria amongst the *Saints*; they all appear as gnats before this specter of blood, this deed towering from hell. After the last father had fallen with his dreams of new opportunity for his family; after the last young mother had been cut off from the horror of her final moments with her terrified children; after the last young man had lost his final, frantic battle for life; after the last young woman, powerless to do anything but plead before God and foe, had fallen easy prey; after the last screaming, clutching child had been denied all spoken and unspoken pleas for mercy; after the eighteen orphaned babes, toddlers, and children too young to testify, had cried themselves to sleep without their mothers, fathers or siblings to comfort them; the horror of this deed rose up as a darkening cloud, overshadowing all claims against the emigrants, concocted or real. Furthermore, the deed overshadows the murder of Joseph and Hyrum Smith, Haun's Mill massacre, and any and all complaints of murder and persecution against the Mormons which I had heard so sanctimoniously recited in religion classes, in Sunday School, and continue to hear broadcast to the world.

I once proudly claimed my place amongst *God's chosen people*; amongst those who considered themselves tutored by the Almighty through prophets and blessed with special gifts of the spirit; amongst those who looked down upon a wicked world, scornfully rejecting their fallen and darkened state. Now I shudder as I awaken to my own hypocrisy, having tried for years to teach others as if they were blind and as if my vision was clear, reliable, and based upon unfaltering integrity.

At first, as I struggled to understand the perpetrators of the bizarre massacre at Mountain Meadows, I found myself aching for the existence of a hell to receive them. Yet, there is nothing to be gained by such hopes. In fact, why even remember or contemplate this repulsive deed? The answer becomes apparent as I watch and read of world events. Eerily, while writing this chapter, on the 144th anniversary of the Mountain Meadows Massacre, the world was once again given reason to remember September 11 as they witnessed the work of a fanatic Islamic group led by Osama bin Laden. I believe that September 11 should be remembered for both events linked to religious devotees. The wages of heartfelt, mindless devotion, at home and abroad, continue to take innocent lives and to heap varying degrees of misery upon the believing and the unbelieving; upon those professing different Gods or different forms of worship for the same God; upon those claiming differing roots; upon those whose offenses have been imagined, exaggerated, or even accurately portrayed.

> **And if the Gentiles wish to see a few tricks, we have "Mormons" that can perform them. We have the meanest devils on the earth in our midst, and we intend to keep them for we have use for them; and if the Devil does not look sharp, we will cheat him out of them at the last, for they will reform and go to heaven with us.**
> —Brigham Young, January 17, 1858, *Journal of Discourses*, Vol. 6, p. 176

The initial success of the cover-up of the Mountain Meadows Massacre was foiled by the rumors of surviving infants living with the Mormons. As the rumors gathered momentum, denials by Mormon leaders intensified. Enough people were fooled to keep justice at bay for nearly two decades. In 1877, twenty years after the massacre, one man was punished for his part in the slaughter. Some people consider John D. Lee to be the single scapegoat for a community of murderers; the Church leaders of Southern Utah, carrying significant responsibility for the deed, were left untouched by Utah justice.

Once I understood the capacity for violence and deceit in the early Mormon Church, I decided to research some of the rumors of foul play which I had so flippantly dismissed my whole life. As I unraveled early Utah history, I realized that Mountain Meadows Massacre was an aberration only in its scope. It was preceded by and followed by a host of murders at the hands of faithful Mormons. A significant step in identifying some of Brigham Young's "meanest devils" came with the discovery of a book, *Reminiscences of Early Utah*, published in 1914, written by R.N. Baskin, an attorney, Salt Lake City mayor, and eventually chief justice of the Supreme Court of Utah. In the book, he documents various threats, deeds, confessions, and testimony given in court involving several brutal murders. Initially, I questioned Baskin's unthinkable claims, but further research—involving early Mormon journals, sermons, and confessions—verified his references and supported his account.[170]

> I will not attack your doctrines nor your creeds if they accord liberty to me. If they hold thought to be dangerous — if they aver that doubt is a crime, then I attack them one and all, because they enslave the minds of men.
> —Robert G. Ingersoll, *The Ghosts*, *The Works of Robert G. Ingersoll*, Dresden Edition, Vol. 1, p. 324

Eventually, I concluded that the blood atonement teaching was a thinly veiled attempt to coerce others. It was also an excuse for some Mormons to rid themselves of those they hated, those they did not trust, or those they found irritating. The teaching was a jumping-off point for the Mountain Meadows Massacre, the 1861 brutal beating of Utah Governor John W. Dawson by Hickman's gang,[171] the annihilation of the Aiken party,[172] the Circleville massacre[173] and a number of other Indian shootings, the killing of a deaf and dumb boy for stealing,[174] the murder of Hartley, the murder of Parrish and Potter by Bishop Aaron Johnson of Springville, the murder of Henry Jones and his mother by Bishop Charles Hancock and others in Payson, the murder of Potter and Wilson in Coalville, the Morrisite murders, and the murder of Yates.[175] Those are only some of the well-documented murders.

Today, Mormon disclaimers of blood atonement include: the teaching was merely rhetoric to motivate the Saints; it was taken out of context; it was applicable only to murderers; Brigham effectively denounced the teaching;[176] it couldn't be true because there are apostates and anti-Mormons who have lived in Utah for years; it is a misunderstanding; it never happened; it is simply material dreamed up for popular and sleazy magazines and literature; it is just another example of Mormons being maligned for their religious beliefs. More troubling still, some Mormons acknowledge the doctrine then fall back on the Old Testament to justify the Plutonian teachings and actions of the early Mormons.

Now, I marvel at how ill formed, passionate, and deceitful—and how effective—the defense appears to be in clearing the names of Brigham Young and other Mormon leaders. I am reminded of a phrase by Church leader Charles W. Penrose in a letter to President John Taylor in 1887: "the endless subterfuges and prevarications which our present condition impose . . . threaten to make our rising generation a race of deceivers."[177]

There is no surer way to judge a man than by his own words, taken in context, repeated time and again while enjoying complete liberty to speak his mind, which he has approved for publication. Yes, Brigham had some good things to say, but I now recognize how much he had to say that was not good. Some defenders say he was only pretending to be ruthless. It may be pointless to argue over where the greater pretense lies: in his noble facade, in his talk of vengeance and violence, or in today's defense of his saintliness.

Few of my family and longtime associates (virtually all Mormons) will entertain the idea that Brigham was anything less than one of the noblest men to have ever lived, a man chosen by God in the premortal existence to guide His Church. Perhaps the passing of time and better access to information will someday bring about a more thorough examination of their ardent beliefs. Because I labored contentedly under these illusions for many years, it is not appropriate for me to complain (although I do) of believers who refuse a deeper look.

At times I become angry over past deceptions, lost confidences, and the altered relationships that I have experienced and which I see in the lives of others; and yet, I recognize that the actions and attitudes that I find offensive were once my own, born of ignorance. And in fact, the Mormon community abounds with wonderful, thinking, considerate, talented people. They are found in the sports

The days come and go like muffled and veiled figures, sent from a distant friendly party; but they say nothing; and if we do not use the gifts they bring, they carry them as silently away.
—Ralph Waldo Emerson, "Work and Days", *Society and Solitude*, 1870, Chapter 7, p.151

world, politics, academia, business, and in every occupation, from the mundane to the exotic. Their total devotion inspires cooperation and facilitates great achievements.

Good principles and fruits coming from today's Church of Jesus Christ of Latter-day Saints will be poorly represented here. The brutal legacy coming from the roots of Mormonism does not reflect the views and feelings of the typical Church member today. The seeds of future changes for the better are still found within the Church. Mormonism emphasizes education, honesty, and compassion. The tools we each use for discovery and the inner motives we nurture are more important than the temporary conclusions we have reached—if we can avoid doing too much harm in the process of discovery.

Sometimes in the late evenings, in the attempt to induce sleep, I take a long walk or bike ride with one or more of my young sons nestled in our stroller/trailer cart. Invariably I will go by the church building just around the corner from our home. It is a beautiful building, especially when lit up at night. During the early months of my religious withdrawal, I teased Cathy, telling her that Caleb and I were going out to throw rocks at the church (thankfully, she recognizes my attempts to lighten harsh reality with a little humor). In fact, the sight of this building generates a mixture of emotions. It invokes memories of late night and early morning basketball games with good friends. (Most Mormon church buildings have a cultural hall with a nice hardwood floor and basketball hoops on each end.) It stirs sweet memories of singing in choirs and of counsel from men and women I revered. It brings back images of leadership meetings in which we contemplated ways to help others with their temporal concerns and to build up the Kingdom of God. Generally, I find myself gently shaking my head at the absurdity of my past, so full of the stuff of life; passionate devotion and rude awakenings, unselfish sacrifices and haunting offenses, thoughtful analysis and short-sighted conclusions, cherished friends and shattered loyalties, confidence and fear.

Occasionally, I return with my sons to the campus of my alma mater, Brigham Young University, to wander the beautiful grounds and visit some of the exhibits there. I cannot visit the campus without fond recollections of a host of experiences and friendships. My sons are always delighted by the experience, quite unaware of my conflicting emotions. As a young boy, I grew up not far from BYU. My paper route bordered the campus, and sometimes after my deliveries, I wandered the grounds and explored the buildings. The students seemed like such nice people.

When I came to BYU as a freshman, I found nothing at which to complain except complainers. I was devoted to the institution and in return benefited from opportunities to learn and grow. In trying to support myself as a freshman, I first worked as an early morning janitor for $1.35 an hour. Much later, I spent several years on the faculty as a full-time mathematics instructor. I loved the experience and the people; at the time, I lamented that my masters degree and devotion to the school were not enough to secure a permanent position.

Now when I visit the campus, I no longer think of it as "the Lord's University" but I still find the people pleasant, the kind of people I would choose as friends. When passing students smile at my boys or make friendly conversation, I am glad for a moment incognito. Unaware of my apostasy, they can share a genuine, unguarded piece of themselves, once again reminding me of how much I enjoyed my years there as a student and faculty member.

In the spring of 1999, upon concluding my investigation of blood atonement, I found myself watching my young sons intently while murder and

> We are all artists painting our own fragile masterpiece on the fabric of life. How foolish to bully—with fear, rhetoric, or false friendship—our sketch of virtue upon another's canvas.
> —blm

massacres shadowed my thoughts. I wondered about the mystery of life, love, hate, and death. I looked at the intelligence which my oldest boy displays and asked myself how it came to be. I wondered at his creativity, his joy, his biases, his sense of humor, his imagination, and his well-developed will. I wondered about his future. I wondered how I would have felt had I and my precious family been a part of the desperate Arkansas wagon train there in Mountain Meadows on September 11, 1857.

I thrilled to see my eighteen-month-old running and jumping down the sidewalk, waving his arms wildly, jabbering with excitement in his little falsetto voice. I marveled at his new fascination with trees as he repeatedly pointed to them, seeking my shared excitement over these big objects with their leaves fluttering in the wind. In the evening, as I turned on the go-to-bed music, I melted in his viselike grip on my neck, with his body squirming in excited anticipation of his nightly last dance with Dad. For me, life defies explanation, but I cherish the experience. I am willing to believe that others feel the same love and thrill for life, whether or not they share my beliefs and passions, whether or not I think they are on the path to greatest happiness.

Chapter 17

Sailing Without a Banner

Chris

Although our headlong investigation into the Mormon Church had set Brad and me on a journey that strained some precious relationships and although our road map for the afterlife had gone up in flames, yet in that same fall of 1998, we found harmony in our new world. I enjoyed an unfettered peace—never before known in my adulthood—which was worth every bit the price I paid. It was, however, a peace that would soon be severely tested.

Take pride in being yourself. Envy no one; copy no one. Rejoice in your original looks, talents, feelings, and thoughts. Listen to others, read widely, and heed counsel; but do your own thinking, draw your own conclusions, speak your own words, determine your own actions.
—Lowell L. Bennion, a Mormon author and instructor of religion. (Search Internet, or see http://www.2think.org/hii/arm.shtml.)

Throughout the fall of 1998 and into the first part of 1999, I kept my religious investigations focused mostly on Mormonism. From the beginning, I had understood that my investigations might give me welcome relief from contradictory beliefs and internal strife. On the other hand, the occasional glance beyond Mormonism had left me apprehensive. What would come of a serious inquiry into the existence of God and the afterlife?

While talking with relatives in late 1998, Connie had defended my belief in God and argued against the notion that Satan governed my actions. I hesitated to reevaluate my view of God, concerned that my conclusion would only reinforce some people's belief that Satan was dragging me ever closer to Hell. However, I had earlier vowed to draw my own conclusions regardless of what others thought, so in spring of 1999 I pulled my questions out into broad daylight and continued my search for honest answers.

In my eyes, Joseph Smith's fall had been a fall from godhood—or near godhood.[178] As Joseph Smith fell, so fell Abraham, Isaac, Jacob,[179] and all the other extra gods. I no longer presumed myself to be a god in embryo. The next question was obvious: Is there *any* god at all? And the all-important question: Is there life after death? As a Mormon, I felt that the afterlife gave meaning to this life; life after death had always been as certain as the sunrise. As I examined the evidence, certitude slowly faded. I did not discard with glee my conviction on this matter; the very best I could do was reluctantly replace it with a wish. When I spoke to Connie of these thoughts, she was alarmed at the turn my investigation had taken.

Losing the Mormon atlas that would guide me through the eternities had been one thing, but losing eternity itself pushed me to depths of anguish I had never known. To experience this life and its simple pleasures, to enjoy the love of family and friends, to have a "knowledge" that it would last forever, and then to have that sure knowledge ripped away seemed the ultimate loss—a most cruel practical joke that the cosmos had played on me.

Suddenly my life had been infinitely shortened. Death will not be the previously anticipated doorway into eternal life. It will be the end of life, the end of love, the end of consciousness, the end of existence. In a few short years, I will be nothing but a memory in a few mortal minds, and soon even the memory of me will be forever gone. My name—eventually buried under the names of those who will follow me—will never again be associated with a man who lived and loved at this time on this part of planet earth. The universe will never know I existed.

Some scientific theories, which I had previously refused to consider, suddenly became credible, thus completing the demolition of my view of eternity. In a few billions or perhaps trillions of years, with no god to command otherwise, the theories of science will be realized: The universe will be crushed into oblivion as it collapses upon itself, or it will continue to expand—stars burning out—into a cold, dark expanse of lifelessness. Even though this process will take eons, it is less than a fraction of the eternity for which I had expected life to flourish.

Mortality is terminal and universal.

Brad also pondered questions about God and searched for evidence of an afterlife. We conversed often, each hoping the other had information to restore our once-cherished beliefs. Even though such information never came, I enjoyed our e-mail exchanges and our phone calls; he was the only person I knew who could both understand the magnitude of my loss and appreciate the validity of my questions.

Although I found some reprieve from my distress as we looked for, shared, and laughed at the humor in our new life, these months were by far the most difficult part of my passage. It was not a matter of trying to get others to understand the facts; it was a matter of recovering from my annihilated expectations. It was no longer a question of what to expect of, and how to best prepare for, the afterlife; I faced a dilemma. How could I pick up the pieces of a shattered faith and move ahead with a meaningful mortality? It was not an ordeal that lent itself well to an external solution. Inevitably, it was a lonely personal struggle.

For months, I lamented the loss of eternity. The sorrow was especially poignant when I thought of my children. If only they could live forever, I could somehow accept my own finite life span. The undoing of my faith had caused Mom and Dad to mourn losing me, and now, ironically, I was mourning for the loss of my children.

A different and relatively minor source of sorrow came as I realized that family members would likely never really understand who I had become. Earlier, I had told myself that at least in the next life, they would recognize that I was not acting under the influence of Satan; they would see me for who I was. Having always believed that death was not the end, I was accustomed to waiting for some things until the next life. But with my assurance in the afterlife now crushed, I saw little chance that their view of me would change—ever. Compared with "losing eternity," worrying about what my siblings think of me seems like a shallow concern; certainly, my ego played a part in making this a difficult pill to swallow.

I had once thought that those who lose belief in God do so out of rebellion. They are angry with God, and the ultimate act of rebellion is to deny his existence. This may be true for some people, but it was not the case with me. I have had a wonderful life, and if there is a creator who is a giver of so many good things, I am most grateful. However, to believe in God because of *my* good fortune seems to be a rather narrow view. If a starving, lonely orphan in a war-torn country were to see *my* good fortune, would she then accept the existence of God? Perhaps she would look at her own situation and conclude that there is no benevolent creator.

Whenever I am reminded of the magnitude of suffering in this world, I long for evidence of an all-powerful god who will put an end to this misery. I shudder when I think of the millions of men, women, and children who have endured atrocities and who, in the end, have faced vicious deaths at the hands of heartless men. As I better comprehend the cruelty suffered by the Jews in the Holocaust, as I better comprehend the inhumanity and violent deaths endured by Blacks on slave-boats and in slavery, and as I better comprehend numerous cases of unspeakably barbaric deaths suffered over the centuries, I think that surely it is impossible that a person's entire existence can end in such horror. There absolutely *must* be a god who can guarantee an afterlife that smothers all the wrongs of this world and delivers the peace and dignity so callously denied some in this life. Yet, despite my ardent hopes and wishes, I have become a skeptic, and I have no anesthetic to numb my anguish. Using faith and hope to determine truth failed me miserably in the past. Now, I feel compelled, by experience, to base my beliefs on evidence and reason.

I do not make the claim that there is no God; it is simply that I no longer accept what I once thought was compelling evidence for the existence of God. I do not claim to know that this life is all there is; I only admit to myself that I see no more evidence of an afterlife than I see evidence that Joseph Smith was a prophet of God.

I do not ridicule others, Mormon or non-Mormon, who find re-assurance through their faith in God. I understand the comfort that comes from faith that God will, in the end, make all things right.

Neither would I take pleasure in seeing the destruction of one's hope of an afterlife (a hope not necessarily connected with a belief in God). I understand that after experiencing the joys of this world, one would hope for the continuation of joy throughout eternity, rather than the annihilation of body and soul at death.

If the sheer force of willpower could turn my wishes into a truth, then for me there would be an afterlife—and it would be similar to the afterlife defined by Mormons. (It would not be *exactly* as the Mormons describe it; I'm sure Connie would never go for that polygamy thing.) Their doctrine of the afterlife is a kind doctrine in which even apostates like Brad and I would eventually inherit a life in a world much better than the one in which we now live—unless, as some personal acquaintances have hinted, we have actually attained the dreaded depths as sons of perdition.

Gradually, I have climbed out of my abyss of lost hopes. I do not have an eternity to look forward to, but I do have something. I have the present. I have a fascinating world of which to learn, a beautiful world in which to live out my life. My thoughts keep returning to my children and the positive influence I can have on them. I can reach outside my small circle of influence to help make life more pleasant for a few others. My good deeds may not be recorded and rewarded by a benevolent god, but they can still be done. Time will march forward, terminating my life; but it can never march backward and erase a single act of kindness or a moment of courage. In that respect, any of my good deeds will be as long lasting as my death. My new mindset gives me a type of eternal life with which I am growing comfortable.

Despite initial feelings of utter devastation, Brad and I have never regretted leaving the Church, nor do we regret our subsequent life-altering conclusions. Earlier in our lives, we had felt compelled to justify our religious beliefs when we encountered a contradiction. Now, we hope to let encounters with truth reshape our views, rather than try to force the facts to fit our faith. We have replaced the discord of contradictions with the harmony of consistency. Our newly found peace is a powerful peace; it has been severely tested, but it has emerged intact.

We realize that people of other faiths—those we had once faulted for not accepting the "truths" we taught—are not our spiritual subordinates. Furthermore, the nonreligious—those that we might have once mistrusted and condemned as unenlightened, closed-minded, or selfish pleasure seekers—are equally likely to have good hearts and the desire to make the world a better place. While we still acknowledge that there are problems in the world, the view we once had of an evil world now appears exaggerated; perhaps people are not naturally wicked. This more optimistic view of the ordinary, everyday man and woman quite suddenly makes the world a better place in which to live; it is a wonderful feeling.

On the other hand, I realize that I am not so noble as I once supposed. I had once taken pride in donating the required ten percent of my income to the Church. When I left the Church, I thought to give that ten percent to organizations that would feed the hungry, house the homeless, educate the masses, and otherwise help those in need. However, now that the threat of eternal damnation is not connected to my charitable giving, my donations have dropped drastically.

It took some time for me to acknowledge that my passage out of Mormonism, however unique it might seem to me, was no more significant than spiritual and personal journeys others have taken. Brad and I were not the first to leave an authoritarian organization. We were not the first to announce a new course in life, only to have cherished relationships become warped, strained, or even severed. We were not the first to agonize over the question of God's existence and the afterlife. We will not be the last to ponder the meaning of mortality.

A man's ethical behavior should be based effectually on sympathy, education, and social ties; no religious basis is necessary. Man would indeed be in a poor way if he had to be restrained by fear and punishment and hope of reward after death.
—Albert Einstein, *The World as I See It*, p. 27, Citadel Press, Translated by Alan Harris. (See also "Religion and Science," *New York Times Magazine*, November 9, 1930)

We had once believed that God knew the perfect answer to each of life's difficult problems, and we prayed for guidance. Yet, we heard no reply to our fervent prayers on some extremely important issues. Perhaps we did not pray with enough faith. Perhaps we did not try hard enough to find the answers ourselves. Perhaps our hearts were just not right, and we were not sensitive enough to hear or understand God's answer. Whatever the case, our prayers were ineffective because we were somehow inadequate. We no longer make these judgments.

Theologically, we seem light years away from where we once were. The spiritual tenets we once embraced included not only teachings of the afterlife, but had guided our thoughts on political, social, historical, and scientific issues. Our new beliefs place us squarely on a path that we once thought was trod only by the unenlightened, the closed-minded self-deceivers who were unwilling to open their eyes to the truth, and sinners who wanted no interference with their selfish pleasure-seeking and evil desires.

In 1997, President Hinckley described the dismal state of a nonreligious person:

> Without acknowledgement of deity, without recognition of the Almighty as the ruling power of the universe, the all-important element of personal and national accountability shrivels and dies . . . Teen pregnancy, abandoned families, failure to recognize the property and rights of others, general incivility have resulted in large measure, I am satisfied, from failure to recognize that there is a God to whom someday each of us must give an accounting.[180]

I had once thought that the good deeds of unbelievers—and to some extent non-Mormons—were a vain attempt to find meaning in a shallow life. I know now, from experience, that belief in a god who metes out rewards and punishment is not a prerequisite for finding joy in doing a good deed. Deception is still distasteful. Injustice is as intolerable as it ever was. My efforts to be forgiving and merciful are not because of some divine decree, but because I recognize my own faults; it seems only fair to give others the forgiveness and mercy that I would want. The real satisfaction in doing good works is found in the doing itself, not in doing it because God expects it. Virtue yields its own dividends, as does vice.

As a Mormon, I had always believed that the god of this earth was once a man on another world, and that he became a god, a perfected man, by "learning to be good." In other words, I believed that: "Good was good, before God was God." I loved God not because it was a commandment, nor because I was afraid of burning in Hell if I did not love him. I loved God because he was merciful. I loved God because he was just. I loved God because he was good. Losing my faith in the existence of God has not affected my love of mercy, justice and goodness.

With my Mormon beliefs peeled away, I have become a humanist. Yet, I believe it is consistent to acknowledge that some Church teachings and members have had a positive influence on my life. In addition, I can accept some teachings of a spiritual leader, such as Jesus, without believing everything said or written of that leader.

As a Mormon, two factors had left me vulnerable to an exaggerated sense of insecurity. First, many of my religious beliefs had either contradicted each other or were at odds with the evidence. Second, my futile attempts to discern the constant inspiration from God—which was my right as a worthy Mormon—had always left me second-guessing myself. Now, with no more expectations of always being right, I am much more comfortable in my beliefs and confident in my decisions.

Brad and I feel that in many ways we have changed very little. We still find happiness in making another's day brighter. We are still pained when we see the suffering of others, whether it is a family member, a friend, a neighbor, or a nameless refugee halfway around the world. Seeing someone who, against the odds, makes a courageous stand for principle still inspires us. Seeing an act of kindness motivates us to be better ourselves. We have not lost our inordinate delight in simple things such as giggles and hugs from our children; their antics still make us laugh. We are skeptics, but we are not cynics. We find life every bit as meaningful as it ever was. We continue to find new and unexpected joys. We have a deeper appreciation for this fleeting life and all it has to offer.

We realize that our religion had not so much been the rudder by which we steered, as it had been the banner under which we sailed. As it turns out, we have not cast off the rudder; we are simply sailing without a banner.

Appendix I

In the Name of God

Brad

It was not a love for violence that led us to research early Mormon history; rather, we yielded to an intense curiosity about the roots of our former religion. After

All absolute power demoralizes its possessor. To that all history bears witness. And if it be a spiritual power which rules men's consciences, the danger is only so much greater, for the possession of such a power exercises a specially treacherous fascination, while it is peculiarly conducive to self-deceit, because the lust of dominion, when it has become a passion, is only too easily in this case excused under the plea of zeal for the salvation of others.

—Professor J.H. von Dullinger [Johann Joseph Ignaz von Dollinger]—who was subsequently excommunicated from the Roman Catholic Church (1871), (See http://www.2think.org/quotes1.html)

giving up our faith as founded on the sands of innocent hope, the ruthless violence we uncovered took us by surprise. Certainly, our allegations from previous pages deserve further documentation for the skeptical reader. To that end, this appendix offers limited, but compelling, accounts of stunning discourses and deeds. It sheds a brief pulse of light on the long dark shadows of early Mormon history, an appalling history that Chris and I had once dismissed as mostly absurd rumors, easily rationalizing the rest into non-significance.

Beyond the need to certify some incredible claims, beyond the need to justify our apostasy, and far beyond the narrow issue of Mormonism, there is a compelling observation to be made. People who are unfamiliar with the conscientious efforts for good, which are found so abundantly within the Mormon Church—today and in years past—may not fully appreciate the point, but in a nut shell it is this: They who worship a merciful god, who love their families and neighbors, who fairly strive to incorporate the noblest of perceived virtues in their lives, can still become hopelessly deluded to the point of horrific inhumanity. If such zealots are not of our faith, we tend to call them evil, putting them in league with the devil. We may make war on them. We may condemn them to prison, death, and even happily to hell. Yet, it appears that many atrocities in the world are committed or allowed by *decent* people, on God's side, who are blinded by intransigent convictions and a fear of the perceived evil within others. Maybe these *decent* people are led astray by a madman or a quorum of madmen in prophets' robes. Maybe they are led astray by almost innocent men who are intoxicated by their exalted callings as God's spokesmen, men who are heady from the sweet reverence paid them by their adoring followers. Too often, we are simply led astray by good men and women whose unfounded, magnified, and contagious fears overwhelm the thoughtful critics of the time, infecting then driving a society to a moment of madness.

At this point then, having done little more than assure the unfamiliar reader of the goodness and virtues found within the Mormon Church, we shall focus on the evidence of a horrific past.

There will be three sections in this appendix. The first section consists of a collection of quotations from the Mormon pulpit, mostly by Brigham Young, as approved for publication by Brigham Young. These excerpts reveal the worst in fanatic, hateful rhetoric. They also further demonstrate that the irrational and chilling doctrine of blood atonement—saving individuals from damnation by killing them—was taught regularly with great emphasis. The second section touches on the aftermath of the Mountain Meadows Massacre, where Brigham Young's duplicity and blind, if not approving, eye insured the escape from justice of every last murderous perpetrator, save John D. Lee. The third section documents additional acts of murder and violence against sinners and enemies of the Church.

God's Chosen Servants Speak

The following collection of unsaintly doctrine and threats is selected from the period preceding and concurrent with the

The Lord is in our midst. He teaches the people continually. I have never yet preached a sermon and sent it out to the children of men, that they may not call Scripture.
—Brigham Young, January 2, 1870, *Journal of Discourses*, Vol. 13, p. 95

Mountain Meadows Massacre. Along with references given previously, they reveal the posture of the Mormon leaders, touted as God's most Christlike sons on earth.

I say again, you Gladdenites, do not court persecution, or you will get more than you want, and it will come quicker than you want it. I say to you Bishops, do not allow them to preach in your wards. Who broke the roads to these valleys? Did this little nasty Smith, and his wife? No, they staid in St. Louis while we did it, peddling ribbons, and kissing the Gentiles. I know what they have done here they have asked exorbitant prices for their nasty stinking ribbons. [Voices, "that's true."] We broke the roads to this country. Now, you Gladdenites, keep your tongues still, lest sudden destruction come upon you.

I will tell you a dream that I had last night. I dreamed that I was in the midst of a people who were dressed in rags and tatters, they had turbans upon their heads, and these were also hanging in tatters. The rags were of many colors, and, when the people moved, they were all in motion. Their object in this appeared to be, to attract attention. Said they to me, "We are Mormons, brother Brigham." "No, you are not," I replied. "But we have been," said they, and they began to jump, and caper about, and dance, and their rags of many colors were all in motion, to attract the attention of the people. I said, "You are no Saints, you are a disgrace to them." Said they, "We have been Mormons." By and bye, along came some mobocrats, and they greeted them with, "How do you do, sir, I am happy to see you." They kept on that way for an hour. I felt ashamed of them, for they were in my eyes a disgrace to "Mormonism." Then I saw two ruffians, whom I knew to be mobbers and murderers, and they crept into a bed, where one of my wives and children woke. I said, "You that call yourselves brethren, tell me, is this the fashion among you?" They said, "O, they are good men, they are gentlemen." With that, I took my large bowie knife, that I used to wear as a bosom pin in Nauvoo, and cut one of their throats from ear to ear, saying, "Go to hell across lots." The other one said, "You dare not serve me so." I instantly sprang at him, seized him by the hair of the head, and, bringing him down, cut his throat, and sent him after his comrade; then told them both, if they would behave themselves they should yet live, but if they did not, I would unjoint their necks. At this I awoke.

I say, rather than that apostates should flourish here, I will unsheath my bowie knife, and conquer or die. [Great commotion in the congregation, and a simultaneous burst of feeling, assenting to the declaration.] Now, you nasty apostates, clear out, or judgment will be put to the line, and righteousness to the plummet. [Voices, generally, "go it, go it."] If you say it is right, raise your hands. [All hands up.] Let us call upon the Lord to assist us in this, and every good work.
—Brigham Young, March 27, 1853, *Journal of Discourses*, Vol. 1, p. 83. (Brackets appear as found in original text.)

Suppose the shepherd should discover a wolf approaching the flock, what would he be likely to do? Why, we should suppose, if the wolf was within proper distance, that he would kill him at once with the weapons of defence which he carries; in short, that; he would shoot him down, kill him on the spot. If the wolf was not within shot, we would naturally suppose he would set the dogs on him; and you are aware, I have no doubt, that thence shepherd dogs have very pointed teeth, and they are very active, very sensitive to know when the flock is in danger. It is sometimes the case, perhaps, that the shepherd has not with him the necessary arms to destroy the wolf, but in such a case he would set his faithful dogs on him, and by that means accomplish his destruction.

Is this true in relation to the shepherd, and the flock, and the dogs? You can all testify to its truth. Now was Jesus Christ the good shepherd? Yes. What the faithful shepherd is to his sheep, so is the Saviour to his followers. He has gone and left on earth other shepherds who stand in the place of Jesus Christ to take care of the flock. When that flock is out on the prairie, and the pasture range extending broad and green before them, and completely cleared of wolves, is not that sanctified and cleansed, when there is nothing to hurt or destroy them? I ask if one wolf is permitted to mingle with the flock, and unmolested proceed in a work of destruction, will he not go off and tell the other wolves, and they bring in a thousand others, more wicked and ravenous than themselves? Whereas, if the first one should meet with his just deserts, he could not go back and tell the rest of his hungry tribe to come and feast themselves upon the flock.

Now don't say that brother Hyde has taught strong things, for I have only told you what takes place between the shepherd and the flock, when the sheep have to be protected. If you say that the Priesthood or authorities of the Church here are the shepherd, and the Church is the flock, you can make your own application of this figure. It is not at all necessary for me to do it.
—Orson Hyde, April 9, 1853, Ibid., Vol. 1, pp. 72–73.

It was asked this morning how we could obtain redress for our wrongs; I will tell you how it could be done, we could take the same law they have taken, viz., mobocracy, and if any miserable scoundrels come here, cut their throats. (All the people said, Amen.)
—Brigham Young, July 8, 1855, Ibid., Vol. 2, p. 311.

Live here then, you poor, miserable curses, until the time of retribution, when your heads will have to be severed from your bodies.
—Brigham Young, October 6, 1855, Ibid., Vol. 3, p. 50.

The time is coming when justice will be laid to the line and righteousness to the plummet; when we shall take the old broad sword and ask, "Are you for God?" and if you are not heartily on the Lord's side, you will be hewn down. I feel like reproving you; you are like a wild ass that rears and almost breaks his neck before he will be tamed. It is so with this people.
—Brigham Young, March 2, 1856, Ibid., Vol. 3, p. 226.

I say, that there are men and women that I would advise to go to the President immediately, and ask him to appoint a committee to attend to their ease; and then let a place be selected, and let that committee shed their blood.

We have those amongst us that are full of all manner of abominations, those who need to have their blood shed, for water will not do, their sins are of too deep a dye. . . .

We have been trying long enough with this people, and I go in for letting the sword of the Almighty be unsheathed, not only in word, but in deed. . . .

Brethren and sisters, we want you to repent and forsake your sins. And you who have committed sins that cannot be forgiven through baptism, let your blood be shed, and let the smoke ascend, that the incense thereof may come up before God as an atonement for your sins, and that the sinners in Zion may be afraid.
—J.M. Grant, September 21, 1856, Ibid., Vol. 4, pp. 49–51.

I know, when you hear my brethren telling about cutting people off from the earth, that you consider it is strong doctrine; but it is to save them, not to destroy them. . . .

I do know that there are sins committed, of such a nature that if the people did understand the doctrine of salvation, they would tremble because of their situation. And furthermore,

I know that there are transgressors, who, if they knew themselves, and the only condition upon which they can obtain forgiveness, would beg of their brethren to shed their blood, that the smoke thereof might ascend to God as an offering to appease the wrath that is kindled against them, and that the law might have its course. I will say further; I have had men come to me and offer their lives to atone for their sins.

It is true that the blood of the Son of God was shed for sins through the fall and those committed by men, yet men can commit sins which it can never remit. As it was in ancient days, so it is in our day; and though the principles are taught publicly from this stand, still the people do not understand them; yet the law is precisely the same. There are sins that can be atoned for by an offering upon an altar, as in ancient days; and there are sins that the blood of a lamb, of a calf, or of turtle doves, cannot remit, but they must be atoned for by the blood of the man. That is the reason why men talk to you as they do from this stand; they understand the doctrine and throw out a few words about it. You have been taught that doctrine, but you do not understand it.

—Brigham Young, September 21, 1856, Ibid., Vol. 4, pp. 53–54.

All mankind love themselves, and let these principles be known by an individual, and he would be glad to have his blood shed. That would be loving themselves, even unto an eternal exaltation. Will you love your brothers or sisters likewise, when they have committed a sin that cannot be atoned for without the sheding of their blood? Will you love that man or woman well enough to shed their blood?

. . . I have known a great many men who have left this Church for whom there is no chance whatever for exaltation, but if their blood had been spilled, it would have been better for them. The wickedness and ignorance of the nations forbid this principle's being in full force, but the time will come when the law of God will be in full force.

This is loving our neighbour as ourselves; if he needs help, help him; and if he wants salvation and it is necessary to spill his blood on the earth in order that he may be saved, spill it. Any of you who understand the principles of eternity, if you have sinned a sin requiring the shedding of blood, except the sin unto death, would not be satisfied nor rest until your blood should be spilled, that you might gain that salvation you desire. That is the way to love mankind.

—Brigham Young, February 8, 1857, Ibid., Vol. 4, pp. 219–220.

I wish that all such characters were in hell, where they belong. [Voice: "They are there."] I know it; and it is that which makes them wiggle so the poor, miserable devils. They would make our Father and God a drudge—make him do the dirty work, kill those poor devils, and every poor, rotten-hearted curse in our midst. With them it is, "O Lord, kill them, kill them, damn them, kill them, Lord." It is just like that, and their course has just as much nonsense in it. We intend to kill the poor curses ourselves.

—Heber C. Kimball, August 2, 1857, Ibid., Vol. 5, p. 135.

I have not a doubt but there will be hundreds who will leave us and go away to our enemies. I wish they would go this fall: it might relieve us from much trouble; for if men turn traitors to God and His servants, their blood will surely be shed, or else they will be damned, and that too according to their covenants.

—Heber C. Kimball, August 16, 1857, Ibid., Vol. 4, p. 375.

If our enemies will behave, themselves, all right; and if they do not, they may take what follows. We could have used up those now in our borders, and have taken their trains; but we do not wish to hurt one of them: but let them undertake to come in here, and they must abide the consequences. And in reality, instead of their speaking against my character, they ought to send in presents for having lived till now.

—Brigham Young, October 7, 1857, Ibid., Vol. 5, p. 333.

Aftermath of Mountain Meadows

The Mountain Meadows Massacre cover-up by Mormon leaders was—and still is—extensive. Civil justice never was served except upon one man, John D. Lee, twenty years later, under great pressure from a

When we undertake to cover our sins, or to gratify our pride, our vain ambition, or to exercise control or dominion or compulsion upon the souls of the children of men, in any degree of unrighteousness, behold, the heavens withdraw themselves: the Spirit of the Lord is grieved; and when it is withdrawn, Amen to the priesthood or the authority of that man.
—*Doctrine and Covenants* 121:37

watchful, irate nation. It took thirteen years for the Church to act on the massacre, at which time they excommunicated John D. Lee and Isaac C. Haight.

Mormons often claim that Brigham had no input or knowledge of an intended massacre beforehand. I have no intent to delve into that claim. It is Brigham's follow-up which I find so telling.

In answer to the urgent message sent from the Southern Utah Mormons, asking Brigham Young for direction in dealing with the Arkansas wagon train, Brigham sent a quick response. He reportedly told the rider: "Go with all speed, spare no horse-flesh. The emigrants must not be meddled with, if it takes all Iron County to prevent it. They must go free and unmolested."[181]

It is reasonable to assume that Brigham would have retained some interest in the outcome of this situation which he perceived as so urgent. As the "Lion of the Lord," he was known to rule with an iron hand. In the eyes of most Utah residents, he wore the mantle of a prophet and commanded considerable respect from his worshipful followers. The fact that the Southern Utah leaders sent a message asking for his input in this situation speaks of their respect for his leadership. It seems doubtful that these leaders would have notified Brigham then made their plans without anticipating his support.

At least three people testified of speaking with Brigham Young about the massacre shortly after it took place. One of these witnesses, Jacob Hamblin, testified in court that soon after the massacre he had informed Brigham Young and George A. Smith of the Mormon involvement.[182] Hamblin, a faithful Mormon and missionary to the Indians, lived in the remote Mountain Meadows area. His home, just a few miles from the massacre site, was where the newly orphaned children were taken immediately following the massacre. Hamblin, not home at the time, had gone to Salt Lake City to marry a polygamous wife, but his connections with the Indians and the Mormons left him well informed on the event. Even more significant, his adopted Indian son had witnessed the massacre.

John D. Lee claimed to have reported the massacre to Brigham toward the end of September, a few weeks after the massacre. This claim is backed up by Wilford Woodruff's journal entry, which talks of Lee telling Brigham on September 29, 1857. Woodruff also mentioned young children who were spared.[183] So Brigham Young, who was Utah Governor and Superintendent of Indian Affairs, knew of the surviving children from the massacre, yet he did nothing to report them or return them to relatives. It was two years before they were reunited with friends or relatives, credit going to Jacob Forney, sent by the U.S. Government in response to the rumors of surviving children of the massacre. The orphans went penniless, with nothing of the substantial wealth that should have been theirs.

Brigham's private reactions differed from his public reaction. Consider this account from Wilford Woodruff's Journal, May 25, 1861, not quite four years after the massacre. (Woodruff was an apostle who later became the prophet.)

> 25 A vary Cold morning. Much Ice on the Creek. I wore my great Coat & mittens. We visited the Mountain Meadow Monument put up at the burial place of 120 persons killed by Indians in 1857. The pile of stone was about 12 feet high, but begining to tumble down. A wooden Cross was placed on top with the following words: Vengence is mine and I will repay saith the Lord. President Young said it should be Vengence is mine and I have taken a little.[184]

Once again, Woodruff's journal says Indians were guilty of the massacre, even four years after the fact; denial was apparently becoming a habit. Furthermore, Indians were never brought to justice, so on whom had God taken vengeance? Rumors had the emigrants guilty of killing Indians and stealing from and threatening Mormons. Brigham seems to be saying the emigrants had received their just due.

John D. Lee faithfully kept a journal. Five days after the above mentioned visit to the Mountain Meadows monument, Lee's diary entry, [30] May 1861, reports Brigham at the monument as saying: "Vengeance is Mine Saith the Lord, & I have taken a little of it." He also records Brigham as saying that any who betray their brethren's involvement in the massacre will be damned.[185]

More than six years after the massacre, Brigham Young said from the pulpit:

Nearly all of that company were destroyed by the Indians. That unfortunate affair has been laid to the charge of the whites. A certain judge that was then in this Territory wanted the whole army to accompany him to Iron county to try the whites for the murder of that company of emigrants. I told Governor Cumming that if he would take an unprejudiced judge into the district where that horrid affair occurred, I would pledge myself that every man in the regions round about should be forthcoming when called for, to be condemned or acquitted as an impartial, unprejudiced judge and jury should decide; and I pledged him that the court should be protected from any violence or hindrance in the prosecution of the laws; and if any were guilty of the blood of those who suffered in the Mountain Meadow massacre, let them suffer the penalty of the law; but to this day they have not touched the matter, for fear the Mormons would be acquitted from the charge of having any hand in it, and our enemies would thus be deprived of a favorite topic to talk about, when urging hostility against us. "The Mountain Meadow massacre! Only think of the Mountain Meadow massacre!!" is their cry from one end of the land to the other.
—Brigham Young, March 8, 1863, *Journal of Discourses*, Vol. 10, p. 109–110.

Eighteen years after the massacre, on July 30, 1875, Brigham signed an affidavit, which was used in the second and final Lee trial. Therein, he claimed to have known nothing of the massacre until some time after it occurred, and then only by floating rumor.[186]

Following God's Chosen Leaders

I want the Gentiles to understand that we know all about their whoredoms and other abominations here. If we have not invariably killed such corrupt scoundrels, those who will seek to corrupt and pollute our community, I swear to you that we mean to, and to accomplish more in a few hours, towards clearing the atmosphere, than all your grand and traverse juries can in a year.
—J.M. Grant, March 2, 1856, *Journal of Discourses*, Vol. 3, pp. 234–235

Research into the Mountain Meadows Massacre led me to a host of new discoveries, starting with a book written by R. N. Baskin, *Reminiscences of Early Utah*, 1914.

Baskin spent time as the chief justice of the Supreme Court of Utah and as the mayor of Salt Lake City. As an attorney he was involved with a number of murder cases in early Utah history. He actively fought against polygamy and was initially disliked by many Mormons. Later, he was acknowledged by some as an honest man. In 1902, Heber J. Grant, a Church leader and later prophet, said: "Robert N. Baskin, one of the supreme court judges . . . is not the only honest, straight-forward man who was once very much opposed to the Latter-day Saints, who today takes pleasure in bearing testimony as to the honor and integrity of the Mormon people."[187] Baskin confessed the good amongst the Mormons, but his praise of them may not have been as flattering as Grant reported.[188] Still, Grant was pleased with Baskin's remarks and called him an "honest, straight-forward man."

I first read a photocopy of Baskin's book. I later found and purchased an original, wanting to remove any chance of fraud in the making of the copy. His was the first book I read that raised substantial suspicions concerning Brigham Young. Baskin quoted extensively (and accurately) from Brigham's sermons and gave testimony that Brigham and his followers had made good on some of their unsaintly threats found in the *Journal of Discourses*.

Baskin came to Salt Lake City in 1865 as an attorney. In just over two years he became prosecutor for two unsuccessful cases involving charges against faithful Mormons for destruction of property and for murder. Baskin gave this account of one of his clients, a Gentile, Doctor Robinson:

> Dr. Robinson was assassinated on October 22, 1866. At that time there were no public or private hospitals in Salt Lake City. He decided to build one, and began by erecting in the vicinity of the Warm Springs, upon unoccupied land situated a considerable distance beyond any habitation of the city, a small frame house to be used as a workshop in the construction of the hospital. Shortly after the workshop was finished a police force tore it down and warned the doctor that it would not be healthy for him to renew his operations there. The doctor subsequently came to my office, and after stating what had occurred, announced that he contemplated bringing suit to recover damages for the destruction of his property and enjoining further interference by the police. He also stated that another attorney whom he had consulted refused to institute a suit because he feared it would subject him, the attorney, to personal violence. Some of his friends had warned him that he would incur great personal hazard by bringing suit.
>
> I replied that the attorney and his friends certainly must be very timid, for I did not believe it possible anywhere in the United States that a citizen would jeopardize his life by applying to the courts of his country for an adjudication of his rights in any case; that while in view of what he had stated I would not advise him to bring suit, if he decided to do so, I would not hesitate to act as his attorney. Shortly afterward he requested me to proceed in the matter, which I did.
>
> A few weeks after the suit was instituted he was called from his bed at midnight by some unknown person, who stated that an acquaintance of the doctor had been severely injured by being thrown from a mule, and that his services were immediately required. Disregarding the dissuasion of his wife, he proceeded with the unknown person, and upon reaching a point near where the Walker dry goods store is

now situated, at the corner of Main and Third South streets, he was brutally murdered. At the inquest held it appeared that seven persons were seen running from the place at the time the crime was committed. The suit instituted was never finally tried, and not having been revived, was abated by the death of the doctor.

Some circumstances antecedent to this murder are significant. A short time before, a crowd of men armed with axes broke the windows, doors, and fixtures of a building belonging to him, and destroyed a bowling alley situated therein. He procured a warrant for the arrest of the chief of police and other members of the police force on the charge of having maliciously destroyed this property, and they were bound over to answer to that charge. Two days before the doctor's assassination he called upon Mayor Wells, who was one of Brigham Young's counselors, and requested him to interpose and restrain the police force. In place of granting that natural and reasonable request, the mayor grossly insulted the doctor and ordered him out of the house.

Doctor Robinson was an educated gentleman of courteous manners and affable disposition. His deportment was in every respect exemplary. He was superintendent of the first Gentile Sunday school in Salt Lake City: was a skillful physician and surgeon: had an extensive practice, and it was generally known that his attendance could always be obtained by anyone, even when compensation was out of the question. He was charitable, and humane motives alone induced him to begin erecting a hospital. He was exceptionally popular, had no known enemy, nor quarrel with anyone except the city authorities. He had done nothing, so far as known, calculated to subject him to any hostility except that of occupying the land before mentioned, which was against the settled policy of Brigham Young respecting the acquisition of property in Utah by Gentiles. That policy will be fully elucidated herein further on.

As at least seven persons were participants in the murder of Dr. Robinson, it is evident that they had previously met and deliberately agreed upon the manner in which it was to be accomplished. It is anomalous, in view of the circumstances

disclosed, that seven or more persons living in a civilized community should conspire to murder such an estimable man as Doctor Robinson.
—R.N. Baskin, *Reminiscences of Early Utah*, pp. 13–14.

B. H. Roberts, a Mormon historian and leader, explains the trouble that Mormons had with Gentile land-jumpers during the latter half of 1866. He conjectures that the intent was to give Doctor Robinson a beating for land-jumping, but that in the struggle, the doctor recognized some of his assailants, so they killed him to insure they were not identified.[189]

In another of Baskin's early cases, in which he was the prosecuting attorney, ten men were charged with murdering two men in Coalville, Utah in blood atonement fashion. (The throat of one was slit from ear to ear.) The chief witness, a third man who had escaped the attack, later disappeared without a trace before the grand jury could convene.[190] Baskin would soon, with little success, tackle bigger cases.

A number of Mormons in those years had formidable reputations. The best known of these is the

> We would not kill a man, of course, unless we killed him to save him.
> —Jedediah M. Grant, *Deseret News*, July 27, 1854

storied Orrin Porter Rockwell. Another was the one-time chief of police, Hosea Stout, whose journal plays an important part in understanding the violence of the day. These men were alleged to be members of the Danite band, a group feared by Gentiles in early Utah. The Danites were a band of avengers established during the Saints' Missouri years. "The organization had been for the purpose of plundering and murdering the enemies of the Saints."[191] Some Mormons claim that Joseph Smith knew nothing of Danite activities, citing B. H. Roberts: "They do not exist, however, and never have existed in the church with the sanction and authority of that church; nor with the knowledge and approval of the responsible officers of the church."[192] The following quotes coming from Joseph Smith and Brigham Young do not corroborate these claims of unawareness.

July 27th [1838] . . . Thus far, according to the order /rev-elation/ of the Danites. We have a company of Danites in these times, to put to right physically that which is not right, and to clense the Church of every [very?] great evil[s?] which has hitherto existed among us inasmuch as they cannot be put to right by teachings and persuasyons. This company or a part of them exhibited on the fourth day of July [-] They come up to consecrate, by companies of tens, commanded by their captain over ten[.]

—*An American Prophet's Record The Diaries and Journals of Joseph Smith*, Edited by Scott H. Faulring, p. 198. (Also see *Brigham Young University Studies*, Winter 1988, p. 14.)

If men come here and do not behave themselves, they will not only find the Danites, whom they talk so much about, biting the horses' heels, but the scoundrels will find something biting their heels. In my plain remarks, I merely call things by their right names. Brother Kimball is noted in the States for calling things by their right names, and you will excuse me if I do the same.

—Brigham Young, July 5, 1857, *Journal of Discourses*, Vol. 5, p. 6.

Have we been disloyal to our country? Have we, in one instance, violated her laws? No. Have we rejected her institutions? No. We are lawful and loyal citizens of the government of the United States, and a few poor, miserable, pusilanimous, rotten, stinking rebels, come here and threaten us with the armies of the United States.
—J.M. Grant, March 2, 1856, *Journal of Discourses*, Vol. 3, p. 235

Bill Hickman was another alleged Danite with a murderous rep-utation. (Neither Chris nor I was familiar with his name, nor were we familiar with the term "Danite," until 1998.) Hickman was close to Brigham Young for many years; his faithfulness to the Church was testified to in part by his having ten wives and thirty-five children. Along with doing Brigham's bidding, he spent time as a school teacher, sheriff, county assessor, tax collector, prosecuting attorney, Utah territorial legis-lative representative, and as a deputy U.S. marshal.[193]

One evening in 1871, Baskin was approached by Samuel Gilson in behalf of Bill Hickman. Hickman, hiding from both the United States marshal and from his former Danite associates, wanted Baskin as his attorney. Baskin reports:

I most positively refused to become Hickman's attorney. Mr. Gilson then stated that Hickman had expressed a desire to make a confession, and that even if I did not accept the offer of employment, that if I would agree to meet him he thought Hickman was in such a state of mind that he would tell me what he knew regarding the numerous murders which had been committed in the Territory. As I was desirous of ascertaining whether such an organization as the Danites or "Destroying Angels"—which was so much talked about and feared, especially by apostate Mormons—actually existed, and as Hickman—if it did exist—would know, I consented to meet him and instructed Mr. Gilson to inform him of that fact. In a short time afterward Mr. Gilson returned to my office and said that Hickman was ready to meet me if I would promise not to have him arrested. This I promised. Hickman, about eleven o'clock at night, in company with Mr. Gilson, came to my office. I had never seen Hickman before. After we had been formally introduced by Gilson, I stated to Hickman what Gilson had told me respecting his inclination to tell what he knew about the matters before mentioned. He hesitated, and I said to him that if, as generally asserted, he was or had been a member of such an organization, and had participated in the numerous murders which had been committed in the territory, that the only atonement now within his power was to reveal the facts, as it might aid in preventing the commission of other like crimes. After deliberating for about a minute, he said that during his seclusion his mind had been greatly disturbed by the matter, and that he had finally concluded to reveal the facts to me, although in doing so he would acknowledge his own guilt. Procuring a pad and pencil I took down all that he said and also cross-examined him closely. We were together several hours. At that meeting he revealed most of the numerous crimes contained in his published confession, but in more minute detail. I told him that I wanted him to meet me again and repeat his statements. This he consented to do. Within two or three weeks thereafter I met him a second time and, as before, took down what he said and cross-examined him. My purpose in doing this was to test the truth of his confession, because if not true, his several statements would in all probability be inconsistent. At various times when I had leisure I critically examined and compared the statements, and while in the second one he mentioned two cases of murder which he had omitted in the first one, and in the second added some details which were not contained in the first, I failed to detect any contradictory statement. The statements of other persons made to me tended to corroborate his confessions. Having become satisfied that Hickman told me the truth, and at my request he having consented to go before the grand jury and tell what he had revealed to me, I placed the statements which I had so written in the hands of Major Hempstead, who was the United States district attorney, and informed him that Hickman was ready to go before the grand jury and testify to the matters therein set forth.

—R.N. Baskin, *Reminiscences of Early Utah*, pp. 36–37.

Hempstead resigned, apparently fearful of retaliation for prosecuting Brigham Young and his band of Danites. Baskin was offered the vacant position of District Attorney. He had no desire for the position, but he took it. Again, he failed in his efforts to prosecute.[194]

As one of Brigham's "meanest devils," Hickman's own account of one of his murders in the spring of 1854 is telling. The following narrative is found in a book written by Hickman in which he admitted to his part in some of the murders in Utah. The account was reproduced in Baskin's book. Baskin claimed that this account matched the one given to him by Hickman.[195]

This Hartley was a young lawyer who had come to Salt Lake from Oregon the fall before, and had married a Miss Bullock, of Provo, a respectable lady of a good family. But word had come to Salt Lake (so said, I never knew whether it did or not), that he had been engaged in some counterfeiting affair. He was a fine-looking, intelligent young man. He told me he had never worked any in his life, and was going to Fort Bridger or Green River to see if he could not get a job of clerking, or something that he could do. But previous to this, at the April Conference, Brigham Young, before the congregation, gave him a tremendous blowing up, calling him all sorts of bad names, and saying he ought to have his throat cut, which made him feel very bad. He declared he was not guilty of the charges.

I saw Orson Hyde looking very sour at him, and after he had been in camp an hour or two, Hyde told me that he had orders from Brigham Young, if he came to Fort Supply to have him used up. "Now," said he, "I want you and George Boyd to do it." I saw him, and Boyd talking together; then Boyd came to me and said: "It's all right, Bill; I will help you to kill that fellow." One of our teams was two or three miles behind, and Orson Hyde wished me to go back and see if anything had happened to it. Boyd saddled his horse to go with me, but Hartley stepped up and said he would go if Boyd would let him have his horse. Orson Hyde said: "Let him have your horse," which Boyd did. Orson Hyde then whispered to me: "Now is your time; don't let him come back." We started, and about half a mile on had to cross the Cañon stream, which was midsides to our horses. While crossing, Hartley got a shot and fell dead in the creek. His horse took fright and ran back to camp.

I went on and met Hosea Stout, who told me the team was coming close by. I turned back, Stout with me, for our camp. Stout asked me if I had seen that fellow, meaning Hartley. I told him he had come to our camp, and he said from what he had heard he ought to be killed. I then told him all that had happened, and he said that was good. When I returned to camp Boyd told me that his horse came into camp with blood on the saddle, and he and some of the boys took it to the creek and washed it off. Orson Hyde told me that was

well done; that he and some others had gone on the side of
the mountain, and seen the whole performance. We hitched
up and went to Weber River that day. When supper was over,
Orson Hyde called all the camp together, and said he wanted a
strong guard on that night, for that fellow that had come to us
in the forenoon had left the company; he was a bad man, and
it was his opinion that he intended stealing horses that night.
This was about as good a take-off as he could get up, it was
all nonsense; it would do well enough to tell; as everyone that
did not know what had happened believed it.
—Bill Hickman, *Brigham's Destroying Angel*, pp. 97–100

Some Mormon defenders dismiss Hickman's book, which covers
a number of murders in which he participated, as a creation of
the editor J. H. Beadle. Others accept the evidence that it was
Hickman's own story and raise the possibility that he was stretching
the truth to get back at Brigham Young.[196] At the least, there remains
little doubt of Hickman's part in the heinous acts to which he confessed to the court and to Baskin. Hickman's reputation was well
known, so one must wonder why he found safe harbor—for so
many years—amongst the elite of the Church.[197]
Baskin had more to say of Hartley's murder.

In the early days of my experience in Utah, I frequently had
cases which required me to go to the city of Provo, and when
attending court there I lodged at Mr. Bullock's hotel. Having
heard of the murder of Hartley, and that his wife was a sister
of Mr. Bullock, I asked him on one occasion, while stopping
at his hotel, whether what I had heard respecting the murder
of Hartley was true. He stated that Hartley had incurred the
displeasure of Brigham Young, who at a public meeting had
used strong language against Hartley, and had ordered him
to leave the speakers stand; that on account of the charges
made by Brigham, which Bullock said were not true, Hartley
was put under the ban of the church, and decided to change
his residence. He joined the company of Judge Appleby, and
while leaving the Territory was murdered by Hickman. I

asked Mr. Bullock if the matter had ever been investigated by the executive authorities, and he said it had not been, although it was generally known that Hickman had committed the crime. I also asked him why he had not instituted proceedings against Hickman. He shook his head significantly and replied, "Don't press me for an answer to that question."
—R.N. Baskin, *Reminiscences of Early Utah*, p. 153

Here is the account of Hartley's wife, as reported by Mormon apostate Etta V. Smith.

I married Jesse Hartley, knowing he was a Gentile in fact, though he passed for a Mormon; but that made no difference with me, because he was a noble man, and sought only the right. By being my husband he was brought into closer contact with the heads of the Church, and thus was soon enabled to learn of many things he did not approve, and of which I was ignorant, though brought up among the Saints, and which if known to the Gentiles, would have greatly damaged us. I do not understand all he discovered or all he did; but they found he had written against the Church, and he was cut off, and the Prophet required as an atonement for his sins, that he should lay down his life; that he should be sacrificed in the endowment rooms, where such atonement is made. This I never knew until my husband told me; but it is true. They kill those there who have committed sins too great to be atoned for in any other way. The Prophet says if they submit to this, he can save them; otherwise they are lost. Oh! that is horrible. But my husband refused to be sacrificed, and so set out alone for the United States, thinking there might be at least a hope of success. I told him when he left me, and left his child, that he would be killed; and so he was.

William Hickman and another Danite shot him in the Cañons; and I have often since been obliged to cook for this man, when he passed this way, knowing all the while he had killed my husband. My child soon followed its father, and I hope to die also; for why should I live? They have brought

me here, where I wish to remain rather than to return to Salt Lake, where the murderers of my husband curse the earth, and roll in affluence unpunished.
—Etta V. Smith, *Fifteen Years Residence with the Mormons*, pp. 309–310

Some early Mormons claimed that blood atonement had to be voluntary and must be done by someone authorized.[198] Apparently, an uncooperative Hartley passed up the opportunity to volunteer.

There has never been a moment when this people have been destitute of the guidance of the Lord, and of the revelations and counsel necessary to enable them to carry out the mind and will of the Lord.
—President Geo. Q. Cannon, October 29, 1882, *Journal of Discourses*, Vol. 23, p. 357

The following account is given by J. H. Beadle, the editor to Hickman's book:

Of all the cowardly and cold-blooded acts which have made the Mormon Priesthood infamous, this wholesale murder of the Aikin party stands pre-eminent. Second to that of Mountain Meadow only in extent, it even excels it in wanton cruelty, treachery, and violation of every principle of hospitality, that virtue held sacred even by marauding Arabs or wild Indians, by all savages except Mormon fanatics. Fourteen years had the blood of these victims cried from the ground before the whole truth was known, and now, with the establishment of national power in Utah, a cloud of witnesses rise, and every incident in the tragedy is fully proved. From the evidence before the grand Jury and in possession of the officers, I condense the history of the Aikin party, and their treacherous murder. The party consisted of six men: John Aikin, William Aikin, ——Buck, a man known as "Colonel." and two others whose names the witnesses do not remember. They included a blacksmith, a carpenter, one or two traders, and others whose business was unknown, but they were supposed to be "sporting men." They left Sacramento early in May, 1857, going eastward to meet Johnston's army, as was supposed. On reaching the Humboldt

River they found the Indians very bad, and waited for a train of the Mormons from Carson, who were ordered home about that time. With them they completed the journey, John Pendleton, one of that Mormon party, in his testimony on the case says: "A better lot of boys I never saw. They were kind, polite, and brave; always ready to do anything needed on the road."

The train traveled slowly, so the Aikin-party left it a hundred miles out and came ahead, and on reaching Kaysville, twenty-five miles north of Salt Lake City, they were all arrested on the charge of being spies for the Government! A few days after Pendleton and party arrived and recognized their horses in the public Corral. On inquiry he was told the men had been arrested as spies, to which he replied, "Spies, h—ll! Why, they've come with us all the way—know nothing about the Army." The party in charge answered that they "did not care, they would keep them." The Aikin party had stock, property, and money estimated at $25,000.

They were then taken to the city and confined in a house at the corner of Main and First South Streets. Nothing being proved against them they were told they should be "sent out of the Territory by the Southern route." Four of them started, leaving Buck and one of the unknown men in the city. The party had for an escort, O. P. Rockwell, John Lot, ——Miles, and one other. When they reached Nephi, one hundred miles south. Rockwell informed the Bishop, Bryant, that his orders were to "have the men used up here." Bishop Bryant called a council at once, and the following men were selected to assist: J. Bigier (now a Bishop.) P. Pitchforth, his "first councillor," John Kink, and ——Pickton.

The doomed men were stopping at T. B. Foote's, and some persons in the family afterwards testified to having heard the council that condemned them. The selected murderers, at 11 p. m, started from the Tithing House and got ahead of the Aikins', who did not start till daylight. The latter reached the Sevier River, when   informed them they could find no other camp that day; they halted, when the other party approached and asked to camp with them, for which permission was granted. The weary men removed their arms and heavy clothing, and were soon lost in sleep—that sleep which for two of them was to have no waking on earth. All seemed fit for their damnable purpose, and yet the murderers hesitated. As near as can be determined, they still feared that all could not be done with perfect secrecy, and determined to use no firearms. With this view the escort and the party from Nephi attacked the sleeping men with clubs and the king-bolts of the wagons. Two died without a struggle. But John Aiken bounded to his feet, but slightly wounded, and sprang into the brush. A shot from the pistol of John Kink laid him senseless. "Colonel" also reached the brush, receiving a shot in the shoulder from Port, and believing the whole party had been attacked by banditti, he made his way back to Nephi. With almost superhuman strength he held out during the twenty-five miles, and the first bright rays of a Utah sun showed the man, who twenty-four hours before had left them handsome and vigorous in the pride of manhood, now ghastly pale and drenched with his own blood, staggering feebly along the streets of Nephi. He reached Bishop Foote's, and his story elicited a well-feigned horror.

Meanwhile the murderers had gathered up the other three and thrown them into the river, supposing all to be dead. But John Aiken revived and crawled out on the same side, and hiding in the brush, heard these terrible words:

"Are the damned Gentiles all dead, Port?"

"All but one—the son of a b— ran."

Supposing himself to be meant, Aikin lay still till the Danites left, then, without hat, coat, or boots, on a November night, the ground covered with snow, he set out for Nephi. Who can imagine the feelings of the man? Unlike "Colonel" he knew too well who the murderers were, and believed himself the only survivor. To return to Nephi offered but slight hope, but it was the only hope, and incredible as it may appear he reached it next day. He sank helpless at the door of the first house he reached, but the words he heard infused new life into him. The woman, afterwards a witness, said to him, "Why, another of you ones got away from the robbers, and is at Brother Foote's."

"Thank God; it is my brother," he said, and started on. The citizens tell with wonder that he ran the whole distance, his hair clotted with blood, reeling like a drunken man all the way. It was not his brother, but "Colonel." The meeting of the two at Foote's was too affecting for language to describe. They fell upon each other's necks, clasped their blood-spattered arms around each other, and with mingled tears and sobs kissed and embraced as only men can who together have passed through death. A demon might have shed tears at the sight—but not a Mormon Bishop. The fierce tiger can be lured from his prey, the bear may become civilized, or the hyena be tamed of his lust for human flesh—religious fanaticism alone can triumph over all tenderness, and make man tenfold more the child of hell than the worst passions of mere physical nature. Even while gazing upon this scene, the implacables were deciding upon their death.

Bishop Bryant came, extracted the balls, dressed the wounds, and advised the men to return, as soon as they were able, to Salt Lake City. A son of Bishop Foote had proved their best friend, and Aikin requested him to take his account in writing of the affair. Aiken began to write it, but was unmanned, and begged young Foote to do it, which he did. That writing, the dying declaration of "Colonel" and John Aiken, is in existence to-day.

The murderers had returned, and a new plan was concocted. "Colonel" had saved his pistol and Aiken his watch, a gold one, worth at least $250. When ready to leave they asked the bill, and were informed it was $30. They promised to send it from the city, and were told that "would not do." Aiken then said, "Here is my watch and my partner's pistol—take your choice." Foote took the pistol. When he handed it to him, Aikin said; "There, take my best friend. But God knows it will do us no good." Then to his partner, with tears streaming from his eyes, "Prepare for death, Colonel, we will never get out of this valley alive."

According to the main witness, a woman of Nephi, all re-
garded them as doomed. They had got four miles on the road,
when their driver, a Mormon named Wollf, stopped the wagon
near an old cabin; informed them he must water his horses;
unhitched them, and moved away. Two men then stepped
from the cabin, and fired with double-barreled guns; Aikin
and "Colonel" were both shot through the head, and fell dead
from the wagon. Their bodies were then loaded with stone
and put in one of those "bottomless springs"—so called—
common in that part of Utah.

I passed the place in 1869, and heard from a native the
whispered rumors about "some bad men that were sunk in
that spring." The scenery would seem to shut out all idea of
crime, and irresistibly awaken thoughts of heaven. The soft
air of Utah is around; above the blue sky smiles as if it were
impossible there could be such things as sin or crime; and the
neat village of Nephi brightens the plain, as innocently fair as
if it had not witnessed a crime as black and dastardly as ever
disgraced the annals of the civilized world.

Meanwhile Rockwell and party had reached the city, taken
Buck and the other man, and started southward, plying them
with liquor. It is probable that Buck only feigned drunkenness;
but the other man was insensible by the time they reached the
Point of the Mountain. There it was decided to "use them up,"
and they were attacked with slung-shots and billies. The other
man was instantly killed. Buck leaped from the wagon, outran
his pursuers, their shots missing him, swam the Jordan, and
came down it on the west side. He reached the city and related
all that occurred, which created quite a stir. Hickman was then
sent for to "finish the job," which he did, as related in the text.

The last of the Aikin party lies in an unmarked grave—
even with Hickman's directions it cannot now be found—and
for fourteen years their murderers have gone unpunished. The
man most guilty is accounted a hero, and even now It appears
that justice may be defeated through the mere indifference of
Government.

—*Brigham's Destroying Angel*, by Bill Hickman, pp. 206–
210.

"During the Blackhawk War in April 1866, the local militia committed a massacre at Circleville, Piute County, Utah. After capturing a group of Piede Indians, Mormon militiamen shot the hand-tied men, then slit the throats of their women and children one by one. Of this incident second counselor [to Brigham Young] and commanding general Daniel H. Wells wrote that these 'brethren' did what was necessary." —D. Michael Quinn, *The Mormon Hierarchy: Origins of Power*, p. 256.

We are a people of peace. We only desire to be let alone to accomplish our mission in peace. God would not permit us to build temples, any more than He permitted David, if we imbrued our hands in blood.
—Bishop Orson F. Whitney, April 19, 1885, *Journal of Discourses*, Vol. 26, p. 203

Another account has the braves being shot while trying to escape. In an effort to keep the deed hidden, the women and children were then killed. One by one, they were brought up from the cellar and their throats were slit. This small group of Piedes, from a nearby village, had no recent history of aggression against the Mormons. They had been friendly and traded freely with the Circleville residents. The accusation against them was of passing information to the tribes at war with the Mormons. (—Albert Winkler, "The Circleville Massacre: A Brutal Incident in Utah's Black Hawk War," *Utah Historical Quarterly* 55, Winter 1987)

As with the Mountain Meadows Massacre, the Mormon need to preserve a saintly image to the world required a brutal silencing of the women and children who could not possibly have been deserving of death.

On December 10, 1858, a Gentile newspaper, Kirk Anderson's *Valley Tan*, raised this question: "What has become of that deaf and dumb boy that used to be around the streets. He has been missing now for two or three weeks. We have heard it rumored that

Do you think it would be any sin to kill me if I were to break my covenants? . . . Do you believe you would kill me if I broke the covenants of God, and you had the Spirit of God? Yes; and the more Spirit of God I had, the more I should strive to save your soul by spilling your blood, when you had committed sin that could not be remitted by baptism.
—Jedediah M. Grant, *Deseret News*, July 27, 1854

he had 'gone under.' Do any of the police know anything about
him? We ask for information."

The next issue of *Valley Tan*, December 17, reported that the boy
had been murdered. The newspaper claims to have received these
two letters:

Mr. Kirk Anderson:
   You inquire in your last paper, the [where]abouts of the
"deaf and dumb boy." That your impertinant inquires may be
satisfied and we hear no more about the matter; I will inform
you that he has been permanently and decently planted, about
one and a half miles north east of your office; in a place called
a Cemetery—where, if you desire, you can find him.
   It was necessary for his salvation, that his existence on
earth should be abreviated, and consequently his sudden transition from this to a better world.
   Having said this much, I would advise you, that it is not
proper that you, hereafter notice such matters in your paper. It
is one of the rights guaranteed to us by the Constitution of our
Government; "to worship God according to the dictates of our
own consciences;" with which right, it is to be hoped you will
not again attempt to meddle.
   I hope you will take the hint, it certainly will be to your
advantage. You see our paper the "Deseret News," does not
make itself objectionable by heralding such things.

Kirk Anderson, Esq:
   Sir:—I have not the pleasure of your acquaintance, but I
am very glad to see the course pursued by you in your paper;
I think it will be approved of by many of our Church members
at least by all those who are opposed to many acts of violence
that are done under a pretended right and color of our faith.
I never did and never can believe in the doctrine that it was
right to take a persons life, for the purpose of saving him; yet
many of my brothers differ with me on this—they think that
when there is danger of Apostatizing they should by a *premature transition* from this world be secured the happiness of
a better one.

You inquire in your paper of last week about the deaf and dumb boy. For your information I will say that he was killed about three or four weeks ago about twelve miles east of here, in the Kanyon on the road to Bridger, and near the house of Ephraim Hanks. The person who killed him, is a Policeman of this City, his name is ----------. The boy was shot through the arm, and also had a second shot through the breast, that not killing him his throat was cut. I am glad to see you notice these things, it may have a tendency to prevent such actions in future.

Not being much in the habit of putting my thoughts on paper, you will look over my disconnected kind of writing, and especially excuse my bad spelling. I thought it was right to let you know that some of us approved of your paper, and thought it my duty to answer your inquiry.

On December 22, the *Valley Tan* gave a fairly detailed account of the testimony of various witnesses. (This particular issue is not on microfilm in the BYU Lee Library. It can be found in the Utah Historical Society Library in Salt Lake City.) On November 9 or 10, the police arrested the seventeen-year-old deaf and dumb boy, Andrew Bernard, for stealing. Four days later, his mother inquired of the police about her son and was told that he had escaped. About two weeks later the mother was informed by John Sharp that a policeman, N.L. Christiansen, had killed her son. In the trial, Christiansen claimed self-defense. The boy's throat had been slit; he had been buried without trial or notification of relatives. When the policeman was acquitted, the Gentiles of the city were furious.

Wells received a subpoena from U. S. Court, while the Judge was sitting as committing Magistrate, though the Court was in Session, to attend as a witness in case of the death of a deaf and dumb man named Bernard,(17) said to be killed by a policeman, who was attacked by the 'dummy', and stabbed. Pres[iden]t Wells knew nothing of the affair, but he was sub-poenaed to annoy him and with an intent to implicate the authorities of the church:

—Brigham Young Office Journals—Excerpts, 1853–62
[December 15, 1858:] Dec. 15, p. 16. (New Mormon Studies
CD-ROM, Smith Research Associates)

[January, 1859]4th I Called at the office at 9 oclok. I attended the Legislature and during the day the Grand Jury
decided that Christiansen was not guilty & wrote on the in-
ditement Ignored. The Deseret Agricultural Board of Directors
met at the House of Brother Winder. S. M. Blair was present.
He was so overjoyed that Christiansen was liberated that He
was filled with excitement. He hollowed shouted horaw for
Israel. He was so excited all the evening that we Could [do]
no business. He said that He had suffered so much through the
trial as that Court had tried to make Brigham Young Daniel H
Wells A O Smoot & many others accessory to the death of
Andrew Burnard Called Dimmy who attempted to kill
Christianson who was on duty as a policeman & Christianson
killed him in self defence. 9 of the Jury was against
Christianson & 12 for Clearing him. Two of the Jury that was
for Condemning him viz David H. B[eck?] & G W. Bayliss
insulted Blair & Blair drove them both out of the street.

Captain Tyler & Mr Tabbott Came in the Council. Capt
Tylor said in the Globe that they were going to send over
24 Commissioned officers of the Armey & Hold a Court
Marshall in this City & hang Just who they pleased. Govornor
Cummings had to meet with the mad Gentiles to keep them
quiet. Many of them were mad because Christion[son] was
Cleared. Their was quite a sensation through the City.
—Wilford Woodruff's Journal, Vol. 5, p. 270–271

It would be difficult for a Mormon jury to convict Christianson
for killing the boy while Brigham Young was preaching death to the
thief.

If you will cause all those whom you know to be thieves,
to be placed in a line before the mouth of one of our largest
cannon, well loaded with chain shot, I will prove by my works

---

whether I can mete out justice to such persons, or not. I would consider it just as much my duty to do that, as to baptize a man for the remission of his sins.
—Brigham Young, May 8, 1853, *Journal of Discourses*, Vol. 1, p. 109.

Soon after leaving the Church I learned of and read excerpts of John D Lee's confessions. They include mention of a gruesome incident in Sanpete

If I am not a good man, I have no just right in this Church to a wife or wives, or to the power to propagate my species. What, then should be done with me? Make a eunuch of me, and stop my propagation.
—Heber C. Kimball, July 12, 1857, *Journal of Discourses*, Vol. 5, p. 29

County. A young man, Thomas Lewis, was castrated in a meeting for supposedly failing to yield his sweetheart to become a polygamous wife to Bishop Warren Snow.[199] I questioned Lee's bizarre account but soon found additional references to such an act in Sanpete County.[200] Another castration was mentioned in the journal of Hosea Stout, a faithful Mormon.[201] I found references within the speeches and journals of Church leaders, advocating emasculation.[202]

My former reverence for early Utah Mormons was based upon wonderful stories of loyalty, courage, sacrifice, generosity, and compassion. Because I still appreciate the noble efforts made by so many early Saints, my discovery of their dark side has given me a new perspective of humanity. As I reassess Nazi Germany, the Taliban, Islam, Christianity, the Ku Klux Klan, and a host of small cults and large mainstream religions, I now see people who consider themselves the chosen ones. I do not see inherently evil people so much as I see leaders and followers who are committed, for the most part and in their myopic way, to their view of a better world, at least for those whom they judge worthy. Commitment to an illusion—made unwittingly or for perceived personal security—can generate blind brotherhoods, fanatic societies, and gross misunderstandings. The results are too often uncivil and even horrific acts in the name of God and virtue.

Endnotes

Chapter 2 notes

[1] Ezra Taft Benson, "Fourteen Fundamentals in Following the Prophets," BYU devotional assembly, February 26, 1980.

[2] Mormons are taught never to question the reliability of the prophet. Consider the following teachings: "The Lord will never allow the president of the Church to teach us false doctrine." (*Gospel Principles*, 1985, Chapter 9, p. 46); "The Lord will never permit me or any other man who stands as President of this Church to lead you astray. It is not in the programme." (*Doctrine and Covenants* Official Declaration–1)

In the Church publication, *Improvement Era*, p. 354, June 1945, we find the following:

> This sort of game is Satan's favorite pastime, and he has practiced it on believing souls since Adam. He wins a great victory when he can get members of the Church to speak against their leaders and to "do their own thinking." . . . When our leaders speak, the thinking has been done. When they propose a plan--it is God's Plan. When they point the way, there is no other which is safe. When they give direction, it should mark the end of controversy, God works in no other way.

[3] A patriarchal blessing is usually given to a person some time in his/her teenage years. The blessing is given by a patriarch, a man who has been called and set apart to that position. The patriarchal blessing "includes an inspired and prophetic statement of the life

possibilities and mission of the recipient." —Elder Richard D. Allred, *Ensign,* November, 1997.

[4] Though missionaries are referred to as elders, in fact, virtually all faithful men in the Church are either elders or high priests and are organized into quorums, the leader of which is called the elders quorum president or the high priest group leader. They meet weekly for an hour in a quorum meeting in which they take care of quorum business and are instructed in gospel principles.

[5] *Teachings of Presidents of the Church: Brigham Young*, p. 81. This manual was in use by the adults in the Church in 1998.

Chapter 3 notes

[6] Once France had been beaten in the North by Ho Chi Minh's forces, a treaty was signed. France pulled out, leaving Vietnam split; Ho Chi Minh's communist government ruled in the North, and the non-communist government, set up by the French, continued in the South. The treaty required free elections in the South within two years. After the French left, a second war began. This battle started within South Vietnam between those who supported Ho Chi Minh (the apparent majority) and those who supported Ngo Dinh Diem, the French-appointed leader of the South. The elections, which had been guaranteed by the treaty, were cancelled.

PBS aired an award-winning series called *Vietnam: A Television History*. The text is available at:

http://www.pbs.org/wgbh/pages/amex/vietnam/index.html.

[7] Consider Mormon Apostle Mark E. Peterson's view about the black man, expressed to a group of religion teachers at BYU in 1954.

He is not just seeking the opportunity of sitting down in a cafe where white people eat. He isn't just trying to ride on the same streetcar or the same Pullman car with white people. It isn't that he just desires to go to the same theater as the white people. From this, and other interviews I have read, it appears that the Negro seeks absorption with the white race. He will not be satisfied until he achieves it by intermarriage. That is his objective and we must face it. We must not allow our feelings to carry us away, nor must we feel so sorry for Negroes that we will open our arms and embrace them with everything we have. Remember the little statement that we used to say about sin, 'First we pity, then endure, then embrace'. . . .

I think the Lord segregated the Negro and who is man to change that segregation?

—*Compilation On the Negro In Mormonism*, compiled by Lester Bush, 1970, pp. 260–261. Also see Mary Lythgoe Bradford, *Lowell L. Bennion*, by pp. 131–132, and the website: http://www.xmission.com/~plporter/lds/disavow.htm.

Though I found the call number, BX 8643.622.P445r, at Special Collections in the Lee Library, the staff were unable to locate a copy of Peterson's remarks, "Race Problems — As They Affect The Church, Convention of Teachers of Religion on the College Level," Brigham Young University, Provo, Utah, August 27, 1954.

The most outspoken Mormon apostle on the Civil Rights Movement was Ezra Taft Benson. Although not all Mormon leaders shared his views, he was a prominent and influential leader who later became the prophet and president of the Church from 1985 to 1994. He claimed that the communists were using the "so-called civil rights movement" to promote revolution and eventual takeover of America. (Official Report of the 137th Semiannual General of the Church of Jesus Christ of Latter-day Saints, Oct. 1967., p. 35.)

Benson spoke out strongly in support of the John Birch Society. The following memorandum reveals this aspect of the environment in which I grew up. The memo was sent to all Utah chapters of the John Birch Society in September 1965, signed by Reed Benson, son of Ezra Taft Benson and an officer in the Birch Society.

It is common knowledge that the Civil Rights Movement is Communist controlled, influenced and dominated. . . . Our founder and guide, Mr. Robert Welch, has instructed us that when necessary we must adopt the communist technique in our ever present battle against Godless Communism. It is urged that in the coming weeks the Utah Chapters begin a whispering campaign and foster rumors that the Civil Rights

groups are going to organize demonstrations in Salt Lake City in connection with the forthcoming LDS conference. . . . A few well placed comments will soon mushroom out of control and before the conference begins there will be such a feeling of unrest and distrust that the populace will hardly know who to believe. The news media will play it to the very hilt. No matter what the Civil Rights leaders may try to say to deny it the seed will have been sown and again the Civil Rights movement will suffer a telling blow.
—Michael Quinn, *The Mormon Hierarchy: Extensions of Power*, p. 84.

(Also, see the remarks of Quinn McKay in, *Political Extremism: Under the Spotlight*, edited by J. Kenneth Davies, pp. 20–21.)
[8] The following Internet site presents material on the Civil Rights Movement.
http://www.useekufind.com/peace/links.htm

Chapter 4 notes

[9] Similarities between the Mormon temple ceremony and the Masonic ceremony are significant. The explanation given for the resemblance is that the Masonic ritual was a relic from the temple ceremony in ancient Israel, so the resemblance is to be expected. On March 15, 1842, Joseph Smith became a Mason (*History of the Church*, vol. 4, p. 551), and a few weeks later, on May 4, 1842, he introduced the full temple endowment (*History of the Church*, vol. 5, pg. 2). This endowment had many similarities with the Masonic initiation ceremony. In recent years, the blood oaths and several other similarities with the Masonic rituals have been removed from the temple ceremony.

[10] The first vision occurred in 1820, according to the account currently recognized by the Church, written in 1838. In about 1832 Joseph Smith had given a handwritten account—sometimes referred to as the "strange account"—of the first vision, which differs in key points from the current story. There are several other early versions of the first vision, written by those friendly to the Church, which also differ from the 1838 account in key points. Confusion about the first vision is discussed more in Chapter 10.

¹¹ The Kinderhook plates were "discovered" in Kinderhook, Illinois, and shown to Joseph Smith. The *Encyclopedia of Mormonism* says:

> The Kinderhook plates created a stir in Nauvoo; articles appeared in the Church press, an illustrated handbill was published, and some Latter-day Saints even claimed Joseph Smith said he could and would translate them. No translation exists, however, nor does any further comment from him indicating that he considered the plates genuine. . . . There thus appears no reason to accept the Kinderhook plates as anything but a frontier hoax.

Scientific tests have convincingly shown that the Kinderhook plates are indeed a hoax as the *Encyclopedia of Mormonism* states. However, the above quotation implies that Joseph never considered the plates to be genuine. The *Encyclopedia* fails to mention Joseph Smith's account, which contains diagrams of the plates. Joseph wrote the following:

> I insert fac-similes of the six brass plates found near Kinderhook, in Pike county, Illinois, on April 23, by Mr. Robert Wiley and others, while excavating a large mound. They found a skeleton about six feet from the surface of the earth, which must have stood nine feet high. The plates were found on the breast of the skeleton and were covered on both sides with ancient characters.
>
> I have translated a portion of them, and find they contain the history of the person with whom they were found. He was a descendant of Ham, through the loins of Pharaoh, king of Egypt, and that he received his kingdom from the Ruler of heaven and earth.
> —*History of the Church*, Vol. 5, p. 372.

See websites;
http://www.mindspring.com/~engineer_my_dna/mormon/indekind.htm
http://www.xmission.com/~country/reason/kinder.htm

¹² Mark Hofmann was a dealer in historical documents in the 1980s, but many of his "finds" were actually forgeries. He was perhaps the most successful forger ever caught—many experts and even the FBI were fooled by his work. The Mormon Church was evidently his favorite customer. His practice was to create a forgery, then leak news of his "discovery"—invariably, the contents would be an embarrassment to the Church. The Church would then pay well for the documents under the condition of confidentiality, and store them in the First Presidency's vault (which reportedly contained other documents that were unflattering to the Church). Among Hofmann's forgeries bought by the Church were the Anthon Transcript, the Blessing of Joseph Smith III, the Far West Letter, and the Stowell Letter.

His forged *Salamander Letter* was perhaps Hofmann's most famous document. It was one of the key elements in a complicated story of deceit and intrigue in which he killed two people with two bombs and seriously hurt himself with a third. Hofmann had met a number of times with some of the apostles, including the current prophet, Gordon B. Hinckley. Even after the two murders—but before anyone suspected Hofmann—Church leaders continued to press Hofmann to complete the McLellin Collection deal. (McLellin was one of the original twelve apostles of the Mormon Church who later apostatized. He supposedly had a significant collection of early Church documents. If this collection existed, it was another potential embarrassment for the Church.)

Although I knew very little of the case at the time, there were two inconsistencies I recognized but then promptly ignored. First, how could Church leaders be duped so many times into acquiring forged documents? As "prophets, seers and revelators," why didn't they receive inspiration about the forged documents or about Hofmann (whom they had met a number of times)? Second, the actions of some of the General Authorities seemed deceptive, including a statement by Hugh Pinnock who, speaking of Hofmann, told the police, "All we know is what we read in the papers." Pinnock had, in fact, met privately with Hofmann several times and had helped Hofmann secure a loan for $185,000 to buy the McLellin Collection.

Incidentally, Hofmann had lied about having access to the McLellin Collection. He had no idea of its whereabouts or even that it existed.

For more on this issue, see *A Gathering of Saints: A True Story of Money, Murder and Deceit*, by Robert Lindsey. Also see website: http://www.xmission.com/~country/reason/hof1.htm

[13] Heber C. Kimball, a polygamist in this life, apparently saw no limit to the number of wives he could have in the next life.

> In the spirit world there is an increase of males and females, there are millions of them, and if I am faithful all the time, and continue right along with brother Brigham, we will go to brother Joseph and say, "Here we are brother Joseph; we are here ourselves are we not, with none of the property we possessed in our probationary state, not even the rings on our fingers?" He will say to us, "Come along, my boys, we will give you a good suit of clothes. Where are your wives?" "They are back yonder; they would not follow us." "Never mind," says Joseph, "here are thousands, have all you want." Perhaps some do not believe that, but I am just simple enough to believe it.
> —Heber C. Kimball, *Journal of Discourses*, vol. 4, p. 209.

[14] Diary excerpts of Abraham H. Cannon, March 28, 1894.

[15] Concerning a man "having many wives and concubines," God revealed to Joseph Smith that those who rejected the principle would be damned. —*Doctrine and Covenants* 132:1–6.

Brigham Young taught, "Now if any of you will deny the plurality of wives, and continue to do so, I promise that you will be damned." —*Journal of Discourses*, Vol. 3, p. 266.

He also taught, "The only men who become Gods, even the Sons of God, are those who enter into polygamy." —*Journal of Discourses,* Vol. 11, p. 269.

[16] *Doctrines of Salvation*, Vol. 1, 1954, p. 188.

[17] N. Eldon Tanner, *Ensign,* August, 1979, pp. 2–3.

[18] *Doctrines of Salvation*, Vol. 1, 1954, p. 236.

[19] Ezra Taft Benson, *Conference Report*, April 1951, pp.48–49.

[20] As a boy attending General Priesthood Meeting, I heard the following statements from Elder Theodore M. Burton. Boys and men throughout the world heard this sermon, which was broadcast to Mormon churches worldwide.

According to the plan of salvation you were reserved or
held back in the heavens as special spirit children to be born
in a time and at a place where you could perform a special
mission in life. . . . God reserved for these days some of his
most valiant sons and daughters. He held back for our day
proved and trusted children, who he knew from their premortal behavior would hear the voice of the Shepherd and
would accept the gospel of Jesus Christ. He knew they would
qualify themselves to receive the priesthood, that they would
use the holy priesthood to limit Satan's destructiveness and
make it possible for God to complete the work he had planned
for the saving of his children.

You young men [boys from 12 to 18 years of age] of the
Aaronic Priesthood represent, therefore, some of the finest men
ever to be born on the earth. You are an elect generation, a royal
priesthood. . . .

This birthright is only possible for you because you have the
finest fathers and mothers ever given to any generation. . . .

Thus, you and your fathers were reserved to be born at a
time and in a place where you could not fail to hear the gospel
preached and accept the holy priesthood.

—Elder Theodore M. Burton, *Ensign*, May 1975, p. 69.

Joseph Fielding Smith—who became the tenth president of the
Church—gave this explanation for the plight of blacks in the 1950s.

There is a reason why one man is born black and with other
disadvantages, while another is born white with great advantages. The reason is that we once had an estate before we
came here, and were obedient, more or less, to the laws that
were given us there. Those who were faithful in all things
there received greater blessings here, and those who were not
faithful received less.

—*Doctrines of Salvation*, Vol. 1, 1954, p. 61.

There were no neutrals in the [premortal] war in heaven.
All took sides either with Christ or with Satan. Every man

had his agency there, and men receive rewards here [on this earth] based upon their actions there, just as they will receive rewards hereafter for deeds done in the body. The Negro, evidently, is receiving the reward he merits.
—Ibid., p. 66.

At the time of this statement, blacks could not hold the priesthood in the Mormon Church, neither could they participate in temple ordinances. That, evidently, is "the reward he merits" for not being as valiant in the premortal existence.

[21] *Book of Mormon*, 1 Nephi 14:10. The quotation in full:

Behold there are save two churches only; the one is the church of the Lamb of God, and the other is the church of the devil; wherefore, whoso belongeth not to the church of the Lamb of God belongeth to that great church, which is the mother of abominations; and she is the whore of all the earth.

[22] *Mormon Doctrine*, 1958 edition. The quotations in full:

It is also to the *Book of Mormon* to which we turn for the plainest description of the Catholic Church as the great and abominable church. Nephi saw this "church which is the most abominable above all other churches" in vision. He "saw the devil that he was the foundation of it" and also the murders, wealth, harlotry, persecutions, and evil desires that historically have been a part of this satanic organization.
—p. 130.

Then, speaking of harlots in the figurative sense, he [the angel] designated the Catholic Church as "the mother of Harlots" (1 Nephi 13:34, 14:15–17), a title which means that the Protestant churches, the harlot daughters which broke off from the great and abominable church, would themselves be apostate churches.
—p. 314.

[23] Joseph Smith History, 1:19. Joseph wasn't the only early Mormon prophet with unflattering views of other Christian churches. John Taylor, who became the third prophet of the Church, said of the Christianity of his day: "It is as corrupt as hell; and the Devil could not invent a better engine to spread his work than the Christianity of the nineteenth century." *Journal of Discourses*, Vol. 6, p. 167.

[24] *Gospel Principles*, 1985, p. 229.

[25] In 1995, the First Presidency and the Council of the Twelve Apostles of The Church of Jesus Christ of Latter-day Saints presented "*The Family: A Proclamation to the World.*" President Gordon B. Hinckley first read it to the General Relief Society on September 23, 1995. It included the following: "By divine design, fathers are to preside over their families in love and righteousness and are responsible to provide the necessities of life and protection for their families. Mothers are primarily responsible for the nurture of their children."

[26] *Gospel Principles*, 1985, p. 226.

[27] One example of a "lost prophecy" is the following statement by Joseph Fielding Smith on May 14, 1961. "We will never get a man into space. This earth is man's sphere and it was never intended that he should get away from it. The moon is a superior planet to the earth and it was never intended that man should go there. You can write it down in your books that this will never happen." A year later he requested that this be taught to the youth of the Church. Six months before Smith became the president of the Church, Neil Armstrong walked on the moon. (See D. Michael Quinn, *The Mormon Hierarchy: Extensions of Power*, p. 848.)

In both of these cases Smith had a relatively small audience; the Church at large was unaware of the "prophecy." If man had failed to reach the moon, I wonder if there is a Mormon who would not have been made aware of Smith's prophecy.

[28] Spencer W. Kimball, *The Miracle of Forgiveness*, 1969, p. 2.

[29] *Ensign*, May, 1997, "Converts and Young Men."

Chapter 5 notes

[30] John 6:68.

[31] The following quotation about the Adam-God relationship is one of many by Brigham Young and other Church leaders. The

italics and the unusual use of upper case letters in smaller font are as they appear in the *Journal of Discourses*.

> Now hear it, O inhabitants of the earth, Jew and Gentile, Saint and sinner! When our father Adam came into the garden of Eden, he came into it with a *celestial body*, and brought Eve, *one of his wives*, with him. He helped to make and organize this world. He is MICHAEL, *the Archangel*, the ANCIENT OF DAYS! about whom holy men have written and spoken—HE *is our* FATHER *and our* GOD, *and the only God with whom* WE *have to do*. Every man upon the earth, professing Christians or non-professing, must hear it, and *will know it sooner or later.*
> —Brigham Young, April 9, 1852, *Journal of Discourses*, Vol. 1, p. 50.

The following websites offer additional references. Or, one can search for *"Adam God Theory"* on the Internet.
http://www.xmission.com/~country/reason/adam_gd1.htm
http://www.mrm.org/multimedia/text/mcconkies-letter.html
[32] The following statement by the prophet would leave the impression, for the average Mormon, that Brigham Young did not really teach the Adam-God theory.

> We warn you against the dissemination of doctrines which are not according to the scriptures and which are alleged to have been taught by some of the General Authorities of past generations. Such for instance is the Adam-God theory. We denounce that theory and hope that everyone will be cautioned against this and other kinds of false doctrine.
> —Spencer W. Kimball, *Ensign*, Nov. 1976, p. 77.

[33] The doctrine of individual *blood atonement* says that murder, adultery, apostasy, and some other sins can be forgiven only if the person is slain in a manner that spills his or her blood. See Chapter Sixteen.
[34] Dunn related some fabricated experiences, as in pretending to have played baseball for the St. Louis Cardinals. He also told several miraculous, personal war stories that were not true. (For more

information and references, do an Internet search on *"elder paul h dunn"*.)

[35] On October 4, 1992, Gordon B. Hinckley spoke of the prophet Ezra T. Benson and said: "He has reached an age where he cannot do many of the things he once did. This does not detract from his calling as a prophet." (—LDS General Conference, Sunday morning session.)

In 1993 I heard a teacher in a priesthood lesson say: "I know that President Benson receives revelations daily." Doubtful of this assertion, I was more inclined to think that Hinckley and Monson could handle the minor revelations needed to run the Church.

[36] *The Salt Lake Tribune*, July 10, 1993, pp. E1, E3; Ibid., August 15, 1993, pp. C1,C2; *Ogden Standard Examiner*, July 13, 1993, p. 4B.

[37] "Documents Show Counselors Control LDS Assets," *The Salt Lake Tribune*, August 15, 1993, pp. C1, C2.

[38] "LDS Church apostle admits giving false information," *The Daily Herald* (Provo, Utah), October 12, 1993, page B3.

[39] The *Pearl of Great Price*, Abraham 2:22–25.

[40] I had heard, without confirmation, that apostles Talmage and Widtsoe believed in a local flood. But, the orthodox Mormon stance is found in the January 1998 *Ensign*, "The Flood and the Tower of Babel." This article justifies belief in the literal account given in the Bible.

[41] "Did you ever realize that previous to the deluge, no such covenant existed between man and his Creator, that the Antideluvians [antediluvians] never saw a rainbow in the heavens." —*Messenger and Advocate*, Vol. 3, No. 7, p. 485. (Also see Genesis 9:12–17.)

[42] Sometime around 1990, while reading in the book of *Alma*, a book within the *Book of Mormon*, I noticed that five of the prophets died (two were apparently taken up by God, similar to Moses) within a ninety-year period. This caught my attention because each succeeding prophet was a son of the previous prophet. From a first estimate, dividing by four (don't mistakenly divide by five), one would guess the difference in age to be about twenty-two or twenty-three years. The fifth prophet in this line may not have lived as long as the first prophet in this line so the conclusion is not reliable, but it sparked my curiosity. I made a detailed breakdown of all the prophets who had kept the records. With few exceptions it was from father to

son, or brother to brother. In all, I counted twenty-one men who kept the records. There were three pairs of brothers, giving us eighteen generations of record keepers over a span of roughly one thousand years. In three cases, the records were passed on to an apparently unrelated person. With other factors to consider, a hard conclusion would be premature, but an initial estimate would put the average age difference between father and son at more than fifty years. (I used those figures to ease my mind about being forty and unmarried.) The significant thing about this discovery is this: For some time I feared to delve into the details for fear of finding something questionable in the time-line or at least for fear of developing a questioning attitude toward the *Book of Mormon.* I was not eager for information that would shake my faith.

[43] Jerald and Sandra Tanner, an ex-Mormon husband-wife team, were dedicated to making the Church look bad, allegedly with their lies and twisted history—or so I believed. I didn't have to read their works to believe the worst about them; rumors were enough for me, as a faithful Mormon. They formed the Utah Lighthouse Ministry and have done considerable research and publishing of early Mormon history. (http://www.utlm.org)

The magazines *Sunstone* and *Dialogue: A Journal of Mormon Thought* are both publications for liberal-minded Mormons and scholars. Most of my Mormon circle considered these journals too open in their unflattering analysis of the Church. Neither Chris nor I had seen either publication before leaving the Church.

[44] Three men claimed an angel appeared to them, showing them the plates. Eight additional men attested that they had handled the plates. The statements and names of these eleven witnesses are available in the front of any *Book of Mormon.*

Chapter 6 notes
[45] "The Mantle Is Far, Far Greater than the Intellect," by Boyd K. Packer. See first endnote in Chapter 15.

[46] A good example of intolerance came from the lopsided debate raging in my community about a lesbian who was teaching in the high school. There was an unsuccessful effort to terminate her for a collection of reasons. One day in a Sunday school class where the issue was brought up, one man suggested tolerance. No one took

his side; rather, emotions flared, and his suggestion was soundly rejected. I felt bad that I had not supported the man encouraging tolerance, but being new in town, I knew few of the circumstances of the case. I used this as an excuse for my silence. Whatever the guilt—or innocence—of the lesbian teacher, I recognized full-blown irrationality in the emotions and logic of some of the excited Church members.

[47] Organic evolution has never been popular in the Church. Today, some Mormons claim that the official Church stand is neutral, while others claim the Church has made a stand against organic evolution. An Internet search on *Mormonism* and *evolution* should produce many examples. Or, see these Internet sites:

http://eyring.hplx.net/Eyring/faq/evolution/

http://www.etungate.com/Evolution.htm

[48] *Doctrine & Covenants*, Sec. 132 introduction.

[49] There is modern-day confusion over Emma's view of polygamy. Emma Smith ended up in a break-off church, which denied that Joseph ever practiced polygamy. Her sons, Joseph Smith's sons, were also apparently convinced that their father did not practice polygamy. They seemed to believe that his additional marriages were "spiritual marriages" and therefore of no consequence in this life.

[50] Todd Compton, *In Sacred Loneliness: The Plural Wives of Joseph Smith*, pp. 396–456.

[51] Ibid., Chapter 22.

[52] In a poem, Helen left evidence of the social burden she carried as a young teen after her secret marriage to Joseph Smith. Yet, in the end she resolves to do God's will, as revealed by the prophet.

I thought through this life my time will be my own
The step I now am taking's for eternity alone,
No one need be the wiser, through time I shall be free,
And as the past hath been the future still will be.
To my guileless heart all free from worldly care
And full of blissful hopes and youthful visions rare
The world seamed bright the thret'ning clouds were kept
From sight and all looked fair but pitying angels wept.
They saw my youthful friends grow shy and cold.
And poisonous darts from sland'rous tongues were hurled,

Untutor'd heart in thy gen'rous sacrafise,
Thou dids't not weight the cost nor know the bitter price;
Thy happy dreams all o'er thou'st doom'd alas to be
Bar'd out from social scenes by this thy destiny,
And o'er thy sad'nd mem'ries of sweet departed joys
Thy sicken'd heart will brood and imagine future woes,
And like a fetter'd bird with wild and longing heart,
Thou'lt dayly pine for freedom and murmur at thy lot;
But could'st thou see the future & view that glorious crown,
Awaiting you in Heaven you would not weep nor mourn.
Pure and exalted was thy father's aim, he saw
A glory in obeying this high celestial law,
For to thousands who've died without the light
I will bring eternal joy & make thy crown more bright.
I'd been taught to reveire the Prophet of God
And receive every word as the word of the Lord,
But should this not come through my dear father's mouth,
I should ne'r have received it as God's sacred truth.
—Ibid., pp. 499–501.

[53] Todd Compton, *In Sacred Loneliness: The Plural Wives of Joseph Smith*, Chapter 4.

[54] Ibid., p. 80–81.

[55] *Farms Review of Books*, 1998, Vol. 10, Num. 2, pp. 67–137.

[56] In 1987 and 1988, the following radio commercial ran on several Utah radio stations in dramatic fashion.

In 1949 [1946] California lawyer, Tom Ferguson, rolled up his sleeves, threw a shovel over his shoulder, and marched into the remote jungles of southern Mexico. Armed with a quote by Joseph Smith that the Lord had "a hand in proving the *Book of Mormon* true in the eyes of all the people," Ferguson's goal was: Shut the mouths of the critics who said such evidence did not exist. Ferguson began an odyssey that included twenty-four trips to Central America, eventually resulting in a mountain of evidence supporting *Book of Mormon* claims.
—Stan Larson, *Quest For The Gold Plates*, 1996, p. 3.

Ferguson had died several years before the commercial. Unbeknown to me and virtually all of the faithful Mormon community, claims that archaeology supported the *Book of Mormon* had already been thoroughly refuted—by Ferguson himself. On March 12, 1975, he completed and signed "Written Symposium on *Book of Mormon* Geography: Response of Thomas S. Ferguson to the Norman and Sorenson Papers." Not published in his lifetime, the document was published by the Tanners in 1988. I first read a copy of it in Stan Larson's book, *Quest for the Gold Plates.* He listed his source as the Thomas Stuart Ferguson Collection, Accession 1350, Manuscripts Division, J. Willard Marriott Library, University of Utah, Salt Lake City.

Apparently, few people knew of Ferguson's turnabout. Even his family remained unaware. Stan Larson's book tells Ferguson's story, that of a public figure who in the end struggled to hide his crumbling faith. We cannot know if his sudden death came before he had resolved his situation or his future course, but his private correspondence and writings are telling. Larson's well-documented book looks in depth at some of the *Book of Mormon* archaeological issues.

[57] Most Mormons believe that in A.D. 385, the Nephite nation fought their last great battle upon and around the hill Cumorah, located in Western New York, where they were completely destroyed. Less than one thousand years earlier, the Jaredite nation had destroyed themselves in the same land, using swords of steel. Because of the lack of modern-day evidence of such events, some Mormon scholars insist that there was another hill Cumorah where these events took place, suggesting Central America or Southern Mexico. Joseph Fielding Smith thoroughly discredits this claim of a hill Cumorah being in or near Central America, citing statements by Joseph Smith and other early Church leaders. (*Doctrines of Salvation*, Vol. 3, pp. 232–243.)

Joseph Smith gives this unusual account of a skeleton found near the Illinois River in June of 1834 during Zion's Camp march from Ohio to Missouri. His discussion extends the *Book of Mormon* civilization to North America.

The contemplation of the scenery around us produced peculiar sensations in our bosoms: and subsequently the visions of the past being opened to my understanding by the Spirit

of the Almighty, I discovered that the person whose skeleton was before us was a white Lamanite, a large, thick-set man, and a man of God. His name was Zelph. He was a warrior and chieftain under the great prophet Onandagus, who was known from the Hill Cumorah, or eastern sea to the Rocky Mountains. The curse was taken from Zelph, or, at least, in part—one of his thigh bones was broken by a stone flung from a sling, while in battle, years before his death. He was killed in battle by the arrow found among his ribs, during the last great struggle of the Lamanites and Nephites.
—Joseph Smith, *History of the Church*, Vol. 2, pp. 79–80. (Another reference is Joseph Fielding Smith, *Doctrines of Salvation*, Vol. 3, p. 238.)

[58] Joseph Fielding Smith, *Doctrines of Salvation*, Vol. 3, p. 239.

[59] John W. Welch, a FARMS scholar, addresses *View of the Hebrews* in "Finding Answers to B. H. Roberts's Questions and An Unparallel." Consider his rationale.

"These parallels, however, are neither as precise nor as significant as some have made them out to be. In fact, it will be shown that the *Book of Mormon* differs from VH [*View of the Hebrews*] far more than it resembles it, making it hard to believe that Joseph Smith relied on VH."

[60] *Teachings of Presidents of the Church: Joseph F. Smith*, p. 277—the Church's lesson manual for the year 2000.

[61] One of the many commendable aspects of the Church is the welfare program—the way in which the Church takes care of its own. There are welfare farms, canneries, storehouses, and more. Church members donate countless hours to the program.

[62] All faithful members of the Church, who have reasonable access to a temple, maintain a current "temple recommend" allowing them admission to Mormon temples. The recommends must be renewed yearly with appropriate signatures from two Church leaders, after each leader has verified the personal faith and worthiness of the member. Without this recommend, one cannot enter the temple to participate in some of the ordinances necessary for personal salvation and for the salvation of ancestors. Without such a recommend, you cannot attend a Mormon marriage ceremony for family or friends.

Chapter 7 notes

[63] Mary Elizabeth Rollins Lightner gave a speech at Brigham Young University in 1905, where she spoke of the principle of plural marriage. She said: "An angel came to him and the last time he came with a drawn sword in his hand and told Joseph if he did not go into that principle, he would slay him." After marrying Joseph, Mary continued to live with her nonmember husband. —"The Life and Testimony of Mary Lightner," Address at Brigham Young University, April 14, 1905.

[64] Free agency is defined as the right to make a choice. It is often touted in Mormonism as a gift that God would never take from us. This "do it or I will kill you" approach sounded exactly like the plan we once supposedly rejected in the big council in our pre-earth life.

Chapter 8 notes

[65] This is the letter from my niece in full.

Uncle Brad,

It is out of love for you as a member of my family that I write this letter. Recently, you have made a life altering decision to leave behind the beliefs you grew up with and a membership in the Church of Jesus Christ of Latter Day Saints. I must say this came as a surprise for me and many others in the _____ family. However, "love is not love that alters, when alteration finds" and everyone here loves and respects you.

When we love someone, we want to give them the knowledge or assets that will bring them joy. Nothing in life has brought me greater inner peace and joy than the gospel of Jesus Christ. So naturally I would hope to give this gospel to those close to my heart. This also means I would be concerned to see loved ones leave this opportunity that in my eyes is priceless. There are questions and thoughts I would want to put before them about this choice. Doing so not to prove my own correctness on the matter, but to make sure they had examined many aspects and made the decision that they would feel best about in the long run.

It is unclear to me why exactly you left the LDS church. I have heard it was influenced by mainly three things: mistakes in church history, thoughts found in "anti-Mormon" literature, and pressures or messages you received from members of the church. Whatever the reason, all three are based solely on the actions or thoughts of other people. As common as it is, I find it strange that you Brad, would base people and not God as your reason for abandoning a personal belief.

Perhaps I am wrong though. Upon choosing to leave the church did you pray to God? And if so, was the answer a feeling of peace and joy and confirmation, stronger than any you have ever felt? Did it outweigh all those feelings you received during a testimony meeting, your mission, a new convert's baptism, the temple, every priesthood blessing you have ever received or given, and the reality that God was listening as you prayed at night and your repentance on various occasions had been accepted? Did you pray with an earnest heart to know if you should leave a church you once swore to strangers was the only true gospel— And did that answer knock you to floor with such an incredible force of assurance that it erased all doubts or sick feelings you had over such a choice? If so, you have an answer I cannot contend with and by all means, stop reading now. If not, I have some other questions.

What glory is promised to you in leaving the church? Does any of the reading and study you have done mention amazing benefits you will receive from the world and other religions? How do these compare with those of your patriarchal blessing and covenants in the temple? As Moses said, you are a child of God and where is the glory in leaving the church? How does giving up the goal to become a perfect being, who lives eternally in a state of joy with those you love, seem glorified in any way?

This may seem a rather strong response from someone who is acting in love, but leaving the truths that are the framework of your soul has many aspects. I just want to you to read this and look in your heart for the answers.

When I look at your life, I see a man who has been given every blessing he could want from his Heavenly Father. You have found a loving wife (once your eternal companion), received a beautiful son, and business is going well. These seem to be a testament of how your prayers were heard. And yet, have you so easily forgotten?

All these years you have prayed to find the eternal companion the Lord has chosen for you. Others in your family have also spent time on their knees in your behalf. When this special daughter of God was found, how did you know? Probably the Spirit of the Holy Ghost gave you this realization that here was someone worthy to enter the temple, who also wanted to return to Father in Heaven, and raise a family in the gospel. But what now? All that waiting and prayer, was it for nothing and do you think that having Cathy in your life is not truly the result of a divine direction? What ties do you now have in this marriage? How will you both raise the children with opposing views? As Kaleb [Caleb] grows older what can he cling to for help in life? Will he be baptized in the LDS church and receive that priceless gift of the Holy Ghost? What exactly are your views on the Holy Ghost, or Jesus Christ or God the Eternal Father?

I thought decisions are supposed to bring clarity, however it seems that this particular choice seems to dig up many confusing and difficult questions. I could go on for pages about various scenarios you will soon face, or outlets of life and personal identity you have now lost. However, my sole purpose in this letter is to help you come to peace with yourself. 1st Corinthians 14:33, "For God is not the author of confusion, but of peace."

I have prayed to Heavenly Father and received not only a hope, but a knowledge that the path I have taken in life is right. My life has challenges, but I know that through my relationship with God I can overcome them all. I want everyone to have this gift, especially my family. This letter is a personal testament for you that I and many others love you and want to help you find joy. Heavenly Father also loves you and I know that He will show you the path to take if you ask Him.

Love _____

[66] Moroni 7:11.

Chapter 9 notes

[67] *Doctrines of Salvation*, Vol. 3, p. 309, 1956. The author, Joseph Fielding Smith, became the tenth president of the Church.

Chapter 10 notes

[68] *Time*, August 4, 1997, p. 56.

[69] Do an Internet search on the quote, or see website: http://www.irr.org/mit/.

[70] Richard N. Ostling and Joan K. Ostling, *Mormon America: The Power and the Promise*, pp. 421, 422. Also see website: http://www.irr.org/mit/hinckley.html.

[71] See *Gospel Principles*, 1985, pp. 6, 293, or the official Church website: www.lds.org/library/display/0,4945,11-1-13-1,00.html. The introduction of the manual states that the manual may be used for personal study, for family home evening lessons or Church meetings, or for talks in Church. The manual is often used to teach a Sunday School class for new members. The first chapter says, "God is a glorified and perfected man, a personage of flesh and bones." The last chapter quotes Joseph Smith as follows: "It is the first principle of the Gospel to know for a certainty the character of God . . . he was once a man like us . . . God himself, the Father of us all, dwelt on an earth, the same as Jesus Christ himself did."

[72] "The only men who become Gods, even the Sons of God, are those who enter into polygamy," *Journal of Discourses*, Vol. 11, p. 269, August 19, 1866.

[73] Ibid. Vol. 2, p. 236.

[74] *The Restored Church*, thirteenth edition, 1965, William E. Berrett, pp. 133, 134.

[75] Egyptology experts had long ago claimed that parts of facsimile 2 were incorrect. The rediscovered papyrus did not contain facsimile 2, but when Joseph Smith's *Egyptian Alphabet and Grammar* was published in 1966 it was seen to contain a drawing of facsimile 2. Much of the upper right part of the drawing had been left blank. Apparently, that part of the papyrus had been damaged; Joseph had filled it in so he could put a complete figure into the Book of Abraham. It was the filled-in portion that the experts had long deemed incorrect.

[76] Compiled by Bob Witte, published by Gospel Truths.

[77] Today, the Church teaches that in 1820, Joseph was visited by God the Father and Jesus Christ. In this *first vision*, Joseph asked which church he should join and learned from Jesus that all the churches were wrong. (Joseph Smith History 1:19) Brigham Young, John Taylor, and Wilford Woodruff were the second, third and fourth presidents of the Church. They all knew Joseph Smith personally and should have had an intimate knowledge of his first vision—the foundation of the Mormon Church. Yet they each taught that it was an angel, not God and Jesus, who appeared in the first vision.

The Lord did not come with the armies of heaven, in power and great glory, nor send His messengers panoplied with aught else than the truth of heaven, to communicate to the meek, the lowly, the youth of humble origin, the sincere en-quirer after the knowledge of God. But He did send His angel to this same obscure person, Joseph Smith jun.[sic], who af-terwards became a Prophet, Seer, and Revelator, and informed him that he should not join any of the religious sects of the day, for they were all wrong;
—Brigham Young, 1855, *Journal of Discourses*, Vol. 2, p. 171.

I had a visit from some of your folks during the session of the Legislature. How was it, and which was right? None of them was right, just as it was when the Prophet Joseph asked the angel which of the sects was right that he might join it. The answer was that none of them are right. What, none of them? No. We will not stop to argue that question; the angel merely told him to join none of them that none of them were right.
—John Taylor, 1879, Ibid., Vol. 20, p. 167.

That same organization and Gospel that Christ died for, and the Apostles spilled their blood to vindicate, is again established in this generation. How did it come? By the ministering of an holy angel from God, out of heaven, who held converse with man, and revealed unto him the darkness that enveloped the world. . . . The angel taught Joseph Smith those principles which are necessary for the salvation of the world. . . . He told

him the Gospel was not among men, and that there was not a true organization of His kingdom in the world. . . . Joseph was strengthened by the Spirit and power of God , and was enabled to listen to the teachings of the angel.
—Wilford Woodruff, 1855, Ibid., Vol. 2, pp. 196–197.

See website:
http://www.irr.org/mit/FVISION.HTML
[78] Ibid. Vol. 13, p. 324.

[79] Whereas the official version of the Joseph Smith story has Joseph seeing God and Jesus in 1820, Oliver's version has Joseph, in 1823, still unsure of the existence of a supreme being.

You will recollect that I mentioned the time of a religious excitement, in Palmyra and vicinity to have been in the 15th year of our Brother J. Smith Jr's, age that was an error in the type—it should have been in the 17th.— You will please remember this correction, as it will be necessary for the full understanding of what will follow in time. This would bring the date down to the year 1823.
. . . Our brother was urged forward and strengthened in the determination to know for himself of the certainty and reality of pure and holy religion.—And it is only necessary for me to say, that while this excitement continued, he continued to call upon the Lord in secret for a full manifestation of divine approbation, and for, to him, the all important information, if a Supreme being did exist, to have an assurance that he was accepted of him.
—Oliver Cowdery, *Times And Seasons*, Vol. 2, no. 4, p. 241, 1840.

Chapter 11 notes
[80] President Ezra Taft Benson, General conference, October 3, 1987. See *The Ensign*, November, 1987.
Joseph F. Smith, the sixth president of the Church, also taught: "This great American nation the Almighty raised up by the power of his omnipotent hand, that it might be possible in the latter days for the kingdom of God to be established in the earth." —Gospel Doctrine, 1977, p. 409.

[81] That Satan and his angels work harder to get Mormons is illustrated by the following analogy, which I heard several times as a youth.

A man is out hunting ducks with his dog. As some ducks fly overhead, he shoots two of them, and they fall into a lake. One of the ducks is dead; the other is wounded and trying to escape. Naturally, the hunter sends his dog to retrieve the wounded duck before it gets away. The dead duck will be retrieved later. So it is with life. Satan sends his angels first after the Mormons. Non-Mormons can always be retrieved later.

[82] Many Mormons have expressed the view that Monday Night Football was Satan's tool to keep Mormons from holding Family Home Evening on Monday evenings as designated by the Lord. President Hartman Rector, Jr. of the First Council of the Seventy was apparently disappointed that Satan (the *other* side) could so easily influence Mormons to compromise their Family Home Evenings.

Last fall the Lord announced through his prophet that the Church would hold family home evening on Monday nights. It is interesting that about the same time, the other side announced that there would be professional football games on Monday nights. You might be surprised to know how many families tried to work family home evenings in between half time of the football games. Of course it cannot be done. It appears the prophet's request required too great a sacrifice.
—*Ensign*, December 1971.

[83] *Roughing It*, p. 102.

[84] *Gospel Principles*, 1985, p. 153.

[85] *Teaching of the Presidents of the Church: Brigham Young*, 1997, pp. 80–82. These were teachings of Brigham Young from long ago, but the introduction to the manual states that Brigham's "words are still fresh and appropriate for us today."

Chapter 12 notes
[86] *Teaching of the Presidents of the Church: Brigham Young*, p. 79, 1997.

[87] *Church Handbook of Instructions*, Book 1, p. 67, 1998.

Chapter 13 notes
[88] The personal stories of a number of Mormon apostates are found on the Internet. Some stories show bitterness; others show relief with no hard feelings. Some ex-Mormons suffer terrible losses in family relationships; others "escape" with their family intact. Some are unreasonable in their criticisms; others are logical and careful in their analysis. Some are well written and utterly fascinating. All the accounts have something to offer. See:
    http://exmormon.org
[89] *Doctrine and Covenants* 84:80.
[90] "Edward B. Clark, medical director of Primary Children's Medical Center, told the group's news conference Monday that he was troubled by the rate of homicides and suicides among youth, particularly males ages 15 to 19. 'Our community's suicide rate is much higher than the national average, more than three times greater,' Clark said." "Report shows Utah kids healthier, safer," *The Daily Herald*, Provo, Utah, 1/14/98.
[91] This statement is attributed to Albert Schweitzer on numerous Internet sites, but no original source could be found.
[92] *Doctrine and Covenants* 104:17.

Chapter 14 notes
[93] See: http://www.lds.org/media2/library/display/0,6021,198-1-168-16,FF.html, or do an Internet search on "revelation church president wilford woodruff declared."
[94] Todd Compton's *In Sacred Loneliness: The Plural Wives of Joseph Smith* cites evidence that Joseph married thirty-three women. FARMS scholars Richard L. Anderson and Scott H. Faulring accept only twenty-nine of the marriages cited by Compton. In Appendix 6 of his book, *The Mormon Hierarchy: Origins of Power*, Michael Quinn names forty-six women whom Joseph married.
[95] Michael Quinn, *The Mormon Hierarchy: Origins of Power*, p. 607.
[96] Ibid., Appendix 6.
[97] "It would please me to see good men and women have families; I would like to have righteous men take more wives and

raise up holy children. . . . Now if any of you will deny the plurality of wives, and continue to do so, I promise that you will be damned." —Brigham Young, *Journal of Discourses*, Vol. 3, p. 265, 266, 1855.

"Some people have supposed that the doctrine of plural marriage was a sort of superfluity, or non-essential to the salvation or exaltation of mankind. In other words, some of the Saints have said, and believe, that a man with one wife, sealed to him by the authority of the Priesthood for time and eternity, will receive an exaltation as great and glorious, if he is faithful, as he possible could with more than one. I want here to enter my solemn protest against this idea, for I know it is false." —Joseph F. Smith, *Journal of Discourses,* Vol. 20, p. 28, July 7, 1878.

[98] Jedediah M. Grant, Ibid., Vol. 1, p. 346, August 7, 1853; Orson Hyde, Ibid., Vol. 2, p. 82, October 6, 1854.

[99] As mentioned in Chapter 9, it is a fundamental Church doctrine that God was once a man and man may become a god. This tenet has been taught since the time of Joseph Smith. Hinckley denied this doctrine on more than one occasion. The Sunday, April 13, 1997, edition of *The San Francisco Chronicle*, reported an interview with President Hinckley that included the following exchange.

Q: There are some significant differences in your beliefs. For instance, don't Mormons believe that God was once a man?

A: I wouldn't say that. There was a little couplet coined, "As man is, God once was. As God is, man may become." Now that's more of a couplet than anything else. That gets into some pretty deep theology that we don't know very much about.

Q: So you're saying the church is still struggling to understand this?

A: Well, as God is, man may become. We believe in eternal progression. Very strongly. We believe that the glory of God is intelligence and whatever principle of intelligence we attain unto in this life, it will rise with us in the Resurrection.

Knowledge, learning, is an eternal thing. And for that reason, we stress education. We're trying to do all we can to make of our people the ablest, best, brightest people that we can.

[100] *Church Handbook of Instructions*, Book 1, p. 72, 1998.
[101] Doctrine and Covenants 132:1–6.
[102] *Journal of Discourses*, Vol. 12, p. 269.
[103] *Discourses of Brigham Young*, p. 193.
[104] *Journal of Discourses,* Vol. 13, p. 271.
[105] Ibid., Vol. 1, p. 219.
[106] Ibid., Vol. 10, p. 110.
[107] Ibid., Vol. 7, pp. 290–291.
[108] Ibid., Vol. 22, p. 304.
[109] Ibid., Vol. 2, pp. 142,143.
[110] Ibid., Vol. 3, p. 247.
[111] Ibid., Vol. 4, pp. 55–57.
[112] "When a sister will be called to a Church position, it may be desirable to confer with her husband first." —Church Handbook of Instructions, 1998, Book 1, p. 36.
[113] *Instructions for the Discussions*, p. 2 and *Instructions for the Stake Missionaries,* p. 2.

Chapter 15 notes
[114] "The Mantle Is Far, Far Greater Than The Intellect," by Boyd K. Packer, was a talk given at the Fifth Annual Church Educational System Religious Educators' Symposium, 22 August, 1981, Brigham Young University, Provo, Utah. Source: Brigham Young University Studies, Summer 1981.
[115] The Mountain Meadows Massacre was the infamous slaughter of approximately 120 men, women, and children in Southern Utah by Mormons and Indians. It is discussed in Chapter 16.
[116] "The Mantle Is Far, Far Greater Than the Intellect," by Boyd K. Packer.
[117] The following prophecies by Joseph Smith are difficult to justify:

And now I am prepared to say by the authority of Jesus Christ, that not many years shall pass away before the United States

shall present such a scene of bloodshed as has not a parallel in the history of our nation; pestilence, hail, famine, and earthquake will sweep the wicked of this generation from off the face of the land, to open and prepare the way for the return of the lost tribes of Israel from the north country. The people of the Lord, those who have complied with the requirements of the new covenant, have already commenced gathering together to Zion, which is in the state of Missouri, therefore I declare unto you the warning which the Lord has commanded to declare unto this generation, remembering that the eyes of my Maker are upon me and that to him I am accountable for every word I say wishing nothing worse to my fellow-men than their eternal salvation; therefore, "Fear God, and give glory to Him, for the hour of His judgment is come." Repent ye, repent ye, and embrace the everlasting covenant, and flee to Zion, before the overflowing scourge overtake you, for there are those now living upon the earth whose eyes shall not be closed in death until they see all these things, which I have spoken, fulfilled. Remember these things; call upon the Lord while He is near, and seek Him while He may be found, is the exhortation of your unworthy servant. [Signed] JOSEPH SMITH, JUN.
—*History of the Church*, Vol. 1, pp 315–316, January 14, 1833.

It was the will of God that those who went to Zion, with a determination to lay down their lives, if necessary, should be ordained to the ministry, and go forth to prune the vineyard for the last time, or the coming of the Lord, which was nigh— even fifty-six years should wind up the scene.
—Ibid., Vol. 2, p. 182, February 14, 1835.

Yea, the word of the Lord concerning his church, established in the last days for the restoration of his people, as he has spoken by the mouth of his prophets, and for the gathering of his saints to stand upon Mount Zion, which shall be the city of New Jerusalem.

Which city shall be built, beginning at the temple lot, which is appointed by the finger of the Lord, in the western boundaries of the State of Missouri, and dedicated by the hand of Joseph Smith, Jun., and others with whom the Lord was well pleased.

Verily this is the word of the Lord, that the city New Jerusalem shall be built by the gathering of the saints, beginning at this place, even the place of the temple, which temple shall be reared in this generation.

For verily this generation shall not all pass away until an house shall be built unto the Lord, and a cloud shall rest upon it, which cloud shall be even the glory of the Lord, which shall fill the house.

... which house shall be built unto the Lord in this generation, upon the consecrated spot as I have appointed
—*Doctrine and Covenants* 84: 2–5,31, September 22, 23, 1832. (This temple is still not built in the year 2003.)

Zion shall not be moved out of her place, notwithstanding her children are scattered.

They that remain, and are pure in heart, shall return, and come to their inheritances, they and their children, with songs of everlasting joy, to build up the waste places of Zion—

And all these things that the prophets might be fulfilled.

And, behold, there is none other place appointed than that which I have appointed; neither shall there be any other place appointed than that which I have appointed, for the work of the gathering of my saints—
—*Doctrine and Covenants* 101: 17–20, December 16, 1833 (Joseph Smith was speaking of Missouri. "They that remain . . . and their children," ended up settling in Utah.)

I prophesy in the name of the Lord God of Israel, unless the United States redress the wrongs committed upon the Saints in the state of Missouri and punish the crimes committed by her officers that in a few years the government will be utterly overthrown and wasted.
—*History of the Church*, Vol. 5, p. 394, May 18, 1843. (The wrongs were not redressed.)

I prophesy, in the name of the Lord God of Israel, anguish and wrath and tribulation and the withdrawing of the Spirit of God

from the earth await this generation, until they are visited with utter desolation.
—Ibid., vol. 6, p. 58, Oct 15, 1843.

I prophesied at the table that 5 years would not roll round before the company would all be able to live without cooking.
—*An American Prophet's Record: The diaries and Journals of Joseph Smith*, Edited by Scott Faulring, p. 445, February 6, 1844.

Revelation given through Joseph Smith the Prophet, at Salem, Massachusetts, August 6, 1836. HC 2: 465–466. At this time the leaders of the Church were heavily in debt due to their labors in the ministry. Hearing that a large amount of money would be available to them in Salem, the Prophet, Sidney Rigdon, Hyrum Smith, and Oliver Cowdery traveled there from Kirtland, Ohio, to investigate this claim, along with preaching the gospel. The brethren transacted several items of church business and did some preaching. When it became apparent that no money was to be forthcoming, they returned to Kirtland. Several of the factors prominent in the background are reflected in the wording of this revelation.
[—*Doctrine and Covenants* 111: Introduction]
I have much treasure in this city for you, for the benefit of Zion, and many people in this city, whom I will gather out in due time for the benefit of Zion, through your instrumentality.
Therefore, it is expedient that you should form acquaintance with men in this city, as you shall be led, and as it shall be given you.
And it shall come to pass in due time that I will give this city into your hands, that you shall have power over it, insomuch that they shall not discover your secret parts; and its wealth pertaining to gold and silver shall be yours.
Concern not yourselves about your debts, for I will give you power to pay them.
—*Doctrine and Covenants* 111: 2–5, August 6, 1836 (The debts were not paid and Joseph and others had to flee Kirtland to avoid prosecution when his illegal bank failed.)

¹¹⁸ A number of books detail Joseph Smith's deceptive polygamous practices. Three books with which I am familiar are *Mormon Enigma: Emma Hale Smith* by Linda King Newell and Valene Tippetts Avery, *In Sacred Loneliness: The Plural Wives of Joseph Smith* by Todd Compton, and *Mormon Polygamy: A History* by Richard S. Van Wagoner.

¹¹⁹ The Kinderhook plates are discussed in the notes in Chapter 4.

¹²⁰ Lucy Smith, Joseph's mother, told of Josiah Stoal employing Joseph to find a silver mine. "He came for Joseph on account of having heard that he possessed certain keys, by which he could discern things invisible to the natural eye." (Lucy Mack Smith, *Biographical Sketches of Joseph Smith The Prophet, And His Progenitors for Many Generations*, 1853 edition, pp. 91–92.) Though she reported that Joseph tried to talk Josiah out of hunting for treasures, Joseph ended up hiring on anyway. The use of a seer stone in pretending to discern the location of treasures was illegal in many states, including New York. Over the years, the claims persisted that Joseph had been arrested and found guilty for his activities with Josiah Stoal and others. Court documents were quoted, and testimony was given by friendly defense witnesses stating Joseph did have the gift to find treasure. It was also admitted that when treasures were found, before they could be unearthed and removed from the ground, they slipped down further into the earth because of a curse having been placed upon them. In 1971, Wesley Walters and Fred Poffarl discovered two court documents which serve to validate the earlier claims of a trial. (—*Inventing Mormonism*, Marquardt and Walters, p. 223. Also see "Joseph Smith and the 1826 Trial: New Evidence and New Difficulties," *Brigham Young University Studies* 12, Winter 1972, pp. 227–233.)

There is much written about the use of seer stones. Consider the following two accounts.

"President [Brigham] Young exhibited the Seer's stone with which The Prophet Joseph discovered the plates of the Book of Mormon, to the Regents [of the University of Deseret (Utah)] this evening. It is said to be a silecious granite dark color almost black with light colored stripes." —*On the Mormon Frontier: The Diary of Hosea Stout*, edited by Juanita Brooks, Vol. 2, p. 593, 1856.

"Preside[n]t Young also said that the seer stone which Joseph Smith first obtained He got in an Iron kettle 15 feet under ground. He saw it while looking in another seers stone which a person had. He went right to the spot & dug & found it." —Wilford Woodruff's Journal, Vol. 5, p. 382, 383.

Some Mormon historians have found it necessary to rethink their explanation of Joseph Smith. Marvin Hill, a professor emeritus of history at BYU, came to the defense of Joseph Smith with his response in *Dialogue*. He made this observation: "For the historian interested in Joseph Smith the man, it does not seem incongruous for him to have hunted for treasure with a seer stone and then to use it with full faith to receive revelations from the Lord." (*Dialogue: A Journal of Mormon Thought*, Vol. 7, No.4, Winter 1972, p. 78)

[121] Oliver Cowdery, an early associate of Joseph Smith, used a divining rod. This was an instrument supposedly used in locating buried treasure, among other things, and for receiving messages from God. BYU emeritus professor of history Marvin S. Hill noted that, "Some of the rodsmen or money diggers who moved into Mormonism were Oliver Cowdery, Martin Harris, Orrin P. Rockwell, Joseph and Newel Knight, and Josiah Stowell [Stoal]." (—Ibid.)

For me, the most shocking piece of information came from early Mormon scripture. God, supposedly speaking through Joseph, told Oliver Cowdery that he had "the gift of working with the rod; behold it has told you things: behold there is no other power save God, that can cause this rod of nature, to work in your hands." (—*Book of Commandments* 7:3) This scripture was later changed by deleting all references to "rod" and replacing it by the term "gift of Aaron." (—*Doctrine and Covenants* 8: 6–9) I had tried for years, unsuccessfully, to find out about the gift of Aaron. It sounded wonderful. I know of no one in the Mormon Church today who claims "the gift of working with the rod."

[122] Consider the following conflicting statements. The first statement is a "revelation" from God, through Joseph Smith, testifying of John C. Bennett's goodness. The second statement is taken from a letter written by Joseph Smith to Illinois Governor Carlin, testifying to some of Bennett's depraved acts. The revelation, God's

testament of Bennett's goodness, occurred several months after the first alleged depraved act.

> Again, let my servant John C. Bennett help you in your labor in sending my word to the kings and people of the earth, and stand by you, even you my servant Joseph Smith, in the hour of afflictions; and his reward shall not fail if he receive counsel.
> And for his love he shall be great, for he shall be mine if he do this, saith the Lord. I have seen the work he hath done, which I accept if he continue, and will crown him with blessings and great glory.
> —*Doctrine and Covenants* 124: 16–17, January 19, 1841.

Dear Sir:—It becomes my duty to lay before you some facts relative to the conduct of our major-general, John C. Bennett, which have been proven beyond the possibility of a dispute, and which he himself has admitted to be true in my presence.

It is evident that his general character is that of an adulterer of the worst kind, and although he has a wife and children living, circumstances which have transpired in Nauvoo, have proved to a demonstration that he cares not whose character is disgraced, and whose honor is destroyed, nor who suffers, so that his lustful appetite may be gratified; and further, he cares not how many or how abominable the falsehoods he has to make use of to accomplish his wicked purposes, even should it be that he brings disgrace upon a whole community.

Some time ago it having been reported to me that some of the most aggravated cases of adultery had been committed upon some previously respectable females in our city, I took proper methods to ascertain the truth of the report, and was soon enabled to bring sufficient witnesses before proper authority to establish the following facts:

More than twenty months ago Bennett went to a lady in the city and began to teach her that promiscuous intercourse between sexes was lawful and no harm in it, and requested the privilege of gratifying his passions; but she refused in the strongest terms, saying that it was very wrong to do so, and it would bring disgrace on the Church.

Finding this argument ineffectual, he told her that men in higher standing in the Church than himself not only sanctioned, but practiced the same deeds; and in order to finish the controversy, said and affirmed that I both taught and acted in the same manner, but publicly proclaimed against it in consequence of the prejudice of the people, and for fear of trouble in my own house. By this means he accomplished his designs; he seduced a respectable female with lying, and subjected her to public infamy and disgrace.

Not contented with what he had already done, he made the attempt on others, and by using the same language, seduced them also.

—*History of the Church*, Vol. 5, p. 42, June 24, 1842.

[123] *By His Own Hand Upon Papyrus*, by Charles M. Larson.

[124] In one of his addresses to the Saints, Brigham recites in detail his dream of cutting the throats of two ruffians with the bowie knife which he carried. —*Journal of Discourses*, Vol. 1, p. 83. Also, see Chapter 16.

[125] The majority of today's Mormons would be surprised to read the following statement by Brigham Young.

I have many a time, in this stand, dared the world to produce as mean devils as we can; we can beat them at anything. We have the greatest and smoothest liars in the world, the cunningest and most adroit thieves, and any other shade of character that you can mention.

We can pick out Elders in Israel right here who can beat the world at gambling, who can handle the cards, cut and shuffle them with the smartest rogue on the face of God's foot-stool. I can produce Elders here who can shave their smartest shavers, and take their money from them. We can beat the world at any game.

We can beat them, because we have men here that live in the
light of the Lord, that have the Holy Priesthood, and hold the
keys of the kingdom of God.
—Brigham Young, November 9, 1856, *Journal of Discourses*,
Vol. 4, p. 77.

[126] "Ask these sisters (many of them have known me for years,)
what my life has been in private and in public. It has been like the
angel Gabriel's, if he had visited you; and I can live so still." —
Brigham Young, April 7, 1861, *Journal of Discourses*, Vol. 9, p. 36.

"I could prove to this congresion [congregation] that I am young;
for I could find more girls who would choose me for a husband than
can any of the young men." —Brigham Young (age 56), September
6, 1857, *Journal of Discourses*, Vol. 5, p.210.

[127] "Elders, never love your wives one hair's breadth further than
they adorn the Gospel, never love them so but that you can leave
them at a moment's warning without shedding a tear. Should you
love a child any more than this? No." —Brigham Young, June 15,
1856, *Journal of Discourses*, Vol. 3, p. 360.

"Are you tormenting yourselves by thinking that your husbands
do not love you? I would not care whether they loved a particle
or not; but I would cry out, like one of old in the joy of my heart,
'I have got a man from the Lord!' 'Hallelujah! I am a mother—I
have borne an image of God!' " —Brigham Young, April 7, 1861,
Journal of Discourses, Vol. 9, p. 37.

"There are probably but few men in the world who care about the
private society of women less than I do." —Brigham Young, August
2, 1857, *Journal of Discourses*, Vol. 5, p. 99.

[128] Brigham Young castigated President Polk for heaping trials
upon the Mormons. His charges were blatantly false and Brigham
knew it. He said:

There cannot be a more damnable dastardly order issued than
was issued by the Administration to this people while they
were in an Indian country, in 1846. Before we left Nauvoo,
not less than two United States' senators came to receive a

pledge from us that we would leave the United States; and
then, while we were doing our best to leave their borders, the
poor, low, degraded curses sent a requisition for five hundred
of our men to go and fight their battles! That was President
Polk; and he is now weltering in hell with old Zachary Taylor,
where the present administrators will soon be, if they do not
repent.
—Brigham Young, September 13, 1857, *Journal of Discourses*,
Vol. 5, pp. 231–232.

There is high treason in Washington; and if the law was
carried out, it would hang up many of them. And the very act
of James K. Polk in taking five hundred of our men, while we
were making our way out of the country under an agreement
forced upon us, would have hung him between the heavens
and the earth, if the laws had been faithfully executed.
—Ibid., p. 235.

Eleven years previous, the Mormon leader Jesse C. Little had
appealed directly to President Polk for assistance to a broken and
destitute people attempting to cross the plains. The call for 500 men
to serve in the war against Mexico was not forced upon the Mormons;
it was a favor extended by President Polk, one which Jesse C. Little
approved. Although the opportunity was not without its drawbacks,
Brigham then wrote: "This is the first offer we have ever had from
the government to benefit us." (—*A Comprehensive History of the
Church*, B.H. Roberts, Vol. 3, p. 79.) Elder John Taylor also quotes
Brigham as saying: "I think the president has done us a great favor by
calling upon us." (—Ibid., p. 87.) Mormon historian, B.H. Roberts,
gives a thorough account of the affair. (—Ibid., pp. 60–103.)

[129] See Chapter 16.

[130] In 1857:

Mormons counted their martyrs as the murdered missionary
Joseph B. Brackenbury in 1832, Joseph Smith's infant son
during a mob attack in 1832, Andrew Barber at the 'Battle
of Blue River' in Missouri in 1833, Apostle David W. Patten
at the 'Battle of Crooked River' in Missouri in 1838, the

murdered and mutilated men and boys at Haun's Mill, Missouri, in 1838, the Smith brothers at Carthage Jail in 1844, Edmund Durfee in front of his home at Morley's settlement in Illinois in 1845, Apostle Parley P. Pratt in Arkansas in 1857, and every other Mormon who suffered and died during these expulsions.
—Michael Quinn, *The Mormon Hierarchy: Extensions of Power*, p. 241.

[131] See Chapter 16. Also, see Michael Quinn's, *The Mormon Hierarchy: Extensions of Power*, pp. 241–261.

[132] In his famous "Salt Sermon," Sidney Rigdon warned Mormon dissenters that they would "be cast out and trodden under foot of men." The next day, Oliver Cowdery, David Whitmer, John Whitmer, Lyman E. Johnson, and William W. Phelps were threatened in a letter signed by eighty-four Mormon faithful. The five men were given three days to "depart, or a more fatal calamity shall befall you." —*A Comprehensive History of the Church*, B.H. Roberts, Vol. 1, pp. 438–439, and —Michael Quinn, *The Mormon Hierarchy: Origins of Power*, pp. 94–95.

Joseph Smith wrote, "These men took warning and soon they were seen bounding over the prairie like the scape Goat to carry of[f] their own sins." —*An American Prophet's Record: The diaries and Journals of Joseph Smith*, Edited by Scott Faulring, p. 187.

Some Mormons love to remind others of Missouri Governor Bogg's order for exterminating the Mormons, but it was preceded by this inflammatory speech (which I had never heard of as a member of the Church) given by Sidney Rigdon on the 4th of July, 1838. "And that mob that comes on us to disturb us, it shall be between us and them a war of extermination; for we will follow them until the last drop of their blood is spilled; or else they will have to exterminate us, for we will carry the seat of war to their own houses and their own families, and one party or the other shall be utterly destroyed." —B.H. Roberts, *A Comprehensive History of the Church*, Vol. 1, p. 441.

A month later, on August 6, 1838, there was an attempt in Gallatin, Missouri to keep Mormons from voting. It led to a brawl. Some Mormon accounts have the Missourians coming out victors, while other Mormon accounts claim the Saints put the Missourians in their place. The aftermath is covered in several accounts. The following is Reed Peck's description of Gallatin's plundering by the Mormons a few days later. Peck was a Mormon at the time but was excommunicated in March of the following year.

On Thursday (18) pursuant to an arrangement made the evening before by J & H Smith and Lyman Wight, D. W. Patten at the head of 40 men made a descent on Gallatin the county seat of Daviess, burned the only store in the place and brought the goods to 'Diahman and consecrated them to the bishop Joseph having taught that the ancient order of things had returned and the time had arrived for the riches of the Gentiles to be consecrated to the house of Israel (Mormons) There were about 20 men in Gallatin who fled at the approach of Capt Patten and his company and these were all that the Mormons saw during the campaign excepting an occasional straggler more ventursome than his fellows

The sitizens had universally fled leaving their all at the mercy of a merciless foe

On the same day a company of 50 men called the First company commanded by Capt Dunhaw (In camp Cap Black Haw) made their triumphal entry into 'Diahman laden with feather beds, quilts, clothes Clothes, clock's, and all varieties of light furniture <taken from the deserted dwellings> making the most uncouth appearance I ever beheld and were greeted as they passed with three deafning hurras from the whole camp On the same day Seymour Brunson Alexander McRae and about 20 others rode 15 or 20 miles to one of the branches of Grand River and called on an old gentleman whom they found at home with his family and after the customary salutations McRae observed that it was a "dam'd cold day" and introduced the company as a party of mobites come from Carroll county to drive out the Mormons The unsuspicious old man invited them to come in and warm amd[and] ordered dinner as he could not furnish them with whiskey which they pretended to be most anxious for After receiving their dinner and a treat of excellent honey they departed slyly taking the old gentlemans great

coat a silk Handkerchief some woollen sheets woolen yarn a powder horn Gun lock some knives and forks and many other articles as a means I suppose of informing their host whom he had entertained The next night A. McRae and a small party went to Gallatin and stripped the best furnished house of all its valuable furniture which they drew to 'Diahman and burned the dwelling to the ground All the property taken from the store in Gallatin and from private habitations was deposited with the bishop of Diahman and afterwards distributed among theSsociety The Fur company and those parties were constantly bringing in plunder and reducing the dwellings to ashes and for ten days the Mormons were employed in this way without opposition, pillaging houses harvesting the corn and collecting the horses, cattle and hogs of the frightened citizens making 'Diahman their place of rendezvous and depository of their ill gotten riches, foolishly flattering themselves that no notice would be taken of these transactions. while a few Some heads among them were wondering that men from other counties were not flocking in by hundreds to stop their mad career in the beginning The Militia that passed through Far West for the protection of the peace in Daviess had returned home having been informed by the Mormons that their presence was not necessary The citizens of Daviess, men women and children fled through the snow in wagons on horseback and on foot after the plundering & burning was commenced as precipitately as though they had been invaded by a hostile band of Indians, but with this flood of testimony their calamitous report was not generally credited in other counties until men specially appointed for the purpose had visited Daviess county and returned with a confirmation of their Story
—*History of Reed Peck*, pp. 85–92.

[133] One of the most telling books dealing with Mormon deceit is *Solemn Covenant: The Mormon Polygamous Passage*, by B. Carmon Hardy. I learned that additional polygamous marriages were sanctioned by Church leaders after President Woodruff's 1890 Manifesto, which supposedly terminated the practice. Nonetheless, public denials continued. The deception was exposed to the nation

when B. H. Roberts, a polygamist and leading authority in the Church, was elected in 1899 as a U.S. Representative in Congress. Congress did not allow him to take his seat. Reed Smoot, a monogamist and a leading authority in the Church, was elected to the Senate in 1903 but not seated until 1907. As the debate raged in Congress over allowing Smoot to serve, additional light was shed on the continuing practice of polygamy. The dispute heightened among Church leaders over the course to take. President Joseph F. Smith issued a second Manifesto against polygamy in 1905. This was the beginning of the end for additional polygamous marriages, but they evidently did not stop immediately.

One significant instance of a polygamous marriage, after the second Manifesto, occurred in February 1906, when William Gailey Sears married Athelia Call in Mexico. William then returned to Arizona with his first wife, Agnes McMurrin Sears, and his new polygamous wife. William later served a mission for the Church with his first wife in Hawaii. Athelia bore nine sons and two daughters. One daughter, Lucille, married Bill Hofmann, and they had a son, Mark. Mark was bothered by the secrecy to which his mother felt obligated concerning her polygamous upbringing. She refused to tell Mark the details. He vowed to find out. Mark Hofmann immersed himself in Mormon history and became the infamous Mormon document forger and pipe-bomb murderer. —*The Story of the Mormon Forgery Murders*, by Linda Sillitoe and Allen Roberts, p. 208–209. (Also see: *Solemn Covenant: The Mormon Polygamous Passage*, by B. Carmon Hardy, pp. 313–314.)

There are still fundamentalist Mormons today who practice polygamy. They have broken off from the main body of the Church; in addition to polygamy, many still advocate Brigham Young's teachings on the Adam-God and blood-atonement doctrines.

[134] John Taylor, *Three Nights' Public Discussion Between the Revds. C. W. Cleeve, James Robertson, and Philip Cater, and Elder John Taylor, of the Church of Jesus Christ of Latter-day Saints, at Boulogne-sur-mer, France*, p. 8.

At the top of page eight, Taylor preceded his false denial with this observation about another individual: "I proved Mr. Caswell to have told one lie, and a man that will tell one falsehood to injure an innocent people, will tell five hundred, if necessary, for the same object."

I located and purchased an original Taylor pamphlet and verified that the alleged passage was accurate and in context. Upon showing my newly acquired pamphlet to a brother, he questioned the authenticity of my purchase. I found a copy of the pamphlet in special collections in the Harold B. Lee Library at Brigham Young University. There I verified the duplicitous claim made by Taylor and saw that if my copy was a forgery, at least it was an accurate forgery.

[135] Michael Quinn, *The Mormon Hierarchy: Origins of Power*, p. 597.

[136] The highlights of the so called "Civil War Prophecy" pronounced by Joseph Smith on December 25, 1832, as found in *Doctrine and Covenants* 87 are these: South Carolina will rebel, leading to a war encompassing all nations; "the Southern States shall be divided against the Northern States" and each will call upon other nations until all nations are involved; slaves will rise up against their masters; the remnants who are left (Indians) will make war with the Gentiles; by the sword and by a combination of natural disasters God will make an end of all nations. The prophecy closed with the admonition to stand in holy places because the day of the Lord cometh quickly.

The historical background to this "prophecy" is telling. In November 1832 (one month before Smith's prophecy), South Carolina rebelled against the federal government because of the high tariff which burdened the South. Claiming the right to ignore any federal law it considered unconstitutional, South Carolina was prepared for secession and war, if necessary. John C. Calhoun, from South Carolina and a champion for slavery and Southern rights, led the political battle. He had resigned as Vice President to Andrew Jackson in 1832 over these issues. The following year produced the famous debate in the Senate between Calhoun and Daniel Webster over slavery and states' rights.

The following Internet sites are sources for this information.
http://odur.let.rug.nl/~usa/B/calhoun/jcc.htm
http://gi.grolier.com/presidents/aae/vp/vpcal.html
http://pinzler.com/ushistory/timeline4.html
Or, do an internet search for *John Calhoun 1832*.

[137] The scholar who left the Church, whose name I did not remember, may have been Jay Dee Nelson, the first Mormon to

translate the re-discovered papyrus. He was one of several scholars who lost faith in the Church, partly as a result of the papyrus.

[138] *Quest For The Gold Plates,* by Stan Larson, and *By His Own Hand Upon Papyrus: A New Look at the Joseph Smith Papyri,* by Charles M. Larson, offer helpful discussions on the Book of Abraham. The Internet is also a good source of information on this issue. An Internet search for *"Joseph Smith papyrus"* will also produce a variety of sources.

[139] In 1981, a modification in the *Book of Mormon* was made by the Church. The expression "white and delightsome" was replaced by "pure and delightsome." The original verse supposedly described the transformations that would take place in the Native American's skin color in the last days after a few generations of membership in God's true church.

Somehow I had been led to believe that this recent change concerning Native Americans had been unprecedented. It turns out that while it had originally read "white," later on in 1840 it was changed to "pure." Sometime before 1920 it had been changed back to "white." Finally (well, maybe not finally) in 1981 it was changed back to "pure" again. Were church leaders modifying the scriptures without divine inspiration? Was an equivocating God going to rethink this again in another sixty years?

[140] 1 Nephi 11:18, 21, 32 and 1 Nephi 13:40. The idea of God and Christ being separate beings remained unclear in the doctrine of the early Church. Neither the *Book of Mormon* nor Joseph Smith's original accounts of the first vision presented God and Christ as separate beings.

[141] The following Internet site is recommended for information about changes in Mormon scriptures.

http://www.irr.org/mit/CHANGINGSCRIPS.HTML

Or, do an Internet search on "mother of god after the manner".

[142] See Thomas Stuart Ferguson, *One Fold and One Shepherd,* pp. 227–229. Also, do an Internet search for *"izapa stela 5"*.

[143] The Compass interview with President Hinckley aired November 9, 1997. Do an Internet search for *"Compass Interview with President Gordon B Hinckley"* or see the Internet site:

http://www.lds-mormon.com/hinckley.shtml

144 *Pearl of Great Price*, Joseph Smith—History 1:19.

145 *Doctrine and Covenants* 76: 101, 105, 106, 112.

146 In July of 1997, the *Wall Street Journal* published an article by Gordon B. Hinckley entitled "The Mormons' Trail of Hope." Hinckley painted a picture of a people persecuted and driven for their religious beliefs. He failed to mention that Joseph Smith and his closest followers were guilty of a few offenses themselves. We have already mentioned their threats and plundering, the establishment of an illegal bank in Kirtland, and the illegal practice of polygamy. We have not mentioned the destruction of the Nauvoo Expositor press, the Danites, and a great many other deeds. Consider the following "revelation" given to Joseph Smith: "And thus, even as I have said, if ye are faithful ye shall assemble yourselves together to rejoice upon the land of Missouri, which is the land of your inheritance, which is now the land of your enemies." (—*Doctrine and Covenants* 52:42, June 17, 1831.) This "revelation" was given before the Saints had been to Missouri. When it was published in the Book of Commandments in 1833 in Missouri, the "enemies" statement could not have endeared the Missourians to the Mormons.

In the spring of 1834, a Mormon army called Zion's Camp organized and set off to right the wrongs against the Saints in Missouri. It was a miserable failure if judged by the revelation given beforehand. The venture also shows the militant attitude of the Mormons early in their history.

And the lord of the vineyard said unto one of his servants: Go and gather together the residue of my servants, and take all the strength of mine house, which are my warriors, my young men, and they that are of middle age also among all my servants, who are the strength of mine house, save those only whom I have appointed to tarry;

And go ye straightway unto the land of my vineyard, and redeem my vineyard; for it is mine; I have bought it with money.

Therefore, get ye straightway unto my land; break down the walls of mine enemies; throw down their tower, and scatter their watchmen.

> And inasmuch as they gather together against you, avenge
> me of mine enemies, that by and by I may come with the
> residue of mine house and possess the land.
> —*Doctrine and Covenants* 101:55–58, December 16, 1833.

[147] Mark Hofmann was a forger of extraordinary ability. His specialty was early Mormon documents, and his favorite target was the Church. With his extensive knowledge of early Mormon history, he could create a believable document that was embarrassing to the Church. Feigning concern for the Church's image, he often worked quietly with Church leaders Gordon B. Hinckley or Huge Pinnock to make certain the documents he "found" stayed out of the public eye. Once the documents reached the first presidency's vault, there was little chance that they would be seen and exposed. But Hofmann overextended himself. Suspicions arose, and the pressure to deliver the McLellin collection, for which he had received an advance from the Church, became too great. In fact, he had neither the original collection nor an imitation of the collection. To give himself time, he killed the individual most likely to discover and reveal his scam. To create a false lead for the investigation that was to follow, Hofmann killed a second person with another pipe bomb on the same morning. A day later, Hofmann was injured when he accidentally triggered the bomb he had designed for a third victim. The accident put him in the hospital and in the sights of investigators. To crack the case, the investigators had to buck popular opinion which favored Hofmann, expose some expertly forged documents, and gather critical facts about additional forged documents hidden by an uncooperative Mormon Church. The Church's involvement with Hofmann and the documents which they had obtained secretly were an embarrassment.

The investigators had a record of Hofmann's cell phone calls. It showed several occasions when he had called Hinckley's office, and it showed how long he had talked. Investigators also knew that Hinckley had called Steven Christensen several times in the days just before Christensen was killed by Hofmann. Yet, Hinckley, when interviewed by investigators, remembered very little. One such interview angered the investigators. "Mike George left Hinckley's office unexpectedly angry. When he interviewed a bandit he expected lies, not when he interviewed a respected citizen and church leader. He soon realized, however, that his anger was simple—his fellow investigators, born and raised Mormons, were furious." —Linda Sillitoe and Allen Roberts, *Salamander: The Story of the Mormon Forgery Murders*, 2nd edition, by, p. 129.

Other sources include *A Gathering of Saints: A True Story of Money, Murder and Deceit*, by Robert Lindsey, 1988; and *Victims: The LDS Church and the Mark Hofmann Case*, by Richard E. Turley, Jr.

For more information do an Internet search on *Mark Hofmann Mormon* or see Internet site:

http://www.xmission.com/~country/reason/hof1.htm

[148] On September 18, 1999, the *Church News* printed an article on the dedication of the Mountain Meadow Monument. It included talk of hallowed ground, reverence, and respect. There was mention of "the forfeiture of the lives," "those who died," "those who fell," and "tragic end." There was no mention of murder or of ruthless deceit, no mention of unbridled fanaticism, no mention of the carefully crafted massacre of 120 people, many of them being women and children. (See Chapter Sixteen.) In fact, Hinckley said: "That which we have done here must never be construed as an acknowledgment on the part of the Church of any complicity in the occurrences of that fateful and tragic day. . . . I come as peacemaker. This is not a time of recrimination or the assigning of blame." His offering would be magnanimous if it were the Mormons who had been massacred by the Arkansas immigrants.

Hinckley said: "The fires of bitterness and suspicion have burned long enough." He talks of removing bitterness but fails to acknowledge Church members' offenses or to ask for forgiveness.

Hinckley said: "Let the book of the past be closed." He appears to want nothing more said about Mormon offenses; yet, in their devotionals, Mormons continue to sanctimoniously recite the occasions and the names of their abusers from the past.

[149] Alma 32:27.

Chapter 16 notes

[150] The Laffertys lost all participants in their study group just before committing their double murder. One person showed up at their last meeting. I will call him Hank so as not to threaten his

current membership and employment with the Church. Recently, I became acquainted with Hank through a friend and heard his story firsthand, a story he does not wish to make public. Hank is still "absolutely certain" of the inspiration in Brigham's Adam-God teachings and has other Mormon fundamentalist leanings. In that last meeting with the Ron and Dan Lafferty, Hank became very concerned for his own life because of the Lafferty brothers' talk of blood atonement and of slitting throats for sins. Wondering if his own life was in danger, he immediately left town with his family.

The Laffertys' act of blood atonement was not an isolated modern-day incident. Some Mormon Fundamentalists still believe in the doctrine. A search on the Internet—Mormon Fundamentalists Blood Atonement—will yield more information.

[151] "The Lord is in our midst. He teaches the people continually. I have never yet preached a sermon and sent it out to the children of men, that they may not call Scripture." —Brigham Young, Jan. 2, 1870, *Journal of Discourses*, Vol. 13, p. 95. (The last sentence was quoted in 1980 by Apostle Ezra Taft Benson in "Fourteen Fundamentals in Following the Prophets.")

"I say now, when they are copied and approved by me they are as good Scripture as is couched in this Bible." —Brigham Young, October 6, 1870, *Journal of Discourses*, p. 264.

"I have never given counsel that is wrong." —Brigham Young, August 31, 1873, Ibid., Vol. 16, p. 161.

[152] Ezra Taft Benson, "Fourteen Fundamentals in Following the Prophets," BYU Devotional Assembly, Tuesday, February 26, 1980.

[153] This twenty-six-volume set is still used and revered by fundamentalist Mormons. An Internet search generally produces an active website where the digital version is available.

[154] For examples, see our Appendix.

[155] "Joseph Smith taught that there were certain sins so grievous that man may commit, that they will place the transgressors beyond the power of the atonement of Christ. If these offenses are committed, then the blood of Christ will not cleanse them from their sins even though they repent. Therefore their only hope is to have their own blood shed to atone, as far as possible, in their behalf. This is scriptural doctrine, and is taught in all the standard works of

the Church." —Joseph F. Smith, *Doctrines of Salvation*, Vol. 1, p. 135, 1966.

Also, see *Mormon Doctrine*, by Bruce R. McConkie, 1966, pp. 92–93.

¹⁵⁶ Neither Joseph Fielding Smith nor Bruce R. McConkie left room for questions in their denials of the practice of blood atonement in the early Church. At one time I would have believed them, even had I known what blood atonement meant.

But that the Church practices 'Blood Atonement' on apostates or any others, which is preached by ministers of the 'Reorganization' is a damnable falsehood for which the accusers must answer.

. . . it was but the repetition of the ravings of enemies of the Church, without one grain of truth? . . .

Did you not know that not a single individual was ever "blood atoned," as you are pleased to call it, for apostasy or any other cause? . . .

Never in the history of this people can the time be pointed to when the Church ever attempted to pass judgment on, or execute an apostate as per your statement.

—Joseph Fielding Smith, *Doctrines of Salvation*, 1956, Vol. 1, pp. 136–137.

From the days of Joseph Smith to the present, wicked and evilly-disposed persons have fabricated false and slanderous stories to the effect that the Church, in the early days of this dispensation, engaged in a practice of blood atonement whereunder the blood of apostates and others was shed by the Church as an atonement for their sins. These claims are false and were known by their originators to be false. There is not one historical instance of so-called blood atonement in this dispensation, nor has there been one event or occurrence whatever, of any nature, from which the slightest inference arises that any such practice either existed or was taught.

There are, however, in the sermons of some of the early church leaders some statements about the true doctrine of blood atonement and of its practice in past dispensations, for instance, in the days of Moses. By taking one sentence on one page and another from a succeeding page and even by taking a part of a sentence on one page and a part of another found several pages away—all wholly torn from context—dishonest persons have attempted to make it appear that Brigham Young and others taught things just the opposite of what they really believed and taught.

Raising the curtain of truth on this false and slanderous bluster of enemies of the Church who have thus willfully chosen to fight the truth with outright lies of the basest sort . . .
—Bruce R. McConkie, 1966, *Mormon Doctrine*, pp. 92–93.

[157] Bruce R. McConkie, *Doctrinal New Testament Commentary*, Vol. 3, p. 345, 1965–1973.

[158] See the website: http://www.mtn-meadows-assoc.com/inmemory.htm.

[159] Some Mormons claim there was no ban on selling to the emigrants. Others claim the ban was only to keep the Saints from selling grain for the emigrants stock. Speaking of the wagon trains passing through Utah in the summer of 1857, Juanita Brooks wrote the following:

Those who came in after the order was issued to sell no grain at any price met great difficulty. One of the first of these was the Fancher Train . . . They followed a few days behind President George A. Smith on his journey south ordering the people to keep their grain and not to sell a kernel to any gentiles. This, of course, was hard on travelers who faced the desert and had expected to replenish their stores in Utah.
—Juanita Brooks, *John Doyle Lee*, pp. 202–203.

Speaking of the first trial of John D. Lee, Juanita Brooks wrote the following:

During the five days before the defense began, a great deal of evidence was presented, much of it very shocking to the members of the Mormon Church who had moved into the

area after the massacre took place and did not understand the passions of 1857. One witness after another testified to the orders not to sell grain or provisions to the company and to the strictness of the military discipline everywhere enforced. One person had been cut off the church for trading a cheese for a bed quilt; another had been struck over the head with a paling from a fence for giving some onions to one of the emigrants with whom he had become acquainted years before, and from whom he accepted hospitality while on a mission. A number of witnesses testified to the inflammatory nature of the sermons of George A. Smith just preceding the arrival of this company.
—Juanita Brooks, *The Mountain Meadows Massacre*, p. 193. (See also R.N. Baskin, *Reminiscences of Early Utah*, pp. 108–111 and Robert Kent Fielding, *The Tribune Reports of The Trials of John D. Lee for the Massacre at Mountain Meadows*, pp. 124–125, 143.)

Some people claim the ban was justified because of the grain shortage, but that position does not match Brigham's assessment in August of 1857 when he wrote to Jacob Hamblin. "All is peace here and the Lord is eminently blessing our labors; Grain is abundant, and our cities are alive with the busy hum of industry." —Juanita Brooks, *The Mountain Meadows Massacre*, p. 34.

[160] Some of the Mormon charges against the Fancher Party included killing Indians, poisoning cattle and springs, stealing supplies, and threatening to come back and fight with the U.S. (Johnston's) Army against the Mormons. Mormon history records that some members of the wagon train claimed to be Missouri-Wildcats who participated in the murder of the beloved prophets Joseph and Hyrum Smith. More realistically, animosity toward the Fancher Party may have been aggravated, in part, because their significant herd of cattle consumed valuable feed on rangeland claimed by Mormons.

In fairness to the Arkansas emigrants, reports of their foul threats and deeds may have been misdirected and/or exaggerated by some Mormons, then willingly repeated. Mormon historian (Apostle and eventually Prophet of the Church) Joseph Fielding Smith said of the Fancher company:

This company consisted of about thirty families numbering one hundred and thirty-seven persons. The Arkansas emigrants appeared to be respectable and well-to-do. With them there traveled a rough and reckless company calling themselves "Missouri Wild Cats," who conducted themselves in keeping with the name.
— Joseph Fielding Smith, *Essentials in Church History*, p. 513.

[161] The following statements were made by Brigham Young, still unaware of the massacre two days previous in Southern Utah. Obviously these words had no influence on the Saints of Southern Utah prior to the massacre, but they reflect the feelings and the attitude prevalent amongst the leaders and general membership of the Church.

We are in a Government whose administrators are always trying to injure us, while we are constantly at the defiance of all hell to prove any just grounds for their hostility against us; and yet they are organizing their forces to come here, and protect infernal scamps who are anxious to come and kill whom they please, destroy whom they please, and finally exterminate the "Mormons." . . .
They had ordered 2,500 troops to come here and hold the "Mormons" still, while priests, politicians, speculators, whoremongers, and every mean, filthy character that could be raked up should come here and kill off the "Mormons." . . .
I do not often get angry; but when I do I am righteously angry; and the bosom of the Almighty burns with anger towards those scoundrels; and they shall be consumed, in the name of Israel's God. We have borne enough of their oppression and hellish abuse, and we will not bear any more of it; for there is no just law requiring further forbearance on our part. And I am not going to have troops here to protect the priests and a hellish rabble in efforts to drive us from the land we posses;
—Brigham Young, September 13, 1857, *Journal of Discourses*, Vol. 5, pp. 226–227.

¹⁶² Hector McLean, a violent man, had apparently been abusive to his wife Eleanor. She joined the Mormon Church; then, with Pratt's assistance, she left Hector. Though she legally remained Hector McLean's wife, she became Pratt's twelfth wife. The trouble started later when Eleanor went to the South in a second attempt, without Hector McLean's knowledge, to retrieve her children from her parents in New Orleans. (Eleanor's parents did not approve of her religion.) Once she had the children, Pratt, also in the area, attempted to join her. They were both caught and jailed. When Pratt was released, McLean chased him down and killed him. The most complete and documented account from a Mormon perspective is given by Steven Pratt in, "Eleanor McLean and the Murder of Parley P. Pratt," *BYU Studies*, Vol. 15, Winter 1975, pp. 225–256.

¹⁶³ Reference to avenging the blood of the prophets can be found in the oaths, journals, sermons, and blessings of the early saints.

> On 27 June 1845, the first anniversary of Joseph Smith's murder, the Quorum of Twelve's prayer circle presented a formal prayer for God's vengeance on those who shed the blood of the prophets. Six months later, this "prayer of vengeance" (often called an "oath") became part of the endowment ceremony in the Nauvoo temple. George Q. Cannon, then only eighteen and later a member of the First Presidency, said that "when he had his endowments in Nauvoo that he took an oath against the murderers of the Prophet Joseph as well as other prophets, and if he had ever met any of those who had taken a hand in that massacre he would undoubtedly have attempted to avenge the blood of the martyrs."
> —D. Michael Quinn, *The Mormon Hierarchy: Origins of Power*, p. 179.

> You shall have wisdom, discretion, and understanding and knowledge to foresee evil, when danger approaches you the Angel of Life shall be with you to forewarn you of those things. If you are faithful you shall assist in avenging the blood of the prophets of God, and assist in accomplishing the

great work of the last days. [Blessing given to Bill Hickman
by church patriarch, John Young, on February 8, 1857.]
—Hope A. Hilton, *"Wild Bill" Hickman and the Mormon
Frontier*, p. 62.

Thou shalt be called to act at the head of a portion of thy
brethren and of the Lamanites in the redemption of Zion and
the avenging of the blood of the Prophets upon them that dwell
in the earth. The Angel of Vengeance shall be with thee, shall
nerve and strengthen thee. Like unto Moroni, no power shall
be able to stand before thee until thou hast accomplished thy
work. [Blessing given to William H. Dame (the highest-ranking
leader in the military and in the Church with direct involvement
in the massacre) by Patriarch Elisha H. Groves on February 20,
1854 in Parowan]
—Juanita Brooks, *John Doyle Lee*, p. 209. (Also see *The
Mormon Hierarchy: Extensions of Power*, D. Michael Quinn,
p. 248.)

The feeling of many Mormons regarding the death of Joseph
Smith is expressed well by Joseph Allen Stout. He wrote:
"Their dead bodies were brought to Nauvoo, where I saw
their beloved forms reposing in the arms of death, which gave
me such feelings as I am not able to describe. But I then and
there resolved in my mind that I would never let an opportunity go unimproved of avenging their blood upon the heads
of the enemies of the Church of Jesus Christ. . . . I hope to
avenge their blood, but if I do not I will teach my children and
children's children to the fourth generation as long as there is
one descendent of the murderers on the earth."
—Juanita Brooks, *The Mountain Meadows Massacre*, p. 55,
footnote 21. (Also see "The Joseph/Hyrum Smith Funeral
Sermon," *BYU Studies,* Vol. 23 1983, No.1 Winter, pp. 225–
256.)

One thing is certain—The Latter-day Saints will never forget
their persecutors who repent not. Though they bear up under

their losses and misfortunes with a degree of fortitude and cheerfulness, yet the fire of indignation burning in their breasts towards their enemies who have robbed, despoiled, and driven them will never be quenched until they are punished, and justice satisfied, even if it should require time and all eternity to accomplish it.

—Orson Hyde (date not given but in all likelihood spring of 1858), *Journal of Discourses*, Vol. 7, p. 51.

[164] The Appendix includes a number of blood atonement quotes by Mormon leaders just prior to the Mountain Meadows Massacre.

[165] The respected Mormon historian, B. H. Roberts, had this to say about the Sunday council before the attack:

It was customary for the local leading men at Cedar and from the smaller settlements in its vicinity to gather in a council meeting after the close of the regular Sunday services of the church to consider questions of local community interest. At such a meeting on the 6th of September the question concerning the conduct of, and what ought to be done with, the Arkansas emigrants was brought up and debated. Some in the council were in favor of destroying them, and others were not. Finally, and largely through the influence of Mr. Laban Morrill, it was 'unanimously decided' in that council to suspend all hostile action relative to the emigrants until a message could be sent to Brigham Young to learn what would be the best course to pursue.

—B.H. Roberts, *A Comprehensive History of the Church*, Vol. 4, p. 149.

[166] Laban Morrill was against killing the emigrants and strongly expressed his views in a council meeting. His daughter wrote:

That night after the council meeting in Cedar [before the deed] Father felt impressed to go a different way home—to Johnson's Fort. He did so, giving the horses the reins, and going in a hurry. Later he found that two men had been sent out to waylay

him. He said that he noticed the two men leave the meeting
before it was out.
—Juanita Brooks, *The Mountain Meadows Massacre*, p. 54.

Perry Liston's record says:

1857. In the fall of this year, a large company of emigrants
partly from Missouri, passed through our quiet settlements.
They made threats, and swore that Johnston's Army was
coming from the East and they from the South and they would
kill every Mormon in Utah. These words I heard myself—but
there was some good people among them, consequently I did
oppose killing them. So much so that I did not have a thing to
do with it and my life was at stake for refusing. But the Lord
showed me my way, and I walked in it.
—Ibid., p. 55.

It appears there may have been one dissenter in the Mormon
militia shortly before the massacre:

A legend is told of young Tom Pierce, who refused to have
anything to do with the affair and turned to walk away. When
his own father, who was an officer, ordered him into the ranks
and he still did not return, the father shot at him. The bullet
grazed the side of Tom's head, leaving a permanent scar just
above his ear.
—Ibid., p. 90.

[167] Convinced that Jacob Hamblin was the source of this story,
Juanita Brooks quotes J. H. Beadle as follows:

Three men escaped the general massacre. The night before
the closing scene the party first became convinced that white
men were besieging them. They drew up a paper addressed to
the Masons, Odd Fellows, Baptists, and Methodists of the States,
'and to all good people everywhere,' in which they stated their
condition, and implored help if there was time, if not, justice.

To this were attached the signatures of so many members of various lodges and churches in Missouri and Arkansas. With this paper three of their best scouts crept down a ravine and escaped, starting on foot for California. The next day Ira Hatch and a band of Indians were put upon their track. They came upon them asleep on the Santa Clara mountain and killed two as they slept. The third escaped, shot through the wrist. He traveled on and was relieved by the Vegas Indians, on the Santa Clara. After a day's rest he started on, but meeting John M. Young and another, they told him it would be madness to attempt the Ninety-mile Desert in his condition, and promised to try and smuggle him through to Salt Lake City. A few hours after, they met Hatch and his Indians on the hunt for the fugitive. . . .

[Brooks inserts: "The Indians promptly killed the man, while:"]

The paper dropped by the fugitive was given by an Indian to Jacob Hamblin, Church Indian Agent, who kept it many years; but one day showing it to Lee, the latter took it from him and destroyed it.

—Juanita Brooks, *The Mountain Meadows Massacre*, pp. 99–100.

[168] "The victims discovered that white men were in league with the Indians, and this knowledge sealed their fate. It was determined by those making the attack that no emigrant should live who could tell the tale." —Joseph Fielding Smith, *Essentials in Church History*, p. 516. (See also B.H. Roberts, *A Comprehensive History of the Church*, Vol. 4, p. 153.)

[169] One of the earliest accounts of the Mountain Meadows Massacre was given by Josiah F. Gibb. It can be found on the Internet.

http://www.utlm.org/onlinebooks/meadowscontents.htm

See also:

http://www.mtn-meadows-assoc.com/

[170] See the Appendix.

[171] Hope A. Hilton, *"Wild Bill" Hickman and the Mormon Frontier*, pp. 99–100.

¹⁷² For an account of these murders, see the Appendix.
¹⁷³ For an account of this slaughter, see the Appendix.
¹⁷⁴ For an account, see the Appendix.
¹⁷⁵ D. Michael Quinn, *The Mormon Hierarchy: Extensions of Power*, pp. 241–261.
¹⁷⁶ One Mormon apologist cites this reference to show that blood atonement was not used.

What has been must be again, for the Lord is coming to restore all things. The time has been in Israel under the law of God, the celestial law, or that which pertains to the celestial law, for it is one of the laws of that kingdom where our Father dwells, that if a man was found guilty of adultery, he must have his blood shed, and that is near at hand. But now I say, in the name of the Lord, that if this people will sin no more, but faithfully live their religion, their sins will be forgiven them without taking life.
—Brigham Young, February 8, 1857, *Journal of Discourses*, Vol. 4, p. 219.

¹⁷⁷ B. Carmon Hardy, *Solemn Covenant: The Mormon Polygamous Passage*, p. 368.

Chapter 17 notes
¹⁷⁸ The Mormon hymn, "Praise to the Man," praises Joseph Smith and states that he is "mingling with Gods."
¹⁷⁹ Abraham, Isaac, and Jacob "have entered into their exaltation, according to the promises, and sit upon thrones, and are not angels but are gods." *Doctrine and Covenants* 132:37.
¹⁸⁰ Gordon B. Hinckley, June 29, 1997, *The Spirit of America*, p. 156.

Appendix
¹⁸¹ B.H. Roberts, *A Comprehensive History of the Church*, Vol. 4, p. 150.
¹⁸² R.N. Baskin, *Reminiscences of Early Utah*, p. 126. (See also Robert Kent Fielding, *The Tribune Reports of The Trials of John D. Lee for the Massacre at Mountain Meadows*, p. 222.)

[183] Juanita Brooks, *The Mountain Meadows Massacre*, pp. 140–141. (Also see Wilford Woodruff's Journal, Vol. 5, pp. 102-103, and Susan Staker, *Waiting For World's End*, pp. 203–204.)

[184] Juanita Brooks, *The Mountain Meadows Massacre*, pp. 182–183. (Also see Wilford Woodruff's Journal, Vol. 5, p. 577, Susan Staker, *Waiting For World's End*, p. 262, and B.H. Roberts, *A Comprehensive History of the Church*, Vol. 4, p. 176, footnote 24.) Juanita Brooks also noted that in the official *Journal History of the Church* the "vengeance" quotation by Brigham is omitted. In addition, her grandfather, Dudley Leavitt, was with Brigham on his visit to the Mountain Meadows monument. He quoted Brigham as saying: "Vengeance is mine saith the Lord; I have repaid." —*The Mountain Meadows Massacre*, p. 182.

[185] "Pres. Young Said that the company that was used up at the Mountain Meadows were the Fathers, Mothe[rs], Bros., Sisters & connections of those that Murdered the Prophets; they Merit[e]d their fate, & the only thing that ever troubled him was the lives of the Women & children, but that under the circumstances [this] could not be avoided. Although there had been [some] that want[e]d to bet[ray] the Brethr[e]n into the hands of their Enemies, for that thing [they] will be Damned & go down to Hell. I would be Glad to see one of those traitors." —D. Michael Quinn, *The Mormon Hierarchy: Extensions of Power*, pp. 252–253,536, footnote180.

[186] Brigham Young's prepared responses for the Mountain Meadows Massacre trials of John D. Lee included the following points:

"Answer Eight: I did not learn anything of the attack or destruction of the Arkansas company until some time after it occurred—then only by floating rumor."

"Answer Eleven: No, I never gave any directions concerning the property taken from the emigrants at the Mountain Meadows Massacre nor did I know anything of that property, or its disposal, and I do not to this day, except from public rumor."

—R.N. Baskin, *Reminiscences of Early Utah*, p. 116. (Also see Juanita Brooks, *The Mountain Meadows Massacre*, pp. 286–287.)

[187] Heber J. Grant, *Gospel Standards*, pp. 83–84, Grant was seventh president of the Church of Jesus Christ of Latter-day Saints. (Also from Conference Report, April 1902, p. 81.)

[188] Baskin did not impress me as a flatterer, and his book, published a few years later, was critical of Church leaders. So, I questioned Grant's summary of Baskin's generous remarks. I found that the Deseret News, the Mormon owned newspaper, had covered the occasion of Baskin's complimentary acknowledgement of Brigham Young and other Church leaders; the celebration was in honor of the late Brigham Young's 100th birthday. If Baskin's remarks were as generous as Grant remembered, they were not reported by the Deseret News. —"In Memory of Pioneer Leader,"*Deseret News*, June 3, 1901, front page.

[189] B.H. Roberts, *A Comprehensive History of the Church*, Vol. 5, p. 205.

[190] R.N. Baskin, *Reminiscences of Early Utah*, p. 9.

[191] William E. Berrett, *The Restored Church*, 1956, page 198.

[192] B.H. Roberts, *A Comprehensive History of the Church*, Vol. 1, p. 508.

[193] Hope A. Hilton, *"Wild Bill" Hickman and the Mormon Frontier*, 1988.

[194] Baskin felt certain that if any faithful, believing Mormons were on the jury there would be no conviction of Brigham Young and his "mean devils." The Mormon view was reflected in Brigham's statement: "I live above the law, and so do this people." (—Aug 1, 1852, *Journal of Discourses*, Vol. 1, p. 361.) Baskin arranged for a jury of Gentiles by eliminating Mormons in the selection process (he established that potential Mormon jurors did not support the U.S. laws against polygamy). This approach was successfully challenged by Church lawyers in the U.S. Supreme Court. The charges against Brigham and his Danites were useless in front of a Mormon jury. Complicating the issue was the pardon which President Buchanan had given the Mormons in 1858 in connection with the Utah war. The charges were dropped.

[195] R.N. Baskin, *Reminiscences of Early Utah*, p. 36.

[196] Hope A. Hilton, a great-granddaughter of Bill Hickman, once felt that Hickman's book was a creation of J. H. Beadle. After years of research, she wrote in the preface to her book, *"Wild Bill" Hickman and the Mormon Frontier*: "I do not question whether Hickman actually wrote *Brigham's Destroying Angel*. It is too ac-

curate in its details to have been written by anyone else. Instead, I try to determine how much of the autobiography was true and how much of it fabrication."

William Kimball claimed that Hickman, while in prison, denied authorship of *Brigham's Destroying Angel*. Yet Hickman, in writing to his daughter Katharine Hickman Butcher on January 7, 1872, said: "I have written a rough book, but no more rough than true." —Hope A. Hilton, *"Wild Bill" Hickman and the Mormon Frontier*, p. 127.

[197] In 1860, Church leader Orson Hyde came to the defense of Hickman for stealing when John Bennion wanted Hickman excommunicated. Bennion's journal entry for October 13, 1860, reports Hyde as saying: "A man may steal and be influenced by the spirit of the Lord to do it, that Hickman had done it in years past. Said that he never would institute a trial against a brother for stealing from the Gentiles." —Hope A. Hilton, *"Wild Bill" Hickman and the Mormon Frontier*, p. 96. (Also see D. Michael Quinn, *The Mormon Hierarchy: Origins of Power*, p. 554.)

Most surviving evidence reveals that Bill Hickman, Brigham Young, and Orson Hyde were close friends.
—Hope A. Hilton, "Wild Bill" Hickman and the Mormon Frontier, p. 19.

Mayor Smoot had a conversation with the President about Wm A. Hickman, observing people see him come in and out the office, and that leads them to suppose he is sanctioned in all he does by the President he also observed that dogs were necessary to take care of the flock, but if the Shepherd's dogs hurt the sheep it would be time to remove them.
—Brigham Young Office Journals—Excerpts, 1853–62 [April 3, 1860], p. 70.

Ormus Bates informed me that Wm. Hickman told him that what he was doing was by the Council of the Authorities of the Church meaning the Crimes which was Committing such as Stealing Cattles &c. I told Bates it was Fals[false]. Their was not a Righteous man in Israel who either Councilled him

to take such a Course or sanctioned his doings. I told Presidet
Young what He had said.
—Wilford Woodruff's Journal, Aug. 31, 1859, Vol. 5, p. 379.

28 Oct 1871   I met with the school of the prophets. D H Wells
was present & spoke & left the school Before it Closed & went
into the street & soon after the school was Closed Presidet
Daniel H. Wells Hosea Stout, & Wm. Kimball were all three
arested for Murder on the Testimony of Wm. Hickman. All three
of the Men were as innocent as Children But Wm Hickman is
trying to Clear himself by laying all of his damnable Murders
upon Innocent Men & the wicked Judges and U.S. Officers
in this City are trying to Murder the Innocent & to Clear the
guilty.
—Ibid., Vol. 7, p. 36.

[198] R.N. Baskin, *Reminiscences of Early Utah*, pp. 97–98.
[199] The following is a graphic account as told by John D. Lee:

Warren Snow was Bishop of the Church at Manti, San
Pete County, Utah. He had several wives, but there was a fair,
buxom young woman in the town that Snow wanted for a wife.
He made love to her with all his powers, went to parties where
she was, visited her at her home, and proposed to make her his
wife. She thanked him for the honor offered, but told him she
was then engaged to a young man, a member of the Church,
and consequently could not marry the old priest. This was no
sufficient reason to Snow. He told her it was the will of God
that she should marry him, and she must do so; that the young
man could be got rid of, sent on a mission or dealt with in some
way so as to release her from her engagement—that, in fact, a
promise made to the young man was not binding, when she was
informed that it was contrary to the wishes of the authorities.
The girl continued obstinate. The "teachers" of the town
visited her and advised her to marry Bishop Snow. Her parents,
under the orders of the Counselors of the Bishop, also insisted
that their daughter must marry the old man. She still refused.
Then the authorities called on the young man and directed him

to give up the young woman. This he steadfastly refused to do. He was promised Church preferment, celestial rewards, and everything that could be thought of—all to no purpose. He remained true to his intended, and said he would die before he would surrender his intended wife to the embraces of another.

This unusual resistance of authority by the young people made Snow more anxious than ever to capture the girl. The young man was ordered to go on a mission to some distant locality, so that the authorities would have no trouble in effecting their purpose of forcing the girl to marry as they desired. But the mission was refused by the still contrary and unfaithful young man.

It was then determined that the rebellious young man must be forced by harsh treatment to respect the advice and orders of the Priesthood. His fate was left to Bishop Snow for his decision. He decided that the young man should be castrated; Snow saying, "When that is done, he will not be liable to want the girl badly, and she will listen to reason when she knows that her lover is no longer a man."

It was then decided to call a meeting of the people who lived true to counsel, which was to be held in the school-house in Manti, at which place the young man should be present, and dealt with according to Snow's will. The meeting was called. The Young man was there, and was again requested, ordered and threatened, to get him to surrender the young woman to Snow, but true to his plighted troth, he refused to consent to give up the girl. The lights were then put out. An attack was made on the young man. He was severely beaten, and then tied with his back down on a bench, when Bishop Snow took a bowie-knife, and performed the operation in a most brutal manner, and then took the portion severed from his victim and hung it up in the school-house on a nail, so that it could be seen by all who visited the house afterwards.

The party then left the young man weltering in his blood, and in a lifeless condition. During the night he succeeded in releasing himself from his confinement, and dragged himself to some hay-stacks, where he lay until the next day, when he was discovered by his friends. The young man regained his health, but has been an idiot or quiet lunatic ever since, and is well known by hundreds of both Mormons and Gentiles in Utah.

After this outrage old Bishop Snow took occasion to get up a meeting at the school-house, so as to get the people of Manti, and the young woman that he wanted to marry, to attend the meeting. When all had assembled, the old man talked to the people about their duty to the Church, and their duty to obey counsel, and the dangers of refusal, and then publicly called attention to the mangled parts of the young man, that had been severed from his person, and stated that the deed had been done to teach the people that the counsel of the Priesthood must be obeyed. To make a long story short, I will say, the young woman was soon after forced into being sealed to Bishop Snow.

Brigham Young, when he heard of this treatment of the young man, was very mad, but did nothing against Snow. He left him in charge as Bishop at Manti, and ordered the matter to be hushed up. This is only one instance of many that I might give to show the danger of refusing to obey counsel in Utah. —Confessions of John D. Lee, pp. 285–286.

[200] "In the midsummer of 1857 Brigham Young also expressed approval for an LDS bishop who had castrated a man. In May 1857 Bishop Warren S. Snow's counselor wrote that twenty-four-year-old Thomas Lewis 'has now gone crazy' after being castrated by Bishop Snow for an undisclosed sex crime. When informed of Snow's action, Young said: 'I feel to sustain him,' even though Young's brother Joseph, a general authority, disapproved of this punishment. In July Brigham Young wrote a reassuring letter to the bishop about this castration: 'Just let the matter drop, and say no more about it,' the LDS president advised, 'and it will soon die away among the people.'" —*The Mormon Hierarchy: Extensions of Power*, D. Michael Quinn, pp. 251-252.

"Thomas Lewis lived long enough to join his younger brother Lewis Lewis and two friends in an attempt to castrate Warren Snow in revenge in March 1872. Snow used a pistol to shoot two of his attackers, and perhaps this was when Thomas Lewis died." —D. Michael Quinn, *The Mormon Hierarchy: Extensions of Power*, pp. 534–535.

²⁰¹ *On the Mormon Frontier, The Diary of Hosea Stout*, edited by Juanita Brooks, Vol. 2, p. 653, February 27, 1858.

²⁰² "The subject of Eunuchs came up & Joseph [Young] said that He would rather die than to be made a Eunuch. Brigham Said the day would Come when thousands would be made Eunochs in order for them to be saved in the kingdom of God." —Wilford Woodruff's Journal, June 2, 1857, Vol. 5, p. 55.

"Wake up, ye Elders of Israel, and purge yourselves, and purge out the filth that is in your Quorums, for we will not countenance unrighteousness in our midst. There are thousands and millions of men that will have to become eunuchs, to obtain the kingdom of God, and God will cut off their posterity, so that when they come up in the resurrection they will find their houses left unto them desolate. God will not have their names perpetuated on the earth, because they have forfeited their Priesthood." —Heber C. Kimball, December 21, 1856, *Journal of Discourses*, Vol. 4, p. 143

For more references on early Mormon brutality, do an Internet search on *"Mormon Blood Atonement"* or see the Internet site: http://www.xmission.com/~country/reason/blood.htm

Index